MARINA REHM

Inescapable

First published by Marina Rehm, c/o COCENTER, Koppoldstr. 1, 86551 Aichach, Germany 2024

This novel is entirely a work of fiction. The names, characters and incidents portrayed in it are the work of the author's imagination. Any resemblance to actual persons, living or dead, events or localities is entirely coincidental.

Designations used by companies to distinguish their products are often claimed as trademarks. All brand names and product names used in this book and on its cover are trade names, service marks, trademarks and registered trademarks of their respective owners. The publishers and the book are not associated with any product or vendor mentioned in this book. None of the companies referenced within the book have endorsed the book.

Printed by: see back matter

First edition

ISBN: 978-3-00-078982-3

Editing by Karen Robinson
Cover art by Hampton Lamoureux

This book was professionally typeset on Reedsy.
Find out more at reedsy.com

For my mom

Contents

I

Berlin, New Hampshire, January 1985

1

An icy breeze made him look up from his book. The door to the convenience store had been opened and in walked the three people he wanted to see the least. The wide smirks on their faces and quick glances at each other told him that they were up to no good.

Dylan sighed. He was working the counter all by himself tonight. Larry, the proprietor, wouldn't be in until ten – three hours away.

The three morons disappeared down the snack aisle, which only increased Dylan's unease. He didn't like them leaving his sight. He strained to at least hear what they were up to, but he couldn't make out anything over the oldies radio station Larry insisted on playing in the store.

He tried to remain calm and focused on his book again but soon found he was only staring at the page rather than reading it. Not that it mattered. He had completed all his reading for school, had sent out his college applications, and taken his SATs. All he needed to do now was wait. Wait for an acceptance letter, wait to turn eighteen, wait to get the hell out of this miserable town, wait to finally start his life.

So, to pass the time, he was reading. He read anything he could get his hands on: thrillers, comedies, comic books but also tons of books on history and criminal justice. Thick tomes like the one before him. They weren't exactly light reading material, but he wanted to be prepared for college. If he wanted to go to law school, he had to know this stuff. Better to get a head start.

And reading was better than being bored at work. He had read four books in the past two weeks alone. It felt like he was already halfway through the local library. But he didn't have much else to do at this point.

A loud buzzing noise from the back of the store made him jump.

The slush machines.

Fletcher Barnes and his entourage had found something to do, it seemed. Dylan's heart raced, and a single bead of sweat was running down his back. He kept staring at the aisle they had disappeared into and listening intently for more sounds coming from the back.

That's probably how he had missed the customer who had just entered the store, only noticing her when she waved a dainty hand in front of his face.

"Hello."

Startled, he looked at her. And blinked. The person standing in front of him looked like a brunette Madonna – only somehow even more flawless. Her brown curls were long and lush, framing her heart-shaped face. The glow of her porcelain skin was rivaled by that of her light gray eyes, her nose was perfectly straight, and the beauty spot on her chin was the only thing that broke up her face's symmetry.

Her black leather outfit was snug around her petite frame yet seemed like a poor choice of clothing to keep warm in New Hampshire in January. But she didn't seem to be cold.

Her demeanor exuded confidence despite her only being maybe five foot four. If Dylan had seen her walking down the street, he never would have dared talk to her. But as it was, this goddess-like creature had somehow stopped at a gas station in the middle of nowhere during his shift.

Her crimson painted lips spread into a grin. "Can I get fifteen bucks on pump one, please?" She looked at him like he was slow, pointing at the store window with her thumb.

Dylan realized his mouth was hanging open. He closed it and rang her up in a hurry. As she slid three five-dollar bills across the counter, he noticed she was wearing fingerless black leather gloves and couldn't help but wonder how her fingers weren't freezing off. But then again, she had come by car.

As he was fumbling with the register, he glanced out to the pumps. A sleek and shiny sports car – the kind nobody drove around here – was parked under the dim lights of the gas station roof. It was a foreign make. An Audi maybe? He couldn't get a good look at it, but even through the hazy windows and in the dark of the early night, it was obvious that vehicle was fast.

Who was this girl? And what was she doing here of all places?

She hadn't come alone though. A guy in the driver's side of the car was idly looking out the window.

Figures. A girl like that can't be single. Not that he would have stood a chance if she had been.

He turned back to his customer and handed her the receipt. "Are you just passing through?" he asked sheepishly, curious to find out how she had ended up here.

She was watching him closely, her eyes boring into his longer than appropriate. It seemed like she was staring into his soul, extracting his deepest darkest secrets. It made Dylan uncomfortable He had to look away.

"Not sure yet. We might stay a while."

As he opened his mouth to say something else to keep her from leaving, Amy Barnes – Fletcher's twin sister – started giggling. She kept her distance, standing between the counter and the snack aisle, one hand fake-coyly pressed on her mouth, her blond perm shaking with her suppressed laughter. Ricky Halston appeared next to her. He held out a half empty cup of blue slush that was dripping at the bottom, leaving a trail of thick blue liquid on the beige tiled floor.

"Sorry, man." Only he didn't sound sorry at all. In fact, he seemed to be trying hard not to laugh. "Something's wrong with the machine. There's blue stuff everywhe—"

He couldn't even finish the sentence. Bursting out laughing, he doubled over behind Amy into the aisle. Amy couldn't hold it together anymore either and leaned onto Ricky.

A cold wave of dread ran from Dylan's head to his toes. The kind of dread when the joke cracking everybody up was on you.

He tried to remain aloof, telling himself that these two looked ridiculous as they laughed like little children would at a fart, but he couldn't entirely convince himself.

Amy's twin casually sauntered out behind them, grabbing a packet of peanuts from the shelf as he went. Walking up to the counter, he noticed the girl, who was still standing there, watching the spectacle. For a split second, his eyes widened and his brows rose half an inch. Then he pulled himself together and winked at her with a half smile. But she gave him an unfazed look.

"You might want to check those machines, Harper. I think there's something stuck in the tap." He grinned that stupid grin of his. The one that said he knew he was untouchable.

Dylan wanted to sock the guy so badly. But that wouldn't end well for him. He was outnumbered. And even if he hadn't been, he never would have stood a chance in a fight against Fletcher Barnes. Dylan had a few scars to prove it.

Although they were the same age, they might as well have belonged to two completely different species: Fletcher was broad-shouldered, with arms the size of his sister's thighs, with blond hair and cheek-bones that could cut glass whereas Dylan was overweight, his skin was breaking out, and he wore Coke-bottle-thick glasses.

So he swallowed his anger and pretended it didn't bother him at all.

"Just the nuts?" He pointed at the packet in Fletcher's hand.

Fletcher tossed the packet on the counter and shrugged. "Sure."

"A dollar twenty."

He pulled out some change from his jeans pocket and counted out one dollar. "Sorry, that's all I got. But Larry sure won't mind." He winked. And before Dylan could say another word to stop him, he turned on his heel and walked away. "Let's go."

His entourage followed like the good little minions they were. As the door slowly shut behind them, another icy breeze made its way into the store. Dylan shivered from the cold, but on the inside, he was fuming.

Disgruntled, he made his way to the back to look at the disaster Fletcher and his friends had caused. It was even worse than he'd expected. The light brown rug in front of the machines had turned blue and made squishing noises when he stepped on it. The sugary liquid was oozing out onto the beige tile floor staining the grout…

This is never going to come off.

He groaned. In moments like these, he wished he were already a successful lawyer. He would make sure justice was served and people like Fletcher and his sycophants were put behind bars where they belonged. What gave them the right to do this? And why did they keep getting away with it? Consequences seemed to be of no concern for the rich.

Dylan shook his head in disgust and grabbed the mop and bucket from the back office.

"Do you need help with that?"

Confused, he looked up in the direction of the voice. The black leather girl was still there, hovering in the aisle, brow furrowed, and pointing at the soaked rug.

For a second Dylan was dumbfounded. He hadn't expected her to stick around. She had already paid. And besides, wasn't she with someone?

"Uh, will your boyfriend not mind?" He was still clutching the mop, his eyes darting in the direction of the front windows and back. He couldn't see the pumps from there.

She shrugged. "My husband can wait for a bit. We're not in a rush. And you look like you could use a hand."

Husband? His brows raised. She looked too cool to be married.

She flashed a dazzling smile at him. Her teeth were as perfect as the rest of her seemed to be. After way too long he realized he was staring at her. He blushed and looked away. *Embarrassing... Come on, get it together!*

He directed his gaze at the slushed-up tiles instead. Why would a girl – no, a married woman – who looked like a movie star want to help him clean up this mess? Was she serious or was she making fun of him?

He looked her up and down, trying to gauge if he could trust her.

"It's okay," she said with a soft smile. And then, as if she could read his mind, she added, "You can trust me. I mean it. I just want to help you." Slowly she walked up to him, reaching for the old mop he was still gripping with both hands.

He swallowed. She was standing so close to him that he could smell her perfume. Some flowery scent. Rose? His gaze met hers again. Her light gray eyes were honest and inviting.

Ah, what the hell. He would probably never see her again anyway. Might as well take her up on her offer. Plus, he was most likely never going to get another chance at hanging out with a girl as breathtaking as her. The corners of his mouth twitched, and he surrendered the mop.

He hurried into the back room for more cleaning supplies. As he stepped back into the store, she had already rolled up the rug and was wiping the floor.

"It's probably best if you wring that out outside and throw it in the washing machine," she instructed with a frown.

Dylan nodded. He didn't know what to say. He so rarely had company other than his mom, and the situation felt awkward. After all, he didn't know this person.

"I'm Marie-Louise, by the way. But everyone calls me Marie. What's your name?" With a splash, she dunked the mop deep into the bucket of water and stirred it.

"Uh, Dylan."

"Nice to meet you, Dylan." She held out her leather-gloved right hand, and he shook it. Her fingers really did feel frozen. Her touch was so cold it sent a shiver through his body. Did that fancy car of hers not have a heating system?

"Likewise," he murmured. He moved to the counter for the slush machines and started cleaning up the surface which was also covered in blue lumpy liquid. "So, what brings you here?" he asked after a beat. He was dying to know.

"Oh, uh…" She hesitated. "I'm on a break from college, and we're just driving through the country, you know… No real destination in mind, just going where the road takes us."

That sounded amazing. Dylan could hardly imagine the immeasurable amount of freedom these two had to be feeling. His heart yearned for it. A trip like that was something he wanted to take once he earned enough money as a lawyer. Then he could maybe also afford to take his mom somewhere as a treat. Maybe even overseas. That would be nice…

"That sounds like fun."

"Yeah. But we might stay here for a while."

"Why?" Dylan asked incredulously.

Berlin was a small town in New Hampshire, surrounded by nothing but forest and mountains. Temperatures were below freezing every day this time of year, and everything was covered in a thick layer of snow and ice. They got fresh snow almost every day. Plus, they were too far off the grid for tourism. Nobody was coming here to visit.

In fact, since the sneakers factory had closed a few years back, people were moving away in droves. The population had dwindled to a little over 12,000. So why anybody would want to stay there was beyond him.

She shrugged and focused on scrubbing the grout with her mop. "No reason. Seems like an interesting place." The way she grimaced at those words told Dylan that she wasn't going to elaborate.

"How old are you, Dylan?" she asked before he could say anything else.

"Seventeen."

Her eyes darted to his face. "Oh. Okay. When do you turn eighteen?"

That was an odd question to ask someone you just met – at least in Dylan's opinion. "In a little over two months."

"Hm." She put her attention on the grout again. "So, you're still in school?"

"Yup. High school senior."

"I see."

He wondered why she bothered talking to him and asking him all these questions. Just to make small talk? Or had Fletcher put her up to it to see if Dylan would make a fool of himself in front of a pretty girl? Dylan's heart sank. Fletcher would tease him about this endlessly…

No, she didn't even know Fletcher. She had shown him the cold shoulder earlier. *Stop being so paranoid, Dylan!*

"How old are you?" he asked, trying to steer the conversation away from himself.

"Twenty" came the quick-fire response.

He had moved on to cleaning the wenge wood cabinet below the counter, the doors of which were lined with blue streaks like veins, and the next question shot out of his mouth before he could stop it: "And you're *married*?"

"Yes." She grinned. Apparently, she hadn't taken it personally. "When you meet the right person, why not make it official?" Her grin deepened as if she were reacting to some private joke.

"Guess so…" Not that he would know. He had never really been in love. Unless you counted the misplaced crush he had had on Amy Barnes in first grade, back before she had turned into her brother's shadow, and the feelings he'd had for his classmate Leonard in fifth grade. But he didn't like to think about that.

"All done," Marie exclaimed. And she was right. The floor no longer looked like a whole village of smurfs had been trampled to death on it. She put the mop in the bucket and leaned it against the wall.

"Thank you. I appreciate your help." He smiled and dumped his sponge into the bucket as well. The water had turned distinctly blue.

"You're welcome. It was really no problem at all."

Neither of them seemed to know what else to say, so they stood there in awkward silence for a moment, The Everly Brothers playing over the scratchy speakers in the background.

"Do you work here every day?" she finally asked.

"Monday through Thursday evenings. Saturday and Sunday during the day," he replied automatically. He had taken on the extra shifts recently to make as much money as possible before college.

Her face fell. "That's a packed schedule. Do your friends not mind that you're so busy all the time?"

Dylan almost scoffed but stopped himself. He didn't want to look like a loser with no friends – even though that was exactly what he was.

He scratched the back of his head, avoiding her gaze, stalling.

"You don't have any friends?" Her voice had taken on a soft tone.

Great. Now she felt sorry for him. He didn't need her pity. "I…" He didn't know what to say. He let his mouth hang open and stuffed his hands in his pockets. He suddenly didn't know what to do with them.

"Well, maybe you just haven't found the right crowd yet. But they're out there. I'm sure. You'll find a place to belong."

He was surprised at the lack of condescension in her voice. When he finally mustered up the courage to look at her again, she was smiling confidently.

He didn't know how to respond to that. Of course she was right. Once he got to college things were going to change for him. Once he got out of this town… But that wasn't going to happen anytime soon.

Embarrassed, he closed his mouth and gave her a tight-lipped noncommittal smile.

"Okay. Then I'll know where to find you." She winked and turned to leave.

Dylan stood there, flabbergasted. Did that mean she wanted to hang out with him again?

Before he had pulled himself together, he heard the door open, and Marie shouted, "See you around!"

* * *

Dylan kept the doorknob tightly turned and slowly released it only once the front door was back in its frame. When he was safely inside the warm cocoon of his house, he took his beanie and gloves off. The walk home had been freezing. Not a soul had been out on the road in the dark, and the blanket of snow and ice had turned the world eerily quiet.

He shivered with the remnants of cold still clinging to his body. His nose was running from the sudden change in temperature, but he was too scared to even sniff too loudly because he didn't want to wake his mom, who usually fell asleep on the couch when he wasn't there to keep her company. And she needed her rest. She worked long hours at the local grocery store – stocking shelves, working the register, dealing with customers – and all that while making nothing more than minimum wage.

Dylan felt bad about that. After all, if it hadn't been for him, his mom would probably still be living in Boston. Maybe she'd even be married and have a few kids. Kids that weren't him.

Still breathing heavily from the strain of bending over and taking his boots off, he tiptoed a few steps to the living room. The television was softly playing commercials in the background. The single shaded lamp behind the couch cast a beam of warm light into the hallway. As he peeked into the room, he saw his mom stretched out on the couch, covered in the threadbare quilt her aunt Elsie had bought on a trip to Canada twenty-five years ago.

Her disheveled brown hair – the same shade as Dylan's – was spread out like seaweed on the sofa cushion beneath her head. Her deep breaths told Dylan that she was fast asleep. He suppressed a chuckle. Susan always insisted that she never fell asleep in front of the TV, but he found her like this almost every night when he came home from work.

He had told her countless times to go to bed when she felt tired, but she insisted on waiting up for him. It was a nice sentiment even if it was completely unnecessary. Nothing was ever going to happen to him in this boring backwater town.

With a sigh, he walked over to the TV set and turned it off. It was probably the most modern thing in the house – one of the only things his mom had replaced after she had inherited the house from Elsie almost eighteen years ago.

As the noise from the small screen stopped, Susan started to stir. She blinked a few times, disoriented. When her gaze landed on Dylan, a small smile spread across her lips.

"Hey, you're home." Her voice sounded like sandpaper. She had obviously been sleeping for a while.

"Yeah. Five past ten. As always. Mom, go to bed. The couch must be really uncomfortable."

She squeezed her eyes shut and rubbed her face. With a groan, she stretched her arms and legs. "In a minute. You can go ahead and use the bathroom first."

She'd already started to doze off again. Dylan chuckled, shaking his head.

He made his way upstairs to the one bathroom in the house. The entire room was tiled red – also courtesy of Susan's aunt. "Not even blue slush could make a difference on these tiles," Dylan muttered under his breath.

One look in the mirror confirmed that he had gained a few new whiteheads, and the zit that had been invisible under the skin of the bridge of his nose had sprouted, creating an ugly red infected bulb. He touched it lightly and winced at the stabbing sensation.

He opened the mirror cabinet to get the face wash his mom had bought for his acne. But if he was honest with himself, he only bothered with that because Susan cared. He had long ago accepted that his skin condition was persistent. After all, it had been there since he had turned thirteen. Nearly five long years of being called 'pizza face' and 'pus-volcano' by Fletcher and his disciples. It seemed unfair that he was the only person in his entire grade who had acne this bad on top of being overweight. The name-calling was basically endless at this point. Not that they were particularly creative with it…

He slipped his pajamas on and didn't bother with brushing his teeth.

One last walk downstairs to wake his mom – "Yeah, yeah, I'm coming up…" – and he grabbed a fresh bag of Cheetos from the kitchen and went back upstairs to his room.

The ceiling of the tiny rectangular space was slanted as it was directly under the roof. He had plastered it with all sorts of posters of fast cars, his favorite rock bands, and at the center of it all, a cutout of the Harvard crest. The place he wanted to go to so badly it almost hurt. If not for college, then definitely for law school.

He had sent in his application a few weeks ago, hands shaking as he had slid the thick envelope into the mailbox. He had barely been able to afford the application fees for his five chosen colleges. That's why Harvard was the only Ivy League school he had applied to. *Better play it safe.*

And if he actually got in, he would have to pay a small fortune in tuition and room and board. Money his mom couldn't afford to spare. He had considered applying for a scholarship, but as it turned out, he wasn't disadvantaged or talented or athletic enough to be eligible for one. So he worked his ass off at the gas station to make as much money as possible as fast as he could.

He lay down on his twin bed which had become too short for him and ripped open the bag of Cheetos. As he munched on the cheesy deliciousness, he gazed around his room. The opposite wall was lined with a long bookshelf that contained stacks upon stacks of worn hardcovers and creased paperbacks. Another tall stack sat on his desk at the foot of the bed, right next to his Walkman.

Ah, so that's where I left it! He had been looking for it all day at school, already half believing that Fletcher had had it stolen.

He got up and put the headphones on. The bag of Cheetos was already empty, so he tossed it into the trash can under his desk. He pressed play. The first soothing notes of Pink Floyd's 'The Great Gig in the Sky' traveled through his eardrums straight into his brain, relaxing him for the first time all day. As he settled back onto his bed, he pulled his thick down covers all the way up to his chin, turned off the light and let Clare Torry sing him to sleep.

2

"How was the cleanup, Harper?" Fletcher shouted from across the hallway, making every head turn toward Dylan, but he pretended not to hear the guy.

He slammed his locker shut, swung his backpack over his shoulder, and walked in the opposite direction. It was the wrong way – his next class was in Mrs. Turner's room, next to where Fletcher was standing – but he was not going to risk a confrontation.

A group of girls looked at him with utter disgust, as if he were an insect or a big hairy spider. One of them – Juliette Wheeler, a junior – turned to her friends and said in a low voice loud enough for Dylan to hear: "I heard he asked Lauren to the winter dance." She snickered. "As if any girl in her right mind would say yes to *that*."

Not true. He hadn't asked anyone out. Hell, he didn't even bother with going to any of these high school dances where it would be so easy for Fletcher to humiliate and degrade him. He wasn't a masochist. But there was no use in correcting Juliette. She would just think he was trying to save face.

What face? he thought bitterly. Everyone already believed the worst of him. It was liberating in a way. If he didn't have any friends, he couldn't lose any either. What did he care what all these assholes thought of him? A few months from now he would most likely never see any of them again.

Still, he didn't like all those eyes following him down the hallway. He turned the corner and made a beeline for the school library. Nobody would bother him there. He could hide between the shelves until the bell rang. He'd be a little late for class, but Mrs. Turner wouldn't mind. She spent the first ten minutes of each period telling Eddie Richter off for not doing his homework, anyway. She probably wouldn't even notice if he got in a little late.

All the way at the back of the library was the foreign language section, filled with thick dictionaries for various languages nobody around here needed to learn. Most people's grandparents were from some European country or French Canadian, so a lot of Dylan's peers had some kind of knowledge of a foreign language. Another thing that set him apart from everyone else. Dylan had taken French for two years, but the only thing he had retained from that was 'bonjour.'

He checked for anyone following him, but the place was empty. With a sigh, he slid to the floor and searched his backpack for a chocolate bar he knew was in there. When he finally glimpsed a corner of the wrapper, he frantically pulled it out, unwrapped it, and stuffed the whole thing in his mouth.

A sense of calm washed over him. He closed his eyes and leaned his head back against the shelves as he chewed the crunchy, sweet goodness. Soon he'd be out of here. Only a few more months…

The bell rang.

* * *

Larry walked into the store, head bent, shoulders drawn up close, the collar of his down jacket up against the icy wind and the rapidly falling snow. He huffed, took his gloves off, and rubbed his hands together. The day's newspaper was clamped under his left arm.

"You're early, Larry." It was only seven. He rarely came in before nine.

The old man huffed again. His cheeks were turning red. "Oh, boy, I didn't want to be out there any longer than I had to." He sniffed.

"Tell me about it. It's been snowing for two hours straight."

"I'm not talking about the weather. Haven't you heard?"

"Heard what?"

Larry's eyes widened and started twinkling. He always got that twinkle in his eye when he was about to tell Dylan the latest piece of gossip.

But today that twinkle gave way to something else. Something darker. A shadow fell over his face.

"Keith, the postman, was found dead this morning," he whispered.

It took Dylan a second to process this information. "What?" He blinked. "Where? How?" The way Larry had broken the news indicated that this hadn't been an ordinary death. No tumble off a ladder, no car accident, no heart attack... No. This had to have been something sinister.

Larry took a deep breath and shook his head in dismay. "They found him close to the O'Shea property. That's always been the first stop on his route. It's pretty close to the woods."

Dylan almost rolled his eyes. Every property in this town was close to the woods.

"Fred Channing found him when he passed the house on his way to work. Said he'd missed him at first, what with all the fresh snow covering the body. But then he noticed Keith's abandoned truck with the door open. He stopped to check it out and, well, he said he couldn't believe what he saw next."

Larry took his beanie off and ran a hand through his tousled white hair. Again, he shook his head.

"Apparently, Keith was nothing but a pale heap of flesh, eyes wide open as if in shock. He had scratch and bite marks all over his body."

The hairs on the back of Dylan's neck stood up. That sounded horrifying. He found it hard to believe something like that had happened in Berlin.

"So it must have been an animal, right?" Not as sinister as murder but still concerning. Usually, the wildlife in the area didn't attack humans.

Larry shrugged. "Nobody knows. Police think so, yes. But they can't say for sure. Something about it didn't seem right." He paused. "I've heard some folks say it was the Yeti." He scoffed. "Well, whatever it was, all I know is I'll be steering clear of these woods till they find this thing." He held up his newspaper menacingly and gave Dylan an emphatic look. And with that he made his way to the back office.

Was Larry's fear justified? Animal attacks like that were rare, after all. But then again, wouldn't an animal have eaten the body and left only a carcass? Or dragged it into the woods to finish it off? Maybe it had been interrupted… Or it hadn't been an animal at all. Maybe it was something else. But what else could it have been?

Dylan shook his head. He was starting to sound just as crazy as those superstitious fools who believed in stuff like the Yeti.

Before he could berate himself any longer, the door opened again and the beautiful girl he had met the day before walked in. Dylan was so shocked to see her again that he couldn't remember her name for a second. *What was it? Mary? No, Marie...*

She was wearing the same leather jacket but no gloves, no beanie, no scarf, not even winter boots. She wore white sneakers instead and a pair of tight jeans. Her jacket wasn't even zipped up. He could see her pink turtleneck sweater underneath. Her curly brown hair hung loosely down her shoulders.

"Hey, Dylan," she said with a wide smile. "How's it going?"

Perplexed, he didn't answer for a few seconds. He hadn't expected her to show up again, much less remember his name. It made him slightly uneasy. He couldn't help but assume she had some ulterior motive.

"Hi… Marie, right?"

She winked at him and nodded.

"Uh, I'm good. How are you?"

"Doing good." She stepped up to the counter and hovered there for half a minute while some country singer was praising his good Christian girl on the radio.

"Can I help you?" Maybe she needed to run an errand. But grocery stores were still open at this time of night.

"I'm just here to hang out for a bit. You don't mind, do you?" She gave him another dazzling smile.

He didn't answer. Something was wrong with her. There had to be. Why would she want to hang out with him? She didn't even know him. *And she probably wouldn't want to if she did.*

"We got a room at Bernie's." That was the only motel in town, just down the road.

Dylan nodded. "Cool. How long are you planning on staying here?" He still couldn't fathom how anybody would want to stay in Berlin for any period of time if they didn't have to.

She shrugged. "We'll see. It's cool for now." She didn't look him in the eyes while she spoke, removing a piece of lint from her jeans instead.

Dylan raised his eyebrows. "I find that hard to believe."

Marie's chin shot up. "Why?"

He hesitated. "Well, because there isn't anything to do here. Not much to see either…"

"Oh, we're not here for the sights." She grinned, but Dylan didn't get the joke. "We like the calm and quiet."

Well, they were married. He could imagine what they'd be doing all day at Bernie's. The thought aroused him a little. She was an attractive woman, after all. He blushed.

She frowned for a split second. Dylan tried not to picture her naked.

To change the subject, he said, "You never told me where you guys were from."

"New York."

"New York City?"

"Yes."

"Really? You don't sound like a New Yorker." In fact, her voice was pretty generic. He couldn't place it at all, but if he had to take a guess, he would go for someplace on the West Coast.

She shrugged. "I moved around a lot as a kid. We lived all over. That's probably why."

"Hm." That made sense.

"Have you always lived here?"

"Yeah. I've never really traveled anywhere to be honest."

Something in her expression changed, but he wasn't sure what it was. She looked a little more somber. "I see."

"But I'd like to change that." He felt the need to cheer her up. "I mean what you're doing sounds really cool. Just going wherever the road takes you." He smiled at her.

She returned the smile. "Yeah, it's been fun." And then, out of the blue, she asked, "Do you have any siblings, Dylan?"

He frowned. "Uh, no. I'm an only child. Why?"

She whipped her hair back over her shoulder. "Just curious. So, you live with your parents?"

"Just my mom."

Her eyebrows shot up. When he didn't elaborate, she asked, "What about your dad?"

Dylan's hands grew sweaty. His heartbeat picked up a little. His father was a sore subject he did not want to get into – especially not with someone he hardly knew.

"He's not around."

"And he doesn't live in the area?"

Why did she care? And besides, that was none of her business. "No." He looked away and thumbed through the book he had been reading before Larry had come in, for no reason other than to avoid her gaze.

"What are you reading?"

"It's a book on criminal justice."

"Dense." He could tell by her inflection that the corners of her mouth had turned down.

"It's for college."

"You want to become a lawyer?"

"Yes." His jaw jutted forward defensively.

"Why?"

He rolled his eyes. He couldn't help it. Whenever people questioned his plans for the future, he got annoyed. They didn't seem to understand that this was the only possible route for him. He was going to become a lawyer no matter what.

But she didn't get offended at his reaction. She patiently waited for his answer.

"Because I'd like to make something of myself." He left it at that. This girl didn't need to know that his goal was to get rich. Not ostensibly rich like Fletcher's family, though. He didn't need a mansion with a garage holding five sports cars and a yacht. He just wanted to make enough money so he wouldn't have to worry about it anymore. Enough to take care of his mom. Enough to have a good life.

Marie raised an eyebrow, waiting for more, but Dylan remained tight-lipped.

"Are you going to go back to college?" he asked before she could shoot another question at him. She had said something about taking a break from college the night before.

She shrugged and looked down at the counter. "Maybe. Not sure yet." After a beat she looked him straight in the eyes. "I'm more into the arts, you know? Music… You don't really need a college degree for that kind of stuff."

He nodded. That made perfect sense. She definitely had the looks of a pop star. And judging by her car, money didn't seem to be an issue for her.

"Do you have a band or something?" Maybe she and her husband were in one together like Fleetwood Mac.

"No. I'm more of a solo artist." She gave him that smile again. The one that made him feel like he was missing the joke.

"What kind of music do you make?" Something about her made him think she was legit. Not one of those boasting wannabes but somebody who actually knew what she was doing.

"Uh, I've dabbled in pretty much everything. I mainly play the piano and the violin, so I'm not limited to one genre."

Yep. She was definitely the real deal. People who played the violin knew music. "That's really cool." He was in awe.

"Do you play an instrument?"

"Not really. My mom suggested I learn the guitar when I was little, but I was never any good at it." He had stuck with it for a few years to humor her, but when she realized he didn't enjoy it, she'd let him quit.

She laughed. "Well, it's never too late to try again."

He sucked in air through the corner of his mouth and made a face. "I don't think the guitar and I are a good fit."

Her melodic laugh rang through the store again.

The door opened and Jake Logan walked in. The man was about the same age as his mom. Dylan knew that because Logan had once tried to date her. The tips of his scruffy reddish-brown beard were tinged white with frost.

When he spotted Marie, he did a double take like Fletcher had the night before. His eyes fluttered from her to Dylan, then back to her and back to Dylan again. As he stepped up to the counter and his face was out of her sightline, he gave Dylan a look, pulling down the corners of his mouth approvingly.

Dylan tried not to roll his eyes. *As if...*

"Have you heard what happened to postman Keith?" Logan asked as Dylan rang him up.

"Yeah. Insane. Must have been an animal, right?"

"I don't know what else it could have been. It's like what happened to Monica Brown twenty years ago. She was out in the woods late one night during the wintertime and got eaten by a wolf. People sometimes forget how dangerous it can get out there." He turned to Marie. "You better watch out."

She smiled her private joke smile again. "I'll be careful. Thanks for the warning."

Logan gave both of them a curt nod and walked out. When the door had swung shut, Marie turned to Dylan with a furrowed brow.

"What happened to the postman?"

"His body was found this morning. Apparently, he was all scratched up and there were bite marks all over him."

Her eyes narrowed. "Does that happen a lot around here?"

Dylan scoffed. "No. Definitely not. But Logan was right. You should be careful."

"Well, so should you!" She looked genuinely worried.

He dismissed her remark with a wave of his hand. "I'll be fine." Despite the warning he had just given her, he was pretty sure what had happened to the postman would remain an isolated incident. Wolves could travel long distances. If Keith had been attacked by one, it would surely be in Canada by now.

She seemed to be caught up in her own thoughts. Her lips were pressed together, and she was staring off into space.

He glanced out through the front windows. Her car wasn't there. "Did you walk here?" Bernie's was close by but still a good fifteen-minute-walk away, and she really wasn't dressed for the weather.

"Hm? Yeah. It's not far and I can take care of myself. Don't worry." She smiled that knowing smile again.

He didn't doubt that for a second, but even a girl like her was no match for a wild animal. "I walked here myself so I can't offer you a ride, but maybe you'd like to use Larry's phone to call your husband to pick you up?"

She contemplated his offer. "And how are you going to get home?"

He shook his head at her concern. "I'll be fine. I literally live round the corner." Two streets. It was a five-minute walk. No need to worry.

She started to say something else, but the door opened again, interrupting her before she could get a word out.

A guy who could be none other than Marie's other half entered. His shoulder-length dark brown hair and dark eyes were in perfect contrast to his skin, which was so pale, it seemed to reflect the fluorescent light inside the store. His features were sharp and angular, making him look like a male model from a commercial for fancy perfume. His mouth formed a tight line, which made it hard for Dylan to even picture him smiling.

He was dressed entirely in black, but just like Marie, he was not equipped for the weather. His boots were fashionable but looked like they provided little protection from the cold, his leather jacket wasn't zipped up and he wore neither gloves nor a beanie.

His whole demeanor was imposing. He easily filled the room with his presence. But it wasn't a calming presence. It made Dylan deeply uneasy.

Nevertheless, this man was strangely alluring. Dylan's heartbeat picked up speed as he made eye contact with him. He wondered what it would feel like to be touched by him but buried the thought as soon as he'd had it.

"Hey, babe. This is Dylan. Dylan, that's my husband, Alec." She smiled and looked adoringly at Alec.

"Nice to meet you." Dylan smiled courteously, but Alec didn't return the gesture.

He stared straight into Dylan's eyes without blinking. After a few seconds, Dylan felt scrutinized under Alec's intense gaze and started fidgeting. When Alec still didn't say anything after what seemed like an eternity, Dylan broke eye contact and looked at Marie instead, who didn't seem to find Alec's behavior odd.

"We have to go." Alec's voice immediately commanded the room. They looked at each other for a moment, silently communicating. Marie nodded earnestly.

She turned to Dylan. "When do you get off?"

He hesitated. Before Alec had come in, he had felt somewhat at ease with Marie, but now his guard was back up.

"Why?"

"You shouldn't walk home. I'll stop by and drive you."

"That really isn't necessary. I told you I live right around the corner. I'll be fine."

"I'm sure the postman thought he'd be fine as well. Come on, it's no inconvenience for me and you wouldn't have to walk."

The stern expression on her face told Dylan that she wasn't going to take no for an answer.

"Well, I get off at ten. So it'll be another two and a half hours." Surely she wouldn't bother coming back for him.

"Okay. I'll be here." She nodded once and followed Alec out the door without another word.

"Sure…" Dylan muttered to himself. He definitely wasn't going to hold his breath.

3

At five minutes to ten Susan's old Chevy pulled up into the gas station. Dylan smiled to himself. Of course his mom had heard about the incident with the postman and of course she would insist on picking him up from work so he wouldn't have to walk home. A warm feeling spread from his heart into his whole body.

He packed his stuff and shouted, "Larry, my mom's here to pick me up. I'm off now. See you tomorrow!"

He could hear Larry shuffling out of his chair in the back office. A few seconds later the old man appeared between the snack shelves. "It's nice of your mom to come and get you." He waved at Susan through the window. She returned the gesture from the driver's seat.

"Yeah. She's swell." He stepped out from behind the counter, swung his backpack over his shoulder, and made his way out the door.

For a fraction of a second, he felt a pang of disappointment that he would never find out if Marie was going to show up. But he shook the thought off. Of course she wasn't going to show. And even if she were, he hardly knew the girl. It didn't matter.

"Hey, Mom, thanks for picking me up," he said with a wide smile as he climbed into the Chevy. The door closed with a loud bang, and the engine howled as Susan hit the gas pedal.

"Of course. I couldn't let you walk home after what happened to Keith this morning."

Dylan didn't have to ask how she knew about the incident. She worked at the busiest grocery store in town, and news like that was sure to travel fast. He had most likely been the last to know – except for Marie of course.

Again, he wondered if she would have shown up, and he started to feel a little bad. What if she did come and he wasn't there? She would have made the trip for nothing.

No, don't be ridiculous. She won't come.

"Did you have a nice day?" Susan asked. She sounded tired but cheerful.

"Uh, yeah, it was good. Pretty quiet. You?"

"Mine was good, too. Robert brought in leftover muffins from his wife's birthday party. They were delicious. I took one for you as well. It's at home in the fridge."

"Aw, thanks, Mom." His mouth watered.

She pulled into the driveway of their little house. Dylan got out of the car and walked inside so fast it bordered on running. He was breathing heavily as he opened the fridge.

"Don't you want to eat a proper meal first? Before you dig into that muffin?"

He always made himself a premade meal in the microwave in Larry's office when he worked this late. Usually, he got hungry afterward though. So he had a few chocolate bars and a bag of chips here and there throughout the night as well. Today he'd had chicken pot pie, three Snickers bars, and two large bags of chips, but he felt like he could eat more.

"Sure, what do we have?"

"I made a casserole." Susan took an oven tin covered in aluminum foil off the top shelf of the fridge. She lifted the foil and held it out to show him the contents.

It looked delicious even though it was cold. "Cool. I'll have some."

She smiled warmly and put the casserole in the oven to heat it up.

Dylan took a seat at the round chestnut kitchen table. It sat four, but they only ever used the two chairs closest to the kitchen counter. His mom folded the tin foil into a neat square and put it into the designated drawer. She hated throwing stuff away. Usually, she reused a sheet of aluminum foil four or five times before she decided it was too crumpled and chucked it out.

"I wonder what it was that attacked Keith," she said to the kitchen counter.

"Must have been an animal."

"I don't feel comfortable with you walking to school tomorrow. It's still dark when you leave the house." She turned around and looked at him admonishingly with a furrowed brow as if it were his fault that he had to go to school.

He shrugged. "What else am I supposed to do?"

"I'll drive you."

"Mom, that's really not necessary." She would have to get up earlier for that, and he didn't want her to fuss. "I'm sure the animal is long gone by now."

"I insist." She took a plate out of the cabinet, closing the door with a little too much fervor. "You never know. Better safe than sorry." She held up her index finger in typical mom fashion and turned to the oven and checked the casserole. She stuck her hand in and patted the food lightly. She closed the oven door and turned back to Dylan.

"How about we cook together Friday night?"

His face lit up. He loved their cooking sessions. But since he had started working so late at the gas station, they had become few and far between. He couldn't even remember the last time they'd had one.

"Yes, that sounds great. Did you have a specific dish in mind?"

She thought about it for a moment. "Maybe we could make steaks with those special potatoes. You know, the ones I saw on the cooking channel with the cream and the garlic."

"Oh yeah, delicious!" He couldn't wait.

"Great." She smiled warmly at him. She removed the casserole from the oven, put the steaming dish on the counter, and carefully placed the food on the plate for him.

He quickly got up, grabbed a fork, and took the plate from her. He hadn't even sat down before he started digging in – and promptly burned the roof of his mouth. He forced himself to slow down.

Susan took a seat next to him. She thrummed her fingers on the table. That was something she did only when she was nervous.

"What is it?" he asked.

Her jaw was working. She hesitated, staring at her hand. Then she took a deep breath and looked at Dylan with apprehension.

"Martin Kirkgaard asked me out on a date."

Dylan's hand holding the fork froze midair. A wave of cold washed over his body, making him lose his appetite.

"Oh." He focused on his casserole so he wouldn't have to look at her. He didn't know why this always caught him by surprise. Susan was still young – only thirty-seven – she was slender, and her blue eyes sparkled with joy. Of course men were going to ask her out.

"Yeah." She sounded contrite, as if she had done something wrong, as if it were her fault somebody had asked her on a date.

Dylan got angry at himself. He had no right to be upset if his mom wanted to date somebody. Hell, she deserved it, and he wanted her to be happy. But he also couldn't help himself. He didn't like it. He wasn't even sure what exactly bothered him about the idea. He just didn't want to share her with anyone.

But then again, soon he would be off to college, and it would be unfair to expect her to sit at home alone with nobody to talk to.

He sighed. "And did you say yes?" He still wasn't looking at her.

"I like Martin. And it's been a year since his wife died…"

She was being evasive which most likely meant yes. Dylan slowly nodded. Martin Kirkgaard. He didn't know much about the man, only that he was an insurance agent who had lost his wife in a car accident last winter. His daughter, Molly, was a senior as well. He couldn't remember ever talking to her, but they did have history together.

"Okay. And when is the date?" He looked up at her and forced a smile, which must have been convincing enough because she beamed at him.

"Saturday night. We're going out for dinner."

"Nice." He nodded, scraping the last of the casserole off his plate. "Well, that's great, Mom. I hope you'll have fun."

She leaned over the table and gave him a kiss on the cheek. "Thank you, darling." She took his empty plate away. While she was rinsing it in the sink, he walked over to the fridge and got out the muffin she had promised him earlier.

But a bitter feeling crept up on him: Had she been trying to bribe him with food to break the news about the date more easily? He didn't like that thought. He didn't want her to feel like she had an obligation to him to stay single.

Was it his fault it had never worked out with any of her previous boyfriends? His stomach tightened painfully for a second. That hadn't been his intention. Sure, he had never been thrilled at the idea of Susan dating because none of those guys were good enough for her. But he had never stopped to think that he was actively ruining her relationships. *Was* he ruining her relationships?

There had been Jake Logan, who had stopped coming over after a month for no apparent reason. Then there was Gary Haakon who she broke up with over something she never told Dylan about. And her longest relationship – with Paul Neuget – who she had been dating for almost a year, ended because she hadn't wanted him to move in with them. Had that been because of Dylan? He had never been warm to any of those men.

She had deserved better, but the bottom line was they had been good guys. And he had most likely driven them away. His heart sank. Well, that wasn't going to happen with Martin.

"I'm looking forward to meeting him. Assuming the date goes well." He gave Susan a tight-lipped smile, and she answered with another beaming one.

"I hope it will, darling."

"That muffin was really good." He had almost swallowed it whole. "And the casserole too. Thank you." He kissed her on the cheek and stretched his arms wide, stifling a yawn. "I'm going to head to bed now. Good night, Mom."

"Good night, darling. Sleep tight!"

"You, too."

Upstairs in bed he stared at the ceiling in the dark, trying to fall asleep and not stress over Martin Kirkgaard.

He forced himself to think about something else, and the first thing that came to mind was Marie and her peculiar interest in him. Again, he wondered if she had shown up at ten only to find him gone. He highly doubted it but still… He was curious.

He had a hunch that she was going to come back in again tomorrow. *Nonsense.* He shook his head at himself. She and her intimidating husband had probably decided this town was too boring to stay in after all and were off to greener pastures. And he couldn't blame them.

* * *

The next morning, his mom got up bright and early to drive him to school as promised. She was pouring herself some coffee while Dylan wolfed down his breakfast cereal, listening to the weather forecast on the radio and staring at the half empty glass of orange juice in front of him without seeing it. Mornings were rough. Especially when they started at six o'clock.

"And we're expecting more snow this weekend, so buckle up and get those shovels ready!" The cheery man's metallic voice blared through the scratchy radio speaker. The radio was a remnant from the sixties, one of the last things Susan's aunt had bought before her sudden death.

"We have to leave, or you'll be late," Susan murmured, taking a huge gulp from her coffee mug and promptly making a face as the hot liquid scorched her mouth.

He gave her a curt nod, put his empty bowl and glass in the sink, and followed her out into the hallway to put his snowproof clothes on. As he slipped into his thick down jacket, he wished for the cold weather to be over, but there was no end in sight at this point. Sometimes they even got snow around his birthday at the end of March.

Fully dressed, he sighed and followed his mom out the door. Their house was small and surrounded on three sides by nothing but forest. Their next-door neighbors' houses were each a good two hundred yards away, and there were no streetlamps. Usually, the snow reflected enough moonlight to illuminate the area, but the moon seemed to be hidden under a thick layer of clouds. Only the porch light cast a weak glow onto the old Chevy in the driveway. Dylan thanked his lucky stars it hadn't snowed during the night so at least they didn't have to shovel the car free.

Its windows were covered in ice which needed to be scraped off before they could go anywhere though. Dylan volunteered while Susan got into the car and turned the engine and the headlights on. The engine's sudden loud rumbling sounded like thunder in the silence of the early morning.

Dylan tried to be quick as they were already running late. He started scraping the windshield, his breath visible in the ice-cold air. Even though he was wearing thick clothes, he was shivering. The cold was relentless.

He was scraping the driver's window when a sudden movement between the dark trees made him stop in his tracks. He looked up but couldn't see anything.

He could have sworn he had noticed something move between the dark trees. He froze in place, staring at the spot for a full minute, heart pounding in his chest, his breath short and visible in the cold air.

Susan tapped the glass from the inside of the car, making him jump. She made a face that said, 'hurry up, we're going to be late.' And she was right. It had probably been nothing. His imagination was running wild because of the attack on the postman.

But his heart was still pounding with the aftershock as he went back to scraping the window.

He did a hurried and sloppy job and quickly moved to the passenger's side. But as he was walking around the car, he glimpsed a pair of eyes staring at him from between the trees. He blinked a few times, sure he was hallucinating, but the eyes were reflecting the light like a cat's. Only they were too big to belong to a cat.

He struggled to see the rest of the body, but when he blinked one more time, the eyes were gone as suddenly as they had appeared. Without meaning to, he stepped toward the spot where they had been, and his feet hit something solid.

There on the frozen and snow-covered ground just off the driveway lay something big and squishy. He kicked it softly to find out what it was and heard the distinct swishing sound of a winter jacket. He frantically stumbled backward, heart pounding, blood rushing in his ears.

"Dylan, what's going on?"

"Mom, call nine-one-one! Someone is lying there in the snow."

He refused to believe this person was dead. They couldn't be. He was still staring at the lump on the ground, but he couldn't make anything out and was unable to move any closer. The horror and shock had cemented him in place.

"What!?"

He heard Susan rummaging for something in the glove box. A few seconds later a flashlight clicked on, and the light briefly created a circle around Dylan. Breathing heavily, his mom came around the Chevy brandishing the flashlight like a weapon. He pointed at the ground where he had stumbled onto the body, and she swerved the light cone over it.

Dylan gasped. The person on the ground was a girl. A girl he knew. Stacy Yelander. She was in Dylan's class and lived down the street. Every morning she walked past his house on her way to band practice before school.

But this girl was never going to walk anywhere ever again.

Her face was contorted into a silent scream, eyes bulging out of their sockets. Her clothes were ripped up by large scratch marks all over her body. Her neck had been all but torn out, causing her head to lie at an awkward angle and staining the snow red with blood.

"Oh my god." Susan covered her mouth with her hand.

For a moment they both stood there, captivated by the sheer horror unfolding before them. Then Dylan remembered he had seen something in the woods. Something large with gleaming eyes. They were sitting ducks out here.

"Quick, Mom, get back inside!"

He grabbed her hand, and they hurried back to the house. He fumbled with his keys, taking way too long to get the house key into the lock. Gasping for breath, he finally unlocked the door, practically diving inside the house dragging Susan close behind. He slammed the door and leaned against it, for fear it might open and whatever had killed Stacy might follow them inside.

"I'm calling the cops." Susan headed toward the kitchen phone.

Dylan's heart pounded so fast it nearly jumped out of his chest. Being safely indoors had apparently sprung her into action whereas it had paralyzed Dylan with shock. He closed his eyes and took deep breaths, trying to calm himself down, but in his mind's eye all he saw was Stacy's mangled body.

"Hello? Yes, this is Susan Harper. Uh, one forty-four Chestnut Street. There—there's a dead body outside my house. I think she was mauled by an animal. Yes. Please come quick! Thank you."

Dylan slid down to the floor and leaned his head back against the door. *Holy shit!* Now that the initial shock had worn off, he realized he was shaking. *That could have been me out there.* He immediately felt bad for thinking it. Somebody was dead and his first reaction was to be relieved it wasn't him? Poor Stacy. She was only seventeen.

"Okay, they're on their way." His mom stepped into the hallway. Her face looked tense, eyes huge, nostrils flared. "Come on, darling, come into the kitchen where it's warmer." She held a hand out to him. It took Dylan's brain a second to figure out what to do with it, but he finally gripped it and let his mom heave him off the floor.

She pulled him into the kitchen and sat him down at the table. He could see the car through the kitchen window. Its lights were still on, and the engine was running, the door on the driver's side wide open. But he sure as hell wasn't going to go out there and turn it off. And he wasn't going to let his mom do it either. Not with that thing still on the loose.

He could barely make out the lump on the ground that was Stacy's body. He shook his head in disbelief. A dead person was lying in their front yard. It was only now starting to sink in.

3

"That's Stacy Yelander, isn't it?" He hadn't even noticed Susan sitting down next to him. She had absentmindedly lit a cigarette but wasn't smoking it, rather holding it up next to her face staring into the distance.

"Yes," he whispered.

They sat in silence until the police arrived, which was only five minutes later but felt like hours to Dylan.

Every squad car in Berlin was parked around their house. The cops fanned out searching the area with flashlights. Dawn was approaching fast, but it was still fairly dark out. A group of policemen in hazmat suits surrounded the body, blocking Dylan's view. The chief of police – a big burly man whose name, Dylan was pretty sure, was Samuel Mangold – took one look at Stacy and walked up to their Chevy, turned the engine and the lights off, and took the keys with him to the house.

Susan let him in. "Thanks for coming over so quickly."

"I'm sorry you had to see this, ma'am." He wiped his feet on the doormat and stepped into the house.

"Sir," Dylan said by the way of greeting. The chief took his gloves off and extended a hand. Dylan shook it.

"Please, have a seat." Susan indicated her usual chair, and the chief sat with a heavy sigh.

Dylan took a closer look at Mangold. His face was lined heavily and deep circles sagged under his eyes, but he couldn't have been older than fifty.

"Do you think this was the same animal that killed the postman?" Susan asked anxiously. She had sat down across from the chief on one of the chairs they never used. She thrummed her fingers on the table again, but it apparently didn't calm her down, so she lit another cigarette.

The chief lit one as well and nodded absentmindedly. He scratched his temple. "It's likely. The bodies show similar injuries." He fished Susan's keys out of his jacket pocket and slid them over the table to her.

"Thanks."

He pulled a notebook and a pen out of the other pocket and jotted something down.

"Can you tell me if you saw anything before you found the body?"

"It's Stacy Yelander. She is—*was* our neighbor," Dylan interjected. Referring to Stacy as 'the body' made him uneasy. Up until – what? A couple of hours ago? – she had been a happy person with a full life and a future to look forward to.

"I see…" The chief made a note.

"We didn't see anything," Susan said. "That is… Dylan? What were you staring at before you found her?"

He gulped. He remembered the gleaming pair of eyes between the trees. Something had been watching him, and for some reason he felt like it had been no animal. But what else had reflecting eyes like those? Certainly not a human.

The chief looked at him expectantly.

"I-I think I saw something move between the trees, but I couldn't make out what it was in the dark." Maybe he had imagined the eyes. Something like that couldn't possibly be real.

The chief frowned but made a note.

He continued before the cop could ask him any more questions about what he had seen. "Then I kind of stumbled over her—"

"And we panicked and ran back inside."

The chief nodded.

"What do you think it was, chief?" Susan asked.

Mangold seemed to be debating how much he could tell her. Eventually he settled on saying, "We think it might have been a mountain lion, but we're still investigating other options."

"But there are no mountain lions in New Hampshire," Dylan cut in.

The chief looked at him with an expression that said 'no shit, Sherlock.'

"What 'other options' are you looking into?" Dylan asked.

"Wolves. Bears." The cop scratched his stubbly chin.

"But bears are in hibernation. And wolves have gone extinct around here." Had this man skipped elementary school?

"We know that," he retorted, clearly annoyed. "But we have to look into everything. Especially now that there are two people dead."

They sat in silence for a moment. Dylan started to get worried. This was clearly exceeding the skill level of the Berlin police department.

"I advise you to stay indoors as much as possible and not to walk anywhere after dark." Mangold got up. "If you remember anything else, let me know." He put his card on the table.

Susan got up as well. "Of course. We will. Thank you, chief." She escorted him to the door. The sun had risen, but the sky was still overcast by a thick cover of white clouds.

It was past eight o'clock. He was missing first period.

"I'm going to call your school and tell them you're not coming in today. And then I'm going to call Robert and tell him I'm not coming in to work either."

Susan's voice sounded definite.

"Okay, thanks." Dylan didn't mind a day off. There was nothing they could teach him at school anyway. At this point, he went just to be present. Besides, he could do without Fletcher's bullying for a day.

He took another look out the window. They were wrapping things up. Stacy's body had been moved, but the imprint she had made in the snow was still there, along with a dark red stain bright as a beacon in the white landscape. That and the empty space seemed to be screaming at him. The hairs on the back of his neck were standing up in response.

He snapped the curtains closed emphatically. Out of sight, out of mind.

Or so he thought. Because when he turned around facing the hallway and the empty living room, he thought he saw those gleaming eyes again, watching him in the dark.

4

Dylan and his mom spent the day watching TV. All the while, Dylan was stuffing his face to calm his growing anxiety. Susan had locked the door twice and made sure all the windows were locked too. It made her feel safe, but it had the opposite effect on Dylan. He felt trapped. The air felt too stuffy, and the house felt too small.

And no matter how much he tried to distract himself, he couldn't get the sight of Stacy's mangled corpse out of his head. What was worse, every now and then, he thought of those gleaming eyes.

It couldn't have been a mountain lion. Those were shorter. And it couldn't have been a cat in a tree either because the eyes had been too big.

Then again, he wondered if he had imagined them. He had been groggy and cold, and with Keith's death the day before, his mind could have played a trick on him. *That's probably what it was.* He tried to banish the image from his mind and focus on the quiz show instead.

His mom had been smoking nonstop all morning – her way of coping with her own anxiety. Apparently, she wasn't as calm as she pretended to be.

This was bullshit! Why were they hiding out in their own home like that? The thing that had killed Keith and Stacy was obviously nocturnal, and it was the middle of the day. And besides, when all was said and done, it was still an animal. They had flashlights and torches and engines and fucking guns to scare it off! Hiding in here like chickens was getting ridiculous.

"Mom, I need to go to work."

She looked at him wide-eyed. "What!? Didn't you hear what the chief said? We're supposed to stay indoors."

"It's the middle of the day." He made a sweeping gesture with the hand that wasn't holding a peanut butter and jelly sandwich. "It's obviously nocturnal." When she still didn't give in, he added, "You can drive me if it makes you feel better."

She considered it. "But by the time you get off, it'll be dark."

He sighed. "I won't be a prisoner in my own house, Mom. How long do you think it'll take till they catch this thing? We can't just put our lives on hold, sit around and do nothing in the meantime. We have bills to pay."

She flinched. As soon as it was out, he regretted saying it. He knew his mom felt bad about having to live paycheck to paycheck although he had told her repeatedly that he didn't mind, that he was happy and that it didn't matter to him, but she worried over it anyway. It seemed like there was nothing he could say that would make her believe him.

"Still. You don't have to put yourself in mortal danger over a few bucks. I'm the one who's supposed to take care of you."

"I know, Mom. But I want to go to work, okay? I need to get out of here. I'm going stir-crazy in this house."

She made a face but seemed to ponder his words. "Okay, then. But I'll drive you and I'll pick you up. No walking home in the dark!" She wagged a finger at him.

"Promise." He held up two fingers like a Scout. "And thank you, Mom."

He rushed up to his room and swapped his sweats for the pair of worn jeans he had put on earlier that day for school – the waistband feeling tighter than that morning – and a thrifted light brown turtleneck sweater that didn't fully cover his midsection. He added a green checkered sweater vest on top, which was large enough to accommodate his belly.

Susan was waiting for him by the door when he came downstairs, holding out his backpack, which she had stocked with more sandwiches. Neither of them said a word as they walked up to the Chevy.

Despite his claims from before, Dylan suddenly wasn't so sure if leaving the house was such a good idea. Anxiety crept inside him again. He fidgeted with the straps of his backpack and took a calming breath, telling himself to suck it up.

But as he got to the passenger's side, the bright red bloodstain in the snow jumped out at him. It seemed to be screaming at him to be vigilant, to stay inside and lock the doors. He squeezed his eyes shut and shook his head, trying to ignore it. *You're overreacting. You're in shock, that's all.* He got into the car without another glance at the blood, taking a deep calming breath.

From the corner of his eye, he noticed Susan's hands were visibly shaking, and Dylan knew that the cold outside had nothing to do with it. The few lines on her face had gotten deeper since that morning, but she didn't say a word. She didn't even look at Dylan. She just diligently drove him to work.

As he entered the store, Connor, the guy who worked the day shift during the week, shouted, "Man, I thought you weren't coming in today. I heard what happened at your house. Damn… Shame about Stacy."

The nonchalance of Connor's comment struck Dylan. 'Shame' didn't seem appropriate. Somebody's life had been tragically cut short. Her family was bereaved. Her parents would never talk to her, never hold her, never hear her laugh again. That was more than a shame. The worst had happened.

"Mhm. But I wasn't the one who was killed, so I figured I'd come in."

Connor laughed. Dylan got angry. That wasn't meant to be funny.

"Sure, man. Then I'll take off. Have a good one!" He flinched at his own words. At least he did have the decency to look contrite. "I mean considering the circumstances…" He cleared his throat and left in a hurry.

Dylan could see Connor's wife Patty waiting for him in the car. The two had been high school sweethearts and had been forced to get married two years ago when she got pregnant during senior year. Whenever Dylan saw the two of them, he couldn't help but think that they were stuck here, Connor working shifts at the gas station and Patty waiting tables at one of the better diners in town. He felt a little sorry for them – while at the same time hoping that wouldn't be him two years from now. Albeit the chances of him knocking anyone up were less than zero.

Well, at least they're alive and well, unlike Stacy...

Business was slow that afternoon, but every customer he knew asked him about Stacy. Maybe the change of scenery hadn't been the best plan to take his mind off things after all. After one of his neighbors had left, he pulled out his book and started reading. But the exemplary case study involved the death of a young woman, so he ended up thinking about Stacy again.

Wasn't it weird? He had never thought about her much while she was still alive. But now she occupied every second of his day. It didn't seem right. She had been a nice person – at least from what he could tell – and maybe he should have paid closer attention to her, when she was still around…

The sun was still setting early this time of year, so at six o'clock it was pitch dark outside. He never would have admitted it in front of his mom, but the dark made him nervous. There was a good chance this thing was lurking out there in the shadows, prowling for its next victim.

A car pulled into the gas station. At first all Dylan could see was a pair of bright headlights, but as it got closer, he recognized the foreign sports car he had seen on one other occasion. He couldn't help but smile a little. Marie was back.

Instead of driving up to the pumps, she parked in one of the designated spots by the windows. He watched her walk up to the door. She was dressed in denim jeans and her leather jacket. He shook his head disapprovingly like an old man. Again, he wondered how she didn't freeze to death.

She spotted him through the glass door, and a smile spread across her face. She waved. He reciprocated.

"Hey! I heard what happened. Are you all right?" There was genuine worry in her eyes. It was the first time anyone had asked him that since he had found Stacy. People either seemed to assume he was rattled so they didn't want to pry or they didn't care at all. They probably just wanted to hear the story straight from the horse's mouth so they could gossip to their friends and families.

"I'm fine, thanks. A little shaken but I can handle it. But news sure travels fast if even you've heard about it."

She looked taken aback for a second. "Yeah… uh…" She ran her fingers through her curls. "Bernie told us to be careful when we go out. He said another dead body had been found at the Harpers' place, so I figured that'd be your house."

"Yeah." He couldn't look her in the eyes. Stacy's face was clouding his mind. "Bernie is right, you know. You *should* be careful."

Her expression became grave, aging her several years. Her eyes turned glassy with a deep sadness. It made Dylan ache for her despite barely knowing her. But the look on her face would have had that effect on anyone.

"So should you." Then the grave expression was gone as suddenly as it had appeared, and the spell was broken, making Dylan wonder if he had misread her. "Especially if you're going to leave work early and walk home alone in the dark instead of waiting for me to give you a ride." A playful smile spread across her lips, and her gray eyes twinkled with challenge.

It took Dylan a moment to process the drastic shift in her mood. "Hold on. Does that mean you actually showed up?"

"Of course," she said with mock disappointment. "But you weren't there."

He laughed uncomfortably. "Sorry, my mom picked me up because she was worried about me walking home. She got here early so she would catch me in time." He paused. "And I honestly didn't think you would come."

She frowned. "What? Why not? I said so, didn't I?"

He shrugged. "Yeah but … still." He didn't want to get into why he hadn't believed her. He didn't want to tell her that he had assumed she was playing a prank on him. He wouldn't have guessed in a million years that she was being serious. But now he felt embarrassed about not trusting her. She was new in town, so she wasn't aware that people his age usually weren't nice to him. As far as she knew, the slush disaster with Fletcher and his friends could have been an isolated incident.

She fixed him with an intense stare, the same as the first time they had met, and slowly nodded. "Well, I'm glad you didn't walk home and that you're still alive."

"Yeah, me too," he said absentmindedly. Stacy's face was there again. She hadn't been so lucky. He pushed the thought away. "So, how come you're still here? With people getting killed, I figured you'd be getting out of here as fast as you can."

She contemplated that for a bit. "You know, it's really no different to places like New York City. Only there you don't really notice people dying because it's not newsworthy." She shrugged. "Besides, now we're invested. We want to know if they catch this animal." She smiled that little private joke smile again but tried to hide it by covering her mouth with her hand.

"Well, I certainly hope they will."

She came closer to the counter, peering at it. "Are you still reading that boring book?" The disdain in her voice was mirrored by the expression on her face.

He snapped it shut and pulled it away defensively. "It's not boring. It's useful."

She arched an eyebrow. They had a little stare-down that Dylan ended up winning. She shrugged. "Fine. If you say so."

He laughed and she joined in. It felt surprisingly easy to be around her. Normally, talking to other people his age was a chore. He obsessed over saying the right things and behaving a certain way, but with her none of that seemed to matter.

They fell into conversation as quickly and effortlessly as the previous times she had been there, and after a while Dylan forgot about Stacy – if only temporarily.

About an hour later, Fletcher and Amy Barnes and Ricky Halston walked in. For a second, Fletcher looked startled when he saw Marie leaning on the counter talking to Dylan like they were close friends. But he pulled himself together quickly, grinning deviously at Dylan.

"Hey there, Harper." His blond hair was slicked back – of course he didn't wear a beanie, so as not to mess it up – and his hands were stuffed deeply into the pockets of his blue bomber jacket.

Amy and Ricky were flanking him on either side and mimicking his stance – as they always did. Dylan wondered if Fletcher thought he needed backup. Maybe he wouldn't be such a massive dick if he didn't constantly have an audience around to cheer him on. Or maybe it wouldn't make a difference. What did he know?

"Fletcher."

Now the bully focused his attention on Marie. He extended his hand to her. "You must be new in town. I don't think we've met. I'm Fletcher Barnes."

She looked at his hand but made no move to take it. She gave him a once-over instead, and her lips twitched. "Good for you."

Fletcher's jaw dropped. And now Dylan was the one mimicking Fletcher's expression. He had never seen anyone reject the bully. Ever. Usually everyone was fawning over him because of his good looks and athletic prowess – especially the girls.

But Marie stared him down until he awkwardly dropped his hand. He seemed to grapple for the right words to save face. Meanwhile Ricky had moved to the snack aisle. He pulled a bag of hard candy from the shelf. The rattling sound snapped Fletcher out of his trance.

He seemed to have decided to ignore Marie and focus on Dylan instead. "So, Harper, I heard your face made Stacy Yelander drop dead on the spot." He shook his head. "Poor girl."

Dylan flinched. How could this asshole make fun of a person's death like that?

Amy snorted, but her snort turned into an uncontrollable chuckle that she tried to hide behind her hand. Ricky came back from the snack aisle and high-fived Fletcher. They genuinely seemed to think that was the funniest joke anyone had ever made.

"It's not funny. She died." Dylan bit his lip. Why had he said that out loud?

Fletcher grinned because Dylan had taken the bait. Dylan closed his eyes in defeat. Now it was only going to get so much worse.

"No, it isn't funny at all." Fletcher sounded dead serious. "You should wear a warning label on your forehead. It could save lives." He turned to Marie again. "I'd be careful around him if I were you."

"Have you seen a dead body before? A person who met a brutal death?" she asked calmly. Her tone was casual, as if she were asking him if he'd ever been to the beach.

Fletcher frowned and huffed scornfully. "No, cause I'm not a freak."

Ricky laughed. He had ripped the bag of candy open and was chowing down on its contents like popcorn at a movie theater.

"Hm, I figured." Marie slowly nodded. "Because if you had, you'd know their eyes are wide open, staring at you like they're pleading for help that you can't give them. Their skin looks ashy and pale like a sheet. They lie there completely still, yet you expect them to move any second because nobody can be that still for too long. The expression on their face will haunt you in your dreams forever, and you'll always ask yourself if there was anything you could have done, had you just been there a little sooner."

While she was speaking, she stepped closer to him. Even though he was more than a head taller than her, he shrank under her gaze. Her voice sounded weirdly threatening, even to Dylan. He could only imagine how uncomfortable it was making Fletcher.

Ricky had stopped eating. Amy looked like she might be sick.

Fletcher gulped. "Whatever…" he mumbled, looking at the ground. "You two seem to be perfect for each other." Without another glance at either of them, he turned and walked to the door.

"Didn't you want to buy anything?" Dylan shouted after him, a little glib.

Fletcher flipped him off. "Amy, Ricky, come on!" he shouted to his entourage.

Amy followed him immediately while Ricky's eyes darted back and forth between Fletcher and Dylan.

Amy held the door for him, urging him on with her eyes. Ricky fished two dollar bills out of his pocket, tossed them on the counter, and hurried after the twins, clutching his bag of candy to his chest.

Once they were gone, Marie turned to Dylan with a sweet smile.

"Do these guys bother you a lot?"

He shrugged and looked at the windows behind her.

"I'm sorry. That sucks." She seemed to mean it.

"Why do you care?" he asked, genuinely confused. She hardly knew him, and she wasn't even from here. Why was she so interested in his life?

Now she was the one shrugging and looking away. "You seem like a good guy. Why not?"

She smiled at him again, and his lips twitched in response. Her words came back to him. She had described Stacy's expression so accurately, as if she had seen it herself. He couldn't help but wonder how she knew so much about dead people. But he was too scared to ask. He didn't want to pry, and it seemed like a personal question.

Silence hung between them awkwardly for a few seconds. When Marie opened her mouth to say something, the door opened again, and Larry walked in. Dylan glanced at the clock on the wall. A quarter to eight.

"Hey, Larry, you're early again."

"Oh, boy." Larry took his beanie off and tousled his gray hair. "It's dangerous out there. Didn't want to take any chances."

Dylan wasn't exactly sure what Larry meant. The old man would still have to close up at three o'clock in the morning. But then again, he couldn't exactly leave the gas station unmanned either.

Dylan nodded. "Good call."

"Who's your friend?" A wide smile spread across his face as he gazed admiringly at Marie.

"Oh, uh, that's Marie. She and her husband are just passing through town. Marie, this is Larry, my boss."

"Nice to meet you." She shook his hand.

"Likewise." Larry gave her an approving once-over and focused on Dylan again. "So… I heard you found her." His tone was grave and low, but his eyes were sparkling with curiosity and excitement.

"Yeah." He didn't want to elaborate. Not again. "It was pretty awful."

Larry nodded. "I heard she was all scratched up." He waited for Dylan to confirm.

"Yeah, she was," Dylan answered reluctantly. That was it. The old man wasn't going to get any more out of him.

"Hm. Very strange… I wonder what kind of animal would do that." They all wondered in silence for a bit. Larry must have realized Dylan wasn't going to tell him anything else or give him the scoop on something nobody else knew about, so he turned to go to his office.

"Oh, one more thing. Why don't you go home early tonight? Take it easy, okay?"

Dylan blinked. "Really? Are you sure you don't need me?" Fear crept inside him. Was Larry firing him for not gossiping about Stacy?

Larry waved him off. "No, I'm sure people are staying indoors tonight anyway. It'll be quiet. I'll just drop off my coat in the back and you can head out. Oh, would you like to call your mom so she can pick you up?"

Before Dylan could answer, Marie chimed in. "I'll drive you."

They both looked at her in surprise.

"Uh… Okay…," he heard himself say. "Sure."

She brandished her car key. "Cool. Let's go."

His body switched to autopilot. He grabbed his book and stuffed it into his backpack, put on his jacket, gloves and beanie, and said good night to Larry, following Marie out into the cold.

He felt nervous about being outside the store with her and having her do him a favor. Everything about this situation was a first for him. But as he got into her sports car, he momentarily forgot his nerves.

"Wow. This is an amazing car." The interior was decked out in expensive black leather, and it emanated that new-car smell. He had never seen a modern cockpit like that in real life. It looked almost like KITT's on *Knight Rider*. Everything was state-of-the-art, even the radio with its cassette tape player.

"Thanks. It's quite new. We bought it last year."

"What kind of car is it?"

"It's an Audi Quattro. Four-wheel drive. Very convenient in this mountain weather." She smiled.

As she turned the key in the ignition, 'Thriller' blared from the speakers – which sounded unsurprisingly crisp. "Sorry." She quickly turned down the volume. "I like to listen to loud music when I drive alone."

"No problem."

She turned onto the road. "So, where do I have to go?"

"Oh, right, uh, it's just down this way." He pointed to a smaller side road leading to the woods.

She took the turn and blurted out, "You know, I didn't have many friends either when I was your age. It's nothing to be embarrassed about."

Her words zapped him like an electric current. His heart started beating faster. He remembered that they had talked about him not having friends the night they'd met. Back then, he had thought he'd never see her again, so he hadn't thought much of divulging his loner status, but her bringing it up made him regret that he hadn't come up with an excuse at the time.

And even though she claimed it was nothing to be embarrassed about, he still felt like it was. Everyone had friends. Finding some couldn't be so hard. He must have been doing something wrong. It made him feel like a total loser.

He tried to push that feeling away and focus on the other thing she had said.

He highly doubted that she had ever had problems making friends with her flawless looks and open-minded artsy personality. She was obviously trying to make him feel better.

He shrugged, trying to play it cool. "Yeah. I don't care. I'm going to go off to college soon anyway, and then I can have all the friends I want." If everything worked out according to plan.

"Hm." She was quiet for a moment, then changed the subject. "Do I just follow this street?"

"Yeah, straight ahead, then to the left again at the end of the street." She took the next turn. They were on his street.

"I'm really sorry you had to find that body."

"It's okay. It's not like you could have done anything about it." He laughed, but she didn't. Her lips were pressed together in a thin line, and she kept her gaze fixed straight ahead.

"Um, the next house is mine." The lights were on in the living room. His mom was probably asleep on the couch. At least, he hoped she was and that what had happened right outside their front door wasn't keeping her up.

Marie stopped in front of the driveway.

"Well, thanks for the ride." Dylan grabbed the door handle, but Marie gripped him by the arm. Her grip was surprisingly strong and firm. The cold of her hand was seeping into his arm even through his thick jacket.

"Wait." There was urgency in her voice. She scanned the woods to Dylan's right. He followed her gaze but saw nothing but a bunch of very dark trees covered in snow. The image of the gleaming eyes came back to him, and he wondered if she had seen them too just then.

"Did you see anything?"

She looked at him as if she had forgotten he was there and let go of his arm. "No, there's nothing."

He opened the door.

"Dylan."

"Hm?" He turned around again. She kept her eyes on the steering wheel. Her guard was up. He felt like she was hiding something.

"Did you see anything this morning before you discovered the body?" She looked at him with big searching eyes.

He contemplated telling her about the cat eyes, but he knew it would sound crazy. No way was she going to believe him. He shook his head. "No. I didn't see anything at all."

She frowned. Something told him that she knew he was lying. His heart started beating faster.

"Okay. Well then, good night. I'll see you Saturday."

"Yeah. Wait, what?"

"I'll drive you home from work." She smiled and winked at him with the confidence only beautiful people had. "Go ahead, you're letting the cold in," she added when he didn't move or answer. He was still holding the door, one foot outside the car.

"Oh, sorry. Okay, see you Saturday, I guess." He scrambled out of the car and shut the door. She waited till he had unlocked his front door and stepped inside, then she drove off, speakers blaring again.

As he closed the door behind him, stepping into his warm house, he wondered if he had just made a friend.

II

Berlin, New Hampshire, February 1985

5

"Mom, where's the strainer?" Dylan hastily opened and closed several overhead kitchen cabinets looking for the item in question while his mom cut off a stick of butter for the sauce she was making.

"On the bottom shelf of the lower cabinet to your left," she answered while watching the butter melt in the saucepan.

He rummaged through the lower cabinet and found the blue plastic strainer. "Got it." He took the boiling potatoes off the heat and strained them.

Both Susan and Dylan were a little on edge. Martin Kirkgaard and his daughter Molly were coming over for dinner. It was the first time they were cooking together for one of Susan's boyfriends. It was the first time both families would be together, and the first time Dylan would actually speak to Molly.

During the past five weeks, as Susan and Martin's relationship had progressed, Dylan had been paying closer attention to Molly at school, and it seemed like she had been doing the same. They had been sizing each other up, but neither of them had gone as far as to talk to the other.

The situation was strange to say the least. Susan had introduced Martin to him two weeks ago. Dylan didn't find anything wrong with the guy besides him being not good enough for her. But reminding himself that he was most likely the reason his mom couldn't tie a man down, Dylan tried to be supportive. He was extra nice to Martin, engaging in conversation, asking about his job. And it was going well. Martin and Susan spent more and more time together. But unlike Susan's previous boyfriends, Martin never stayed over, always claiming he didn't want to leave Molly alone at the house all night.

And he wasn't wrong. Two more people had been killed since Dylan had found Stacy dead outside their house – both had died the same way as Stacy and the postman. And still, neither the police nor Fish and Game knew what kind of animal was attacking people. Although investigations had dead-ended, there hadn't been another victim in almost two weeks, but people were still careful. Nobody left the house at night unless they absolutely had to.

That made Dylan's shifts at the gas station even less busy than they already were. Some nights he had no customers at all. But he didn't mind because he had Marie to keep him company. At least twice a week she came in to hang out with him. And she drove him home every night.

He had to suppress a smile as he thought about his newfound friend – his only friend. He had gotten to know her more over the course of the past few weeks: He knew that she liked to run, that she didn't like candy, that she ran her fingers through her hair when she was nervous, and that she got a little wrinkle between her eyes when she was focused on something.

He hadn't met Alec again though, which was a relief. He would never have admitted it to Marie, but her husband gave him the creeps. Something about Alec made the hairs on the back of Dylan's neck stand up.

"Are you almost done with that?" Susan peeked curiously into Dylan's pot, where he had mashed the potatoes and was adding some hot milk.

"Yup. Butter, please!" He held out his hand, and his mom passed him the butter without missing a beat stirring her sauce. They worked in perfect tandem as always when they were cooking.

The timer went off with a loud ring.

"The meatloaf's done," Dylan exclaimed. He bent down in front of the oven, breathing heavily from the exertion, and looked through the glass at the sizzling tray. The meatloaf looked just right.

Susan handed him a pair of oven mitts, and he carefully took out the tray, placing it on the kitchen counter. He wiped his glasses on his apron as the steam emanating from the oven had caused them to fog up.

"The peas are almost done, too." She stirred the contents of a tiny saucepan with a spoon. Dylan cleared the sink area so she could get to the strainer.

"The potato mash is ready. I'll put it in a bowl and set the table."

"Perfect."

He did just that and took off his apron. He was wearing his only button-down shirt for the occasion. His mom had bought it for him about a year ago, which meant it had grown tight around his midsection and his arms. He had gained at least six pounds since last year, and it made him feel a little uncomfortable. For fear of ripping the seams or popping off a button, he tried to move his arms as little as possible.

"Okay…" Susan sighed. She had poured the sauce in a tiny boat they normally used only at Thanksgiving and Christmas and placed it on the table. "We're all set," she declared, looking over the feast with satisfaction, hands on her hips, fingers of one hand thrumming nervously.

"It's perfect. They'll love it." Dylan rubbed her back, trying to calm her down.

She didn't react but turned around and started to clean up the mess they had made cooking. As she rinsed the big pot they had used for the potatoes, Dylan heard a car door fall shut outside. Moments later, a knock sounded at the door.

"They're here." Susan hurriedly stripped off her apron, revealing the flattering dark blue dress she was wearing, and rushed to the door.

Dylan stayed behind in the kitchen, taking a deep breath and bracing himself for an evening of scrutinizing and being scrutinized.

"I'm so happy you're here," he heard Susan exclaim.

"We're happy to be here." That was Martin. Kiss on the cheek.

"Nice to see you again, Molly. Come in, come in."

There was some rustling as they took their jackets off – it was still freezing outside – and they came into the kitchen: First Martin, a man in his forties, receding blond hair, small round glasses, big smile showing off his crooked eyeteeth. Then his daughter Molly, short girl, long blond hair tied into a ponytail, big hazel eyes, and a permanent frown on her face which made her delicate pale face look even more fragile.

"Hey, Dylan. How are you doing?" Martin shook Dylan's hand firmly.

"Good. How are you, Martin?"

"Doing well. You know my daughter, Molly, right?" He put an arm around Molly, who looked like there were a million places she would rather be right then.

"Yes, we have history together."

She nodded, staring at the table.

Susan came in, urging them to take a seat. "The food is going to get cold."

They sat, the Kirkgaards on the two chairs by the walls that Dylan and Susan never used, Susan closest to the kitchen counter, and Dylan closest to the door.

"Mm … meatloaf!" Martin exclaimed with hungry eyes. He started moving to serve himself but stopped, looking a little embarrassed.

"Oh, please, let me!" Susan hastily cut the loaf and served everyone a slice. Dylan put a giant heap of mashed potatoes on his plate. He was starving. He couldn't remember the last time he had eaten. It couldn't have been long ago, but it felt like days.

For a second, he forgot he was in the company of people he didn't know well and dug in like somebody who had been marooned on a desert island for a month. And the meal tasted incredible. His mom always made the best food, but her meatloaf deserved an award. The blend of meat juices and her special secret sauce was just the right amount of savory.

"This is delicious. Thank you, Susan." Martin's voice reminded Dylan that he wasn't alone. He tried to slow down.

"Are you sure? Doesn't it need more salt?" Her plate was still untouched.

"No, it's perfect. This is amazing." He pointed approvingly at his food with his fork.

She smiled with obvious relief, and he winked at her.

"Isn't that right, Molly?" he asked.

"It's good." Molly answered flatly without looking at him, stabbing her peas with more aggression than necessary.

What's the matter with her? 'Good' didn't cut it. And insulting his mom's meatloaf felt like blasphemy to him.

"Oh, would you like some more sauce, Molly?" Susan asked. An awkward smile was plastered onto her face. It seemed to Dylan as if she was afraid a bomb might go off any second.

"No, thanks." Same flat tone.

Everyone stared for a moment at Molly, who was focused on her food and seemed to ignore everybody else around the table. Dylan could hear the faucet softly dripping.

Martin finally broke the silence clearing his throat. "So, Dylan, Susan told me that you applied to Harvard." Dylan nodded. "I hope you get in. My dad almost went Ivy League, but he didn't pass on the 'smart' gene to my brother and me." He laughed.

Dylan joined in. "Well, I hope so, too. But it'll probably be a few more weeks before I hear back from them."

"I'm keeping my fingers crossed." Martin smiled at him encouragingly.

Dylan smiled back. "Thank you."

"Have you applied to any colleges, Molly?" Susan asked.

Molly sighed. "Yes, to a few. Mainly out west."

"She's sick of the weather around here, you know," Martin added with a laugh when Molly didn't elaborate.

Susan huffed. "I get that."

"I'm mainly sick of people getting murdered," Molly retorted dryly.

Silence. *Drip, drip, drip* went the faucet.

Something Marie had said a while back about crime in New York City came back to Dylan. "You do realize that homicide rates in California are way higher than in New Hampshire, right?"

"Who says I'm going to California?" Molly finally looked up, straight into Dylan's eyes. Her signature frown had deepened.

"Then where are you going?"

"Don't know yet. Utah maybe."

"Yeah, you should be safe there, with all the Mormons," Martin interjected before Dylan could say anything else. Susan half smiled, as if unsure whether to laugh at his joke, but Molly was looking daggers at her father. He didn't seem to notice.

"It is awful, though, what happened. With the animal attacks, I mean…" Susan seemed to have settled on siding with Molly.

"Oh, yes, definitely," Martin mumbled between bites of meatloaf and mashed potatoes.

"My friend from out of town said she saw something similar in Pennsylvania a while back. Apparently, someone had been attacked by a wolf that had wandered down there. But there was only one victim." Marie had told Dylan that story only a few days earlier.

"Did that girl from New York tell you that?" Susan asked. She hadn't met Marie yet, but Dylan had been talking about her a lot.

"Girl from New York? You have a girlfriend, Dylan?" Martin's obvious surprise stung Dylan a little.

"She's not my girlfriend. She's married. We're just friends." Embarrassed, he blushed when he saw Martin's facial expression go from confused to ah-that-sounds-more-likely.

"Married? She must be a little older than you, then."

"Yeah, a little. She's twenty."

Martin's expression went back to confused. "And what is a twenty-year-old married woman from New York doing here in Berlin?"

"She and her husband are taking a break from college and traveling around the country. They're staying at Bernie's for now."

"Ah, I see!" Martin greedily shoveled more mashed potatoes onto his plate. Dylan was already on his third serving.

They ate in silence for a bit, and Susan said, "I'm so happy we get to do this today. Bring everyone together like this, I mean."

"Mm," Martin mumbled; his mouth too full to speak. He looked at her adoringly instead and put a hand on hers, resting on the table.

Dylan suddenly felt a little sick. He took a deep breath, reminding himself that his mom deserved to be with someone and that he wanted this thing with Martin to work out.

"Yeah, it's nice." He forced a smile.

Molly scoffed, shaking her head while picking at her food. *Drip, drip, drip.*

Ignoring her, Martin swallowed and said, "Feels like we're a family, doesn't it?"

Susan smiled, and it was the most genuine expression of happiness Dylan had seen on her face all night. His heart sank. He had always considered the two of them a family. They didn't need anybody else in his book. But apparently, Susan thought differently. And he had been denying her that all these years. He felt terrible.

"No, it doesn't."

Everyone looked at Molly. *Drip, drip, drip.* Had she really just said that? Dylan was gaping at her in shock.

"We're just two broken ones having dinner together." She stared her father down.

But Martin didn't even flinch. "Molly. We've been over this."

"No. *You've* been over it. You don't listen to me." She crossed her arms. "It's only been a year since mom died, and you've already forgotten all about her."

"That is not true." Martin put down his fork. It seemed like they'd had this conversation several times before. "Your mom will always hold a special place in my heart, but I can't be alone forever. She wouldn't have wanted that."

He turned to Dylan and Susan. "I'm sorry."

"No, *I'm* sorry," Susan said hastily. "Molly, I don't want to replace your mom. I know I would never be able to do that. But I really like you and your dad, and I would love it if you gave me a chance."

It sounded like she had rehearsed that speech. Dylan wondered how long that had been weighing on her. He'd had no idea. What else did he miss when it came to his mom?

Molly didn't say anything, but she uncrossed her arms. *Drip, drip, drip.* What was up with that faucet?

Dylan felt the need to stick up for his mom. "For what it's worth, I don't think our family is broken. I've never felt like I've been missing out because I don't have a dad."

Susan's lips twitched, and her eyes started glistening.

"Well, good for you." Molly sounded almost bored. "Where's the bathroom?"

"Uh, upstairs, first door to the right."

She got up and stomped upstairs.

"I'm really sorry about that," Martin muttered as soon as the bathroom door shut.

Susan waved it off. "Oh, no, please, don't be. It's hard for her. I understand."

"No, you went out of your way to make this exceptionally good meal for us, and she insulted you in your own home." He scratched his temple, frowning, and sighed. "I'm really sorry."

Susan smiled understandingly. "It's okay, Martin. I appreciate you coming over."

He laughed. "Are you kidding? With food this good, I'll be coming over every day. You'll be sick of me in no time."

She laughed as well. "I could never be sick of you, Martin."

Dylan felt like throwing up as the two of them were gazing at each other longingly. He wished he could hide out in the bathroom like Molly.

No, he was doing the right thing. He had to suck it up. This was only going to be for tonight.

Until Martin came over again. And again. And then maybe moved in with them. And he and Susan got married. Oh, why did it have to be so hard to do the right thing?

He put his fork down on his plate so the soft clatter would remind them that they weren't alone. It worked. Both their heads snapped in his direction. They seemed a little startled.

Martin took a deep breath. He had finished his food and seemed to be thinking about what to say. "So, Dylan, do you follow the hockey league at all?"

"Uh, no." *Do I look like I care about sports?*

"Oh… Football?"

Dylan pulled one corner of his mouth back and audibly sucked in air. "Not really."

"Right." Martin fidgeted with the end of his fork.

"Dylan isn't really one for sports. He prefers to read." She smiled approvingly at her son, pride in her voice.

"Comic books?" Martin asked hopefully.

"Among other things." Dylan wasn't too much into comics. He had only read a few editions of the popular ones, like *Superman* or *Spider-Man*.

But apparently *Superman* was exactly what Martin had read – and loved – as a boy. He launched into a monologue about his favorite stories. Dylan only had to nod and grunt in approval occasionally. It didn't matter that he didn't know half the editions Martin talked about.

Susan was clearing the table as Molly came back into the kitchen.

"Oh, Molly dear, are you done with that?" Susan pointed to Molly's half-eaten food. Molly nodded, and Susan took her plate away while Martin was still talking about *Superman*.

"Dad, can we please leave now?" Molly was hovering in the doorway, arms crossed again.

Startled, Martin interrupted his stream of consciousness. "But we just got here, sweetheart. Come on, sit down! Join us!"

Molly's permanent frown turned into a scowl. And then, as Susan was throwing the leftovers on Molly's plate into the garbage under the sink, a stream of water shot out of the faucet, splashing Susan in the face. She shrieked.

As suddenly as it had started, the water stopped.

"What the hell was that!?" Dylan jumped up.

Susan wiped her face with the back of her arm. "I don't know. It's like the water turned itself on…" She looked at the faucet, puzzled.

Martin laughed, but it sounded forced. "Well, it's an old house."

"Not that old. And we've never had any issues with the tap," Dylan replied.

"Well, there's a first for everything," Molly declared disinterestedly.

Susan grabbed a kitchen towel and wiped up the water that had splashed onto the floor.

"Dad? Are we going?" Molly looked pointedly at her father.

Martin's eyes darted from her to Susan and back again. "Well, it *is* late. And it's a school night." He got up with a grunt. "It's probably best if we continue this another time. Susan, thank you for the incredible meal." He walked over and gave her a kiss on the cheek.

She blushed. "Oh, it was nothing. You're more than welcome."

"Dylan, I'd love to get more into *Superman* with you next time."

Dylan cringed internally. "Can't wait." He shook Martin's hand.

"All right, sweetheart, let's go." With one arm outstretched to his side, he gestured to Molly to walk into the hallway.

As the Kirkgaards put on their jackets, Martin thanked Susan profusely again and promised to come back soon. He apologized for the hasty exit. All the while Molly was tapping her foot impatiently.

"Bye" was all she said to Dylan and Susan.

Once they had left, Dylan helped Susan clean up the kitchen. Puzzled, he examined the faucet. Everything looked normal.

"That was weird."

Susan sighed. "I know. I hope she'll come around."

"No, I meant the tap."

"Hm. Yeah… I probably knocked something over and it turned the tap on."

"Probably." It sounded like the only reasonable explanation. Yet something about it bothered Dylan. He hadn't been paying close attention, but he was pretty sure she hadn't even come near anything that could have fallen over.

But then what? Had the faucet turned itself on like magic? The thought made Dylan smirk. That was crazy. Something had to be wrong with the plumbing. Some issue with the water pressure, for sure.

Because what else could it have been?

III

Berlin, New Hampshire, March 1985

6

On the first day of March, five days after the disastrous dinner, Dylan decided to go to the library for some more editions of *Superman*. If that was the only topic he could talk to Martin about, he wanted to expand his knowledge of it. He was trying to make an effort for his mom's sake.

It was Friday afternoon – his day off from work – and he had walked to the public library off Main Street straight after school so he would be done and home long before nightfall.

Breathing heavily, he climbed the five wide steps to the entrance of the familiar colonial style brick building. As soon as he stepped through the door, he relaxed. The warmth indoors enveloped him like a blanket, and the calm made him let his guard down. The familiar smell of old paper and carpeted floors gave him a sense of safety, like nothing could harm him.

He stepped up to the counter, taking off his backpack and pulling out the latest book he had borrowed, a nonfiction title on World War II.

"Oh, hi, Dylan dear, it's so good to see you," the middle-aged librarian greeted him with a smile.

"Hi, Mrs. Foster. Good to see you, too. I wanted to return this." He handed her his book. "And then I'll just browse a little."

She signed his library card and gave him another smile. "Of course.

Go ahead."

On his way over to the comic book section, which was at the far end of the big hall filled with books from floor to ceiling, he had to pass the history section, where the cover of a large coffee table book caught his eye. It showed an intricately detailed painting of two opposing armies, consisting of musketeers and pikemen. The title was sprawled across in big gold letters: *War on Faith – The Thirty Years' War*.

He was sure he hadn't seen that one before. It must have been new. Intrigued, he stepped closer. He took it off the shelf and thumbed through it. The illustrations were beautiful, and he'd never heard of that war before... But he was supposed to read *Superman*. With a sigh, he put the book back on the shelf.

But another new title caught his eye: *Knighthood in Medieval England*. And next to it was *Pre-Imperial Europe*. The book titles lured him into the aisle. He pulled out one book after another, letting himself be captivated by the unfamiliar worlds they were opening to him.

After a while – he was reading through the first chapter of *War on Faith* – he heard a female voice coming from the counter.

"Anything occult. Anything at all." He couldn't place the voice at first but then a delicate face with a frown and a pair of hazel eyes appeared in his mind's eye.

"You have to have something!" Molly sounded exasperated, almost upset.

"Well, there is a section on religion. You might find something on pagan and heathen traditions there. But I doubt we have much. You shouldn't really read stuff like that anyway, young lady," Mrs. Foster admonished her. Dylan had never heard her be this short with anybody.

Molly sighed. "All right then. Where do I have to look?"

"Fourth aisle to your left."

Dylan peeked out from behind the shelf and saw her stomp off in his direction. She didn't seem to notice him, as she walked straight past him and disappeared into the religion section two aisles farther down.

What was she looking for? Had she said occult books? Was that for a school project, maybe? But for which class?

She seemed to have found something because she didn't come back out. Curiosity got the better of him, and since it was getting late and he needed to move on to the comic book section anyway, he decided to investigate. He shut *War on Faith*, put it back on the shelf, and made his way to Molly's aisle.

He spotted her crouched on the floor, head bent forward at an awkward angle trying to read the titles of the books on the bottom shelf.

"Hey." He could talk to her, right? Her dad was dating his mom. She had been to his house. That should put them squarely on speaking terms.

She looked up. But when she realized who had spoken to her, her head went back down immediately. "Hey," she replied.

"Looking for anything specific?"

"Why don't you mind your own business?" She pulled out a book, looked at the cover, shook her head, and put it back.

"Maybe I can help you." Why did he even bother? She clearly didn't want anything to do with him.

"I doubt it."

"Okay then … suit yourself." He shrugged and turned to leave.

"Wait."

Surprised, he turned back to her. She sighed. She was giving him her undivided attention now, her face contrite.

"I'm sorry, I didn't mean to be rude."

Dylan shrugged again. "Don't worry about it."

She seemed lost for words for a moment. "I mean, not just a second ago, but also at your house. You know, with everything that happened last year, I'm kind of on edge. All the time. It's not your fault and it isn't your mom's. You just got caught in the crossfire. I'm sorry."

He felt deep sympathy for her, but he didn't really know how to respond to that, so he shrugged again. "It's okay. I get it."

"I don't think you do. But thanks for trying anyway."

"It must be very hard for you. I don't blame you." Truth was, he didn't like Martin and Susan's relationship either, albeit for different, entirely selfish reasons. He wished he could be as openly hostile as Molly.

Molly's lips twitched, and she looked at the floor. "Anyway, I'm looking for books on Wicca. So I don't think you can help me."

Dylan frowned. "What is that?"

"You know, witchcraft. Modern day witchcraft anyway. It's a religion." She ran her fingers along the line of books on the second shelf.

"Never heard of it. Sorry." *Witchcraft?* "What do you need that for?"

"For a project for English class."

When she didn't elaborate, he said, "Well, good luck with that." He half smiled at her. "I'll leave you to it."

She murmured something in response that he didn't understand, already focused back on the books.

Dylan turned and walked up to the end of the hall to meet *Superman*.

The comic book section was small but well stocked. He grabbed two editions of *Superman*. And even though he was technically done after that, he lingered because the colorful covers drew him in. He flicked through a few editions of *X-Men*. Before he knew it, he had started reading, and three comics later, Mrs. Foster came up behind him.

"I'm sorry, Dylan dear, but we're closing. Do you need me to check anything out for you?" Her smile was so wide, he could see all her teeth.

"Oh, yes, thanks, Mrs. Foster. I'll take these." He held up the two editions of *Superman* and three more editions of *X-Men*.

"Great." She gestured for him to follow her. When they got back to the counter, they found Molly waiting for Mrs. Foster, two small hardcovers in hand.

"Just these?" The librarian asked her coldly.

"Yes."

She checked Dylan's comics out first.

He nodded at Molly's books. "So, you've found something! Great."

"Yeah, I'll see if they're any good."

"Here you go, dear." Mrs. Foster handed Dylan his comics.

"Thanks." He turned to Molly. "Well, I guess I'll see you around."

"Mhm." She kept her gaze on Mrs. Foster as the woman handed her the books.

Realizing he wasn't going to get anything else from her, he turned on his heel and walked away. Outside, he reflexively pulled the collar of his jacket up against the cold. And only then did he realize he had completely lost track of time. It was six o'clock and the sun had already set. Streetlamps were illuminating the narrow street, which was almost deserted save for the occasional car driving by. But his mom was still at work, so he had no choice but to walk home.

At least, she wouldn't know about it…

As he took the few steps down to the sidewalk, a familiar-looking truck drove by. Only a couple of buildings down, the truck stopped and pulled into a parking spot. Dylan didn't want to pass it, but he didn't have anywhere else to go. He contemplated pretending to have forgotten something inside so he could turn around and hide in the library. Maybe they would leave while he was in there. That was probably his best bet.

But as he turned around, Molly came out through the heavy double doors, and he heard Mrs. Foster hastily lock them behind her. Molly, who was wrapped in a thick down jacket, stopped on the stoop and slid her books in her backpack.

"Hey, Harper!" Dylan cringed as he heard the voice coming closer. "Why are you just standing there? Are you stalking Molly?"

Somebody laughed behind him. Another voice said, "Creep."

Bewildered, Molly glanced over to where Fletcher's voice had come from. And even though he didn't want to face his tormentor, Dylan didn't like having his back to a threat. So he turned.

Fletcher – flanked by his twin and Ricky – was walking toward him, hands in his jacket pockets. All of them had eager smiles on their faces. This wasn't looking good for him.

"I don't want any trouble, Fletcher."

Fletcher laughed. "Why would there be trouble, Harper? I just want to talk to you." He winked at Dylan. "And make sure you don't attack Molly." He glanced at Molly. "Are you all right? Is he bothering you?" He sounded overly concerned, laying it on thick.

Dylan blushed. *What must she be thinking?* He didn't dare turn around to face her.

"No." She sounded confused. "Why don't you mind your own business?"

That seemed to be a phrase she used on people a lot. Fletcher's eyebrows shot up. He laughed. "Oh, she's a feisty one. I see why you like her, Harper."

Dylan blushed even more. He obviously didn't like Molly in that way, but if he told Fletcher so right then it would make him sound pathetic.

But he didn't have to stand there and take it. He wasn't at work; he could leave. So, he did just that – or tried to do just that. He had to squeeze past Fletcher and his gang to get anywhere. He tried Amy's side, but Fletcher was quicker. He caught Dylan's arm and yanked him back.

"Let me go!" Dylan shouted.

The three idiots laughed. *"Let me go."* Amy imitated him in an exaggerated whiny voice. "I think he's scared, Fletch. Careful, he might piss himself." She chuckled at her own joke, whipping her blond perm back with her manicured hand.

Fletcher grinned, stepping closer to Dylan. He frowned. "Hey, I think you got something on your face, Harper." He pointed to his own nose. "Right there."

Dylan didn't make a move. He kept staring at Fletcher like a rabbit in front of a snake. Fletcher squinted, leaning in slightly.

"Oh, sorry, no, that's just a giant zit. I should have known."

Without warning, his hand shot forward, snatching Dylan's glasses right off his face. Dylan had no time to react.

"Give them back!" He grabbed at the glasses, but Fletcher held them up over his head.

"Damn, Harper, you're blind. Can you even see how many fingers I'm holding up?" He waved his other hand in front of Dylan's face.

Without thinking, Dylan slapped the hand away, lunging for his glasses.

"Whoa! Hey, you want to throw!?" Fletcher's voice held more aggression, which should have warned Dylan of what was to come, but he was still snatching at his glasses, fully focused on retrieving them.

Before Dylan realized what was happening, Fletcher's fist came crashing down on his face with a loud smack. The power of the punch sent him tumbling onto the library steps. He clumsily caught himself with his hands, scraping his left shin on the sharp edge of a stone step. His hands were stinging from the impact.

Only then did he feel the dull throbbing in his right cheek from the impact of Fletcher's fist.

"What's wrong with you!? Leave him alone!" Molly shouted from the top of the stairs.

"Why don't you mind your own business?" Fletcher retorted with a smirk.

That was it. Dylan needed to get out of there, no matter what. With all the strength he could muster, he pushed himself off the steps and used the momentum to barrel through Fletcher's gang, bulldozing past Amy and running as fast as he could down the street.

He had to leave his glasses behind. He felt like he was running for his life.

But without his glasses, everything was blurry. So he missed the icy patch on the sidewalk, just a few feet away, and slipped. He lost his balance, windmilling, fighting to stay upright, but he had hit the ice too fast.

He faceplanted on the icy sidewalk, the searing pain shooting through his skull into his brain.

Behind him, everyone burst out into roaring laughter. "Why is it so hilarious when fat people fall?" Amy shouted between laughs. He wished for the sidewalk to open up and swallow him whole.

"Leave him alone!"

Embarrassed, Dylan froze when he recognized the voice. He looked up, but all he could make out was a dark, slender figure moving toward him. As it got closer, he could distinguish long curly hair but no facial features. Yet he knew exactly who it was.

Marie walked past him, standing protectively between him and the bullies, towering over Dylan. He scrambled to his feet. His head was still throbbing, and he felt blood trickle out of his nose.

"Or what?" Fletcher asked menacingly. His laughter had died off. The rest were silent too. "Are you going to give me another speech?" He snorted, trying to seem aloof, but his words sounded insecure.

"No," Marie replied calmly. She stepped closer to him. They seemed to be staring each other down. Dylan's heart was pounding in fear for his friend.

Out of nowhere, Fletcher bent over backward at a weird angle, screaming in pain.

"You're going to leave him alone from now on. Is that clear?"

He was still wincing in pain, his upper body bent backward. Was she holding his arm? All he could do was squeeze out a "yes!"

"Good." She let him go.

"Bitch dislocated my shoulder," he mumbled breathlessly, holding his arm.

"Oh, don't be ridiculous. You're fine. But I can and will dislocate your shoulder if you mess with Dylan again. Understood?"

"Yes," he mumbled, and he and his gang scurried off to their truck, giving Dylan a wide berth.

Marie bent down, retrieving something from the ground, and walked up to him. She held out his glasses.

He took them from her gratefully and put them back on. "Thank you."

Now he could see the worried expression on her face. "Are you okay?"

A mix of feelings ran through him: relief that he had gotten out of the situation, pain from the punch and the fall, embarrassment that she had witnessed the whole thing, then more embarrassment that he had needed the help of a girl to get out of this instead of helping himself, and finally gratitude. She didn't have to save him. At the end of the day, it was of no concern to her what happened to him, but she had done it anyway. And Dylan appreciated that massively.

He smiled. "Yes, I'm fine. Thank you for…" He blushed. "Thanks for saving me," he mumbled, still a little embarrassed, sniffing to suck the blood back into his nose.

She frowned. "Of course. You're my friend and you were in trouble.

I'm just glad I was there."

Her modesty reminded him of the superheroes in the comics he had just borrowed. In a way, Marie was his own personal superhero, like an avenger that had been sent by some higher power to save him from his tormentors. It wasn't a stretch to think of her that way. It took super strength to go up against a guy as tall and athletic as Fletcher.

"Uh, what exactly did you do to his arm back there?"

She shrugged and gave him a half smile. "It's a simple self-defense move. If you twist somebody's arm at the right angle, they can't move and it's very painful. Doesn't even require much force." She winked at him.

He had heard of moves like that before, but he had never seen one in action. "I see."

"Do you need a ride home?" She gestured behind Dylan, presumably at her car.

"Yeah, that would be nice. Thanks." He sniffed again, wiping his nose with his hand. At least the bleeding seemed to have stopped.

She walked in the direction she had pointed to, moving out of Dylan's sightline, and his gaze traveled to Molly, who was still standing on the stoop, watching them intently. Her eyes were wide with shock, and she looked pale standing stock-still.

As Dylan was about to ask her if she was okay, a car pulled up in front of the library and the driver rolled down the window.

"Are you coming, Molly?" It was Martin.

Molly hesitated, her eyes still trained on Dylan.

"Dylan?" That was Marie behind him.

"Coming." He told himself Molly would be fine with her dad there. So he pulled himself away from her and followed his friend to her car.

7

As Dylan got into the warm vehicle, his face was throbbing even more. He gingerly touched his flaming cheek and winced. That was going to become a bruise.

"Are you sure you're okay?" Marie glanced at him worriedly from the driver's side.

"Yeah, don't worry." He tried to laugh it off, but his face hurt too much.

"Your hands are bleeding."

He looked at his palms and saw the skid marks for the first time. *How had she noticed that?* "Oh, yeah, you're right but just a little. It's nothing."

She frowned again, looking him deep in the eyes. "Are you sure?"

"Yes," he said with a nod. He wanted her to drop it. It was bad enough that he let himself get hurt like that; he didn't need her pity on top.

"Okay." She put the car in reverse and backed out of the parking spot.

They sat in silence for a bit as she drove down the dark Berlin streets.

The farther they got away from the library the more Dylan relaxed. Marie had saved him. He didn't even want to imagine what would have happened if she hadn't gotten there when she did.

"Hey," he started. "Thanks. I really appreciate it."

She smiled. "That's what friends are for."

Friends. The thought warmed his heart.

"What were you doing in the area anyway?"

"Not much. Just driving around." She pressed her lips together. "Why were *you* in the area?"

"Oh, I borrowed some comic books at the library." He desperately wished he had gotten something a little cooler or at least something more impressive.

"Comic books?" She sounded confused. "Like, books about comedy?"

Now Dylan was the confused one. "What?" Was she joking? "No, I mean comic books…"

She frowned at him. *Who doesn't know what a comic book is?*

"You know, stories about superheroes…"

Understanding washed over her face. "Ah, I see." Then another frown. "Aren't those for children?" She didn't say it in a reproachful way; she seemed genuinely unsure.

"Uh, not really. Some of them are pretty dark."

She nodded slowly. "Interesting."

It fascinated him that she didn't know what a comic book was. "I mean, if you want to see for yourself, I can lend you one." He felt stupid as soon as the words were out of his mouth. "Or not. Dumb idea. Sorry."

"No, I'd love that." She smiled at him, her heart-shaped face lighting up. "Thanks."

He hadn't expected that, so he stared at her in surprise.

"What?" she asked.

"Nothing." He rummaged in his backpack for one of his *X-Men* editions. "I'll just leave it here for you." He put it on the dashboard.

"Thank you."

They had reached his house by then. All the windows were dark.

"Is your mom not home?"

"No, she's still at work. She usually gets home around seven."

"Mm."

He unbuckled his seatbelt and gripped the door handle. "Thanks again for your help and for driving me home."

"You're welcome." She smiled warmly. "Since I saved you"—she winked—"can I maybe come inside?"

"Uh…" He was dumbstruck. "Why?" Rude. The least he could do was offer her something to drink. Besides, she was his friend. Didn't friends sometimes come over to their friend's house?

"I mean sure you can. Of course." He blushed.

She laughed. Her tone turned playfully sarcastic. "Thanks for the invitation." He blushed some more.

They got out of the car and walked up to the house. He couldn't believe Marie wanted to see inside his home. His heart was fluttering with nerves as he clumsily unlocked the front door and held it open for her.

"Thank you." She stepped inside.

He flicked the light on in the hallway. Marie looked decidedly out of place between his great-aunt Elsie's dark hardwood furniture, her dated decor (mainly consisting of white lace placemats and tacky vases), the dark green carpet covering every floor except for the beige linoleum in the kitchen, and their family photos plastering the flowery wallpaper.

As usual, her only protection against the cold weather was her flimsy leather jacket. Dylan took off his down jacket and beanie, hanging both on a hook by the door.

"You can hang up your jacket here."

"Oh, no, it's fine. I don't need to take it off." She gazed around. "So, this is your house?" The frown had returned.

"Yeah, my mom inherited it from her aunt when I was only a couple months old. She never really updated any of the furniture or wallpaper. I think she's nostalgic about it." From what Dylan knew, Susan had loved her aunt dearly. There were still lots of photographs of her and her late husband scattered around the house.

Marie nodded slowly, lost in thought.

Realizing they were still standing in the hallway, Dylan asked, "Would you like something to drink?" Without waiting for an answer, he marched into the kitchen and opened the fridge. "Or are you hungry? Cause I'm starving…"

"No, thanks, I'm good."

His attention was focused on the contents of the fridge. There were leftovers from yesterday's rice dish. He and his mom were most likely going to cook together later, so a little snack would do. He grabbed the jelly, some bread, and a jar of peanut butter and made himself two peanut butter and jelly sandwiches.

"Where is your room?" Marie suddenly asked from behind him.

"Upstairs." He blushed again. For some reason the idea of Marie in his room made him even more nervous. "But it's messy, so I'd rather not show you," he added preemptively.

Sandwiches on a plate in hand, he turned to her. She had sat down at the table, one arm propped up, head resting on her palm. She smiled. "Okay."

He sat down next to her, feeling uncomfortable with eating in front of her. "You really don't want anything?"

She smiled her little private joke smile, her gray eyes twinkling. "No. I'm good."

"Okay." He dug into his sandwich, painfully aware that she was watching him.

Out of nowhere, she asked, "So, what about your dad?"

The shock of this question made him accidentally bite his tongue.

The pain drove tears to his eyes. He hastily rose for some cold milk from the fridge to try and quench the pain, glad for the excuse to turn away from her.

She had asked him that question before, but that had been weeks ago, before they had become friends. He still didn't want to get into the topic of his father, but the curious look on her face when she had asked the question told him it was unlikely she'd let it go. He sighed and took a big swig of his milk to stall her.

She waited patiently.

"Well, there isn't much to tell," he mumbled once he had swallowed. She raised both eyebrows expectantly.

"He left my mom before I was born. They were never married. One day he was there, the next he was gone." He shrugged. "Guess the responsibility of a kid was too much for him. I never met him."

His tone was detached, but that was a façade. Anger was boiling inside him. It was true, he had never met the man. He didn't even know what his father looked like. Dylan strongly resembled his mother – for which he was glad – and she had no photographs of his father. But he still hated him for what he had done to Susan. Knocking her up and then leaving her high and dry was unforgivable.

"Hm." She looked thoughtful. "I'm sorry."

He shrugged, shoving the last of his second sandwich into his mouth.

"Can I meet your mom? I'd really like to get to know her."

"Uh, sure. She should be home any minute anyway. You're welcome to stay and wait." He took his plate to the kitchen sink and started washing up the breakfast dishes piled there.

She came over to him and grabbed a towel.

"Oh, you don't have to help!"

"But I'd like to." She smiled warmly, drying Dylan's plate. They worked in companionable silence for a bit. Then Marie asked, "When exactly do you turn eighteen? Wasn't it this month?"

He nodded. "Yeah. March thirtieth."

"Twenty-nine days," she murmured.

"Yeah." He grinned. It would still be another month after that until he finished school and was finally free of this place, but turning eighteen was a huge milestone for him.

"Do you have any birthday plans?"

"Not really." Hard to have plans when you didn't have any friends. "It'll probably be just like any other day except with more cake."

She snorted. "Well, that sounds good, but turning eighteen is a pretty big deal. Are you sure you don't want to do anything special?"

He shrugged. "What did you do for your eighteenth birthday?"

She hesitated. "You know, uh…"

He looked at her, puzzled. Not such a special day after all, it seemed, if she couldn't even remember it.

"I was with my then boyfriend and we were … having a good time."

"Oh." He blushed. Not something that would happen on his birthday. But then he realized something else. "So, you weren't with Alec at the time?"

"No."

That meant Marie and Alec had only been together for two years at the most. He had assumed they'd been high school sweethearts.

"You must have gotten married pretty quickly then."

"Oh, yeah, we didn't waste much time." She smiled.

A key turned in the lock of the front door, and Susan stepped inside the house, huffing and wiping her feet loudly on the doormat.

"Dylan, can you please help me with the groceries?" she shouted from the hallway.

"Oh, sure!" He was looking for the towel to dry his hands when he realized Marie was using it. As he reached for it, she offered, "No, let me."

Before he could protest, she rushed into the hallway.

"Hi, Miss Harper, I'm Marie, a friend of Dylan's. Let me help you with that."

"Oh… Hi." Dylan heard Susan's confused voice from the hallway. He quickly dried his hands off and rushed to the door. Susan stood in the doorway, heavy grocery bags in both hands, hugging two more to her chest.

Marie held out her hands. "May I?"

Before Susan could respond, Marie took two bags from her and carried them into the kitchen.

Susan gave Dylan a confused and questioning look, but he shrugged and took the remaining bags. He couldn't explain her interest in him either.

As Susan was studying his face, her confusion turned to alarm.

"What happened to you!?" She reached out and not so gently cupped his chin, turning his bruised cheek toward the light.

Dylan struggled to get out of her grip. He couldn't look her in the eyes. "It's nothing. I slipped on the sidewalk outside the library and fell on my face. No big deal." He gave her a reassuring smile.

She frowned. She knew he was lying. Too many accidents had happened all throughout his childhood and adolescence for her to believe him. But Dylan didn't want to admit that he was being bullied. It wouldn't make a difference, and he didn't want his mom to think he had a hard time. She already worried enough.

Susan sighed but let the blatant lie slide.

"It's nice to meet you, Marie," she said to their guest as she walked into the kitchen. "Dylan talks about you a lot."

Dylan bit his lip. Did she have to say it like that?

"It's nice to meet you, too, ma'am." Marie smiled warmly at Susan, but for a second Dylan thought he saw something else in her face. Yet before he could be sure, it was gone.

"Oh, please, call me Susan!"

Susan started unpacking the grocery bags, which Marie had parked on the dining table. She handed Dylan a gallon sized tub of ice cream to put in the freezer. As he took it from her, his mouth started watering. Maybe he could sneak some before dinner…

"Okay, Susan."

"Would you like to stay for dinner?"

"Uh, no, I have to head out. My husband is probably wondering where I am. But thank you."

"Mm. Sure. The invitation stands, though. I'd love to get to know you sometime."

Marie laughed uncomfortably and ran her fingers through her hair. "Thanks, that sounds nice." She inhaled deeply. "Well, I really have to go, so…" She suddenly seemed eager to leave.

"I'll see you tomorrow, Dylan." She lightly brushed his shoulder with her hand as she squeezed past him out the door.

"Yeah, see you." He trailed behind her, watching her from the front door as she walked down the driveway to her car.

As she was speeding away, he was overwhelmed with gratitude. Not only had she stood up for him, but she hadn't ratted him out to his mom either. Nobody had ever been there for him like that.

"Dylan? It's cold. Can you shut the door, please?"

"Sure. Sorry."

As he turned to close the door, he glimpsed something shiny between the trees across the street. But when he looked again it was gone.

"Today, please!"

"Right." He hastily shut the door and went back into the kitchen.

Weird. He could have sworn he had seen a pair of gleaming eyes.

8

The bell rang, signifying the end of another tedious history lesson. Dylan had been watching the rain through the window the entire period, desperately trying not to fall asleep while Mr. Kline was droning on and on about the Civil War.

"And remember to hand in your essays by Wednesday!" Mr. Kline shouted over the bustling noise of the students in the room. Dylan gathered his things and made his way to the door, his mind already on his next class.

But as he was about to step outside, somebody behind him gently touched his arm with intention. He whipped around in surprise. Molly Kirkgaard stood there, deep circles under her eyes, gaze fixed on him.

"Can I talk to you for a sec?" Her gaze darted around the emptying room. Others were squeezing past them, some sighing dramatically, making a point of showing them that they were blocking the exit.

Even more surprised, Dylan nodded. Molly gestured for him to move. "Not here."

They walked through the crowded corridor, Dylan following Molly sheepishly. He wondered what she wanted to talk to him about. Susan had stayed the night at their place on Saturday. Maybe something had happened? She hadn't mentioned anything, and Dylan hadn't noticed anything off about her, but it wouldn't be the first time she was hiding something from him.

Molly kept glancing over her shoulder periodically, scanning the crowd. She was probably embarrassed to be seen with him. And people did give them looks. Some even whispered to each other, not so subtly watching the two of them. Dylan tried to ignore them as best he could, but he still felt dread.

She walked him into an empty science classroom, shutting the door behind them. Then she just stood there, biting her lower lip, avoiding his gaze.

"Okay, what is it?" he asked when the silence between them became too heavy.

She sighed. "It's about your friend from out of town." Raindrops were hitting the windows loudly.

He frowned. "Marie?"

She nodded. "Have you noticed anything … weird about her?"

Dylan blinked. He almost laughed. Several things came to mind: her ability to stay warm in thirty-degree weather, her incredibly good looks, the ease with which she carried herself… But Molly was serious. Her gaze was intense. She had pressed her lips together, fixing him with her stare. She seemed deeply worried.

He shook his head. "Why?" he asked, a tad more hostile than he had meant to.

"She seems … dangerous." The rain pelted the windows harder.

"Dangerous? Are you talking about her kicking Fletcher Barnes's ass?" He smiled at the memory. "Yeah, I guess she can be dangerous but only to people who deserve it."

Molly shook her head. "That's not what I meant."

Dylan crossed his arms in front of his chest. *This better be good.*

"I mean, what do you really know about her?"

Dylan shrugged. "I know enough." Marie had been nothing but kind to him so far. He was not going to let this angry girl who had never cared about him spoil their friendship.

Molly arched an eyebrow. "Are you sure? Has she never told you anything that didn't quite add up? Didn't you say she was married? Isn't it a little strange for a married woman to travel the country like that? What about that husband of hers? Have you ever even met him?" Now the rain almost drowned out her voice. Some girls outside were shrieking about their hair getting wet. He had to strain to hear her words.

But he also wished the noise would drown her out. She was getting on his nerves. Who did she think she was? He decided to ignore her questions. "How is any of this your business?"

She sighed, rubbing her temple. "Look, all I'm asking is that you be careful, okay?"

The bell rang, announcing the start of second period.

"I've got to go. I'm late." Dylan rushed out of the room before Molly could say anything else.

As he walked to algebra, he tried to remain calm, but inside, he was seething.

Molly hadn't intervened when Fletcher had attacked him. She had just watched. Marie was the only one who had stepped up and helped. She was his friend. Not once had she tried to take advantage of him in any way. She had been nothing but kind and generous.

"Sorry…" he mumbled as he opened Mrs. Goff's classroom door. The teacher gestured for him to take a seat without interrupting her monologue.

All eyes were on him. He tried to ignore them, but he felt them follow him as he walked through the rows to his seat at the far end of the room. He hated being on display like that. His heart was pounding.

As quickly as he could, he sat down, trying not to make a sound. Slowly everyone's attention went back to whatever they had been doing before, some focused on Mrs. Goff, others on their doodles and daydreams…

The only one who was acting strange was Molly. She had gotten scared by Marie's performance the other day, and now she took it out on him. This girl had some serious issues. What was the big deal? Sure, Marie might be mysterious and different, but that didn't make her dangerous.

What do you actually know about her?

He knew plenty. She was from New York, she was on a college hiatus, touring the country with her husband, she was a musician…

Have you ever heard her play? What's her college major?

Well, he had never bothered to ask, but surely, she would tell him if he did. Nothing suspicious about that. And what exactly did Molly mean by 'dangerous' anyway? Physically dangerous? He found that hard to believe despite her having kicked Fletcher's ass. She wasn't a violent person. Besides, how violent could a girl really get anyway?

He took a deep breath to calm himself. Molly was clearly overreacting, and he wanted no part of it.

He started to relax into his chair.

"…which will be relevant for the quiz," Mrs. Goff trilled. He didn't care. He was top of the class anyway. Algebra was his least favorite subject, but he had suffered through it and studied so hard to keep up that he was ahead of the curve now, thus able to relax.

He cranked his neck to relieve the last remaining tension in his body. As he turned his head to the side, he noticed Fletcher staring at him. When their eyes met, the bully quickly averted his gaze, focusing on his notes instead.

Dylan hid a smile. That was a first. Marie must have left a lasting impression. Served him right. That guy needed to feel some consequences for once.

Molly was clearly full of it. He pushed her concerns aside, basking in the knowledge that Fletcher and his crew wouldn't bother him for a while.

$*\,*\,*$

At ten p.m. sharp, Marie pulled up at the gas station. He could see her car's distinctive headlights through the store window.

"Hey, Larry," he shouted. "I'm taking off. See you tomorrow!"

"All right, good night, Dylan!" Larry shouted back from his office.

He grabbed his backpack and rushed outside. She greeted him with a warm smile as he got into the car. The speakers were turned to a sensible volume, playing a Queen song.

"Hey," he said, slightly out of breath.

"Hey. Oh, before I forget…" She leaned over the middle console into the back of the car, fishing for something on the backseat. "I really enjoyed it. Thank you." She handed him the copy of *X-Men* he had loaned her.

His heart jumped with joy. "You liked it?"

"Yeah, it was cool. A group of mutant outcasts finding family and community with each other? That's a really nice sentiment."

He smiled. "It is." He slid the comic into his backpack.

As she was driving, Molly's words came back to Dylan. They seemed even more ridiculous now, but she had managed to feed into his insecurities nonetheless. Why did Marie care about him? It just didn't make any sense.

"Can I ask you something?" He didn't want to reveal his doubts, but the need to know outweighed the desire to come across as cool.

"Sure." Her tone was cheerful, but her hands tightened around the steering wheel.

"Uh, the other night, in front of the library…"

"Yeah?"

"Why did you save me from Fletcher and his friends?"

She frowned but kept her eyes on the road. "Why wouldn't I help you? You're my friend."

"Yes, but why are you friends with me?" The question came out more aggressive sounding than he had intended. It seemed like it had been simmering inside him for so long it now came to a boil.

Without missing a beat, she answered, "Why wouldn't I be? You're a great guy, Dylan."

Dissatisfied with her nonanswer, he retorted: "But you could be friends with literally anyone. Why me?"

She shrugged. "Do I need a reason?"

He didn't say anything. Technically, she didn't need a reason to be friends with anyone, but why she would pick him of all people still eluded him.

She sighed. "Well, you were the first person I met here. We're almost the same age and you seemed like a nice guy. That's all there is to it. Is there a reason why you're suddenly asking me this?"

That made sense. It was simple. He was nothing special to her. It could have been anybody. He had put too much thought into it. He needed to be careful; otherwise, Molly's words would drive him full-on crazy.

Now he was the one shrugging. "It's just something that's been on my mind for a while and with the incident on Friday… It just made me wonder."

She turned to him and gave him a dazzling smile. "I like you, Dylan. That's it."

His heart pounded in his chest, and blood rushed to his cheeks. No girl had ever told him that she liked him, especially not a beautiful one like her. Married or not, she affected him.

"I like you, too," he mumbled, looking away.

That's when she made a turn and the car headlights hit a section of the woods, illuminating a large gray shape that wasn't supposed to be there. Dylan could hardly believe his eyes. His jaw dropped.

Right in front of them was the biggest animal he had ever seen outside of a zoo. It must have been the size of a bear, but it was slender with long limbs, and its fur looked scruffy and spiky. It had a long snout, and its teeth were sharp and gleaming in the headlights.

The sudden presence of the car didn't seem to scare it at all. It stared at them from the shelter of the trees.

"Holy shit! What is that!?"

Marie didn't answer. Instead, she hit the gas and sped past the thing. Dylan turned in his seat so as not to lose sight of it. It threw its head back and howled, and that's when it clicked. That thing was a wolf.

And the wolf started chasing them.

"It's coming after us!" Dylan screamed.

Marie floored the gas pedal. The sudden acceleration pressed Dylan deeper into his seat. He gripped hold of the door and the center console, adrenaline flushing his body.

The trees outside flew by in a blur, the remaining snow on the ground merged into an endless streak of white along the road. How they weren't hitting anything was beyond him. They must have been going a hundred miles an hour.

And Marie kept driving. A sudden cuss on her lips woke Dylan from his paralysis.

"Is it still chasing us?"

"Yes," she replied calmly.

Without warning, she jerked the steering wheel to the left, making a tight U-turn in the middle of the road. Dylan gripped the side of his seat and held onto the car headliner with his other hand, but the change of direction still slammed him into the door.

They were barreling toward the beast, closing the distance. And the wolf held its course. Running toward them with its teeth bared.

Why wasn't it running away? What kind of suicidal animal was that?

They hit it with a loud crunching noise. The force of the collision catapulted the beast into the air. Marie hit the brakes, and they shrieked to a halt. Dylan would have gone through the windshield if he hadn't been wearing his seat belt. The straps were digging uncomfortably into his flesh.

Outside everything was still and quiet. They had come to a complete halt. The engine was crackling, and smoke was rising from the hood.

He looked around, trying to get his bearings. They were on Walnut Street. At the other end of town.

Houses sat to the left and more forest to the right. And there, a few feet away from the car lay a giant gray heap of fur. Dylan fumbled for his seat belt, wanting to get out there and see the dead wolf up close, but Marie blocked him with her arm hovering in front of his chest.

"Stop. Wait."

He froze, looking at her in surprise. What did she mean? Surely, this thing wasn't alive anymore. But her gaze was fixed on the furry heap by the side of the road.

It twitched. No, he had imagined that. It couldn't have.

But again, it stirred. This time the movement was distinct. Dylan stared at it in horror as its head snapped up and it howled in pain. Next thing he knew, it jumped up and huddled off into the woods, much faster than it should have been possible for an animal that badly injured.

"How the hell did it…" He didn't even know how to put into words what he had just witnessed, but there was no doubt in his mind: This had to be the animal attacking people.

"Okay, it's gone." She turned the key in the ignition to restart the car. But the engine stuttered and fell silent. "Shit." She unbuckled her seat belt. "I'm going to look for a payphone and call a tow service."

"What!? Are you insane? You can't go out there! What if it comes back?"

"It won't."

"How can you be so sure? It seemed tenacious."

She pressed her lips together for a second and said, "It would have attacked already. But it didn't. It went back into the woods."

Dylan turned his gaze to the forest again. He was staring hard at the spot where the wolf had disappeared into the shadows but saw nothing. No movement, nothing.

His breath was shaky, and he realized his hands and feet were trembling.

"Hey…" She put a hand on his thigh. "Calm down. It won't come back, I promise."

Embarrassment turned his cheeks crimson. Marie was calm and put together and had reacted in the best way possible when the animal had started chasing them, whereas he'd acted like a child who needed to be comforted by their mother. Pathetic. He swallowed hard.

"We can knock at the door of that house there." He nodded toward the nearest house behind Marie. "They'll let us use their phone."

She looked at the house and back at him, smiling slowly. "Yeah, good idea. Let's do that."

Giving a piece of helpful advice made him feel braver and more competent. He inhaled deeply and took his seat belt off.

His limbs felt stiff and wobbly at the same time when he got out of the car. But the fresh air was like a cooling balm on his face. He cast one more glance in the direction of the woods but still saw nothing.

By the time he had walked around the car to join Marie, she was already ringing the doorbell. After what seemed like an eternity, a weary-looking middle-aged man in a robe opened the door. When he saw Marie, his eyes widened.

"Good evening, sir," she said. "Sorry to bother you this late, but our car just broke down." She pointed with her thumb over her shoulder.

The man's eyes fluttered to the still smoking car on the street and back to her. He made a face that was supposed to express sympathy.

"Could we maybe use your phone to call a tow service? It would only take a minute."

"Of course. It's right here in the hallway. Come in."

They stepped into the hallway. Marie went straight for the phone, dialing the tow service.

"Shouldn't we call the police? Or Fish and Game?" Dylan asked after she had finished the brief call.

She frowned. "No, I don't think that's necessary."

"Marie, that was clearly the animal that has been killing people. We need to tell them what we saw."

That made the robed man's ears perk up. "What are you talking about?"

Dylan turned to him. "We hit a huge wolf – and by that, I mean enormous. It didn't even die after the collision. It just walked off into the woods. It was crazy."

The man looked at him with furrowed brows. "Are you serious?"

"Yes."

"No," Marie said at the same time. She turned to Dylan. "It's fine. Trust me."

He shook his head at her incredulously. *She must be in shock.* "What are you talking about? People need to know. This thing is dangerous and it's still out there."

She closed her eyes and rubbed the bridge of her nose. Dylan didn't understand her hesitance.

But the robed man was already ahead of them. He grabbed the phone and dialed the police. As he was waiting to be transferred, he held the mouthpiece to his chin and whispered to Dylan and Marie,

"Why don't you two take a seat in the living room? It'll probably be a while till they get here."

Dylan nodded and urged Marie on to walk into the adjoining room. They sat on the couch while the robed man was talking to the chief of police. "He said it was huge. … A wolf of some sort. … Mhm. … Mhm."

Dylan sighed with relief. He leaned back into the couch, the tension of the incident falling off. But Marie sat on the edge of the sofa. Her posture was rigid, and she didn't move a muscle.

The events had finally caught up with her. Dylan moved to put a hand on her shoulder, but he chickened out. Instead, he said in – what he hoped was – a soothing voice, "Relax. It's over. We're safe."

She didn't look at him.

The robed man hung up the phone. "Can I get you guys anything while we're waiting? You must be in shock."

"No, thank you," Marie replied flatly.

Dylan shook his head with a slight smile. "Thanks."

He nodded. "Then excuse me for a minute. I'm going to get changed." He walked off without waiting for a reaction.

When Marie still didn't move, Dylan asked, "Are you okay?"

"I'm fine." The curtness of her tone told him to stop speaking. So they sat in silence till the police came.

The cops were prompt. They beat the tow service by several minutes.

Just like the time Dylan had found Stacy, there was a whole squadron of police cars – way more than the town of Berlin should even have. A group of policemen fanned out into the woods while the chief was questioning Marie and Dylan at the house.

"A wolf, you say?" He jotted something down on his notepad.

"Yes. It was big. Probably twice the size of a regular wolf. And it survived getting hit by a car."

"Hm…" He made another note. "Can we take a look at your car, ma'am?"

"What?" Was that panic in Marie's voice?

"Maybe there are traces of the animal left on your bumper."

"I doubt it," she said resolutely. "And what if there is? How would that help you in any way?"

The chief scratched his head. "Well…" He paused for a moment. "Can you tell me anything about the animal that your friend here hasn't mentioned yet?"

"No. That's it. He told you everything." Dylan had never heard that much annoyance in her voice. But the chief tended to bring that out in people.

"Okay, then." He stowed away his notepad in his inside jacket pocket. "The tow service is going to take your car to the shop. Do you need a ride home?" He indicated his car.

"Thanks, that would be great," Dylan answered. It was already past eleven o'clock. *Mom must be worried.*

"I'd like to stay with my car, thank you," Marie said.

The chief frowned at her. "It's going straight to the shop, I assure you, ma'am."

"Still." She flashed a smile that looked more wicked than charming. "My husband will pick me up from the shop. It's no big deal."

When she mentioned her husband, the chief's eyebrows shot up. "Uh, sure. Then … have a good night, ma'am. And take care!"

"You, too." This time, her smile was dazzling.

"Are you sure?" Dylan hated to leave her behind like that. She had saved their lives, but that thing was still out there.

"Yes," She answered emphatically. "But you go ahead and get home. Get some sleep. I'll see you tomorrow." She smiled warmly and rubbed his upper arm.

"Okay." There was no changing her mind. "See you tomorrow."

He followed the chief to his squad car. As he sat on the passenger's seat in the warm cabin, he took in the scene before him. Police cars were everywhere, red and blue lights flashing in the dark. Some neighbors had come out of their houses to see what all the commotion was about.

All the policemen were scouring the woods for the beast. Marie stood with her arms crossed next to her car as the tow people hooked it up to their vehicle. She looked worried. Dylan wasn't sure if it was for the car or because of the wolf. Maybe both.

The chief started the engine and pulled out of his parking spot. As they got farther and farther away from the scene, the streets became darker. The town lay silent against a backdrop of snow-covered mountains and forest. The very place where this thing thrived. It was like they were trapped.

Dylan scanned every bit of landscape they passed for the wild beast but saw no sign of it.

"Don't worry, kid." Apparently the chief had noticed Dylan's anxiety. "We'll catch this thing."

9

"How big did you say it was?" Lana Waskowski gripped the back of her chair so hard her knuckles had turned white as she was half turned toward Dylan in her seat. Her wide brown eyes were fixed on him.

He struggled not to groan. Being repeatedly asked about the wolf sighting was bad enough but all this attention was giving him anxiety. He wished they would all just go back to ignoring him.

"Like, twice the size of a regular wolf, I'd say," he repeated for the hundredth time. Everyone within earshot stopped what they were doing and listened in on their conversation. Dylan automatically tensed and shrank into his seat. Too many eyes were on him.

For the first time in his life, he wished Mr. Kline would start the class, but the teacher was being held hostage by Amy Barnes, who was trying to negotiate an extension for her essay that had been due today. So everyone else was free to question Dylan about the wolf incident.

And he hated everything about it. Not just the unwanted attention, but also knowing that all of these people were only nice to him because they wanted something from him.

The wolf encounter had creeped him out. Now that he had slept on it, the craziness of the situation had sunk in. This wolf had been able to keep up with a car going over a hundred miles an hour, and then it had survived getting hit by said car at almost as high a speed.

If he hadn't seen it with his own eyes, he wouldn't have believed it.

"That sounds awful. Imagine that's the last thing you see…" Maureen Cohen shivered. She was sitting on the desk next to Dylan's, feet propped up on her chair, elbows resting on her knees, face in hands.

The hair on Dylan's neck stood up, and he gulped. If it hadn't been for Marie's presence of mind, that might have been true for him. He involuntarily imagined the beast lunging at him, its long sharp teeth bared… He wondered if he would have felt its rank breath on his face seconds before it chowed down on him. Stacy's body appeared in his mind's eye, and he shivered. Now that he had seen what had killed her, he felt even sorrier for the girl.

"Yeah, and my dad said he and his colleagues couldn't find a trace of it. You might think an animal this big would leave a trail behind, but there was nothing. It's like it disappeared into thin air." Lana snapped her fingers for dramatic effect.

Her dad was a police officer. Apparently, he had been on call the night Dylan and Marie had run into the wolf. A tiny part of Dylan wondered why Lana even bothered to ask him questions when she had a much better source of information right at home.

"My dad and his buddies want to go out there and shoot that animal," Sandra Brown said to Lana with a furrowed brow. That ripped Dylan out of his reverie. They couldn't do that. That thing had survived getting hit by a car, for crying out loud! A gun would hardly make an impact.

"No. That's way too dangerous." He barely recognized his own voice. It had dropped to a husky whisper.

Sandra's kind round face fell with worry. "My mom doesn't want him to go, but he won't hear it."

Maureen nodded gravely. "Yeah, my dad wants to go out there, too." Nobody said anything for a moment, clearly concerned for their fathers' lives.

"No, no, no. You have to stop them." But even as he said it, Dylan realized there was nothing he or anyone else could do. If these guys wanted to go out and play big-game hunters, nobody could stop them.

"All right, everyone! Let's start. Please, open your books to page thirty-two."

They all scattered to their seats as Mr. Kline started the class. But Dylan could tell nobody was listening – and not for the usual reasons. They were all still thinking about their dads going out to hunt a lethal animal and potentially getting hurt or even killed in the process.

And he couldn't blame them.

He tried to focus on Mr. Kline to distract himself, but the man was like a walking sleep aid. As Dylan let his gaze wander around the room over his equally drowsy peers, his eyes met Molly's.

She sat in the same row two desks away from him, but she was facing him, staring intently, her hazel eyes unreadable. She didn't even blink.

Dylan didn't know why, but her gaze gave him the creeps. He had to look away. He felt watched, threatened even. Something about Molly wasn't right.

That thought almost made him snort. There was nothing to be afraid of after all. Molly was just a girl. And she had never been mean to him. Granted, she had never stuck up for him either, but neither had anyone else but Marie.

Something was weird about her though. She seemed on edge, with her face even paler than usual, dark circles under her eyes, her cheeks hollow. If Dylan didn't know better, he would think she was on drugs. Was all of that just because of her mom's death?

And why was she so obsessed with Marie?

* * *

Marie was leaning on the counter, arms crossed, watching Dylan flip through his comic book.

"My mom won't even let me leave the house unaccompanied anymore. She insists on driving me to school every morning." He pretended to be annoyed because he didn't want to admit how scared he was in front of Marie, but the truth was, he understood perfectly where Susan was coming from, and not having to walk to school in the early morning hours did make him feel safer.

"Hm… I mean, she's not wrong. Better safe than sorry, right?"

Dylan avoided her gaze, focusing on the colorful panels in front of him without really seeing them. He shrugged. She had been so brave when the wolf had been chasing them that it made him feel like he had somehow failed, like he was inadequate.

"Hey…" She put a hand on his that was still flipping pages. Startled, he looked up.

Her heart-shaped face was full of concern. She hadn't been fooled for a second. "It's okay to be scared. That thing was really scary." She smiled empathetically. "Besides…" She nodded toward the comic book. "The *X-Men* look out for each other, too."

Dylan couldn't help but smile at her comment. She answered with a dazzling smile of her own. Her hand was as cold as always, and her lingering touch made him shiver uncomfortably. He tried to hide it, but she noticed and pulled her hand away.

"Yeah, but the *X-Men* also have superpowers," he said, trying to lighten the mood.

She pulled up one corner of her mouth, her gray eyes sparkling with mischief. "Who says I don't?"

He almost didn't laugh. It felt like she did have superpowers sometimes. His own personal superhero. But then she burst out laughing, and he joined in.

That's when the door opened, and Molly entered the store. She wore her blond hair in her usual ponytail and was wrapped in a thick down jacket. Her cheeks were slightly flushed from the cold night air, but her eyes still had that eerie look and dark circles underneath.

"Hey," Dylan said in surprise. She had never come into the store before – at least not during his shifts.

"Hey," she replied a little unsteadily.

Marie turned around briefly and turned back to Dylan.

"What are you doing here?" he asked when Molly didn't move.

She pointed with her thumb over her shoulder. "I was going to pick you up. Your mom is at my house, and I figured we could all hang out together for a bit."

It took Dylan a second to process her words. That was new. When she had been invited to dinner at his house, she had been dying to return home the entire time, and she had never hidden her disdain for Susan and Martin's relationship. And now she wanted all of them to hang out?

When Dylan didn't react, Marie straightened, appraising Molly with curiosity.

Molly's chin jutted forward. She took two steps toward Marie, offering her hand. "You must be Dylan's friend. I don't think we've met. I'm Molly."

Marie looked at Molly's hand for a second, like she had done with Fletcher so many weeks ago. For a moment, Dylan wondered if Marie wasn't going to take it, but she stepped forward and shook Molly's hand.

"Marie. Nice to meet you." Dylan could hear the smile in her voice.

Marie's action snapped him out of his trance.

Molly wanted to take him to her house to hang out with his mom and her dad. He could think of a few things he'd rather do, starting with standing stark-naked outside in the cold for an hour, but he reminded himself that he wanted to make an effort for his mom.

"Uh, okay. But I still have ten minutes on the clock." He pointed over his shoulder to the clock on the wall to emphasize his point.

Molly shrugged. "That's fine. I'll wait."

He scratched his head in confusion. And now she wanted to hang out with him and Marie? Something was definitely up.

"What were you two talking about?" She stepped up to the counter, leaning on the opposite end from Marie's spot, looking only at her.

"The *X-Men*," Marie replied with a sweet smile.

"Who?"

Dylan chuckled. "Never mind. It's a comic book series."

"Oh." An awkward silence stretched out between them. Dylan tried to think of something else to say, but he felt tense. This didn't seem right.

Finally, Molly broke the silence. "So, you both saw a wolf the other night?" Marie's lips formed a narrow line at Molly's words while a wave of dread hit Dylan. *Not again.*

"Yes," he answered curtly.

"Have you heard that they're organizing a hunting party?"

Dylan sucked in air. He had tried to forget about that. He said, "Yeah…" as Marie said, "They really shouldn't do that. This thing will rip them to shreds."

The image of the long sharp teeth coming at him flashed in Dylan's mind again. He squeezed his eyes shut and rubbed the bridge of his nose. Marie was right. They should leave the hunting to the police. But then again, what could the police do that these guys couldn't? Everyone was at risk. And none of them even had an inkling of how dangerous this beast was.

"I think there are more dangerous things out there than this wolf,"

Molly said, all the while staring at Marie without blinking.

That made Dylan angry. "What are you talking about? You didn't even see it. It's incredibly strong and fearless. It's going to eat those guys for breakfast, I assure you."

Marie threw a worried glance his way. "You know, maybe it has moved on by now." It was a feeble attempt to calm him down.

He snorted. "Right."

Marie ignored his sarcasm, her gaze fluttering from him to Molly. "Anyway, how do you two know each other?"

And now she was changing the subject. Dylan thought about protesting, but he realized there was no use. Arguing his point wouldn't stop anyone from going out after that wolf, so he gave up and kept his mouth shut.

"His mom is dating my dad." Molly's eyes had slightly narrowed, and her posture was rigid.

"Hm." Marie nodded. "Funny. He has never mentioned you." She looked reproachfully at Dylan whose head bobbed back automatically.

"I didn't think it was important."

She shrugged and turned back to Molly. Something flickered in her eyes, but it was gone so quickly Dylan thought he might have imagined it.

With a loud plop, the cap of Dylan's half-full soda bottle on the counter popped off and the soda foamed and spewed out of the bottle as if somebody had shaken it.

"What the hell…?" Dylan tried to cover his face from the geyser of soda but neither Molly nor Marie reacted.

"How could this happen?" He hadn't touched it in at least twenty minutes. Had he shaken it before? But why would it spontaneously explode?

A few moments later, the soda stilled, but most of it had splashed all over the counter and a puddle had formed around the bottle. Some of it trailed toward the edge of the counter.

"I'll go get paper towels," he said to the girls but neither one of them paid attention to him.

He rushed to the bathroom, pulled a bunch of paper towels from the dispenser, and rushed out again. As he made his way through the snack aisle back to the counter, he heard Marie speak in a hushed voice: *"Stay out of this, little witch. If you don't get in my way, I won't get in yours. Live and let live, okay?"*

He froze for a second. Her cold, hard tone caused the hairs on the back of his neck to stand up. It had been similar to the tone she had used on Fletcher but somehow even more menacing.

And what did she mean? The thought that she had an ulterior motive to be friends with him crept up on him again. But that was ridiculous. Maybe this wasn't even about him. He had only overheard a fragment of a conversation. It would be foolish to jump to conclusions. He shook his head, trying to banish his fears.

As he stepped out between the shelves, he noticed the two girls were staring at each other. Marie looked relaxed, one elbow resting on the counter, all her weight on one leg while Molly stood as rigid as before, not moving a muscle.

"Is something wrong?" he asked before he could stop himself, curiosity getting the better of him.

"No, we're all good here, Dylan." Marie's tone was sweet as sugar again. She winked at him as he stepped behind the counter and gingerly wiped the soda spillage.

"Well, I won't keep you guys. Enjoy the rest of your night! It was a pleasure meeting you, Molly." She gave Molly a wide smile and made her way to the door.

"I'll see you tomorrow, Dylan. By then I'll have my own car back!" she shouted over her shoulder as she exited the store.

"Awesome! See you tomorrow!" He smiled warmly, already looking forward to being in the fancy Audi again instead of her busted-up rental.

When he had wiped off the last bit of sticky liquid, he glanced at the clock. His time was up. Turning toward the back of the store, he shouted, "I'm taking off, Larry! Good night!"

"Good night, Dylan."

"Okay, you ready?" he asked Molly even though he wasn't eager to leave at all.

Molly's face looked ashen. Tiny pearls of sweat beaded along her hair line, and her lips were pressed together.

"Yes. Come on, let's go."

* * *

"So, what where you two talking about earlier while I was in the bathroom?" Dylan asked when they were on the road to Molly's house. He wasn't entirely sure where she lived and how long they'd be alone in the car together, so he didn't want to waste any time. He needed to know what was going on.

Molly's perpetual frown deepened. "Nothing. You were gone for, like, five seconds." She pressed her lips together, staring straight ahead into the night.

"Okay…" For a second, Dylan doubted his own perception, but he was sure he had heard Marie talk to Molly. "It's just … I thought I heard her say something to you."

"She didn't." But Molly's answer came too quickly, betraying the lie. She was clearly hiding something. What had they been talking about that he wasn't allowed to know? Marie was *his* friend after all.

Had Molly said something rude to provoke her? It seemed likely.

Molly wasn't the friendliest person. But Marie had called her a witch, which seemed harsh. Even if Molly had insulted her in the two seconds he had been gone, wouldn't Marie just have ignored her?

Without looking at him, Molly let out a sigh. "Just please be careful around her, okay?" Her voice had become small, her usual bite completely gone.

Dylan refrained from rolling his eyes. "She's harmless, Molly." Her hands visibly tightened around the steering wheel. "Seriously. She's never given me any reason not to like her." On the contrary. She had been his fierce protector, but he wasn't going to say that in front of Molly – besides, she had personally witnessed the incident with Fletcher in front of the library.

"And it still doesn't seem strange to you that a married woman who's supposed to be traveling has befriended you and is voluntarily staying in a town haunted by a series of mysterious killings?" Molly asked after a beat. Her voice was firmer now but not as standoffish as usually.

The truth was he had thought about that a million times, and he had asked Marie about it. And even though, she had reassured him that he was just being paranoid, he couldn't shake the feeling there was something she wasn't telling him. And Molly feeding into those fears wasn't helping.

He shrugged. "Why? Do you think I'm so awful nobody can like me?" He had meant to sound sarcastic, but it came out like an accusation.

"No." She hesitated. "It's just…" She took a sharp turn onto Seventh Street. "What do you really know about her? I mean really?"

She had asked him that before, but that had been prior to his encounter with the wolf. Back then he had quickly discounted her question, but now that he thought about it… After seeing how well Marie had reacted when faced with that animal and how she seemed to know the car crash wouldn't kill it… It did seem strange.

"What do *you* know about her?" If Molly knew something, she might as well tell him instead of beating around the bush. She seemed sure that she knew something Dylan didn't. But if it was so important, why didn't she just come out with it? It seemed like she was purposefully being mysterious.

She pressed her lips together again, all the while keeping her gaze fixed on the street. "I know it sounds weird, but I kind of have a sixth sense about people. And right now, it's telling me not to trust this girl."

Dylan didn't say anything. He wanted to tell her she was crazy, but something held him back. Marie had called her a witch and now she was talking about having a sixth sense. But those were metaphors, right? He was being ridiculous.

He saw the wolf again, sharp teeth coming at his face. That thing wasn't supposed to be real. What if there were *other* things that weren't supposed to exist?

His rational mind rebelled against the thought.

"Think about it, Dylan. Why would I tell you to stay away from her? What's in it for me?"

She had a point. In the past, she had made it abundantly clear that she didn't care about him. It didn't make sense for her to tell him to stay away from his only friend.

"Why do you suddenly care?"

"Because too many people have died." She squared her jaw.

"You don't think..." He scoffed. "You don't think Marie has something to do with the killings, do you?" Now that was truly ridiculous.

She didn't respond.

"Molly, it was the wolf. I saw it with my own eyes."

"Did you?"

"What!? Of course, I—"

"She was with you that night, wasn't she? And she's the only other person who's seen it."

"So?" He was getting angry. She didn't believe him. *What the hell?* "It's not like we could have imagined it."

She pulled into the driveway of a sky-blue two-story middle class family home. "We're here."

Dylan didn't want to let her off the hook, but she killed the engine and got out of the car before he had a chance to stop her. Why was she so obsessed with Marie? As he followed Molly inside, he couldn't shake the feeling that she was the one hiding something.

10

The Kirkgaards' living room was modern. Two comfortable flower-patterned pastel pink couches sat in an L-shape on the dark hardwood floor. Susan had curled up on one of them, feet tucked under her buttocks, facing the TV. Dylan could tell she was trying not to touch Martin who sat next to her, one arm resting on the backrest behind her. He looked content. Dylan hated it. And he hated himself for hating it.

He stuffed some freshly made popcorn into his mouth, trying to make himself be okay with the situation. But the sinking feeling in his stomach told him he'd need way more than a salad bowl full of the salty crispy snack on his lap for that.

Molly shared the other couch with Dylan, legs and arms crossed, eyes trained on the TV screen, where they were watching *On Golden Pond*. She seemed to be as uncomfortable as he was, which annoyed Dylan to no end. After all, this whole thing had been her idea.

He grabbed another handful of popcorn. Nobody else was having any. He couldn't let it go to waste. And it seemed to be the only thing that could stop his mind from going to places he didn't want to go.

Susan leaned forward and grabbed one of the two bottles of beer on the coffee table. When she let herself sink back into the couch, Martin casually moved his arm from the backrest to her shoulder. Susan turned to him, beaming, and he smiled and winked at her.

Dylan wanted to throw up.

Molly scoffed next to him, and Susan's beer suddenly spewed from the bottle. With a shriek, she held the bottle away from her body and the couch, leaning forward and leaving Martin's embrace.

But unlike Dylan's soda at the gas station, the beer stopped spewing immediately.

"How did that happen?" Martin exclaimed with an uncomfortable laugh, his eyes shooting to Molly for a split second.

Dylan froze.

The faucet at his house, the rain on the classroom windows, the soda at the gas station, and now the beer… Molly had been there every single time. What if she was somehow connected to these strange incidents?

A part of him told him he was being ridiculous, but he couldn't shake the thought.

As Susan was wiping at her turquoise cable knit sweater, trying to disperse the drops of beer and reassuring Martin – who was fussing over her – that everything was fine, Dylan was watching Molly from the corner of his eye.

She hadn't moved, her posture still as rigid and standoffish as before but – and Dylan wasn't sure if he was reading too much into it – her face looked a little smug. The frown had smoothed out a bit.

"It's fine. This sweater is old anyway…" Susan waved Martin off. "I'm so clumsy, I don't know how this happened." She laughed, holding up her beer and shaking her head. "I'm sorry, I hope I didn't spill anything on the floor." She leaned over, scanning the hardwood floor between the couch and the coffee table.

"It's fine, don't worry about it." Martin put his arm around her again, squeezing her shoulder. "It happens."

Molly shot up and mumbled, "I need to use the bathroom…"

Before anyone could react, she disappeared into a room beneath the stairs, slamming the door behind her.

Her sudden absence made Dylan even antsier. He couldn't shake the thought that he was on the right track, thinking Molly had somehow caused the accident. But how was that possible?

He needed to think.

"Do you have another bathroom I can use?" he asked before he had really decided to do so. Martin smiled courteously and pointed upstairs.

"Upstairs. Third door on the left."

"Thanks."

He placed the bowl of popcorn on the couch and rushed upstairs, taking two steps at a time, too eager to get away from the happy couple on the couch and to be alone so he could organize his spinning thoughts.

On the upper floor, a *Flashdance* poster on the second door to the left made him stop. This had to be Molly's room. The door was shut, taunting him, tempting him to open it and take a peek inside…

He scolded himself for even considering it. He wasn't going to violate another person's privacy.

But then again, he needed to know the truth.

And how will her room tell me?

He stared at the doorknob. All he had to do was reach out and turn it.

Molly wasn't going to volunteer any information. After all, she hadn't been forthcoming so far. And she was clearly hiding something. He needed to find out what was going on. And he could use any clue he could get.

She was still in the bathroom downstairs, but there was no telling how much time he had left. He needed to hurry.

His heart pounded in his chest as he reached out a shaking hand and grabbed the doorknob. He twisted it slowly, careful not to make a sound, and pushed the door open.

The room was dark. He quickly stepped inside, silently closing the door, shutting out the light from the hallway.

He awkwardly felt for a light switch by the side of the door, flipping it on as silently as possible – even though he knew nobody would be able to hear it.

The sudden illumination made him jump. He felt caught for a second, knowing full well he was doing something he wasn't supposed to. His heart was racing as he tried to take a few calming breaths, telling himself he just needed to get it over with.

He let his gaze wander around the room. It was big, almost twice the size of his own. The walls were painted a light pink and covered in movie posters. Matching frilly white furniture decorated the room, with a queen-sized bed as the centerpiece. Molly's clothes were spilling out of her open closet onto the floor, the back of her desk chair, and her vanity. Dylan was shocked by the mess. He had pegged Molly for a tidy person.

He didn't want to look at her stuff too closely, feeling like he was already intruding enough but he had to find something…

But he didn't even know what he was looking for. Everything looked normal enough.

He didn't know what he had expected. A cauldron and a black cat maybe? He scoffed at his own foolishness. In this pink explosion of a room, it seemed even more ridiculous that Molly somehow had something like supernatural abilities.

He needed to get out of there before he got caught and forget about this nonsense.

But as he turned to leave, his gaze fell onto Molly's desk by the door, where several items of stationery had been pushed aside to make room for a bowl with a half-burnt incense stick and an open notebook.

Dylan peered at it and saw the words *protection spell* written in fine cursive on the first line of the page.

His heart skipped a beat.

With a start, he remembered the books Molly had checked out at the town library. The ones about Wicca. She had called it modern witchcraft.

He gulped. This couldn't be real.

His heart was doing somersaults in his chest and his hands were shaking violently. His already tight turtleneck sweater suddenly felt even tighter, the collar seeming to cut into his throat. He stuck a finger inside his collar and pulled it off his neck a few inches, squeezing his eyes shut and taking a few deep breaths, trying to calm himself down. He needed to get out of this room.

He wiped his clammy hands on the sides of his jeans and silently opened the door.

All he could hear from downstairs was the movie.

He flipped the lights in Molly's room off and stepped out, shutting the door behind him. Once he was no longer where he wasn't supposed to be, he felt immediately calmer. He took one more deep breath to steady himself and made his way back downstairs.

If Molly really had magical powers – he hated to even think it, but everything was pointing toward it – what did that mean? Was she dangerous?

She was back on the couch now. He took his time walking toward her, scrutinizing her from behind. She sat in the same position as she had before – arms and legs crossed – and her eyes seemed to be glued to the screen.

Everything about her seemed normal.

"Is everything okay, Dylan?" Susan's voice interrupted his thoughts. He realized he had stopped walking and was standing a few steps behind the couch, staring intently at Molly.

He blushed. "Uh, yeah, yes, of course, I was just … I was just wondering if anybody wanted anything from the kitchen?" He pointed with his thumb over his shoulder.

Molly turned around, looking him up and down.

"Oh, no, thanks, buddy," Martin chimed in.

Dylan nodded and made himself move toward the couch again, all the while trying not to stare at Molly.

But he couldn't help himself. Sitting next to her, he kept peering at her from the corner of his eyes. At some point, she grabbed a glass of soda from the coffee table, taking a sip and keeping the tumbler in her hand.

And as she was holding it, her eyes back on the screen, the liquid in the glass started moving, faster and faster, forming a swirl. She was holding the tumbler completely still. There was no way the liquid could have started to swirl on its own.

Dylan tried not to react, but he was hypnotized by the swirling soda. Molly didn't even seem to notice, sitting there beside him, all calm and quiet. But the liquid didn't slow down. Instead, it started bubbling. And small drops were shaking loose from the bubbles and rising to the top of the tumbler.

And they weren't wandering upward on the glass wall. No. They were floating upward.

When they reached the top of the tumbler, they popped like air bubbles and the liquid fell back down to join the rest, as if the soda was juggling tiny bubbles of liquid. Dylan couldn't tear his eyes off the display.

His hands grew sweaty, and his heart raced.

This was real.

* * *

That night he couldn't sleep. He kept tossing and turning in his bed, thinking about what he had learned. Molly had supernatural abilities. Even as his brain still rebelled against the thought, there was no use denying the facts.

She was able to control water the way Magneto was able to control metal. His mind was grappling for a logical explanation. He thought about what he knew about the scientific properties of water from science class, but he couldn't come up with anything that might explain how a person might be able to control it the way Molly did.

Dowsing rods were a thing. Was Molly some sort of water-witch? Marie's words rang in his head again. She had called Molly a witch. But witches weren't real. They existed in fairytales where they lured children into their houses or where they were melted by water…

But then again, he had seen what he had seen.

He automatically thought of the Wicked Witch of the West and snorted. But then his laughter died on his lips. He remembered the way the rain had been pelting the classroom windows the day he and Molly had talked about Marie. He might be imagining things, but he was more and more sure that she could control the rain.

Dylan pictured her in his head: her delicate face and skinny body, the sad hazel eyes… She certainly didn't look abnormal. And even though she was rude at times, she seemed like a regular girl.

And what was her deal with Marie, and why didn't she believe he had seen the murderous wolf?

He couldn't fathom that Marie might be dangerous. She had been nothing but nice to him. She had protected him and gotten Fletcher off his back.

But she seemed to know something. She certainly knew Molly was a witch. But how? Had she figured it out when she saw the soda explode at the gas station? Maybe she had known other witches in the past. She got around a lot after all, and Molly couldn't be the only one, could she?

Marie had also known the wolf would be able to keep up with the car and that it would survive being hit. It was strange and made Dylan curious, but it didn't mean Marie was dangerous.

She knew things, that was certain.

And if she really were dangerous, what did she want with him? He owned nothing worth taking and if she had wanted to hurt him, she'd had enough chances to do so.

Telling himself to stop worrying, he drifted off into an uneasy sleep, haunted by dreams of a wart-faced cackling Molly chasing him on a flying broomstick through the woods till he was face to face with the growling wolf, which was staring him down with gleaming eyes.

11

Dylan was sleepwalking through the entire day. At school, he couldn't focus on anything, his mind drifting off to Molly again and again.

During history class, he kept sneaking glances at her, looking for anything out of the ordinary. Of course, there was nothing. Molly was doodling in her notes the whole time, not once looking in Dylan's direction.

If she knew about Dylan's discovery from the previous night, she didn't let on. Or maybe Dylan was imagining things. He still couldn't quite believe that Molly was a real-life witch. Besides, he was unsure what that even meant.

A part of him was panicking, wanting to run from the unknown, but another part of him wanted to know more. And curiosity won out. He was going to confront her about it and ask her to explain.

He spent the rest of the class hyping himself up, but when the bell rang and everyone jumped up from their seats, he chickened out.

How was he going to broach the subject? *Hey, Molly, awkward last night, wasn't it? By the way, can you control water with your mind by any chance?* No, that would not go over well. He had to formulate a proper plan. A strategy.

He was still mulling that over during his shift that evening, when Jake Logan walked into the store, packing a shotgun over his shoulder.

"Hey, kid."

"Hey."

"I just need some cigarettes." He nodded as Dylan handed him his usual brand. "Going to go out to get that wolf tonight. That thing's head will look great on my wall."

Dylan shuddered and his pulse picked up speed. The thought of Logan going up against that beast was terrifying. The man didn't know what he was getting himself into.

Dylan nodded toward the shotgun. "A shotgun won't do much against that thing. It survived getting hit by a car."

Logan scoffed, stuffing the packet of cigarettes into the chest pocket of his hunting jacket. "Don't worry, kid. This baby has never let me down." He patted the gun's strap on his shoulder. "It's like magic."

"Well, you're going to need a fucking miracle." But as he was saying it, he registered Logan's words. What if you needed actual magic to get rid of this wolf?

He shook his head, taking a deep calming breath. He was sounding crazier and crazier.

Logan scoffed at Dylan's remark. "I'll see you around, kid." He tipped his baseball cap and left.

Dylan sure hoped he would see Jake Logan around and that the man wasn't going to get eaten that night.

But he didn't have time to dwell on the thought because as Logan exited, Marie entered to pick Dylan up. She was wearing her regular leather jacket over a tight green sweater and light denim pants and white sneakers. Her long brown curls were framing her beautiful heart-shaped face.

"Hey, Dylan, are you ready to go?" She smiled from ear to ear, revealing her perfect teeth. That smile was contagious. And for the first time since last night, all the tension fell off him.

"Sure." He grabbed his backpack from beneath the counter. "Larry, I'm off!"

"Have a good night, Dylan!" the old man called from the back room.

Dylan followed Marie to her car, which didn't show any signs of the run-in with the wolf anymore.

As soon as he was wrapped in the warm cocoon of the luxurious interior, he sank into his seat, sighing contently.

But the moment of reprieve didn't last long because when Marie turned the key in the ignition the radio started playing 'Psycho Killer' by Talking Heads, cutting in right at the first verse, and the lyrics triggered his anxiety.

A deadly animal was on the loose and people were out to hunt it down. His mom's boyfriend's daughter was most likely a real-life witch, and she had made some serious allegations against the woman he was currently sitting next to in an enclosed space.

He rubbed the bridge of his nose, squeezing his eyes shut, to silence the panicked voice inside his head.

"Are you okay?" Marie asked with genuine concern in her voice.

"Yeah, yeah, I'm fine." Dylan let go of his nose and took a deep breath, trying to calm himself down. He exhaled a little shakily.

"Are you sure? Is something on your mind? Is that blond airhead bothering you again?"

Dylan laughed despite his fear. "No, no, he hasn't bothered me since you… Well, you know…" The words *since you saved me from him* still didn't come out easily. The embarrassment ran deep.

Thinking about that incident brought back Molly's warning. And he remembered that he wanted to ask Marie about the wolf.

"Then what is it?" she pressed.

But they had already reached his driveway. She had turned off the engine and was looking at him expectantly. The radio had cut off with the engine, so they were sitting in silence.

Dylan debated what to do. She was his friend, and he didn't want to upset her or, worse, lose her. But he needed answers. So he gathered all his courage and asked, "Would you like to come in? We can talk about it then. My mom is at her boyfriend's tonight, so I'll have the house to myself." He nervously pulled at his jacket collar.

Her face lit up. "Yes, I'd love to."

Dylan's pulse sped up. Now there was no turning back.

He led her inside. This time, she shrugged her jacket off and hung it on one of the hooks by the door. Dylan took off his jacket and boots, but then he wasn't sure what to do.

"Why don't you take a seat in the living room? Can I get you anything? Water? Coffee? Soda?" He was trying to buy time. He hadn't thought this all the way through.

Marie pursed her lips. "Mm… Can I see your room?"

Dylan's heart skipped a beat. He frantically tried to remember what his room had looked like that morning when he left for school. It was presentable enough, but the thought of Marie – of any girl actually – inside his room made him sweat with nerves. What if she thought it looked childish and laughed at him?

He gulped. There was no time to think about that. He needed answers, and giving her what she wanted might make her talk.

"Sure… It's upstairs. Just follow me…" He led the way, trying to hide the fact that his entire body was shaking. On the landing, he took one last deep breath and opened the door for her, flicking the light on. When she stepped inside, he wondered what the room looked like to her.

His tiny twin bed, the walls and ceiling plastered with posters and the Harvard crest, which he was now a little embarrassed about…

He paused. Normally, he didn't care what people thought of his Ivy League plans, but somehow, Marie's opinion mattered.

She stopped in the middle of the tiny and tidy space on the worn navy blue carpeted floor and looked around.

After a few seconds that felt like eons to Dylan she declared, "I like it. It's very you." She gave him a smile and winked.

His heart stuttered and relief washed over him. "Thanks." He blushed. "Uh, make yourself comfortable." He hurried past her, cleaning off a pile of books from his desk chair and sliding it out to her. "Can I get you anything now?"

"No, I'm good but get whatever you need for yourself." She plunked down on his chair, still gazing around the space.

He nodded once and fled the room. His anxiety levels were through the roof. There was a girl in his room. Right now.

He grabbed a bottle of soda and a large bag of chips from the kitchen and practically ran back upstairs.

Marie was sitting nonchalantly – with one ankle resting on her other leg – on his great-aunt's wooden desk chair with the curved backrest in this room full of outdated furniture where all his personal belongings didn't quite fit. He tried not to see it, to consider this situation as nothing but normal. After all, he was on a mission. He sat on his neatly made bed and ripped open the bag of chips. The first mouthful of salty goodness calmed his nerves.

His guest eyed him curiously.

He held out the bag to her, feeling rude not sharing, but she shook her head.

"So, what is going on?"

He took his time chewing his snack, internally debating how to proceed. Best to start off easy. He swallowed. "You know, I've been worried about the wolf. The entire neighborhood is out hunting it, which is just insane. They're all going to get themselves killed."

Her expression turned grave, and she pressed her lips together. She nodded. "Yes, it's unlikely that they can kill it." She avoided his gaze, fixing on a point above his shoulder.

"I've been wondering…"

She met his gaze, her gray eyes boring into his blue ones. It made him unable to continue.

"What?" she prompted.

"It's just…" Now or never. He inhaled sharply. "How come you knew the wolf would survive getting hit by your car?"

She shrugged without missing a beat. "It seemed sturdy. Tenacious. I didn't know for sure; I was just being careful."

Dylan thought back to that night. She had reacted immediately after spotting the wolf, she had stayed calm while it was chasing them, and then after the crash, she had stopped him from getting out of the car.

What she said was reasonable and made sense. You wouldn't leave the car after hitting a wild boar either, but knowing what he knew now about Molly, he couldn't shake the feeling that there was more to it.

"But you seemed to know. You seemed very sure about it." It sounded pathetic, even to his own ears, but he didn't know how else to press the matter. And he didn't want to bring up Molly yet for fear of sounding utterly crazy.

Marie shrugged again. "I don't know what to tell you." She looked him squarely in the eye. Dylan wasn't sure, but it seemed like her expression had hardened the tiniest bit, turning defensive. "It might have come across that way, but I didn't know."

She left him no choice. "And what was that between you and Molly?" He stuffed more food into his mouth to calm his nerves.

Her head bobbed back in surprise. "What are you talking about?"

He swallowed. "Yesterday, when she came to the store and the soda spontaneously exploded, I left for a few seconds to get paper towels, and I overheard you call her a 'witch.'" That much he was sure about. And he needed her to explain.

Her brow creased, and her gaze wandered to the top right corner. It looked like she was trying to remember. "I did?"

"Yes."

"Are you sure?"

"Yes."

She paused. "Well, she was very rude. Maybe I got a little hostile, but I don't remember the exact words I said to her."

That was news to Dylan. Molly had sworn she hadn't said anything to Marie while he was gone, and according to her own words, he had only been gone *for like, five seconds*.

"Really? What did she say?"

Marie crossed her arms in front of her chest. "I don't want to repeat it." For the first time, since he had met her, she seemed rattled.

He didn't know how to reply, but Marie interpreted his silence as prompting, so she elaborated: "She told me in pretty clear words that I wasn't welcome here and that I should leave you alone."

Dylan's pulse picked up speed. It definitely sounded like Molly. Miss Why-don't-you-mind-your-own-business was blunt like that. And she hadn't liked Marie from the beginning. He was suddenly mad at the little witch. No wonder Marie had been so abrasive toward her!

"That's awful. I'm really sorry."

She answered with a weak smile. "It's okay. It's not your fault. I didn't want to upset you, so I didn't bring it up."

Dylan believed her. It all added up. Maybe she didn't know anything after all. Neither about the wolf nor about Molly.

But that didn't mean his conclusions were wrong. He had clearly seen Molly influence the soda in her hand, and then there was the stuff he had found in her room… He might still be right about the witch part.

"Stop worrying! I don't give a shit what some girl in high school thinks about me." She grinned, her posture relaxing. "And I'm pretty sure that wolf is long gone by now. We must have scared it off. Your neighbors are safe."

He desperately wanted to believe her. Things just had to go back to normal. Enough people were dead.

"I hope you're right." He ate another handful of chips.

She nodded at the Harvard crest hanging over his bed. "You never lose sight of your goals, do you?"

Dylan was glad she was changing the subject. He didn't want to think about the wolf or Molly anymore. Or about magic.

He grinned. "Sure don't. I'm going to get in. I just know it."

Her answering smile was dazzling. "That's the spirit."

They continued talking about college and the *X-Men* for another hour till Marie said Alec was probably wondering where she was and left.

After the conversation Dylan felt lighter, like a weight had been lifted off him. He clung to Marie's optimism, and for the moment, he forgot all about Molly and her magic.

12

No deaths or wolf sightings in over two weeks. The neighborhood hunters got more and more frustrated with the lack of action, but Dylan was relieved none of them had been hurt or killed. It seemed like the beast had finally moved on.

Dylan had been antsy for a few days after the conversation with Marie, but when it became clear the wolf wasn't going to make a reappearance, he had let himself relax.

At least, as far as the threat of the wolf was concerned.

Winter had finally loosened its tight grip on the town, and Dylan had exchanged his heavy snow boots for a pair of worn ratty sneakers. His peers were getting their college acceptance letters, but he hadn't had any so far. During a quiet minute at work, he was reading up on Harvard's admission policy in a leaflet from school, telling himself that there was nothing unusual about the delay. As long as he hadn't heard from them, there was still a chance he had gotten in. He hadn't been turned down yet.

But still.

For the first time in his life, he was wondering if he might not make it into the college of his dreams. He was facing the very real possibility of that.

No.

He just had to get in. He'd been working toward this his entire life.

There was no other way.

He folded the leaflet and stuffed it into his backpack underneath the counter, trying to be patient, when he heard the door opening.

Business had picked up, now that being out at night was safe again, but even the pre-murder level of clientele had been low, what with the size of the town. So Dylan usually still had a lot of time to himself.

He shot up to greet the customer, but when he saw it was Larry, he checked the time in surprise. Eight thirty. That was strange. Larry hadn't come in this early in a while.

"Hey, Larry! You're early."

Larry's face was drawn, his short white hair sticking up. His eyes looked haunted.

"W-what happened?" Dylan asked. But he already knew the answer before Larry spoke.

"It struck again." Larry whispered dramatically, stepping closer to the counter. "And this time, two people are dead."

Dylan's blood ran cold. "Who?" He managed to choke out.

Larry shook his head and ran a hand through his hair, tousling it even more. "Two guys who were out hunting it. Hikers found their bodies in the woods this morning, all scratched up like the others." He paused, and it took everything Dylan had not to urge him on. "It was the Brown fella. You know, the one who owned that carpenter business on Main Street."

Sandra's dad. The girl from his history class. The one who had been worried about her dad going out there in the first place. Dylan balled his fists to keep his hands from shaking.

"Who else?" Dylan braced himself. Larry had said there were two bodies.

"Jake Logan. You know, the one, who—"

"I know." So, his magical shotgun hadn't provided much protection in the end. Dylan felt sick.

Larry shook his head again. "It's awful. When will this finally end...?" he muttered as he made his way to the back room.

Dylan's head was spinning. He gripped tightly to the counter to steady himself and closed his eyes, taking a few deep calming breaths.

This was insane. Something needed to be done. Somebody had to stop this animal.

Dylan was sure that neither Sandra's dad nor Jake Logan had been surprised by the attack. They had known what they were looking for, and they had been armed. Maybe Logan had even fired a few shots at it, before the thing ripped him to shreds...

He shuddered. It seemed like this beast was unstoppable. But why wasn't it moving on? What was it still doing there?

Well, why wouldn't it stay? It was clearly at the top of the food chain. Cars didn't scare it off, neither did guns or any other human gadgets. It seemed to feel comfortable in the Berlin woods. So why would it go anywhere else?

Dylan rubbed his forehead, trying to get a grip. Somehow it had to be stopped. But it really looked like only a miracle could do that.

Or somebody who could do miraculous things. But he couldn't ask Molly to put her life on the line. Enough people were dead. And what could she do anyway? Drown it in soda?

The more he thought about it, the more Dylan realized how little he knew about Molly's magic. He had tried to put it out of his mind for almost three weeks, not wanting to deal with it. It still made him deeply uncomfortable. Even just contemplating the fact that something like magic existed made him question everything he thought he knew about the world. It unsettled him. He'd rather ignore it and go on with his life.

So he had been avoiding her.

But it seemed like that was no longer an option. He had to talk to her and find out more. For everyone's sake.

12

***

When Marie picked him up later that night, he was still thinking about Molly and how to approach her. Marie asked him what was wrong.

"Another two people have been killed."

Dylan had expected more of a reaction from her, but her expression didn't change. She kept her eyes on the road and asked, "When?"

"They found their bodies this morning. It was clearly the wolf again," Dylan answered tonelessly. He was starting to feel numb.

After a moment of silence, Marie answered, her voice betraying much more emotion than her face. "I'm sorry this keeps happening, Dylan."

He turned to her. Her gaze was still fixed on the road, hands gripping the steering wheel tightly.

"It's not like it's your fault."

She shrugged. "Still."

"Well, if I were you, I'd get the hell out of here," he mumbled, wishing he could pack up and leave, too. Take his mom with him and never come back.

"And leave you behind all by yourself? Never." Her answer was more fervent than he would have expected, considering he wasn't one of the hunters risking their lives out in the woods on a nightly basis.

But he understood the sentiment. Even if he could take his mom with him, there were so many other people who would still be at risk. Larry, Connor, even Martin … and Molly. He didn't want her to get hurt.

He didn't want Marie to get hurt either, but he felt like nothing could harm her. She always seemed so confident and carefree. The idea of anything hurting her seemed absurd. But even she wasn't invincible.

"I don't want you to get hurt," he whispered, surprising himself.

She smiled weakly. "Don't worry about me. I'll be fine."

* * *

The lights in the kitchen were still on when Dylan got home, and his mom was sitting at the dining table. She was beaming at him. Dylan spotted a large, thick envelope on the table next to her, and his heart skipped a beat.

"Finally you're home. Look, this was in the mail for you." She held out the envelope with both hands like something precious. That's when Dylan spotted the Harvard crest on the envelope. He took it with shaking hands.

His mom jumped up from her chair, wringing her hands. "I mean, they wouldn't use an envelope this big if they were turning you down, right?"

He couldn't move. This was it. Once he opened this letter, he would find out if his wildest dreams had come true. Suddenly nothing existed but him and the envelope in his hands. His heart was pounding with anticipation. This was the moment of truth.

Susan clapped excitedly. "Open it!"

He slid a trembling forefinger under the flap of the envelope and ripped it open, peeking inside. It contained a booklet and a piece of paper. He pulled out the letter and read:

Dear Mr. Harper,

Congratulations! I am delighted to inform you that the Committee on Admissions has admitted you to the Harvard College Class of 1989.

"I got in." His heart stopped. He couldn't believe it.

But there it was in cold print.

Susan shrieked with glee and threw her arms around him. She planted several kisses on his cheek, but he hardly felt any of it. He had gotten into Harvard. It felt like he was having an out-of-body experience.

"I knew it. I knew from the start that you would get in!"

He read the letter again, checked the address and the name twice, but they definitely meant him. They wanted him. A boy without a father who had been poor all his life. A boy who had been ridiculed and humiliated since he could remember.

But all of that would be over for good now. With this acceptance letter, his life would finally take the course he had intended for it.

Tears sprang from his eyes. He hugged his mom back, burying his face in her shoulder, trying to hide them.

He was going to Harvard come fall. He would leave Berlin behind and start the life he had always dreamed of. This was it. Nothing was going to hold him back anymore.

"We need to celebrate!" his mom shouted. She let go of him and turned to the fridge. She took out a bottle of something cheap and fizzy and a tub of cookie dough ice cream from the freezer compartment.

"When did you buy this?" Dylan was amazed at how well she had prepared for this occasion.

"I told you. I knew it from the start." She laughed, pouring two glasses of the cheap stuff. Dylan grabbed two spoons from the drawer and started eating the ice cream straight from the tub.

Susan handed him a glass and held out her own. "To you! And to Harvard!"

"Cheers!" They clinked glasses. Dylan tentatively sipped his drink. He had never had alcohol before. It tasted funny. Too bitter for his liking.

"Thanks, Mom."

"Of course, darling." She stroked his cheek lovingly and squeaked in delight again. "I'm so proud of you."

He smiled at her. Seeing her being this happy for him made him even happier.

He handed her the other spoon, and they both sat down at the table and ate some ice cream, all the while discussing his future life on campus, wondering what it might be like to study among America's elite, all his worries about the wolf killings forgotten.

When he finally went to bed two hours later, he stared at the Harvard crest on his wall in pure bliss. He had done it. He had taken the first step on his path to success.

He felt like he could take on the entire world.

13

Mr. Kline was as boring as ever, and half the people in class were sleeping with their eyes open, but Dylan had never been more alert. He was resolved. His acceptance letter had given him a surge of confidence, so he had decided to confront Molly after class. No excuses, no chickening out. Something had to be done against this wolf.

Sandra Brown's noticeable absence fueled him on. Her dad's death had been completely avoidable and pointless. Dylan had had enough. Nobody else was going to die on his watch.

When the bell rang, he stood, taking a deep shaky breath. *Here goes nothing...*

Molly was gathering her things. He squeezed through the narrow aisle past his classmates toward her.

"I need to talk to you." No time to beat around the bush. And she needed to know that he was serious.

She eyed him curiously but nodded. They made their way to the same classroom they had gone to for their previous conversation, and Dylan closed the door behind them. The last thing he wanted was for someone to overhear what he was about to say to her.

Molly was leaning against a desk, arms crossed in front of her chest. She was dressed warmly for the weather. Spring had melted the last remnants of snow and temperatures had steadily been climbing these past weeks, but she was still sporting a thick winter jacket and a black turtleneck sweater. Her long, delicate face was like a mask. If she knew or suspected what he was about to say she didn't let on.

Dylan gulped. "I don't really know how to say this, so I'm just going to be blunt."

She frowned.

"I know you have magical powers."

Her frown deepened. For a beat, nobody said anything.

"What?" she finally asked with an incredulous smile.

"Don't pretend." Dylan knew what he had seen. "You can control water. I saw you with the soda at your house. It—" He suddenly felt embarrassed for saying these things out loud. He blushed. "It swirled in the glass in your hand and drops were floating up. And I suspect it was you who made my soda explode at the gas station…"

She had gone pale. Paler than her usual shade of porcelain white. Her eyes had grown wide, and she was stock-still. *Gotcha!*

He waited for her to respond. "I…" She hesitated but seemed to pull herself together. Her expression became more severe. "What makes you think that? That is ridiculous."

"Oh, please. You already gave yourself away." But when he glimpsed the panic in her eyes, he added, "I don't mean any harm. I haven't told anyone and I'm not going to." He held out his hands in a calming gesture, palms facing the floor. "I just want to know the truth."

Her eyes narrowed. "Why?"

"Because it's not every day that one meets a real-life witch, and you might be the only person who can do something about these killings."

Her face relaxed a little. "You might be right."

Dylan could hardly hide his excitement at her confirmation. His heart was racing. He tried to organize his thoughts. "So, how does this work? Is your magic limited to bodies of water?"

She shook her head. "No. All witches can control water because water is the basis of all life, and our magic is connected to the earth and nature. At least, that's how my mom explained it to me."

"Hold on. Your mom was a witch, too?"

Her jaw started working and tears were welling in her eyes, but she nodded. "Yes. She taught me some things when I was little, but when I turned eleven, I refused her lessons because I just wanted to be normal." She paused. Dylan waited. "She was way more powerful than me. I've only gotten back into the practice recently."

"When you borrowed those books from the library."

She nodded again, dropping her hands. "My magic had been acting up, and I needed to find answers. Not that the books helped in any way…"

"What do you mean by 'acting up'?"

"The night at your house when I turned the faucet on, I hadn't meant to do that. My dad got spooked. He doesn't know about my powers, but I'm sure he suspects. Too many strange things have happened around me for him not to know. But I think he's trying to ignore it."

So, she had turned the faucet on by magic. The hairs on the back of Dylan's neck stood up. What else was Molly capable of? What else had he missed?

He had never heard Molly speak so freely. It seemed like she was glad to finally have someone to talk to about these things. It had to be hard for her, losing the only other person on the planet who knew her secret and could help and guide her. No wonder she was in such a horrible mood all the time. His heart suddenly ached for her.

"So, nobody knows?"

She shook her head. "No."

"And what else can you do?"

She scratched her brow. "Well … I'm supposed to be able to do simple things like protection spells, but I'm not sure if they're working…"

He thought of the notebook entry he had found in her room and immediately felt bad again for snooping. "Supposed to?"

"Yeah… Like I said, my magic has been acting up lately. When I want to use it, nothing happens, but when I don't want to use it… Well, you get the idea."

The room they were in was a science classroom, so a sink sat in one corner. Dylan pointed at it. "Try it now." He wanted to help, but he also needed to have more proof. He needed to see it with his own eyes. "Try to turn the faucet on."

Her eyes fluttered from him to the sink and back again. She took a deep breath and closed her eyes. Dylan waited, not daring to move a muscle, but nothing happened.

She pinched the bridge of her nose, letting out a frustrated groan. "Wait. I've been practicing. This should be easy." She took another deep breath and let it out, cracking her neck. This time she focused on the sink with her eyes wide open, and Dylan did the same.

After a few agonizing seconds, the handle slowly started to turn. Panic flooded Dylan's system. This was really happening. It was moving all by itself till the water started flowing.

"Holy shit…" Dylan muttered under his breath.

The handle moved again, slowly stopping the water flow.

He shook his head in amazement. "That is insane." He turned back to Molly, who was watching him with trepidation.

"Please don't tell anyone," she whispered.

"No, of course not," he quickly responded. "What else can you do?" She was his only hope against the wolf, he knew it in his bones.

"Uh, I don't know." She shrugged. "I have my mom's notebook of spells, but I haven't tried most of them."

"Is there anything on getting rid of murderous animals in there?"

"What?"

It was Dylan's turn to be truthful. "It's about the wolf I saw. It's killed again. And I'm beginning to think the only thing that can get rid of it is magic. It can withstand a car crash, bullets… I don't know how else we could stop it. And we have to do something; otherwise, it'll just keep killing people."

Molly looked at him like he was missing something. "So, you know about me, but you don't know about her?"

"What are you talking about?"

"Your 'friend.'" She made air quotes "You still don't think it's weird that the two of you are the only ones who have seen this wolf?"

"No." And they were back to Marie again. "Look." He sighed. "I don't know what's going on between you and Marie, but can you leave her out of this? We need to focus on the real threat here—"

"Oh, I couldn't agree more." She crossed her arms again. "She's the one who has been killing people."

"Wha— No." Dylan ran one hand through his hair in exasperation. "I'm telling you, I saw the wolf. And I saw Stacy, too. Those marks on her body could only have come from a wild animal. No human could do that."

"But she isn't human."

Dylan froze. His rational side told him that Molly had lost her marbles, but after everything he had seen these past few months, he couldn't outright dismiss her words.

She continued, "Think about it. When did the killings start? When she got into town. Who else has seen this animal? Nobody. Have you ever seen her during the day? I doubt it."

His thoughts started racing. He had never seen Marie during the day, but nightfall was still early at this time of year so that didn't mean anything. And Molly had just ignored all of the evidence he had brought up.

"Why would she kill random people, Molly?" Anger seeped into his voice.

"Because she's a vampire." She stared at him triumphantly, like she had just made the closing argument in a trial, sure that she was going to win.

Dylan almost laughed. The word vampire immediately conjured up pictures of Dracula in a cape with long sharp canine teeth, saying in a heavy Romanian accent, 'I vant to drink your blood.'

But Molly was serious. Unbelievable…

But then again, she was an actual witch, so vampires might be real, too. But Marie? It didn't fit.

"And what makes you think that?" He crossed his arms in front of his chest as well, mimicking Molly.

"The night she saved you from Fletcher and his goons, I saw her eyes turn crimson."

He waited for more. When she didn't say anything else, he asked, "That's it?"

"My mom had warned me about vampires. Marie fits the description in her notes."

Dylan scoffed. "Are you hearing yourself right now? All of that is conjecture. You think you saw something, but it was a dark evening, you were standing several feet away, and it might have been a trick of the light. And now you're making accusations based on the conclusions you drew entirely from your own assumptions." All the law books he had read were starting to pay off. "Even if Marie was a vampire – which she isn't – then the marks on the victims' bodies still indicate an animal of some sort. Plus, I have seen the thing with my own eyes—"

"While she was there!" Molly half-shouted, throwing her hands up in exasperation. "Maybe it was an illusion. Maybe she made you see it to plant a false lead. Ever think of that?"

"But why would she do that?" Dylan knew deep down that Molly was on the wrong track. Marie was the kindest person he knew. She certainly wasn't a murderous monster.

"To distract from herself. To make everyone venture out into the woods in search of an animal that doesn't exist. That way, there's more prey for her. She can just pick them like ripe fruit."

Dylan shook his head. "The car was totaled. If the wolf was an illusion, how could it dent the car?"

"Maybe that was an illusion, too!" She threw her hands up in the air again.

"Now you're just trying to make it all fit. Do you even know if vampires have that kind of power?" For a split second, Dylan got scared. If Molly's mom had warned her about them and had even written about them, they were probably real. Of course, that didn't mean that Marie was one of them, but the thought of bloodsucking monsters out there, prowling the night, made his skin crawl.

But his question had thrown Molly off. She hesitated. "No, I don't know for sure, but I can't rule it out either."

Dylan laughed. "You just don't like her, and now you're lashing out. It's pathetic."

Her jaw hardened, and she glared at him icily. "I know I'm right, Dylan. I'm a witch. I can sense that she's not human. And I can sense that she's a threat."

He shook his head. Marie had never threatened *him*. If she really were a vampire, then she'd had dozens of opportunities to hurt Dylan, but she had never done so. Molly was reaching. She was reading too much into her animosity. "You're wrong," he simply stated.

She kept glaring at him. "No, *you're* wrong."

This was frustrating. He needed her help, but her hatred made her blind to the real danger. Somehow, he needed to convince Molly that Marie was harmless and that the wolf was real.

"I'm going to prove it to you."

She scoffed. "Sure. Good luck with that."

There was nothing more to say, so Dylan turned and left. When he stepped into the empty hallway, he realized he was very late for his next class. He started to panic, but then he remembered that he had already gotten into Harvard. It didn't matter if he missed half of his algebra class.

As he walked to his classroom, he thought about how he could prove to Molly that Marie wasn't a vampire. Somehow, he had to get them both in the same room, preferably during the daytime and with more people around. That way Molly would see that Marie was normal.

He smirked. 'Normal' wasn't a word he'd usually use to describe Marie. It was true, she was inhumanly beautiful and confident, but that didn't make her a bloodsucking monster…

"Mr. Harper. Thank you for gracing us with your presence. Would you please take a seat?" Mrs. Goff greeted him sarcastically. "You're not eighteen yet as far as I know, so you can't just stay away without an excuse."

"I'm sorry, won't happen again," he murmured as he sat. He couldn't wait to finally be eighteen. Only four more days…

That's when it clicked. He suddenly knew exactly how to prove Molly wrong.

* * *

He watched the seconds tick by at the gas station all evening. Now that he had formulated a plan, he couldn't wait to put it into action, even if he was a little nervous that Marie would decline his invitation. She might have something better to do than celebrate his birthday with him. And there was Alec to consider…

As he tried not to think about his insecurities, the door opened and someone he hadn't seen outside of school in weeks walked in. Fletcher was wearing a dark blue athletic jacket with two large horizontal white and red stripes on the front. His blond hair was perfectly coiffed as always. But, unusually, he wasn't surrounded by his entourage.

Dylan immediately went into high alert, his body turning rigid and his hands balling into fists.

Fletcher came up to the counter with a nonchalant expression on his face, as if he did this every day. He looked Dylan squarely in the eye, his cold eyes boring into Dylan in a way that made him feel like Fletcher could read his mind. Had Marie's threat worn off?

Dylan gulped. Were they back to the way things had been before?

"What can I do for you?" He tried to stay calm, but his voice shook the tiniest bit.

Fletcher didn't respond for a beat, looking Dylan up and down. Dylan refused the urge to fix the collar of his sweater. His heart was pounding so hard he could hear it.

"I just need some gas." He reached for his wallet, taking his time fishing out a ten-dollar bill. "Ten bucks on pump one." He tossed the bill onto the counter. Dylan took it with a shaking hand and released the pump.

"Anything else?" he asked, his voice steadier this time.

Fletcher pretended to think. "No. That's it." He smirked. "For now." He turned on his heel and left, chuckling to himself.

Dylan wiped his sweaty palms on his jeans and let out the breath he'd been holding since Fletcher had walked in. Something told him that the bully was up to something. Dread washed over his body. He should have known that Fletcher wouldn't be intimidated for long. At some point he was going to bounce back. And Marie wasn't always going to be there to save Dylan. He had gotten so used to her presence that he had forgotten she didn't actually live in Berlin.

He inhaled sharply. This was pathetic. He was relying on a girl to fight his battles. This needed to stop. He needed to learn how to best Fletcher and get rid of him once and for all. After all, he still had to stay in town for a few months before he could leave for campus.

But he would figure that out later. He had more important issues to think about right then. The wolf for one. And his plan to get Molly on his side.

"Dylan? Are you coming?"

Dylan's head jerked up. He hadn't even noticed he'd been staring at the counter, one hand hovering over the register. Fletcher had clearly shaken him.

Marie was standing in the doorway, holding the door open with one hand, an impatient expression on her heart-shaped face.

"Sorry, I was… Sorry." He grabbed his backpack, shouted a quick good night to Larry, and hurried after her to her car. Trying to focus on his plan, he organized his thoughts.

As he sat next to Marie on the passenger seat and she pulled out of the gas station, he thought about how to broach the subject.

"What's up?" she asked, breaking the silence.

The radio was off, which struck Dylan as weird. He paid closer attention to his friend and noticed she seemed nervous. She gripped the wheel tightly; her shoulders were rigid and her jaw set.

"Nothing," he answered. "Is everything okay with you?"

Her eyes darted to him, and she put on a smile, but her posture didn't relax. "Of course. I'm fine. What makes you think I'm not?"

Dylan shrugged. "There's no music." Something was up, he was sure, but he wasn't going to make her talk about it if she didn't want to.

She smiled. "I needed some quiet earlier. I sometimes do." And then she added, "So, what's new?"

That was his chance. "Uh, Saturday is my birthday."

She nodded. "Yeah, I remember."

"Really?" He couldn't hide his surprise.

"Of course." She grinned.

"Well, I was thinking of having a little gathering."

"A party? Nice."

"I wouldn't call it a party." He felt the heat rush to his cheeks. "My mom will make some food, and I was going to ask Molly and her dad to come over…" He trailed off, curious to see her reaction when he mentioned Molly, but her face remained neutral. "And I was wondering if you would like to come, too?" His mouth felt dry, and he couldn't get another word out.

"Sure! I'd love to." Her shoulders relaxed.

Relief washed over him. "Great! Uh, we'll start in the late afternoon, I think…" He hated that he was watching her face for a reaction again. Why would it be a problem for her to come out during the day? Why would he believe Molly's accusations for even a second?

She nodded enthusiastically. "Okay, sounds good."

There. No reaction whatsoever. He felt smug, imagining Molly's face when Marie showed up at his house during the daytime. It would hopefully shut her up and make her realize what the true threat was.

"Awesome. Can't wait."

14

"Dylan, baby, wake up…" Susan softly nudged his side. He didn't want to open his eyes at first. The bed was so comfortable and warm. But something dawned on him.

Today was Saturday, March 30, 1985. His eighteenth birthday.

His eyes flew wide open. His mom was standing next to the bed, fully dressed, wearing a little party hat and holding out a birthday card.

"Happy birthday, darling!" It seemed like she hadn't stopped smiling since he had gotten his acceptance letter from Harvard.

"Thanks, Mom." He opened the birthday card. She always found the sappiest Hallmark cards. It had become something of a tradition. This one read, 'You're sweeter than birthday cake, but let's have some anyway!' Underneath the writing was a frothy pink cartoon cake with a smiley face on the front and stick-figure arms stretched out to the sides.

Dylan smiled. "This is great, Mom. Thank you."

"Wait until you see your gift!" She clapped in excitement. "Come on, get up!" She bustled over to the window. "Come on!" She gestured for him to follow.

He untangled himself from his covers and walked over to her. She pointed to the driveway. "Surprise!"

There in the driveway stood an old pickup truck. He couldn't make out the brand from where he stood. "What?" He couldn't believe it. "Mom, are you giving me a car!?"

She nodded enthusiastically.

He didn't care that he was still in his pajamas and barefoot. He rushed downstairs and outside to get a closer look at *his* new car. Okay, 'new' was a stretch, but it was new to him.

"Oh my god!" The truck was unlocked. He opened the driver's door and looked inside. The interior was as old as the exterior.

"It's thirteen years old..." Susan said sheepishly from the front door.

"It's amazing!"

"I figured you'd need a car when you go to college. And then you could come up here on the weekends to visit, too."

He felt a pinch in his heart. He hated the thought of leaving her behind when he went off to college. But she was right. Harvard was only three hours away. He could come up whenever he wanted.

"I will, Mom. Thank you so much!" He went over and hugged her tightly, inhaling her scent, trying to memorize it forever.

She hugged him back. "Happy birthday, darling." She broke the hug and held him at arm's length. "Come back inside! I've made you pancakes for breakfast. And afterward you can take your new truck out for a ride."

It looked like it was going to be a warm, sunny spring day. After Dylan had finished his two delicious stacks for breakfast, he showered and got dressed. He was standing in front of his new truck, keys in hand. He had gotten the day off from work. So he had nowhere to be, which left him free to drive around town.

He had to be back in the afternoon. As per his plan to convince Molly of Marie's innocence, he had suggested that Susan invite Martin and Molly over for a little birthday gathering. And Marie was going to join them, too, as promised. Maybe Molly would finally see reason and help him get rid of the wolf.

She had been avoiding him since they'd had their little chat. Dylan didn't know what to make of it, but he was sure she would come around after today. Everything was going to be fine now.

His car didn't have a tape deck, so he turned on the radio. REO Speedwagon's 'Can't Fight This Feeling' blared through the speakers. He turned the music down a notch and backed out of the driveway.

He loved everything about his truck. As he was driving through town, he rolled the windows down and hummed along to the radio. The sun was shining brightly in the sky, all the snow had finally melted, and he could hear birds chirping over the music.

Main Street was busy – as usual on a Saturday. So he turned onto one of the smaller side streets and out of town. The mountains, half covered in forest, looked dramatic, looming high over the rooftops of the houses of Berlin. The paper mill was quiet today, the old sneakers factory had been quiet for years…

After a while he got hungry, so he christened his truck with its first drive-through, getting himself a birthday meal with all the works. He couldn't remember the last time he had felt this happy. His heart was so big, he was afraid it might burst out of his chest any second.

When the time came, he drove back home. Martin's car was already parked in the driveway, so he parked his truck on the street. Marie's car was noticeably absent. He tried not to worry about it.

"Happy birthday!" A chorus greeted him when he entered the kitchen. They had hung streamers that spelled out 'HAPPY BIRTH-DAY' across the room. The table was graced by a massive birthday cake with his name and eighteen candles on it – not yet lit – and Martin and Susan were standing next to it with wide smiles on their faces, whereas Molly stood slightly apart from them with her signature frown.

"Thank you, guys," he exclaimed laughing.

Martin stepped forward, extending his hand. Dylan shook it. "And congratulations again on getting into Harvard. I know I had nothing to do with it, but I'm proud of you anyway."

"Thanks." Maybe Martin wasn't so bad after all. He seemed to be genuinely happy for Dylan, and he treated Susan right.

"Oh, your friend Marie called earlier while you were out," Susan said.

"Oh?" His heart skipped a beat.

"Her husband had a little accident and cut up his hand. She had to take him to the emergency room, but she'll be here for dinner."

"That sounds bad. Will he be all right?"

Susan waved his concern off. "Yes, she said he'll probably need stitches but that's all there is." She tapped the pockets of her jeans, pulled a lighter from her right front pocket, and lit the candles.

"Everyone, gather around the cake! I want to take a picture!"

They all got into position while Susan set up the camera on the tripod.

"I'll count to three. One, two, three, cheese!"

After that she insisted that they sing 'Happy Birthday.' While they serenaded him, Dylan sat awkwardly at the table and didn't know what to do.

Susan told him to blow out the candles. "And don't forget to make a wish!"

What could he wish for? He had everything he'd ever wanted. He was so happy, he had momentarily forgotten all his fears and worries. So he closed his eyes and wished for this moment to last forever. He blew out the candles.

The afternoon went by in a blur. They all had cake, and Martin talked for most of the time, even Molly seeming more comfortable than usual.

"I made lasagna for dinner. I'll just heat it up, and then we can dig in."

"Sounds delicious!" Martin exclaimed with a hungry look in his eyes.

At a quarter past six – the sun had just started setting – the doorbell rang.

"I'll get it," Dylan shouted.

Marie stood outside, carrying a gift bag. "Happy birthday!" She hugged him before he could react, making his heart skip a beat.

"Damn, you're cold. Come in! You're just in time for dinner."

"Perfect." She held out the bag to him.

"You didn't have to get me anything."

"I know, but I wanted to."

"Well, thank you." He blushed.

The gift bag was filled with his favorite candy alongside a copy of *X-Men*. He chuckled. "Thank you, this is perfect."

They stood there, smiling at each other for a second.

"Is that your truck out there?" she asked, pointing over her shoulder.

His face lit up. "Yes. My mom gave it to me this morning."

"Neat." She smiled.

"Come in, come in…"

When Martin saw Marie, his jaw hit the floor. For what Dylan assumed was probably the first time in the man's life, he was utterly speechless.

Molly openly glared at Marie, but Susan greeted her warmly.

"We don't have enough chairs," Dylan said. A problem they had never had before in this house.

"Oh, don't worry! I'll take the stool from the living room."

"Are you sure, Mom? I can take it, it's fine."

"No, it's your birthday. Go ahead! Sit!" She slapped him playfully with the kitchen towel.

Dylan took a seat between Molly and Marie, sitting closest to the hallway. Marie – closest to the kitchen counter – moved her chair a little toward Dylan's side to make room for Susan, who put the stool between her and Martin.

"How is your husband, dear?" Susan asked after she had served everyone. Molly scoffed but everyone ignored her.

"Oh, he'll be fine. Thanks. The cut wasn't that bad after all. He's all stitched up." She grinned. "He took some Tylenol for the pain, and now he's out cold."

"I hope he'll feel better soon."

"How long are you planning on staying here?" Everyone looked at Molly in surprise. Those were probably the first words she had said all afternoon.

Marie shrugged. "Still not sure. Now that spring is coming in, this area has a completely different vibe to it. We might stay a while longer."

"And you're still staying at Bernie's? I can't imagine you're very comfortable there."

Marie shrugged. "It's all right. We don't need much." She took a bite of lasagna. "Mm, this is really good, Susan."

"Thank you." Susan looked genuinely delighted at the compliment.

"You're taking a break from college, right?" Molly asked pointedly. Marie nodded.

"Where do you go?"

"Columbia."

"What's your major?"

"History."

"Oh, really?" Dylan interjected. He had never bothered to ask her. He'd always assumed she was doing something artsy or something related to music. "I'm most likely going to major in history, too." It was a good way to get into law school later on.

"Nice. Maybe I can transfer to Harvard next semester. Then we could keep hanging out."

Dylan was stunned. "You would do that?" He couldn't believe he'd asked her that in front of everyone. He bit his tongue.

Marie laughed. "Yeah, of course. Might be fun." She smiled that little private joke smile again.

Dylan smiled back. "Yes, for sure."

"Where are you going to go, Molly?" Marie asked, taking another bite of her lasagna. Seeing her eat made Dylan feel vindicated. He glanced at Molly, but it didn't seem to appease her.

"I'm still undecided. I have a few offers. I'll see which one I like best." Her tone was biting.

"This is delicious, as always, honey," Martin chimed in.

"Thank you, honey." Susan blushed. "I'm glad you all like the food. It's one of Dylan's favorites."

Dylan nodded, his mouth too full to speak. "Mhm."

"What's your favorite food, Marie?" Molly asked innocently. Dylan refrained from rolling his eyes.

"Anything meaty, really. Anything you can sink your teeth into." Marie gave Molly a saccharine smile, and while Martin and Susan laughed, Molly paled. Dylan swallowed hard. Knowing how Molly would interpret the words, he felt uneasy.

Marie turned to Susan and Martin. "How long have you two been dating?"

"Oh, let's see…" Martin said. He seemed to be counting off the weeks in his head. "A little over two months, isn't that right, honey?"

"Yes, something like that." Susan smiled. "And how long have you been married?"

"Not long. Just a little over a year."

"You're from New York, right?" Molly asked. Dylan noticed she hadn't even touched her food yet while he was already on his second serving.

"Yes."

Molly frowned. "You don't have a New York accent."

"Military family. Moved around a lot. I grew up all over."

"So, you met your husband in college?"

Marie nodded. She looked a little annoyed.

"Hey, Molly, can you stop giving her the third degree, please?" Dylan tried to communicate to Marie how sorry he was without saying the actual words. It hadn't been his intention to make his friend uncomfortable. Why couldn't Molly just accept she was wrong?

Molly held up both hands in defeat. "Sorry. Just making conversation."

"Well, stop."

"Dylan!" Susan admonished.

"No, this is my birthday and Molly is making my friend uncomfortable with her questions."

"Why would my questions make her uncomfortable? I'm asking normal things."

"No, you're being petty because I didn't believe your bullshit story."

"Dylan! Language!"

Molly snorted. "Are you too blinded by the pretty face to notice? Open your eyes, Dylan!"

Dylan blushed with anger, but before he could retort, Martin said, "Molly, what has gotten into you?" He laughed uncomfortably. "I'm sorry," he said to Marie.

"Oh, it's fine. No worries." She smiled warmly at him. Dylan saw Martin swallow and stare. He was clearly dazzled.

"I'm sorry," Marie said to Dylan. "I didn't want to ruin your birthday."

"You are ruining it, though," Molly said before Dylan could respond.

"Molly!" Now Martin's voice got louder.

"You're ruining everything."

"What the hell, Molly!? Marie, I'm so sorry." Dylan moved to pat her arm but stopped himself. He wasn't sure if she was okay with him touching her.

"It's okay," Marie said. She wiped her mouth with her napkin and put it on her empty plate. "Thank you very much for your hospitality, but I think it's best if I leave now."

"Yes." That was Molly. Everybody else fell into a chorus of "What? No, please… I'm so sorry. Stay. I apologize…"

Marie got up from the table.

"No, Marie, wait…" But by the time Dylan had gotten up, Marie was already in the hallway. "I'm sorry, I don't know what's gotten into her."

She waved him off. "Don't worry. I have to check on Alec anyway." She opened the front door.

Dylan wanted to make her stay but didn't know how. This was a disaster.

"I'll see you around, Dylan," she said warmly and walked out the door.

Did that mean goodbye? Was she so offended she never wanted to hang out with him again? In his desperation he called out, "Are we still friends?"

She stopped in her tracks halfway across the front yard and turned. "Of course, silly." She winked at him. "I'll see you on Monday."

A huge weight lifted off him. "Okay, see you on Monday!" He waved and shut the door behind her.

"You go and apologize to her!" Martin shouted from the kitchen.

"No way."

"What has gotten into you? Are you jealous of her?"

Molly snorted. "Jealous? Hell no!"

As he stepped back into the kitchen, he saw that Martin and Molly were both on their feet and in each other's faces. Susan sat awkwardly on her stool. It was obvious she was out of her depth.

"Guys! Can you please stop!?" Dylan shouted over their bickering. Everyone looked at him.

"I hope you're happy now, Molly."

She stared at him, lips pressed together, and turned to her dad. "Can we leave?"

"Yes, we're leaving right away, and you're grounded."

"What!?"

"You heard me!" He lowered his voice and turned to Susan and Dylan. "I am so sorry about all this. I'm going to take her home. You two try to enjoy the rest of your night."

"Thanks, Martin." Dylan was furious. He glared at Molly, but she gave him an icy stare in response.

The Kirkgaards got their jackets, Martin all the while apologizing profusely to Dylan and Susan for his daughter's behavior.

Dylan eyed Molly, but she seemed to be ignoring him. She put on her jacket and went ahead of her dad out to their station wagon.

Was she so hellbent on being right that she ignored the hard facts? How could she still believe Marie was a vampire after this? He ran a hand through his hair in frustration. If she didn't believe him, she wouldn't help him get rid of the wolf and more people were going to die.

But what could he do to change the witch's mind?

15

The next day at work, all he could think about was Molly and Marie. He was working through several scenarios, where he was trying to change Molly's mind, but the only thing he kept coming back to was enlisting Marie's help. If he told her about Molly's secret and about her crazy vampire theory, Marie might be able to make the witch come around.

The only problem was that he had promised Molly he wouldn't tell anyone about her magic, and he had no way of proving this craziness to Marie. He'd probably look like a first-class idiot when he told her, but it was his only shot. And he was getting desperate. With every passing night that they sat idly by, the chances grew that another body would turn up.

So he was planning to stop by Bernie's after he finished to have a talk with Marie. The thought made him anxious, but he tried to ignore it. For the first time ever, he didn't want his shift to end.

But at four p.m. sharp, Larry walked through the door of his convenience store. "Hey there, kid. Happy belated birthday! That's a nice truck you got there."

"Thanks, Larry." The old man always came in early on weekends so he wouldn't have to pay anyone for the night shift. "I'll see you tomorrow. Have a good one."

"All right then! You, too!" Larry gave him a curt wave, and Dylan made his way out to the parking lot.

As he exited, Amy Barnes jogged up to the door. He politely held it open for her, without saying a word as she passed. She didn't acknowledge him either. He exhaled in relief. After Fletcher's visit earlier that week, he was nervous around the bully and his gang again. But no time to dwell on that – he had something else to do that made him infinitely more nervous.

He rounded the corner of the store to his truck, burying his hand in his pocket looking for the keys. That's when Fletcher stepped out from behind the truck bed.

"Hey, Harper."

Startled, Dylan froze.

"Nice truck you have here. If you're into old and decrepit … I think we should take it out on a ride. What do you say?"

Dylan took a deep breath, trying to calm himself. He didn't want to show fear. "Leave me alone, Fletcher."

Fletcher smiled deviously in response. "I don't think so. It's still daytime, so your girl can't save you now."

Dylan frowned. "What?" Did Fletcher also believe that Marie was a vampire? How would he even get to that conclusion?

"Don't play dumb. Come on, we're going." He gestured for Dylan to follow as if they were two friends hanging out together on a Sunday afternoon.

"No way. What do you want?"

He sighed. "She said you might be difficult."

"What? Who?"

Instead of answering, Fletcher closed the distance between them and with one swift motion put Dylan in a headlock, forcing him to bend forward at an awkward angle.

Dylan struggled to break free, but Fletcher was much stronger than him. The more he tried to rip Fletcher's arm off his neck, the tighter

Fletcher squeezed.

"Let me go!" Dylan grunted.

"Ricky!" Fletcher called out.

Ricky Halston, who had been hiding behind the truck, rushed up to them. He shoved one hand into Dylan's pocket and pulled out his keys. Dylan could do nothing to stop him.

How come nobody was here to witness this? Larry should be able to see them through the windows.

"Larry!!" Dylan shouted at the top of his lungs, but Fletcher kneed him in the stomach. The impact made Dylan groan with pain and his stomach churn. He almost vomited.

"Amy is talking to Larry. He won't come out to help you. Now come on! Let's go."

Ricky had unlocked Dylan's truck and gotten in on the driver's side. Fletcher maneuvered Dylan toward the other side. Dylan couldn't fight him off. He was still reeling from the pain of getting hit and breathing heavily from the exertion, heart pounding.

With a shove, Fletcher made Dylan climb into the truck and got in himself. Dylan was squeezed in between Ricky and Fletcher inside his own truck. Fletcher held down Dylan's arms for good measure and yelled to Ricky, "Drive!"

And Ricky did.

"What the hell, Fletcher!? This is kidnapping! Where are you taking me!?"

"Shut up," Fletcher replied flatly.

"No! This is a criminal offense. You could get locked up for this."

Ricky and Fletcher looked at each other for a second, and they burst out laughing. Dylan knew these two were used to getting away with everything they did, but even they had to realize how out of line they were. This was more than some schoolyard bullying. They could get into serious trouble.

"Relax, Harper," Fletcher said when he could speak again. "We're just going on a little adventure. You'll be back home safe and sound by tonight. With your ugly-ass truck."

"What are you talking about? Where are we going?"

"To the old sneakers factory," Ricky answered. His tone was way too chipper for the situation.

"What?"

They both snorted.

"What is going on!?"

"You'll see," Fletcher said ominously.

He and Ricky remained silent after that. Dylan kept prodding them with questions, trying to make them let him go, but neither one of them reacted to anything he had to say.

The old factory was deserted. Ricky pulled up in front of the main warehouse that stood a little apart from the factory building. He parked in the middle of the loading dock. The warehouse was sealed, and it was clear from the graffiti on the walls that this place hadn't been used in years.

Fletcher opened his door and dragged Dylan out of the truck with him. Dylan considered screaming for help but thought better of it. The factory was remote enough that nobody would hear him, and he'd only earn himself another kick from Fletcher.

But then another truck drove up the road and Dylan, filled with hope, seized his chance. He ripped himself free from Fletcher's grip and ran toward the truck as fast as he could, arms waving to make it stop.

The truck did stop, and Dylan sighed with relief. But then he recognized the person sitting in the driver's seat.

Amy Barnes. And next to her, Molly.

Confused, he stopped dead in his tracks.

Molly and Amy got out of the truck, which he now recognized

as Fletcher's. Dylan felt Fletcher's hand close around his arm again, yanking him in the direction of the warehouse.

That woke Dylan up. "Molly, what the hell is going on here?"

"It's for your own good, Dylan."

"What!?"

Before he could say anything else, Ricky shoved open the side door to the warehouse, which must have been broken into before as it gave way much too easily. Then Dylan remembered that Fletcher's dad owned this building.

"Does your old man know you're here?"

"No. Stole his key." He shrugged.

This was insane. His mind was racing but Dylan couldn't – for the life of him – figure out what they were doing inside an old warehouse and why Molly was in cahoots with his nemesis.

Fletcher yanked Dylan hard by the arm again, pulling him into the empty building. Inside, metal shelving sat empty against the walls, with a few units stretching into the room, but most of it was empty space which was surprisingly well lit. A thick layer of dust on the shelves was clearly visible.

Dylan looked up. A row of skylights along the length of the ceiling was illuminating the area.

"Okay, we have thirty minutes till sunset," Molly said.

"Come on, Harper, we're going to take a seat and wait."

Fletcher pulled him along to the back of the room and pushed him onto one of the metal shelves. He sat down beside Dylan, laying an arm around his shoulders, which would have looked like an embrace to an outsider but felt like a boa constrictor to Dylan. He was panting from the struggle and his ears were ringing, whereas Fletcher didn't seem bothered at all. *Fucking athletes!*

"So, what do we do now?" Amy asked. She was standing with her arms crossed and her back to the doorway, clearly disgusted at all the dust in the room.

"We wait," Molly said decisively. She had opened her bag and pulled out the notebook Dylan had seen in her room and a piece of coal.

Ricky scratched his head. "For thirty minutes?"

"Yes." Molly sounded exasperated.

Well, that's what you get for working with idiots.

She opened her notebook, read something, moved to the middle of the room and crouched down. Using the coal, she drew a circle on the floor, filled it in and added a half-moon horizontally to the top. She repeated this three more times, forming a circle. The symbols were hardly visible on the dirty floor. If he didn't know they were there, he would have missed them entirely.

She looked up at the ceiling. "Perfect," she murmured.

"What the hell are you doing, Molly?" Dylan shouted.

She turned to him with an icy glare. "I'm going to prove to you that your friend is a vampire, and then I'm going to kill her."

Dylan's blood ran cold. He tried to jump up, but Fletcher held him back.

"No, no, Harper. You're staying right here." He patted Dylan's shoulder with his other hand.

"Are you insane!?"

Molly shook her head in disappointment. "Even they saw it, Dylan. Fletcher, Amy, and Ricky all saw her eyes turn crimson. They believed me when I told them about her."

"Because they're idiots! And they hate Marie!"

"Who are you calling an idiot?" Fletcher's fist landed in Dylan's belly with such speed and strength that he gasped for air.

"You're blind, Dylan. She's using you for something. I haven't figured out what, but it can't be good."

"And what if you're wrong, Molly?" Dylan rasped between coughs. "Hm? Are you willing to kill an innocent woman just to prove a point?"

"No." Molly looked at him with indignation in her eyes. "If she's human – which she isn't – nothing will happen to her. Sunlight only kills vampires. When the sun comes up tomorrow morning, we'll know the truth."

"So you're just going to keep us here till tomorrow!? My mom is going to look for me!"

She sighed. "You're free to go once she's in my trap. I don't wish you any harm, Dylan. I'm trying to protect you."

He snorted. "You have a funny way of doing that." He rubbed his bruised belly for emphasis.

She didn't respond. Instead, she started pacing. As they all fell silent, Dylan tried to come up with a way to get out of this place.

Fletcher still held him in his death grip, and Ricky still had his car keys. Getting through both of them would be nearly impossible, but he was desperate.

Maybe if he elbowed Fletcher in the ribs and tackled Ricky? It was worth a shot. He took one deep breath and shoved his elbow back as hard as he could into Fletcher's ribs. Fletcher groaned in pain, but instead of loosening his grip on Dylan, he tightened it.

"Nice try, Harper, but you're not getting out of here." He hit Dylan in the belly again in retaliation.

Dylan winced in pain. Tears stung his eyes.

"Ricky, go and make the call," Molly said out of nowhere.

Ricky nodded and left the warehouse.

"What call?" Dylan asked.

"He's going to walk to the payphone down the road and call Bernie's. He'll pretend to be you and tell Bernie to tell Marie that your car broke down by the old sneakers factory and that you need her to pick you up."

"Totally believable with that piece of junk out there." Fletcher laughed at his own joke.

"Amy, hide your truck!"

Amy nodded, clearly glad to get out of the dusty warehouse.

After what seemed like forever, Ricky and Amy returned. Then they all waited in silence. Dylan could tell they were nervous. They seemed to be genuinely afraid of Marie. Molly was still pacing frantically.

The sun had started to set.

Dylan's entire body was aching thanks to Fletcher's treatment. But he couldn't sit idly by and watch them commit a felony. He tried to reason with them again.

"Guys, you don't have to do this. Just let me go. I'll pretend that my car actually broke down and you guys can leave. I won't say a word about this to anyone, and we can all forget this ever happened."

Amy looked unsure. "I mean, he's got a point. Maybe this isn't such a good idea…"

"No," Molly interrupted. "She's a killer. We need to put an end to this."

That's when they heard a car pull onto the loading dock.

"Quick! Everyone, gather next to Dylan and Fletcher!" They all did as Molly asked.

"Dylan?" That was Marie's voice outside. Dylan heard her footsteps come closer.

He took a deep breath. He wanted to shout for her to get away, but Fletcher held a hand over his mouth.

Marie appeared in the doorway. When she spotted him sitting on the shelf, with Fletcher's hand on his mouth, she shouted, "Dylan!"

She ran toward them, but three feet before she reached them, she ground to a halt. Surprised, she looked around. She tried to take another step but couldn't. It looked like an invisible wall was stopping her. She held up her fists and banged them against the invisible wall like a mime, unable to move any closer.

Dylan was stunned.

"It worked!" Molly cheered. "It actually worked."

"Hold on. Does that mean there was a chance it wouldn't work!?" Amy asked.

Molly waved her off. "It worked. That's what's important."

Marie looked at her with such hatred in her eyes it gave Dylan chills. "You bitch," she whispered.

Molly ignored her. "Okay, now all we have to do is wait till dawn and she'll go up in flames."

Marie crossed her arms. "Seriously? You really believe that?" She snorted.

Dylan struggled again to get free.

"Let him go," Molly ordered. "We don't need him anymore. Just make sure he doesn't step into the circle. And you don't either!" she added, looking sternly at the others. They all gave Marie a wide berth, walking past her, not letting her out of their sight.

Fletcher maneuvered Dylan around her, too. He gave him a shove in the direction of the exit.

"Get out of here, Harper!"

Dylan caught himself at the last second before tumbling to the floor. He turned around, his heart hammering in his chest. As his eyes met Marie's, she was silently pleading for him to help her.

He nodded once, hoping the others didn't catch it.

"Harper!" Ricky shouted. "Your keys!" He threw them at Dylan.

He tried to catch them, but his hands were so shaky, he dropped them on the floor.

Fletcher chuckled.

Dylan picked them up and made a run for it. Marie's car was parked behind his truck. There was no sign of Fletcher's truck anywhere. Amy must have hidden it well. He climbed into his and drove away. He needed to figure out what to do next.

His heart was still pounding, his ears ringing, and his breathing labored from the run. The farther he got away from the warehouse though, the calmer he became.

Should he go to the police? But what was he going to say? *Hi, my witch friend used her powers to trap my best friend in a circle of symbols because she thinks my best friend is a vampire and wants to kill her.* No, they would never believe him. That story was just too crazy. But what then? He couldn't ask his mom for help, and Martin was unlikely to believe him as well. And hadn't he grounded Molly? She must have snuck out.

But he needed to tell someone. He would never be able to get Marie out of there by himself. If only she hadn't come to get him alone…

That was it! He needed to find Alec. Her husband would help him. He could make them see reason. Or at the very least, he could tell the police his wife had been kidnapped, and they could go and get her.

Determined, Dylan took a turn onto First Street, making his way to Bernie's.

16

He rushed into the old roadside motel's reception room like a man possessed. Bernie looked up from his magazine in surprise. Behind him, the room keys rattled on their hooks on the wall as the door fell shut.

"How can I help you, son?"

Dylan panted. "My friend and her husband are staying here. Is he in? Can you tell me his room number?"

Bernie frowned. "I'd be happy to, but you have to tell me his name."

"It's Alec." That's when Dylan realized he didn't know their last name. "His wife's name is Marie. She's about this tall." He gestured with his flat hand next to his shoulder. "She has dark curly hair, and Alec has dark shoulder-length hair…"

He felt foolish. Bernie would never believe they were his friends if he didn't even know their full names.

"They're both, uh…" He blushed. "Very good looking." He looked at the floor. Bernie probably thought he had lost his marbles.

"Oh, those two… Yeah."

Dylan looked up in surprise.

"It's room twenty-four. On the second floor to the right. But you just missed the girl. She left about half an hour ago to pick up some kid who got stranded—"

"Thank you." Without saying goodbye, Dylan rushed out of the room and to the nearest stairwell. It was pitch dark now. And the harsh fluorescent lighting on the wall outside the rooms gave the old whitewashed building an eerie greenish tint.

He counted down the room numbers. Twenty-eight, twenty-seven, twenty-six, twenty-five, twenty-four…

He gave up on steadying his breath at that point and knocked at the door. As he waited, he realized he was covered in sweat and dust from the warehouse. *No time to dwell on that now.*

Two seconds later the door opened, revealing the guy he had met over two months ago. He seemed just as imposing as he did back then, dressed in black jeans and a black T-shirt. But Dylan was so happy to see him he almost cried with relief.

Alec surprisingly recognized him right away. "Dylan? What are you doing here?"

"I need your help. They trapped Marie and-and-and—"

"Calm down. Come in and tell me what's going on." He stepped aside, allowing Dylan to cross the threshold into his room. He shut the door behind him.

"It was a ruse. They kidnapped me to lure her out there. Molly trapped her in some weird circle. They're convinced she's a vampire, and they want to kill her."

Alec didn't laugh. He didn't react at all.

"Where are they?" he asked calmly.

"In a warehouse by the old sneakers factory."

"Can you take me there?"

"Yes, but don't you want to call the police? There are four of them, and they're committing a felony. Who knows what else they're capable of?" He wouldn't put anything past Fletcher, and Molly seemed so far gone that she didn't know right from wrong anymore.

Alec gave him a stern look. "No. I'll handle it. Come on."

"But…"

"Come on." He held the door open for Dylan, urging him to get going with nothing but his posture, not leaving room for argument.

Something about Alec's demeanor gave Dylan the creeps. It silenced his protests. He nodded and led the way downstairs to his truck.

"So, they trapped her in a circle, you said?" Alec asked once they were under way.

"Yes." He hesitated, unsure what to tell Alec. "I know it sounds crazy, but my friend Molly, she… Well, she isn't exactly a friend, but she can do magic. Like, real magic."

Alec didn't react to that bit of news. "And there are four of them?" he asked.

"Yes." Silence. *He probably thinks I'm insane.* "Are you sure you don't want to call the cops? It's—"

"Yes. I'm sure."

"Okay…"

Dylan looked Alec over from the corner of his eye. The man seemed emotionless, which was weird, considering his wife had been kidnapped. Was he even taking Dylan seriously? He probably was, otherwise, he wouldn't be in the car with the teenager right then.

Either he was really this calm or he was hiding his concern well.

That's when Dylan noticed there was no bandage on Alec's hand. Hadn't Marie said the previous night that he had cut up his hand and had needed stitches?

Well, the wound is probably on his palm, and he might have forgotten to put a bandage on…

Dylan tried to shake off the bad feeling creeping up inside him and focus on the mission.

Marie's car was still parked on the loading dock. Dylan stopped at a generous distance from it so the others wouldn't be alerted by the sound of his truck engine.

"Wait in the car. I'll be back in a minute." Alec opened his door.

"No. I'm coming with you."

Alec arched a brow at Dylan. "No, you're not. You'll wait in the car till I get back," he stated, not leaving room for argument.

Dylan was getting annoyed. Alec might have been intimidating, but he didn't know what he was dealing with here. He didn't even know Fletcher and his gang or Molly. But Dylan did. Together they might be able to defuse the situation. Besides, Marie had stood up for him before. He wasn't going to sit on the sidelines when he had a chance to return the favor.

"I'm coming with you," he said decisively.

Alec looked him up and down. He sighed. "All right then."

They got out of the truck as quietly as possible, which was silently in Alec's case and minimally noisily in Dylan's. As they walked up to the warehouse, Amy's voice trailed over to them.

"Do we really have to wait here all night? Why don't we guard her in shifts? I mean, she's not going anywhere…"

The door was ajar. Taking the lead, Dylan pushed it open and shouted, "This stops now! Let her go!"

Molly, Amy, Ricky, and Fletcher stood spread out in a half circle between Marie and the door. They all turned to Dylan when he entered. They had put up flashlights on the shelves around the room so they wouldn't be stuck there in the dark, but the scarce light made the empty dusty room look creepier than no light at all. Marie stood with her arms crossed in the middle of the circle. She looked annoyed but didn't seem to be hurt.

"What are you doing here, Harper?" Fletcher asked with a snort. "You're not going to get her out of there."

Dylan half turned to the door. But where Alec should have been, there was just empty space. He frowned in confusion, wondering where the guy had disappeared to. Hadn't he said he wanted to talk to them?

A loud crack in the corner of the room caught his attention, making his head jerk in time to see Molly fall to the ground like a marionette whose strings had been cut. Her head rested at a weird angle to her body, her limbs splayed awkwardly.

Amy, who stood closest to her, rushed over, crouched down, and shook her. "Molly? Molly, wake up!" Amy gasped and rose to her feet again as if she had been stung.

Dylan took a few steps closer. Molly lay motionless, her eyes staring at nothing. He had seen empty eyes like that before: two months ago, outside his house, when he had found Stacy Yelander's dead body. A cold shiver ran down his spine.

Molly was dead.

No.

She couldn't be.

He crouched beside her, shaking her, trying to wake her up like Amy had done, but all that did was make her head loll like it wasn't connected to her body. Like her neck had no bones. But how? His gaze darted around the room frantically, looking for what had caused this.

"What was that?" Fletcher asked, his voice slightly trembling.

That's when Dylan heard a squelching sound to his right where Ricky had been standing. He jumped to his feet, twisting around, and couldn't believe what he was seeing.

Alec stood right behind Ricky, his hand buried deep in Ricky's back. When he wrenched it out, Ricky groaned, dropping to the floor just like Molly.

Dylan blinked. Alec was holding Ricky's heart in his hand. It was oozing blood, the liquid trickling down his bare forearm. Dylan's body went numb with shock. Nobody possessed that kind of strength.

"What the…" Fletcher said.

Amy and Fletcher were staring at Alec. But after a split second,

Fletcher made a run for it, leaving his sister behind.

Alec cut him off. One moment, he was standing in the middle of the warehouse holding Ricky's heart and the next, Ricky's heart lay on the floor next to its owner and Alec stood in the doorway, blocking the exit.

How was that possible? Dylan's heartbeat picked up speed, his survival instincts screaming at him to get the hell out of there, but he was trapped. The murderer was blocking the only way out.

Fletcher froze. He slowly walked backward, presumably to put as much distance as possible between himself and Alec.

"That was one step too far," Marie whispered as she wrapped an arm around Fletcher's chest and pulled him closer. Her irises turned a bright crimson, and as she opened her mouth, long sharp fangs gleamed inside.

Dylan's stomach turned in disgust. He felt like retching. This couldn't be real. He was having a bad dream. Panicking, he squeezed his eyes shut, trying to force himself awake, telling himself that once he opened his eyes, he'd wake up in his bed at home.

But that didn't happen. He was still in the warehouse, looking at Marie pulling Fletcher close to her.

Fletcher was screaming in terror, trying to fight her off, but she buried her face in his neck. He screamed again, this time in pain. He struggled harder, scratching and pulling at her arms, but she didn't budge an inch. With every passing moment, he got weaker and weaker until he stopped fighting altogether and his body went limp.

Amy suddenly whimpered loudly behind Dylan. He spun around in terror. Alec was towering over her. She was inching back toward the wall, tears running down her face.

"Please…" she begged.

With one swift motion, Alec bent her head to the side, baring her neck and biting into it. Amy shrieked so loudly it made Dylan's ears ring. But like her twin brother, she went still and limp only a few moments later and the light left her eyes. Alec let her body drop to the floor unceremoniously.

He looked at his bloodied hand, bent over, and wiped it clean on Amy's clothes. Dylan's mind couldn't process what he was seeing. All he could do was gape at the massacre around him, wide-eyed.

"Dylan." That was Marie's voice. He wheeled around automatically. She was swiping Fletcher's body over one of the symbols, smudging it in the process. She stepped over the bully as if he were a toy a kid had left on the floor.

She had left the circle. She was free.

Dylan tried to make sense of it. She had been held back by nothing but symbols which Molly had claimed could trap a vampire, she had fangs, and she seemed to have drained Fletcher of his blood.

He stared at Marie intently, fear creeping inside him.

Her eyes showed deep concern. She held out both hands in front of her in a gesture to show she was unarmed.

Slowly she stepped toward him. "It's okay. It's over. Everything will be all right." As she closed the distance between them, he automatically took a step back. She froze.

"Molly was right," he whispered. "She was right." And now she was dead. His heart was threatening to burst out of his chest, and he felt like he was hyperventilating. He crouched, reached behind his head with both hands, and pulled it toward his knees, trying to catch his breath.

"Dylan, look at me," Marie commanded in a soothing tone. That startled him momentarily, and he looked up. She was crouching two feet away from him, her expression reassuring. "You saved my life. Okay? They were going to kill me. You saved my life."

Her eyes were the same light gray they had always been. And her expression held a warmth that reminded him that this girl was his friend.

But she had just killed someone in front of him. Her husband had killed three people right there in this room. And they both clearly were something other than human.

Still breathing heavily, he looked at the dead bodies spread around the room: Fletcher pale and bloodless lying sprawled out on the floor, Ricky facedown with a hand-sized bloody hole in his back, Molly with a broken neck, and Amy awkwardly leaning against the wall, eyes staring at him accusingly.

He was responsible for this. He had done this. He had led Alec there. His heart pounded again.

"Dylan, calm down. They were going to kill me. There was no other way."

He teared up. What had he done?

"We're not going to hurt you. Please, don't be scared."

That made him pause. He sucked in a breath and held it. "Don't be scared? You guys are vampires," he whispered. He didn't even recognize his own voice. It was thick with terror.

She flinched. His survival instinct kicked back in. He jumped to his feet, wanting nothing more than to get away from there, but as he wheeled around, he almost bumped into Alec, who was standing there, arms crossed, expression bored.

"Shut up. We have more important things to do than cater to your sensitivities." His tone was biting. The polar opposite of Marie's.

His brashness made Dylan see red. He snapped at Alec. "My sensi—You just murdered four people in cold blood!"

"Why don't you shout a little louder? I don't think they heard you at the other end of town."

"Alec," Marie admonished.

Her husband sighed, rubbing the bridge of his nose. "I told you to wait in the car, but you wouldn't listen." He sounded exasperated, which made Dylan even angrier.

"What!? So you could murder them in peace?"

"Yes," he replied flatly. That knocked the wind out of Dylan's sails. Flabbergasted, he just stared at Alec. But the vampire had turned his attention to Marie. "We need to act now," he told her emphatically.

"I can't. Not yet. I'm not ready," Marie said behind Dylan. Her tone wasn't pleading but desperate. She sounded deeply broken. He couldn't help but halfway turn and look at her. Her face was contorted in pain, and she had tears in her eyes.

Alec appeared next to her as if out of nowhere, taking her in his arms. He stroked her back soothingly with one hand, holding her head close to his chest with the other. The tenderness stunned Dylan. How could they be capable of such cruelty one moment and show so much affection the next?

"I'll do it," he murmured.

She pulled away from him in surprise. "What? Really?"

"Yes." He squeezed her hands.

She threw her arms around him, hugging him tightly. "Thank you."

Dylan had no idea what this was about, but he knew this was his one chance to get out of there. As silently as possible, he edged toward the door.

"Where do you think you're going?" Alec asked into Marie's shoulder.

Dylan froze. They split. Marie sighed and looked at him with contrition in her eyes.

"I'm sorry, Dylan. I thought you'd have a few more years… But this is too messy."

His heart was hammering again in panic. "What? What do you mean? Are you going to kill me now? I thought we were friends."

She frowned. "No. No, we would never kill you."

"Then…"

Before he could say anything else, Alec said, "We need to clean this up. Fake his death. We need another body."

"There's still the dead wolf in the trunk." Marie pointed over her shoulder.

"What!?" Dylan asked while Alec said "Perfect" at the same time.

Dylan blinked, and Alec appeared right in front of him. He held out his hand. "Give me your keys and your wallet."

"No."

Alec sighed. "Give them to me or I'll take them by force." The vampire's gaze was so intense, it sent a shiver down Dylan's spine. Fear clenched his throat tightly. He pulled his keys and his wallet out of his pocket with trembling hands and handed them to Alec.

Marie strode back inside through the warehouse door – Dylan hadn't even noticed her leave – a naked dead man slung over her shoulder. She dropped him next to the others.

This man looked wild. He had long hair and a scruffy beard and thick body hair. His body was covered in faded scars, and his fingernails and toenails were long and clawlike. He had several deep gashes all over his body. One of them went from his right shoulder all the way down to his left hip. Probably the cause of death.

"Who is that?" Dylan asked.

"The better question would be 'what' is that," Alec corrected. "It's a dead werewolf."

The wolf. Dylan's heart was racing again. "Hold on. Werewolf?"

They both looked at him innocently. "Yes."

Dylan's head swirled. This couldn't be real. Werewolves didn't exist. But neither did vampires. Or magic. He panicked again, drawing in short breaths.

Alec tossed Dylan's keys and wallet onto the dead werewolf. Marie appeared beside Dylan. She tentatively reached out with both hands, letting them hover over his shoulders. "Come on, let's get you in the car."

When he didn't make a move, she laid her hands on his shoulders. The cold of her fingers was seeping through his jacket, but the tenderness of her touch melted every resistance. He was exhausted, and grief and shock were gnawing at his consciousness. He felt utterly powerless.

He let her guide him to her car. She opened the passenger side door, collapsed the seat forward, and motioned for him to get in the back.

He looked at her, trying to gauge her intentions. Her eyes were innocent and warm, and she gave him a gentle nudge. He pressed his lips together.

"What's going to happen to me?" he whispered. Saying it louder would have overwhelmed him with fear.

Empathy rested on her face. "Nothing. You'll be fine."

Maybe Dylan was losing his mind, but he somehow still trusted his friend. He had grown to love this girl over the past two months. And even though he felt betrayed, he couldn't let go of his feelings toward his first and only friend. So he got into the car. She put the front seat back into place and got in herself.

Alec came out of the warehouse, retrieved something from the trunk, and went back inside.

"What is he doing?"

"Burning it down," she answered as nonchalantly as if he had asked her what she was having for dinner that night.

A moment later, smoke emerged from the warehouse. Alec came out shortly after; flames were already licking at the door frame.

He got in on the driver's side and started the car. They were driving back into town. Alec shot a glance at Dylan through the rearview mirror and said something in a foreign language to Marie.

She answered in the same tongue, and they were having a back and forth. Dylan strained to understand what they were saying, but he couldn't even identify the language. It sounded like Swedish or Norwegian… German maybe?

At some point in the conversation, Alec got agitated. He switched back to English. "No, I'm not leaving you here. What if there are others?"

"There aren't. She was the only witch in town; otherwise, she would have asked other witches to help her instead of those moronic humans."

He looked at her reproachfully. "You also said the witch wasn't dangerous. And you were clearly wrong about that."

She sighed. "I'll be more careful from now on. But really, I smelled no magic on her father, and we killed all the wolves, so this town is clear of all supernatural beings."

They shot quick glances at Dylan, but it was over so fast that he thought he'd imagined it.

"What about her mother?"

Marie started to say something but turned around to Dylan instead. "Do you know Molly's mother?"

"Uh, she died over a year ago." He wasn't following. What did Molly's mother have to do with all this?

Marie gave Alec a look that said, "See?"

When he didn't say anything, she added, "Somebody needs to stay and tie up all the loose ends."

"Then we'll do that together. We hide out at the motel, then once the coast is clear we leave." His eyes darted to Dylan, and he added something in the same foreign language as before.

She fell silent, her eyes fluttering from Alec to Dylan and back again. "Dylan, how did you know where to find Alec?"

"I asked Bernie for your room number." He had answered without thinking but now he was afraid for Bernie's safety. "I didn't tell him anything," he added hastily. "Please don't hurt him."

"I won't. We can alter his memory."

"What!?" He leaned forward. "Then why didn't you just do that to the others?"

"Because it's complicated. Human minds are tricky. And a witch's mind can't be altered at all. She would have just kept coming for us."

This was insane.

"And once an idea has taken root in somebody's mind, it can't be plucked out without causing serious damage. The others would have ended up as vegetables had I tried."

"Is that why you can't do it to me?" He desperately wished he could forget witnessing these murders. He wanted everything to go back to normal.

Alec and Marie looked at each other.

"No, there's a different reason for that."

"What reason?"

But they had arrived at the motel. Marie spun into action, but Alec stopped her with a hand on her arm. "I'm not leaving without you." The intensity and the urgency in his voice made Dylan shrink into his seat.

She rested her hand on his and gazed into his eyes. "Then we'll stay and make it work." She leaned over the middle console and kissed him on the mouth. It was just a peck, but the emotion she put into it made it seem so deep that Dylan had to look away because he felt like he was intruding.

Alec squeezed her arm and smiled weakly. Then the moment had passed, and they sprang into action, getting out of the car. Marie collapsed her seat, gesturing for Dylan to get out as well.

His heart was racing. He tried to figure out what to do next but couldn't think straight. He needed to get away from these two, but how?

He heaved himself out of the car, breathing heavily from the exertion. They could outrun him, that much was certain. Even without supernatural speed, they probably would have been able to. He could only hope for a distraction that would allow him to sneak away.

Marie led them up to their room, and Alec followed closely behind Dylan. Having his back to the vampire made Dylan's palms sweat.

"You know, you can just let me go home. I won't tell anyone about this, I swear."

Alec snorted. "Sure."

"I swear!" Dylan was ready to say anything if it got him out of this.

"As long as I can't use mind control on you to make sure that you won't tell, you're not going anywhere," Alec whispered so low only Dylan could hear.

He balled his hands into fists to stop them from shaking. Cold sweat was drenching his sweater. They had reached the room, and Marie held the door open for him.

Dylan stopped before the threshold, unwilling to go any farther, but Alec shoved him, so he stumbled inside. Marie flipped on the lights and shut the door. He was trapped.

Alec stepped around him and into the en suite bathroom. He left the door ajar. Dylan could hear him turn on the sink faucet and wash his hands. The image of Ricky's lifeless body on the floor next to his heart came back, and he realized Alec was washing the residue of the boy's blood off his hands. He shivered.

Marie had started making the queen-sized bed in the middle of the room, throwing the flower-patterned blue bedspread over the rumpled white sheets. "Take a seat, Dylan." She gestured toward the bed.

"What are you going to do with me?" he asked, surprised at the bravery in his voice.

Her mouth twitched and her brow creased. "We'll explain everything, okay? Just take a seat." The sympathy in her eyes made him comply. He sat on the edge of the bed, facing a tiny TV sitting on a dark brown wooden cabinet. Next to it was an unused desk and a threadbare chair. There was a closet to Dylan's right next to the bathroom door, its wooden sliding doors shut.

Marie took a seat on the two-seater couch in front of the large window next to the door. The window's mauve curtains were tightly shut. She looked worried.

Dylan was about to ask again what they were going to do with him when Alec came back from the bathroom. He pulled out the desk chair and sat across from Dylan, their knees almost touching. Dylan automatically inched back.

When neither one of them spoke, he tried reasoning again. "I'm still in school. My mom doesn't know where I am. People will be looking for me."

"That's why we've faked your death," Alec stated matter-of-factly.

That hit Dylan like a ton of bricks.

"All they'll find in that warehouse will be five bodies burnt beyond recognition. Your car is at the scene. Even the Berlin police department can figure that one out."

"But we'll make sure anyway," Marie added, as if that was reassuring to Dylan.

Dylan frowned. "But why?" He didn't even try to hide his desperation. He needed answers. Now.

Alec pursed his lips. "Well… It's probably best if I start at the beginning."

Dylan rubbed his hands on his thighs, waiting.

"Most legends and folklore about us immortals are made up and unsubstantiated. Among many things, the belief that any human being can become one of us after death given the right circumstances."

He paused. Dylan was trying to process that Alec had just referred to himself and Marie as immortal. He took a deep breath. How was he supposed to get away from them if they could just come after him till the end of time?

"As a matter of fact," Alec continued "only very, very few people can be made immortal. The condition is extremely rare but" – he looked Dylan straight in the eye – "you're one of them."

17

Dylan blinked. He pointed at himself. "Me?" He snorted. "Yeah, right. I think if I was special in any way, I would know about it."

"No, you wouldn't," Alec replied calmly. "I didn't know until I was turned. Neither did Marie."

He looked at Marie, who was still sitting on the couch by the window. She nodded, giving Dylan a tight-lipped smile that he supposed was meant to calm him down.

"But … that doesn't make sense…" Dylan shook his head. "Then how do *you* know? How do you know I'm one of these people?"

"An aura surrounds you. It's like a black mist that clings to your skin. You yourself can't see it, but immortals can."

Dylan looked at his hands, trying to see what Alec was talking about, but they looked perfectly ordinary. No mist.

"We don't know why some people are born with it. Sometimes it's genetic, but most of the time it seems completely arbitrary," Marie explained.

Alec added, "When we find such a mortal, we alone have the power to unleash their potential. To set them free." On these last words Alec fixed Dylan with an intense stare.

Dylan saw where this was going. "You want to turn me into a vampire."

Alec flinched. "Please don't use that word. It's a term humans and witches came up with. It's derogatory."

Dylan arched an eyebrow. There was political correctness among vampires?

"We are neither soulless monsters nor undead. We're simply immortal."

"Not soulless monsters, huh?" He snorted. "You just killed four people in cold blood, and you don't seem fazed by it at all."

"We're not bound by human morals." Alec smiled.

"And they threatened to kill me," Marie chimed in. "We had no choice." She shrugged.

Dylan shook his head. "I'm not buying that, and I certainly won't let you turn me into a monster."

Alec stared at him, unmoved. "Who said you had a choice in the matter?"

The next thing Dylan knew, Alec was towering over him, shoving his wrist between Dylan's jaws. It all happened too fast for him to react. One moment he was sitting there looking at Alec, and the next something cold and wet trickled into his mouth.

When he realized Alec was feeding him his blood, he struggled against the vampire's arm, but it felt like fighting an iron bar. It didn't budge an inch. Dylan tried to spit the blood back out, but Alec placed his other hand on the back of Dylan's head, pressing him harder onto his wrist. Dylan had no choice but to swallow if he didn't want to choke.

His jaw protested in pain and the metallic taste made him gag, but he couldn't move. After an agonizing minute that felt like an eternity, Alec let go of him.

For a second, Dylan didn't feel anything. He almost laughed, thinking Alec had been wrong and he wasn't one of the few after all. Relief washed over him.

But then a sharp pain in his heart made him keel over, and that pain rapidly clawed its way out of his chest and into the rest of his body, knocking the air out of his lungs. It felt as if millions of sharp needles were piercing every cell in his body. He clutched his chest, gasping for breath. His survival instinct was screaming at him to do something. But he was powerless against the onslaught of pain. He was sure he was going to die. Nobody could survive such intense pain.

He hugged himself, moving into the fetal position, desperate for it to end. But it didn't. Instead, the stinging became crushing, making him feel like he was being squeezed between two cement blocks, each one the size of a building. His ears were ringing, and panic tightened his throat… And he still couldn't breathe. Any moment now, his organs would collapse under the weight of this agony.

But when he felt like he couldn't take it any longer, the pain turned into something else.

Dylan felt a tingling sensation in his stomach first. Like the feeling of going down on a roller coaster. A wave of pure bliss washed over him, driving out all remnants of suffering. He was finally able to take a deep breath and found himself unwinding and stretching out on the bed. The ecstasy inside his belly felt like an entire universe was being born inside him. It promised to be infinite. A rush of endorphins made his limbs heavy in a comforting way, like being wrapped in a warm fuzzy blanket.

He wanted to laugh to let the feelings out. He was overflowing with happiness. It needed to escape, but he also wanted to hold on to it. It slowly subsided, dissipating like smoke. Dylan was struggling to catch the last wisps of pleasure, not wanting to let go. He opened his eyes and stared at the ceiling, the room spinning around him. His heartbeat slowed to a regular rhythm, and then everything stopped.

No more pain, no more pleasure.

The room seemed brighter than before – and it was blurry and … smudged? He took off his glasses and, after blinking at the ceiling a few times, realized he saw more clearly than before.

His vision was better than perfect. He could see every tiny crack in the ceiling, every brush stroke on the paint, every dust particle on the light fixture, every tiny imperfection on the glass shade. When he stopped focusing, it all went back to normal, like his eyes had zoomed out. But the room still seemed to be brighter than before, even though the curtains were drawn and it was still the middle of the night.

He heard running water. Somebody was washing their hands. He could hear the squelching sound of lathering hands and the water drops hammering on the porcelain of the sink. Startled, he looked around, but nobody was there besides Alec, who was rummaging in the cabinet under the TV, not paying attention to Dylan, and Marie who sat next to him on the bed. She was watching him, her eyes glistening, her face lit up with a bright smile.

He realized the sound was coming from the room next to theirs. He shook his head in amazement and disbelief.

"It's okay, Dylan," Marie whispered encouragingly, reaching out and squeezing his forearm lightly. He jerked his arm back, not wanting her to touch him.

Alec had found what he was looking for and threw a glance at Dylan. His eyes widened in shock. "Now *that's* a transformation!" He laughed, shooting Marie a glance. "That'll make things a lot easier."

Dylan frowned. He had no idea what Alec was talking about.

"Go ahead and look in the mirror."

Intrigued, Dylan got up, sitting right back down when he realized his pants were slipping. He looked down at himself in confusion. His body was half the size it had been; he was drowning in his clothes. He awkwardly tightened his belt a few notches, noticing how slender his hands were, and tried to stand again.

He expected to be wobbly on his feet, but he wasn't. He threw a glance at Marie, who was still staring at him with teary eyes and that stupid, creepy smile on her face. He wanted to put as much distance between himself and her as possible.

The bathroom was small and clean, with beige tile; the bathtub spanned the whole length of the back wall. A tiny window in that wall was covered with cardboard. He turned to the left, where the sink and the mirror were.

When he saw his reflection in the mirror, he did a double take. He had lost about sixty pounds. His face was no longer chubby but slim, his features more defined than before. His jaw and cheekbones seemed sharper, and his skin was not only clear, but also radiant and pale, almost like porcelain. Had his eyes always been that blue? He looked closer. Yes, they had. It just hadn't been as noticeable behind the thick glasses. The only thing that looked just as before was his brown hair.

Other than that, the guy in the mirror had absolutely nothing in common with him. His heart sank. He felt like he was trapped in somebody else's body.

Dylan didn't want to look at himself a second longer. He turned his back on the mirror and returned to the bedroom.

"Oh, now, don't look so glum. You'll get used to it in no time, trust me." Alec stood smirking next to the TV, arms crossed. Marie was still beaming at Dylan.

"And yes, this is what you'll look like forever. You won't age, you won't lose or gain weight, you won't get scars or blemishes. Your hair and nails will still grow though." Alec shrugged. "You're welcome."

"*You're welcome?* Are you serious? What have you done to me?" Dylan shouted in horror. To his relief, the sound of his voice hadn't changed.

Alec huffed, shaking his head in disdain. "Twentieth century immortals… Such an ungrateful bunch…"

Marie laughed at Alec's remark. "Don't be so hard on him. It's really quite a change. It's going to take some getting used to." She scooted across the bed and stood in front of Dylan. "It's amazing," she whispered, reaching out to touch his face but stopping herself halfway.

Dylan's heart sank. Marie seemed so different now that he knew what she was. He felt like he didn't know her at all. And she had killed someone. Before that night he wouldn't have thought her capable of murder, but apparently, he had been wrong. And how many others had she killed before?

"You must be hungry." Her expression turned serious. "Come. Sit." She put her hands on his shoulders, maneuvering him to the bed, making him sit down. He tried to shrug her hands off, but she was much stronger than him.

Alec stepped closer, and now they were both towering over Dylan, making him want to jerk back, but he didn't. He didn't want to show weakness. Alec thrust something at him. It took him a second to realize what it was. But there was no mistaking the red liquid inside the transparent plastic bag for anything other than blood.

Dylan flinched, knowing what they expected from him. But there was no way he was going to drink that.

But as he breathed in, a sweet scent like flowers mixed with strawberries entered his nostrils. There were notes of something salty in it too. Peanut butter? He sniffed. Yes, definitely peanut butter. The scent was enveloping him, creating images in his mind of sunny strawberry fields and colorful candy stores.

Dazed, he reached for the blood bag. It felt like he was under a spell. A part of him was screaming not to do it, but it was like the smells were singing to him, drowning out the other voices, drawing him in. His hand guided the bag's opening to his lips automatically, and he started drinking the liquid.

The taste was even more intense than the smell. It was as sweet as the fragrance had promised. The fruitiness made his cheeks tingle and his heart sing. He lapped it up like a starved dog, tilting his head back and shaking the blood bag so even the last drops would come loose and roll onto his tongue.

He tossed the empty bag aside. Alec was already holding out another bag for him. This one exuded an earthier, almost bitter scent. Was it walnut? And traces of dairy. He had never consciously smelled dairy before, but he immediately recognized it. Sweet notes, too, almost like honey. He greedily gulped down the liquid, relishing the taste explosion on his tongue.

When it was empty, he tried to shake out the last remaining drops again.

A laugh broke his focus, and he suddenly became aware of what he was doing. He lowered the empty blood bag and looked into Marie's smiling face.

"I'm glad you're not squeamish about the blood. Makes things a lot easier," she said.

Dylan quickly licked the blood residue off his lips. Embarrassed, he crumpled the blood bag in his hand. "Why did they each have such different tastes?"

Alec and Marie looked at each other, frowning. Marie asked, "You could taste a difference?"

Dylan made a face. Wasn't it obvious? Surely, they had smelled the difference, too. "Of course, they were completely different. The first one was light and fruity and the second was nutty and heavy."

Alec stared at him in surprise. "You have a fine palette for a newly turned immortal. Usually it takes years for that to develop." Marie nodded in agreement.

The aftertaste was wearing off, and Dylan realized with a start that he had drunk two pints of blood – and what was worse, he had enjoyed it.

Disgusted, he wiped his mouth, trying to remove the taste from his lips.

"Don't be ashamed," Alec said. "Aversion to blood is a human notion you need to abandon. It serves no purpose for us at all."

Dylan didn't want to do that. He felt horrified at the idea of becoming an uncaring monster like Alec.

Marie looked him up and down. "You need new clothes." She pursed her lips, tapping her chin, her eyes wandering to the closet.

Alec followed her gaze. "You can borrow some of mine. I think we're the same size now."

"No." Dylan couldn't accept this. "This is not happening." He covered his face with his hands, pressing the heels of his palms to his eyes. His fear from earlier had turned into confusion. He dragged his hands down his face.

Alec was rummaging in the closet, but Marie was still standing in front of him. She had taken a step back and was watching him with knitted brows. "Dylan…"

"You need to turn me back. I don't want this." He shook his head vigorously.

"Hush…" Marie gently put her hands on his shoulders, trying to soothe him. "Dylan, we can't turn you back. Immortality is irreversible."

He was avoiding her gaze, staring past her right shoulder, but he could hear the smile in her voice. He wanted to throw up.

"You'll be all right. Once you get the hang of it, you won't want anything else, trust me."

He looked at her then. Not even the slightest hint of insincerity showed in her eyes. But then again, she hadn't been honest with him since they'd met. "Don't touch me," he spat.

She took her hands off him reflexively, and Dylan thought he saw her cringe with hurt for a second, but he couldn't be sure.

"Why don't you go ahead and take care of Bernie, darling?" Alec stepped up to her, lightly squeezing the fingers of her right hand.

She kept her gaze trained on Dylan, staring him down. Dylan didn't blink. In that moment, he hated her more than anything.

Alec ran his hand up and down her forearm, which broke her attention. She gave him a curt nod and with three quick strides exited the room. The door fell shut behind her, leaving Dylan alone with Alec.

The vampire was clutching a pair of jeans and what looked like a gray shirt in his left hand. He dropped the clothes on Dylan's lap.

"Why don't you take a shower?" He had phrased it like a suggestion, but it was clearly an order.

Dylan didn't move a muscle. He glared at Alec. "What do you still want with me? You turned me. Now let me go."

Alec's eyebrows shot up. "You don't know the first thing about being immortal. We can't just leave you unsupervised."

Dylan didn't like the sound of that. It made him feel like a child or a criminal. Ironic, considering there was only one murderer in this room, and it surely wasn't him.

"What does that mean?"

Alec sighed theatrically and took a seat on the chair across from Dylan. "Well…" He steepled his fingers. "If you leave now, before you know how to control the bloodlust, you'll inevitably kill someone."

Dylan shivered involuntarily. "I would never," he huffed.

The vampire half smiled. "Oh, you would, trust me. With the way you just lapped up that blood, you'd probably go through at least five people without stopping."

Dylan gulped. He wanted to argue, but deep down he felt Alec was right. And it scared him. "So, what do you care? You guys just murdered four people."

Alec's face darkened. "Yes, because we didn't have a choice. And it's going to be one hell of a cleanup. Nobody can find out about us. We have to blend in as best we can. And you'll need to learn how to do that."

"And then you'll let me go?" Dylan didn't want it to sound like a plea. He tried to tell himself that he was bargaining.

Alec took his time contemplating Dylan's words. Without revealing any of his thoughts or emotions, he said, "Yes. Should you wish."

Dylan nodded, incapable of imagining a world where he would want to stay with Alec and Marie.

"Okay. Now, go shower and get dressed." Alec nodded toward the bathroom.

Dylan considered refusing, but he needed to put some distance between himself and the vampire. He needed to gather his thoughts and figure out what to do next. His mom was probably worried sick. Had the authorities already discovered the warehouse fire? Would they really assume he was one of the bodies?

The bodies.

Molly's death weighed heavily on his heart. And Fletcher, Amy, and Ricky might have been assholes, but they hadn't deserved to die. Before dread and grief could overcome him in front of Alec, he retreated to the bathroom carrying his borrowed clothes.

He had momentarily forgotten that his body had changed beyond recognition. But when he caught a glimpse of himself in the bathroom mirror, he cringed. The face staring back at him mimicked his expression, but it didn't seem to belong to him.

He turned his back on the mirror and took off his now-oversized jeans and sweater. Even the undershirt hung loosely down his torso, stretched out to a size he could no longer fill out.

When he was naked, he inspected his new body with morbid curiosity. He was lean and lithe, his muscles clearly defined. Every blemish was gone. His skin was nothing but porcelain white. The large scar he'd had on his left upper arm from a fight with Fletcher that had ended with him cutting himself open on a pointy rock had all but disappeared.

That's when he remembered Fletcher was dead, and his stomach churned. He ripped his gaze away from this strange flawless body that felt so alien to him and stepped into the bathtub.

The warm steady stream of water running down his body calmed him some, even if looking down at himself made him feel dizzy. And the water felt different too. If he focused, he could feel each drop individually, the difference in size, speed, and shape.

But the water was loud. The splatter on the ceramic tub sounded like a hurricane to his ears. He found it extremely hard to ignore. But at least it drowned out his thoughts.

When he stepped out of the tub, his reflection gave him a start again. He touched his smooth face in disbelief. All his pimples had vanished. He stared into his unfamiliar eyes, trying to find some piece of himself in them. How was he ever going to get used to this? And hadn't Alec said his body would never change? That meant this was it. Like it or not. And Dylan did not like it.

In addition to the drastic change, it didn't feel right that he was still breathing while the others were dead. Molly's face appeared in his mind's eye. He saw her pleading with him to believe her that Marie was a vampire. The way her eyes had been bulging when she tried to convince him. But he hadn't believed her. Instead, he had helped the bad guys. And she was paying the price for it. She was dead, while he was going to live forever.

It wasn't fair. She hadn't done anything wrong. Tears stung his eyes and his jaw clenched. Her face turned from pleading to accusing in his head, her perpetual frown deepening. *This is your fault*, she sneered. A wave of guilt washed over him.

He leaned on the sink and took a deep breath that was supposed to calm him, but he didn't experience the usual relief. Surprised, he stopped breathing altogether, blinking at his reflection.

Even after two full minutes, his lungs felt fine. His hands didn't tingle with the absence of oxygen. His heart was beating at a normal rate. He realized he no longer needed air.

Anxiety gripped him. This was insane. He ran both hands through his wet hair, staring wide-eyed at his unfamiliar face. Everything that had happened came crashing down on him at once. Nothing was ever going to be the same. What was he going to do?

A knock at the bathroom door interrupted his panic.

"Dylan?" Alec's voice was calm against the door. "What is taking you so long in there?"

"Nothing. I'll be out in a second."

Alec didn't reply, but Dylan didn't hear him leave either. He grabbed a towel from the rack and hastily dried himself off, then he tied it around his waist.

"What?" he asked when he opened the door.

Dylan couldn't read the look on Alec's face.

"If you have any questions about your new body or immortality, you can ask me. I'm going to teach you everything I know…" He trailed off, avoiding Dylan's gaze.

"I don't need to breathe anymore." It wasn't a question but the first thing that came to his mind. Articulating his thoughts relieved some of his anxiety, it seemed.

Alec became his usual composed self again. "No. Our bodies don't need oxygen. But since we rely on our sense of smell, we breathe just like humans anyway."

Dylan tried to process this information.

"Get dressed." Alec nodded encouragingly. "Come out when you're ready."

Dylan shut the door on him. He quickly slipped on Alec's light blue denim jeans and the gray V-neck shirt. Both fit him perfectly. He tried not to think about how weird that was.

Pushing down all his feelings, he tried to figure out his next move. The breathing incident had scared him, and he realized there might be lots of other things he didn't know about his new body yet. Like it or not, he needed Alec and Marie to show him the ropes before he could do anything else.

But then what?

He needed to make sure Molly hadn't died for nothing. Somehow, he had to make Alec and Marie pay for what they had done.

A cold shiver ran down his spine as he realized something else. What if Molly had been right and Marie and Alec had been the ones behind the murders all along? They had said something about a werewolf, but that guy had looked human… And maybe the wolf *had* been an illusion after all. He needed to get to the bottom of this and, most importantly, make sure nobody else got hurt.

Having found new purpose made him feel more determined and less confused and scared. Trying hard not to look in the mirror again, he fled the bathroom.

18

A part of Dylan's brain noticed that he could feel each individual fiber of the carpet under his bare feet as he stepped into the motel bedroom.

Alec sat on the couch by the window, legs crossed, like he was waiting at a doctor's office. Dylan walked around the bed, taking a seat across from Alec.

The vampire looked at him expectantly, so Dylan asked, "Where is Marie?"

"She came back from downstairs while you were showering. She decided to go check on the warehouse, see if the authorities have been alerted yet and if the fire has erased all the traces."

Dylan wondered if Alec was telling the truth. He realized he had no way of verifying anything the vampire told him.

"Aren't they going to get suspicious of her if she shows up there?"

"They won't see her."

Dylan scoffed. "Right. You might not be aware of it, but your car attracts attention. And frankly, so do you."

Alec smirked. "She's not using the car. And trust me, they won't even know she's there."

Dylan didn't know what to make of that, but thinking about Marie made him antsy. He felt betrayed. He had trusted her, and she had lied to his face.

Besides, there were plenty of other things he wanted to know.

"Why do I look like this? I mean why did my body change so much?"

"The transformation puts your body in its prime condition."

"Why?"

Alec shrugged. "We're not sure. Probably a side effect of keeping us immortal. Another theory is that it's to attract prey."

Dylan frowned. "What do you mean?"

"Humans are drawn to us because we look beautiful to them. It's easier to hunt when your food comes to you willingly."

Alec's cold smile made Dylan shiver. He didn't want to lure in unassuming humans to take advantage of them. He remembered the blood he had drunk earlier.

"Where did you get the blood bags from?"

Alec uncrossed his legs. "We get them from blood banks. They're convenient." Another shrug. "But it tastes much better when it's fresh, I assure you."

"But then you— *we* don't have to kill, right?"

Alec arched an eyebrow. "No, we don't. And we rarely do these days. It's become rather difficult to get away with murder in the twentieth century." He smirked.

That answer raised a trillion more questions. But Dylan asked the most pressing one. "So, I can survive without killing people?"

Alec's mouth became a hard line. For a moment, disdain flashed in his eyes, but as soon as it was there, it was gone again. "Yes, you can."

Dylan could have sung with relief. This was the first piece of good news. He didn't have to be a monster. He could live on blood bags. All wasn't lost.

He remembered something Alec had said earlier. "How exactly did Marie 'take care' of Bernie?"

"Through mind control. She made him forget that you'd been there earlier looking for me."

No matter how hard Dylan tried, he couldn't wrap his head around that. "How? And why couldn't you just do that to the others?"

Alec pursed his lips. "It's complicated. Mind control isn't easy. It takes a lot of skill, and you can't just randomly delete things from people's minds. You could easily damage them in the process. Your friends knew too much. There was no other way." His expression had hardened, leaving no room for argument.

Dylan wasn't sure whether he believed that. "Will you show me how that's done?" He needed to see it for himself.

Alec nodded. "Of course."

Dylan didn't feel comfortable with the thought of bending people to his will or altering their memories and he never intended to use that power, but he needed to know it was possible and they weren't lying to him.

"Was that everything you wanted to know?" Alec asked, brow furrowed.

"No. I…" Dylan thought about all the vampire myths he knew from books and movies. What was real and what was fiction? "I don't even know where to begin…"

"Then why don't I explain some things to you? You can interrupt me if you have questions." The vampire leaned back, smiling warmly at Dylan. Alec's patience surprised him. It seemed at odds with the vampire's cold efficiency.

"So, let's start with the folklore you might have been exposed to. As you've seen for yourself, we do have reflections."

Dylan hadn't even thought of that. Considering how unhappy he was with his body, he would have preferred not to have a reflection.

"Holy items, such as crucifixes, crosses, holy water, or any other Christian paraphernalia have no effect on us." He counted the items off on his fingers. "Garlic doesn't bother us." He smirked. "We don't sleep in coffins. Although before there was modern transportation, we sometimes used to travel in them. Journeys could be long and arduous, and it was the best way to stay out of the sun."

"So the thing about the sun is real?" Dylan interrupted.

Alec swallowed. He got a faraway look in his eyes. Avoiding Dylan's gaze, he answered, "Yes, it is very real." He returned his gaze to Dylan. "The sun is the only thing that can kill us."

"So, no stake through the heart?" Dylan asked half seriously.

Alec smiled. "No, that would only make you lose consciousness. But as soon as somebody pulls it out, you'd come to."

"What about beheading?"

"Our bones are like steel. They are indestructible. Even if a human could muster up enough strength to cut off your head, they wouldn't be able to sever your spine. And the wound would heal. It would require a lot of blood, but it would heal. You might be incapacitated for a few hours though. We can't lose limbs either, by the way."

Dylan struggled to believe this. "Are you serious?"

Alec's expression remained neutral. "Dead serious. No pun intended."

Some sick part of Dylan's brain wanted to test this. He stared at his hands and wondered if he could try to break a finger to see if Alec was telling the truth…

"Can my bones break?"

Alec rolled his eyes. "Did you not listen to what I just said? Your bones are indestructible. Of course they cannot break."

Dylan slanted his eyes at him. "That is impossible."

Alec laughed. "Well, you'll find out sooner or later."

That sounded vaguely like a threat, but Dylan decided to let it slide. "But the sun is deadly?"

Alec sucked in a sharp breath. "Oh, yes." He paused. "Sunlight is also one of the few things that cause us physical pain. Direct sunlight, that is."

Dylan frowned. "It burns you?"

"Us," Alec corrected him with a smile.

The door opened, and Marie hastily stepped inside. When her eyes met Dylan's, she smiled. It made him uncomfortable. He fidgeted under her gaze. She was happy that she had ruined his life. He had been so wrong about her.

"So?" Alec asked.

"They just got there. The fire got a little out of control… I think it'll be a while till they can put it out. How are we doing over here?" She smiled warmly and took a seat next to Dylan on the bed. He scooted away from her.

Alec answered when Dylan didn't. "We're doing okay." Dylan was far from okay, but he didn't want to show any weakness, so he remained stoically silent. "Just covering the basics."

Marie nodded. "We should go and have some fun."

She beamed at Dylan, who couldn't stop himself from showing his outrage at her suggestion. People had been killed and she wanted to have fun! Unbelievable!

"Like what? We're in the middle of nowhere," Alec stated before Dylan could say anything.

She shrugged. "Everything is new to him. Let's go into the woods and stretch our legs. Now that the wolves are gone, we have the whole place to ourselves."

Alec looked thoughtful. "What about the human hunters?"

She waved him off. "There are hardly any out there anymore since two of them were killed. We can steer clear of them."

She was talking about Sandra Brown's dad and Jake Logan. Anger flared inside Dylan. Two more pointless deaths. It sounded like Marie and Alec had nothing to do with them, but maybe they were just putting on a show to convince him. He knew better than to trust Marie.

"Okay, let's go." Alec stood.

Dylan jumped to his feet. He couldn't wait to get out of this dreary motel room, and a plan was formulating in his head. He grabbed his beat-up sneakers from the bathroom – glad he could still wear some of his own stuff – and slipped them on.

He followed Marie and Alec out into the night and immediately stopped in his tracks. For a second, he wondered how long he had been inside. Had he been in there all night? No, that was impossible. But it was as light as day out. The sky was dark blue, like on a clear summer's day in the mountains. It was strange because there didn't seem to be a light source. Dylan scanned the sky for the sun, but the only thing he could see was the moon, which seemed to shine almost as brightly as the sun.

He noticed specks of light sprinkled on the firmament, each one a slightly different color: blue, pink, red, yellow, and shades he couldn't even name. He had never seen a starry sky like that, even though he had lived there all his life looking at the same sky every night. But the sky hadn't changed – he had.

He swallowed, following Marie and Alec down the stairs, and took in his surroundings. Lamps were on in several rooms, their light illuminating the curtains behind the windows. The motel's parking spots were lit by streetlamps, like earlier in the evening, but Dylan realized he would be able to see just as well without the electric help. In fact, the bright lights looked like flares to him now and obstructed his view.

"It's incredible, isn't it?" Marie was watching him, eyes lit up and beaming.

Dylan didn't know what to say. He agreed but didn't want to admit it.

"That's what the night looks like to us," Alec explained.

"And out here, there is only little light pollution so we can even see the stars. It's different in big cities," Marie continued.

Dylan nodded, wondering what the daytime sky would look like to him now.

"Come on. We shouldn't be standing here for too long." Alec nervously glanced at the motel windows surrounding them. Marie lightly touched Dylan's elbow, nudging him on.

Dylan thought they were heading to their car, but they walked past it and up the slope on the other side of the road straight into the woods.

After having had to avoid the woods for weeks, Dylan felt the hairs on the back of his neck stand up as he was strolling behind Marie and Alec under the conifer canopy. Not that he had frequented the forest much before. He could remember going on a few little hiking trips with his mom when he was little, but those had stopped when he had reached puberty and started preferring the indoors to the outdoors.

But this was nothing like the trips of his childhood. The night should have been pitch black in the forest, but instead, he could make out every branch, every crack in the trees' bark, every needle on the boughs. He could hear tiny paws clicking on wood and a heartbeat that sounded quicker and lighter than a human's. He turned his head this way and that, glancing up into the thicket of the trees looking for the source. And there, about twenty feet up, a tiny squirrel was scurrying up a branch.

He huffed in amazement. He shouldn't have been able to hear its tiny heart from this distance, but he did.

He also noticed that he wasn't feeling cold, even though he should have been. The night air was crisp, and he was wearing nothing but a T-shirt, but he might as well have been taking an afternoon stroll in the sun. It dawned on him how Marie had survived a winter in New Hampshire in nothing but a leather jacket.

They reached a clearing, where a fallen tree had created an open space in the forest. Marie stepped on the thick trunk and smiled mischievously at Dylan.

"Let's play a little game."

"What?" Dylan was still stunned by how new everything felt to him. His senses were overpowering him, and he had trouble processing Marie's words.

Alec leaned against the fallen tree trunk, crossing his arms in front of his chest. "What do you have in mind?" he asked Marie, eyes trained on Dylan.

"I was thinking we could play catch."

Dylan tilted his head. "Are you serious?"

She flashed him a grin. "Of course."

And without further explanation, she ran a lap around the clearing, only she was so fast, she seemed to blur. She completed the lap in under two seconds. Dylan blinked at her in amazement.

Then he remembered Alec disappearing and reappearing in the warehouse, snapping necks, ripping out hearts, and tearing throats open. He gulped, balling his fists to keep his hands from shaking. "How did you do that?" he whispered sharply.

Alec grinned, while Marie said, "It's easy. You just run." She made a limp gesture toward the trees behind Dylan.

Dylan arched an eyebrow. "Just run?"

"Just run." She hopped off the tree trunk. "And we'll try to catch you—"

Before she could finish her sentence, Dylan took off.

This was his chance. He darted through the forest, dodging the trees which came at him at a neck-breaking speed. A part of him was wondering how he didn't hit anything, but it seemed almost too easy to see the obstacles appearing in his path.

He was acutely aware of Marie and Alec chasing him. There was no way to outrun them, but he didn't need to. He only needed to make it far enough...

18

He didn't know exactly where he was, but he knew the approximate location of the old sneakers factory. He jumped over a creek, picking up speed.

As he glanced up to the sky, he could see an enormous cloud of black smoke. He was getting closer. He didn't know how many miles he'd run, but it had to be a couple at least. Never in his life had he run that far. Had he still been human, he would have collapsed from the strain, but in this strange new body, the exertion felt more like a leisurely stroll – or a nap.

Tiny forest creatures hid in fear as he raced through their territory. He picked up speed, realizing that Marie and Alec had noticed where he was headed, knowing they would try to stop him.

But when he broke out of the woods, the scene before him made him freeze: The warehouse, where he had been only a few hours earlier, was nothing but a charred ruin. The fire had been extinguished, but dark clouds of smoke were still emanating from the remains of the building.

Blue lights were flashing in the dark, irritating Dylan's newly sensitive eyes. Police officers and firefighters were swarming the place. Only a few yards away, the chief was squatting in front of a black husk, his back to Dylan.

He gulped. He didn't know what he was going to say or how he would explain what had happened, but he needed to talk to the chief. Determined, he approached the man, who abruptly stood as Dylan came up behind him.

The sudden motion sent a wave of his scent Dylan's way. He inhaled automatically. It smelled like a chicken breast grilled to perfection and … bread. Freshly baked bread rolls. He sniffed and realized those were just the underlying notes of something bigger. A scent so heavenly, he couldn't even place it.

The chief scratched his head, sending more of the delicious smell

Dylan's way, mesmerizing him, pulling him in. He inched closer, all the while breathing in the intoxicating scent. He was hovering right behind the chief. If he reached out, he would be able to touch him.

He suddenly felt his canine teeth pierce his lower lip. He opened his mouth. Now he could taste the smell on his tongue. It taunted him. He had to have a try. He leaned in…

Two ironlike arms pulled him back into the cover of the trees.

"What the hell!?"

"Shush!" Marie held a finger to her mouth, staring at Dylan intently. "They'll hear you," she whispered. Dylan was struggling against Alec's embrace, but the vampire didn't loosen his grip.

"You can't just bite the chief of police in front of a dozen witnesses," Alec whispered in Dylan's ear.

Dylan froze. Had he been about to bite the chief?

Alec let go of him. Dylan spun around so he could face both of them, pressing his lips together in trepidation. And again, something sharp pierced his lip.

He ran his tongue over his teeth. When he reached his left canine tooth, he paused. It was significantly longer and sharper than usual. He prodded it with his finger, and the sharp tip cut into his flesh. Startled, he snatched his hand away.

Alec and Marie grinned at him. Embarrassed and angry, Dylan turned his back on them.

"They come out when you're about to feed or when you're very hungry or when you're aroused," Alec explained.

"Sometimes also when you're angry," Marie added. "Your irises turn red, too. It's a nuisance, but it is what it is."

Dylan wanted to retch. He was glad he couldn't see his own face right then, but he squeezed his eyes shut anyway.

The touch of a hand made him jerk. Marie pulled him by the shoulder, forcing him to face her. But he avoided her gaze anyway.

"It's okay, Dylan. It's perfectly natural. Don't beat yourself up. Being around humans is really hard in the beginning."

Dylan shook his head vigorously. Nothing about this was natural. He was about to shout that in Marie's face, when a voice interrupted his thoughts.

"We've got five bodies."

The three vampires froze in their hiding place and listened. The voice sounded like it belonged to a young man.

"All burned beyond recognition. Maybe we can pull dental records, but it's not looking good..."

"All right. Thanks, Turner," Chief Mangold answered.

Dylan had no problem seeing every detail from where he stood. They had lined the bodies up on the ground. Their flesh had been charred black, fat tissue had melted off, and bones were gleaming white and protruding from the black mass. It was hard to tell that the heaps on the ground had been human once. He felt sick.

He swallowed hard. Not even Fletcher, Ricky, and Amy had deserved this, much less Molly. But there they were. And he was standing there, hiding in the woods, right next to their killers.

He balled his fists. "What did it accomplish?" he hissed.

"What?" Marie asked behind him, not seeming to understand his question.

He whipped around. "You could at least have given them a dignified death, but they're unrecognizable. What about their parents?" He wanted to say more, but he choked.

He thought of Martin having to identify Molly, seeing nothing but charred human remains. And then his own mother... He had to go see her so she'd know he was still alive to spare her that experience.

"They're dead. They don't care. And we had to do something to hide the cause of death," Alec grumbled, shrugging. "They started it."

Dylan almost exploded with rage. "What do you mean, they started it!?" he shouted way too loudly.

Marie held out her hands, palms down, in a calming gesture, shushing Dylan again. But he didn't care. He wanted the cops to find them.

"They wouldn't have gone after you if you hadn't been killing people left and right!"

Alec yanked him by the arm, and the next thing he knew, they were half a mile deep into the woods.

"What the hell are you talking about?" Alec was gripping Dylan's arms and shaking him. If Dylan had been human, Alec's vise-like grip would have cut off his blood circulation and left ugly purple marks, but to his immortal body it felt more like an inconvenience. No pain, but he would much rather be free to move.

"We didn't kill anyone, Dylan." Marie loosened Alec's hold on him, squeezing herself between the two males, her back to Alec.

Dylan crossed his arms in front of his chest, waiting for an explanation. This should be good.

"It was the wolves." Marie's gray eyes were big and round, her expression pleading with him to believe her.

"How do I know you're not lying to me?"

She shook her head, pressing her lips together.

"You ran into one of them!" Alec exclaimed, rubbing his temples. Marie gave him a look. "What?" He threw up his arms. "He's being an idiot."

"Hey!" Dylan shouted while Marie said, "He has been through a lot."

Alec hissed and shook his head. "You've been nothing but kind to him since you guys met. Then you get attacked, and somehow, we're the bad guys for fighting back?"

"Alec…"

Alec inhaled loudly and pinched the bridge of his nose, closing his eyes for a few seconds. "All right." He went on, much calmer. "I'll take a step back." He turned away, ripping a bough from a nearby tree that looked much too sturdy to be broken off the trunk by hand, and proceeded to tear off the twigs that had grown from it.

Dylan was unimpressed. He was still furious at the two of them and didn't believe a word they were saying.

Marie sighed, turning her attention from Alec to Dylan. She folded her hands as if in prayer. "You saw one of them, Dylan. The one that chased us in the car. Remember?"

How could he forget? That encounter had seared itself into his memory. But had it even been real? "How do I know that wasn't a hallucination?"

Marie looked taken aback. Her brow furrowed. "What makes you think that?"

"Molly, she…" He hesitated. She had been right about everything else, but what if she had gotten that one wrong?

Marie's face darkened. "That witch didn't know anything."

"She knew plenty!" Dylan uncrossed his arms, balling his hands into fists at his sides. "She knew what you were. She tried to warn me—" *But I didn't listen.* Her death was his fault. At least partly. But he couldn't handle that guilt right now. It was easier to be mad at the two vampires in front of him. The ones who had murdered four people in cold blood. "She knew you were responsible for the murders."

Alec shook his head again, proceeding to shave the bark off the bough. Marie stared at Dylan with knitted brows, her eyes betraying her anger.

"It wasn't us, Dylan," she said calmly. "It was a pack of werewolves we had been trailing since Pennsylvania."

Dylan scoffed.

"It's true," she said. "Alec and I were hunting a pack of werewolves, trailing them all the way north. When we stopped for gas in your town, I noticed that you had the aura, so I wanted to make sure they wouldn't hurt you."

"Why would they hurt me?"

"Because they can sniff the aura out. They would have known you were a potential immortal and killed you."

"But why?" Dylan was confused. What had he ever done to provoke a werewolf?

"Because they were created to hunt us." He was going to ask another question, but she stopped him. "It's a long story. Just know that they are dangerous to immortals. Drinking their blood will make you sick for weeks, and their bite is venomous. In high doses, it can incapacitate us, making it possible for them to leave us baking in the sun."

Dylan's mind was racing. If this was true, he had been in more danger than he had thought. But wouldn't Molly have known about the werewolves?

"Of course, killing a mere mortal is a piece of cake to them," Marie added. "You saw what they did to those humans."

A memory of Stacy Yelander's torn and scratched up body flashed in his mind, her eyes staring up in horror. "So you're telling me the murders were committed by men who can turn into wolves?"

"And women, yes. You saw what that girl in your driveway looked like. We don't kill like that." She had a point. Molly and the others hadn't been scratched up, and none of the bodies had been drained of blood. And wouldn't that have been the whole purpose of killing them?

A memory of the mad chasing wolf flashed in his mind. He was inclined to believe Marie, but it didn't change anything: They were still killers and they had turned him against his will.

"They had sniffed you out the night we arrived. They knew we were going to protect you, so they played a little game of cat and mouse, going after humans and then going back into hiding in the woods. It took us a while to find them, and when we did, we couldn't eliminate all of them at once."

"You were protecting me by driving me home every night."

"And by keeping watch over your house." She nodded gravely. "If they had gotten to you…"

"Wait!" He held up a hand. A pair of gleaming eyes between the trees had popped into his head. "It was you I saw that morning. Your eyes were reflecting the light like a cat's."

His blood ran cold. Finding out he had been watched was a shock. Up until then he had believed he had only imagined the gleaming eyes.

"Yes, our eyes do that…" She trailed off. "Anyway, during this time I got to know you and I liked you." She smiled weakly. "I still do, Dylan." He didn't say anything, just stared at her coldly.

"We tend to turn every mortal with an aura we meet, but you were so young… I was planning to enroll in the same college as you, keep an eye on you, and then turn you when you were a little older."

"And you never thought to ask me if I even wanted this?" he interrupted angrily. It was his life. Why didn't they let him choose his own path?

Her expression turned serious. "You can't choose what you don't know."

"That's bullshit. People do it all the time. Otherwise, nobody would ever advance in life!"

"This is different. An uninformed mortal would never choose this life, but it *is* better. You only realize that once you live it though."

He was lost for words. How could she believe that?

"You were born for this," she said. "We all were. You were never human, Dylan."

He realized there was no point arguing that with her. Her zeal rivaled that of a cult member. So he changed tactics. "Why didn't you just tell me?"

She tilted her head.

"I asked you outright if you knew about Molly and what you knew about the wolf. And you lied to me."

"Would you have believed me?" she asked. Her gray eyes softened with sympathy. It made Dylan even angrier.

He couldn't say for sure he would have believed her at that point, but she could have convinced him. They could have avoided this whole mess. And Molly would still be alive.

"You could have convinced me."

She shrugged. "I didn't want to scare you. I thought it was for the best if you didn't know that the wolves were coming for you."

Dylan scoffed. "Well, look how that turned out."

"Oh, come on! Don't pretend like you would have been okay with her being immortal!" Alec hurled what was left of the bough past Dylan like a spear. Dylan didn't flinch. Alec clearly wanted to intimidate him, but he wasn't going to let him.

The truth was he didn't know if he would have been okay with it. He might have been if she had been honest with him. He shrugged. "Guess we'll never know."

He had had enough. Without another word, he turned on his heel and stalked off. Or tried to stalk off. After three steps, Alec appeared in his path, blocking the way.

"Where do you think you're going?" he asked, glaring at Dylan.

"Home." Dylan stepped around Alec, determined not to be held back.

Alec grabbed him by the arm. "Oh, no, you're not."

Dylan struggled to shrug him off. "Watch me!" He wasn't going to be pushed around anymore. All the pent-up anger came to a boil. He shoved Alec hard with his free hand. So hard that the vampire stumbled backward. But he didn't loosen his grip on Dylan, yanking the younger immortal with him.

Dylan lost his balance and crashed into Alec, who took Dylan's move as an attack and finally let go of him. But before Dylan could run off, Alec jumped him and pinned him to the hard ground.

The younger immortal struggled, limbs flailing. "Let me go!"

Alec fixed him with an ice-cold stare, his hands pressing down on Dylan's shoulders. His brown eyes were boring into Dylan's, willing him to stop fighting, which only made him fight harder.

"Dylan, stop!" Marie shouted. "You can't see your mom right now."

"Remember what you almost did to the chief! Do you want that to be her?" Alec spat.

That made Dylan pause. He imagined his mom. Her face was tear-streaked but she was elated to see him. She threw her arms around him, hugging him tightly like she never wanted to let him go. He hugged her back and buried his face in her neck. When he inhaled, the sweet scent of her blood overpowered him, filling every cell of his body with the need to drink.

He shuddered, squeezing his eyes shut, and stopped fighting. Alec finally stood, reaching out a hand to Dylan. He didn't take it. He scrambled to his feet, trying to banish the images from his mind.

Avoiding Alec's gaze, he wiped off the dirt from his borrowed clothes.

"You don't want to kill her, do you?" Alec asked coldly.

"I would never hurt her," Dylan assured himself.

But the truth was he didn't know what he might do. He'd had no intention of hurting the chief, yet the policeman's blood had called out to him in a way that had stripped him of any sense of himself, any shred of decency – of humanity.

Deep down, he knew there was nothing he had wanted more than to sink his teeth into the man's flesh and drain him of all his sweet-smelling blood. He closed his eyes and hung his head in horror and disgust.

"It's okay, Dylan. It will get easier. You'll be able to be around humans again very soon." Marie patted his back, and this time he let her.

But he didn't believe her words. A feeling of hopelessness spread from the pit of his stomach out into his entire body, and his heart clenched with sadness. For the first time, he envied Molly. He wanted to die, too.

19

"So, what's going to happen now?" Dylan asked as they got back to the motel parking lot. His head was still spinning with all the new information about vampires and werewolves, and all of it still seemed too fantastical to be true. But he himself was living proof that it was real – not to mention the two vampires at his side.

"Now, you're going to sleep. You've been up all day and it's late," Alec said.

Dylan didn't know what time it was – he had left his watch with the rest of his old clothes – but he guessed it was around three o'clock in the morning. He didn't feel tired though. Not with the bright sky suggesting to his brain that it was daytime. And besides, who was Alec to decide when his bedtime was? He wasn't a kid.

"You can't just send me to bed. I'm a full-grown adult."

Marie and Alec exchanged a look that Dylan couldn't interpret, and Marie said, "It's just that your body is still transitioning. Every cell in your body is reacting to the immortal blood you ingested."

Dylan scoffed. The blood he was force fed would be putting it more accurately.

"New immortals need a lot of rest. That's just how it is." She stepped in his path, seeking eye contact. He could see her exasperation in the crease between her eyebrows.

He smiled internally, every bit of her discomfort making him feel vindicated. He crossed his arms in front of his chest defiantly.

Alec sighed, stepping next to Marie. Now they were forming a strangely parental unit, both sternly glaring at him, making it known that they wouldn't take no for an answer. Dylan grinned, wanting to provoke them further, but movement in one of the motel rooms caught his eye.

A blond bearded man had opened the curtain of his window and was looking curiously at the trio. Only he wasn't a man. Dylan could clearly see his crimson irises. His grin washed off his face as the vampire slowly started to smile, flashing Dylan his fangs.

"What are you staring at?" Alec asked and turned around, following Dylan's gaze.

But the strange vampire had already zipped the curtain back into place, disappearing from view.

"Nothing…" Dylan answered absent-mindedly. If Marie and Alec didn't know that there was another vampire in the motel, he wanted to keep it this way. Maybe he could talk to this guy and get some help…

But what if the other vampire was dangerous? Then again, what could he possibly do to Dylan that hadn't already been done to him? He had nothing left to lose.

Caution was advised here though. He needed to think about his next moves. And for now, anything he knew that Marie and Alec didn't seemed like an advantage.

"Okay, got it." He memorized the vampire's room number. "Let's go then." Dylan quickly moved around his wannabe-parents and marched off toward their room, trying to lead them away from the other immortal.

"What time is it?" he asked as he was waiting by the door for Alec to unlock it.

"It's four thirty in the morning," Alec grumbled as he turned the key.

"The sun will come up in about an hour and a half."

"You need to get used to sleeping during the day," Marie added from behind him.

The whole sunlight thing still sounded unbelievable to Dylan. How could something most organisms on Earth needed to survive be deadly to him?

"You can take the bed," Alec offered with a nod toward it.

"And where are you going to sleep?" Dylan eyed the bed, puzzled. The sheets had been rumpled earlier before Marie had hastily made it. She and Alec had obviously slept and probably also done other things in it. He hated that the thought of them hooking up aroused him a little.

"The bed is big enough for two and then there's the couch." Marie gestured to the piece of furniture by the window.

Dylan couldn't help but feel claustrophobic. He had never spent this much time with people who weren't his mom. Usually, he was by himself. He had never minded being alone, he was used to it. But now he was crammed into close quarters with two people he barely knew.

He desperately wanted to have a moment to himself. No, not a moment, an hour – at least! He needed time to think, to process, to grieve.

Only, there was no way he would get that. He realized he couldn't even have a bathroom break because his body didn't need to use the bathroom anymore.

Deflated, he plunked down on the bed.

"Tomorrow night, we'll get you some new clothes." Marie's tone was encouraging, like a mother promising her kid ice cream after a visit to the doctor's office. Dylan shook his head in denial. All of this was absurd.

"I need a shower," she said to Alec. Her tone sounded somewhat suggestive, her raised eyebrows adding a *care to join?*

Alec smirked, but his eyes darted to Dylan and his expression soured. "Guess I'll go after you…"

Marie sighed, grabbed some fresh clothes from the closet, and disappeared into the bathroom. Alec was watching her walk away from him, sighing deeply when the door closed behind her. Turning to Dylan, his expression went from longing to disdainful.

"I can tell you're dead-tired. Go to sleep."

There was no use arguing, and he did feel tired now that he was sitting on the soft mattress. He slipped his sneakers off and scooted back until he could lie flat on the bed.

Staring up at the ceiling, he counted the cracks in the plaster, listening to the splashing of the water on the ceramic tub in the bathroom. The water made him think of Molly, and he had to fight back tears.

Alec moved over to the couch. Dylan could see from the corner of his eye that the vampire had picked up a book. Disgusted, he turned on his side, toward the closet doors, facing away from the immortal.

He still felt angry, helpless, betrayed, confused but also strangely numb. Exhaustion enveloped him like a heavy blanket, making his head droop and his eyelids fall shut.

* * *

His limbs felt leaden. He could barely move. He wanted to rise… He needed to rise. He tried to lift his head but couldn't.

A wheezing sound drew his gaze to the side. The candlelight created dancing shadows on the walls, scarcely illuminating the row of sick immobile monks. Brother Ignatius lay next to him on the stone floor, the straw underneath him as filthy as his habit. Ignatius coughed and attempted to speak, but no words left his lips.

He tried to reach out to his brother, but his hand didn't budge. He tried again, focusing all his willpower on the one simple motion of lifting his hand off the floor and swiping it a mere ten inches to the side to touch his brother's. Slowly his hand obeyed. It inched sideways, moving into his sightline. He registered without emotion that it had turned a deadly shade of purple. Not long now. *If only the pain would end! His entire body ached.*

He had finally reached his brother's hand, but Ignatius had stopped wheezing. As he touched him, the latter didn't react. Ignatius's unblinking eyes were fixed on the ceiling. With a start, he realized his brother had stopped breathing altogether. He was dead.

The shock of that realization caused a jolt of energy. He needed to go to the chapel. He couldn't die here like this. He hadn't received the sacrament yet.

None of the healthy brothers would touch him now. If there were even any left... But he had to get inside the house of the Lord at least. Surely that would count for something.

He crossed himself sloppily and mumbled a Bible verse for his deceased brother. He was unable to stand, let alone walk. Everything felt too heavy. But he could crawl. So he rolled onto his belly and dragged himself along the flagstone floor. The door to the main corridor was ajar. From there, it wasn't far to the chapel. He had made the journey a thousand times before. Since he had been a novice. Through the corridor, out the main door, around the building, into the chapel. But now that short walk felt as arduous as a pilgrimage to Rome.

But he had to succeed. This was the last journey he would ever make. So he crawled.

The corridor was housing about twenty refugees from the north. All of them were sleeping, huddled together in small groups, trying to keep warm.

It was a cold winter's night after all. Not that he could feel it. He felt like he was being burnt from the inside. The disease laying siege to his body.

He had almost reached the heavy wooden doors – and like magic they opened before him. Not entirely, just wide enough for a woman to poke her head through and peer inside. Was he hallucinating? Was he asleep and only dreaming?

The woman spotted him on the floor and paused. Silently, she stepped into the hallway. He could only see her silhouette in the dark, but as she stepped closer, he could tell she was wearing a simple dress and cloak. She knelt in front of him and – with surprising force – turned him around onto his back and let his head rest in her lap. He wanted to protest but couldn't muster the strength. Her long fingers caressed his cheeks, and she bent down low. Her face was so close to his now that he could see her features in the moonlight streaming in through the windows. She was the most beautiful woman he had ever laid eyes on. So beautiful in fact that he immediately chastised himself for his impure thoughts. Her skin was like porcelain, her eyes big and round, and her lips full. He quickly averted his gaze.

"You poor thing," she whispered. She looked around. "I'll save you." He wanted to tell her to go away, to save herself while she could, but he couldn't form the words. His mouth was dry, his tongue swollen.

The woman rose, picking him up like a child. Stunned at her strength, he wondered again whether he was dreaming. Perhaps he had already died, and this angel would carry him to heaven. But that didn't explain why he was still in so much pain.

She carried him outside, around the building and into the chapel, as if he weighed nothing. Candles were ablaze in the house of God. Now he could see his angel's light red hair and hazel eyes. Her nose was long and straight and her jaw set. It gave her a cruel look, but it didn't take away from her beauty. He squeezed his eyes shut, sending a silent prayer to God to forgive him for his sins.

She laid him down on the stone floor of the center aisle and caressed his cheeks again. "It's all right…"

He opened his eyes tentatively. She knelt beside him, smiling down at him. But there was no warmth in her smile. On the contrary, it was deeply unsettling. He wanted to recoil but had lost all feeling in his body.

Panicking, he watched her eyes turn a bright crimson. She opened her mouth, revealing a set of enlarged canines, and proceeded to bite her own wrist. His heart was pounding in fear.

This wasn't an angel; this was the devil incarnate!

He started praying. His mouth had stopped working but his mind was still sharp. I will not succumb to thee. I am a man of God. Credo in Deum, patrem omnipotentem, Creatorem caeli et terrae. *Her wrist was dripping with blood. To his horror, she shoved it into his mouth, forcing the liquid inside. He wanted to fight her off, but he was still unable to move. He couldn't even lift his hand to swat hers away. He tried to turn his head, but he was too weak and her grip too strong. His throat was too swollen for him to even swallow. Her blood trickled down his throat, making him gag. His eyes teared up. He kept praying, renouncing the devil, pledging his loyalty to God.* Credo in Deum, patrem omnipotentem, Creatorem caeli et terrae. *Finally, she let go of him.*

He had assumed the pain he had experienced in the previous few days was all a human being could bear, but now he realized he had been sorely mistaken. The pain he felt in every fiber of his being in this moment was ten times worse than anything he had experienced before. It was crushing him, suffocating him. His bones threatened to snap under the immense pressure of this agony.

And then it all stopped. Even the pain from the disease was gone.

The relief made him almost giddy. Was he dead now? Had the suffering finally ceased? A wave of joy washed over him. His body was singing with pleasure. He couldn't recall ever feeling so joyful in his entire life.

He could feel his body again, and his limbs obeyed his commands. He examined his hand which was no longer purple but had gained back its normal pinkish tone. Surely he had to be dead. But he still lay on the stone floor of the chapel, gazing up at the high vaulted ceiling.

"It's nothing short of miraculous. Every time."

His head jerked to where the voice had come from. The devil was still there, sitting on the floor beside him, her back leaning against a pew, ankles crossed. She smiled at him knowingly. He scrambled to his feet, trying to get away from her.

It had been days since the last time he had been upright. He had been dying, but now he felt like he could run a mile.

She tilted her head, frowning. "You must be hungry." She jumped to her feet. "Come."

How had she even been able to enter the house of God? She had to be a strong devil indeed. His eyes darted left and right, looking for a weapon to defend himself with. But the only useful thing he spotted was the basin of holy water on the opposite side of the nave. He dashed to it in a flash and grabbed the sprinkler, pivoting and splashing the devil woman with holy water. But she merely blinked in irritation and wiped a few drops from her face.

"Oh, dear. No need to douse me with that sacred water of yours." She stepped toward him.

Terrified, he took a step back. How could she resist the power of God? "Begone, devil!" he shouted, crossing himself.

She scoffed. "I just saved your life, and you treat me thus?" Before he could react, she closed the distance between them and dragged him by the arm to the chapel doors. He grunted, trying to fight her off, but her grip was ironclad. Only the devil would be able to exert such force...

She manhandled him back into the main building's corridor, closing the heavy doors behind her. A delicious smell he couldn't place entranced him momentarily. So much so that he stopped fighting. She let go of his arm and walked over to the first group of sleeping people, cowering by the wall. It was a man and two women, all dressed in rags. He had no idea how far they had traveled to escape the horrors of the war. All of them were haggard and filthy, but the exquisite smell seemed to emanate from them nonetheless. One of the women stirred in her sleep. Without warning, the devil grabbed her by the shoulders and dragged her to her feet. The woman gasped and was about to scream, but the devil held a hand over her mouth and bit her neck.

He was hypnotized by the display. Something deeply sensual about the gesture awoke feelings inside him he had kept buried for years. And the delectable smell crashed into him tenfold. The devil shoved the woman at him so forcefully that he didn't have a choice but to catch her lest she fall. She stared at him with wide eyes, terror written all over her face. Blood was oozing from the wound on her neck. He inhaled deeply. That's where the smell came from. Mesmerized, he lowered his head. He needed to get closer, he needed a taste...

His lips found her skin, and the wetness of her blood bathed his tongue. The taste almost sent him into a frenzy. This was what he imagined the blood of Christ to taste like: salvation. He drank greedily, sucking every last drop of blood from the woman till she went limp in his arms. When she took her final breath, a feeling of euphoria washed over him, sending him straight to paradise. He had never felt so alive.

He dropped the woman and moved on to the man the devil was presenting to him. He seemed dazed, as if in a trance. He could hear the man's heartbeat drumming steadily, the rhythm drawing him in, inviting him to take a sip. And he was eager to oblige. He felt his canine teeth extend with his anticipation. They cut through the man's skin with ease, freeing the scrumptious liquid underneath.

The body emptied too quickly. So he moved on to the next one. He kept feeding, draining one person after another, not caring if they screamed or begged for their lives. He only cared for the blood flowing through their veins.

But once all the refugees had been drained, all the heartbeats silenced, the spell the blood had cast on him was broken.

He stared at his bloodied hands in horror. His habit was drenched in blood. He looked around at the dead bodies piling up around the corridor. All of them had sought refuge within these walls, and he had murdered them.

Suddenly he was overcome with despair. It made him whimper. Tears filled his eyes, clouding his vision. He cried for the innocent children of God he had killed. He was supposed to guide and comfort them, yet he had been their demise. How could he have done something so vile?

"What have you done to me?" he murmured, sobbing.

The devil laughed at him. Her crimson eyes were glistening derisively. She slowly and delightfully ran her tongue over her teeth, reveling in his despair. "I've set you free."

Dylan awoke with a start. He felt disoriented for a second. His gaze frantically darted around the room, but it was only when he saw Marie peacefully sleeping next to him in bed that it all came rushing back.

The warehouse. The murders. The fire. The vampires.

He rubbed his face and stared at his unfamiliar hands. He had been turned into a vampire. His mom most likely thought he was dead. He needed to get home and set things right.

Determined, he tossed the bed sheets aside and sat up. That's when he realized he didn't remember getting under the covers… Alec or Marie must have tucked him in. The thought of them hovering over his sleeping body made his skin crawl.

He glanced around the room, trying to get his bearings. Marie was lying on her side, facing Dylan. She wore a black T-shirt that was way too big for her – probably one of Alec's – but her legs were bare. Dylan's gaze lingered on her flawless skin a little too long. She was sleeping soundly, her left shoulder rising and falling with her breath.

He tore his gaze away from her and found Alec dozing on the couch.

It was too small for the vampire. He was curled into a ball, facing the backrest. Alec wasn't wearing a shirt and the rhythmic movement of his toned bare back mesmerized Dylan in a way that made him blush.

He had no idea what time it was or how long he had slept. No light seeped through the curtains, but Dylan was pretty sure it was daytime. Maybe he could catch his mom at the grocery store. Unless she wasn't working that day after everything that had happened… He would try the house first and then go to the store.

Nodding to himself, he slipped on his sneakers, trying to be as quiet as possible, and tiptoed to the door. He gingerly turned the key in the lock and unhooked the chain. And then, with one swift motion, he opened the door and bathed himself in blindingly bright sunlight.

He shielded his eyes reflexively against the stinging light. It felt like he had been looking through a telescope straight into the sun. But once the initial shock had worn off, he realized the exposed skin of his arms and face had started to sizzle and sting. The pain grew more intense by the second, paralyzing him on the spot. He screamed in agony, feeling his skin steadily melt off his flesh and his flesh slowly melt off his bones. The searing pain went straight down into his core, like he was being skinned with steel wool. It was worse than the agony he had felt when he had been turned. He wanted to move away from the light so badly, but the sun mercilessly held him in place.

The realization hit him that he was going to die if he didn't move. He screamed louder. He didn't want to go out like this.

He had only just turned eighteen. His entire life lay ahead of him!

But then he thought of Molly and realized with a pang that he might deserve this. He wondered if he would see her again on the other side and if she'd be mad at him when he did.

20

The door banged shut with a loud thwack. The shadow enveloping him felt like a cooling balm on his melted flesh. But the pain lingered. He sank to the floor, still blinded by the sunlight.

"What were you thinking!?" Alec sounded panicked.

"I…" Dylan couldn't form a coherent sentence through the burning pain on his face, neck, and arms. He felt like his hair had melted into his skull. He blinked obsessively, trying to banish the lights dancing before his eyes, but his vision didn't clear.

Something hard and smooth touched Dylan's mouth.

"Drink," Marie commanded. "It'll heal you."

Dylan took a whiff. The metallic smell of blood hit his nostrils and then a soft note of something like vanilla. His lips had burnt off, so Marie helped him gobble up the delicious liquid. With every sip the burning sensation seemed to ease. Soon his vision cleared.

Alec hastily handed him another blood bag. His expression was serious. "Here. Can you hold it?" He closed Dylan's fingers around it. They were charred; his nails had melted off completely.

Dylan tried to grip the blood bag but couldn't. "No…"

Alec kept holding the blood bag and helped Dylan empty that second portion. He felt his flesh regenerating, a tingling sensation, like tiny air bubbles under water dancing on his skin – only he didn't have any skin. Marie grabbed another blood bag from the mini fridge. This time, Dylan took it from her and chugged it.

His skin reappeared in blossoms that grew steadily and melded into each other till it was smooth and flawless. He marveled at his hands that had been charred to the bone a moment ago and were now completely restored.

"Here, have another one for good measure." Marie handed him another blood bag. Dylan didn't protest. He finished serving number four just as quickly as the ones before.

He touched his face to make sure it had healed, even though he could clearly feel that it had. He looked at Alec and Marie in wonder. The vampires were frowning at him, the crease in Alec's brow so deep it seemed to leave a permanent imprint.

"Were you trying to kill yourself?" Alec asked in a subdued voice, almost a whisper.

Dylan was taken aback. "No. It was an accident. I wanted to—" He stopped, unwilling to reveal his plan. "I wanted to go outside, and I had forgotten about the sun…"

If he was honest, he hadn't entirely believed the part about sunlight being deadly. It had been too difficult to fathom that something as natural and omnipresent as the sun could be lethal to him. But now he had proof that it was. His stomach tied itself into a knot. That meant he would never be able to go outside during the daytime again.

Marie and Alec exchanged worried glances. She fixed Dylan with a stern look. "Don't ever do that again." She stared at him without blinking, waiting for an answer.

Dylan gulped. "No… No, of course not." He didn't want to die.

Seemingly satisfied with his answer, she got up, swiping the empty blood bags as she went, and tossed them in the trash can next to the TV. She rubbed her temples, closing her eyes and drawing in a deep breath.

As Dylan was watching her, he realized Molly had planned to burn

Marie alive, and now that he knew what that felt like, he shuddered at the thought. He hated that he felt for Marie, but he didn't wish a death like that on anyone.

But then again, they were immortal. How long had they been alive? How many people had they killed? Maybe they did deserve a death like that.

He turned to Alec, who was still eyeing him suspiciously. "How old are you guys?" His voice had dropped to a whisper. He was somehow scared of the answer.

Before Alec could respond, Marie said, "I'm twenty and Alec is twenty-four." Dylan raised an eyebrow at her, but she shrugged. "We're forever frozen at the age we were turned."

Alec smirked. "I guess you'd like to know when we were born, right?"

Dylan nodded.

Alec stood, reaching a hand out to Dylan, helping him up. "I was born in 1608, and Marie was born in 1695," he stated matter-of-factly like it wasn't a big deal.

Dylan's heartbeat picked up speed. He tried to do the math in his head. "So, you're three hundred and seventy-seven years old?"

"I've been alive for three hundred and seventy-seven years, but I am forever going to be twenty-four years old."

Dylan tried to wrap his head around that, but he couldn't. "How have you survived over three hundred and fifty years of night?"

Alec stretched his arms over his head, showing off his torso. His upper body was as defined as Dylan's new body. In fact, if their heads were cut off, they would be indistinguishable. Was his body just some generic cookie cutter version of a handsome man? That made Dylan feel even worse.

Alec grabbed last night's shirt off the floor and put it on. "You've seen what the night looks like to us, or have you already forgotten?"

Dylan remembered the strangely dark blue sky from the previous night. "Yes, it looks like daytime but still. Don't you ever want to take a stroll in the sun? Lie on the beach?"

Alec flinched. "No." His face distorted to a mask of pain as if he were being burned by the sun right that second. Then Marie was by his side, rubbing his arm soothingly. He immediately calmed down. He closed his eyes and his face relaxed.

Marie seemed to contemplate her next words. "The sun is our worst enemy, Dylan."

Alec nodded, his eyes snapping open again. "Remember what the sun felt like. How it burnt you alive. Remember the pain." His gaze bore intensely into Dylan's. "That'll prevent you from making that mistake again."

Marie squeezed Alec's arm. "Will you two be all right? I need to take another shower. I still feel dirty from that warehouse…"

Alec nodded and they kissed.

"Thank you for saving me," Dylan mumbled as she turned to the bathroom. Granted, he had only gotten into this position because they had turned him into a vampire, but he still felt grateful to them for saving him from the fiery sun. He didn't want to die.

Marie smiled sweetly. "You're welcome. Just don't do it again."

Dylan shook his head. "I won't."

When they were alone, Alec asked, "Have you had any weird dreams?"

Dylan's ears perked up. Now that Alec mentioned it, he did remember the strange dream about the monk. "Yes. As a matter of fact, I have."

Alec half smiled. "Okay. Let's talk."

He indicated for Dylan to sit on the bed and took a seat on the couch. Dylan obliged, curious where this was going.

"I forgot to warn you last night. My blood is still coursing through your veins, your body is still adjusting. It takes two, sometimes three, nights. During this time, my blood will cause you to see some of my memories in your dreams."

Dylan tried to process that information. His blank expression prompted the vampire to continue to explain. "You'll see events from my past through my eyes. I can't control which ones you'll see, but it's usually important ones. Events that shaped my life in some way."

Dylan thought back to his dream, trying to remember the details. He had been inside a monastery, before the invention of electricity or heaters. He had been sick and … a monk? That couldn't be right. If that was a memory of Alec's… That guy could not have been a monk.

Alec cleared his throat. "So, what did you see?" It seemed like he was trying to hide the anticipation in his voice.

"I-I'm not sure…" He thought about what to say. If he started talking about monks, Alec would laugh at him. He was sure of that. Then he remembered the woman. Undoubtedly a vampire. She had turned him…

"I saw a beautiful woman with light red hair. And she turned you?"

Alec's eyes glinted knowingly. "Ah. You saw Arianne." A weak smile spread across his lips. "The night I was turned."

Dylan nodded tentatively. "I think so? It was all very hazy…"

"Of course it was. I was dying from the plague, and she saved my life."

"What?"

Alec pursed his lips, thinking. "I guess I'll have to elaborate a little." He leaned back and crossed his legs. "As you now know, I was born in 1608."

Dylan nodded, curiosity making him forget his hatred for Alec momentarily.

"I'm originally from what is now south Germany. Back then, it was the duchy of Bavaria. My family—"

"Hold on. You don't sound German at all."

Alec didn't look happy about being interrupted. He scowled at Dylan. "No, because I've lived in the United States for eighty-five years."

Dylan mulled this over. He thought about some of the older people in Berlin, who still had accents even though they had immigrated decades ago.

Alec seemed to be reading the skepticism off Dylan's face. "Our memories are impeccable, and our heightened senses allow us to accurately hear and reproduce sounds. Humans lose this ability when they reach puberty, but we keep it all our lives. That allows us to learn as many languages as we want with ease and without a foreign accent."

That explained his generic voice. And Marie's.

"May I go on now?" Alec asked pointedly.

Dylan nodded.

"My family was part of the aristocracy of the time. My father was a baron, a wealthy landowner, who was blessed with many children. I was his third son, so I wasn't going to inherit the title or any of the land. Instead, I was bred to become a cleric."

Dylan's eyebrows shot up in surprise, but he didn't interrupt.

"The reformation and the resulting rift in the church still had tremendous effects on the region, and my father – a devout Catholic – wanted to gain points to get into heaven." He grinned. "So I was to become a monk."

"Was that something you wanted?" Dylan asked skeptically. He still couldn't imagine Alec as a monk.

Alec tilted his head. He looked puzzled. "What do you mean?"

"I mean was that something you envisioned for your future? Or would you rather have done something else?"

Understanding washed over his face. "Times were different then.

It was my destiny. There was no other path I could have taken. Of course I embraced it." He paused. "This might seem strange to you considering all the possibilities young people have these days. But back then, nobody had a choice. You became what you were born to be." He got a faraway look in his eyes. "And I was very pious. My faith was everything to me. It gave me solace in a time of war, you see? From the time I was ten, a terrible war ravaged central Europe."

"The Thirty Years' War," Dylan murmured.

Alec paused in surprise. "Yes."

"I read a book about it," Dylan explained. He thought back to the book he had eventually borrowed from the library a couple of weeks ago. It seemed like a different lifetime now. "From what I read it was extremely hard on the population."

Alec scoffed. "That's one way to put it. The enemy troops raided the villages, leaving nothing behind but bare land. And they brought disease, including several outbreaks of plague. Those who hadn't been killed by the enemy or driven from their homes soon perished from disease. Very few survived."

Dylan felt lucky that he had been born in the twentieth century. He couldn't imagine anything like that.

"The monastery I lived in became a stronghold. We took in refugees from the entire region and tended to the sick. But in the winter of 1632, it looked like our side was going to lose. Things were dire. The monastery was overrun with refugees. And then one of them showed signs of plague." He paused, clearly caught up in a memory. "It spread fast. People were dropping like flies. But more refugees came in by the day. We had our hands full. I was caring for a sick brother when I noticed the first bump on my neck. That was early one morning. By evening, I ran a high fever and my entire body ached."

"I think that's where the dream started..."

Alec nodded. "I see. Then you saw how Arianne found me and

turned me and then lured me into killing roughly twenty people." His tone was matter of fact, detached from the terror he had felt during the experience.

Dylan frowned.

"What?" Alec asked.

"It's just … you seemed so different."

"It's been three hundred and fifty years. I've evolved." He paused. "Let me give you this piece of advice: Accept what you are. Don't fight it. I spent way too long fighting against my nature, and I paid dearly for it in the end."

"So, what? I'm just supposed to go out and joyfully murder people?"

Alec sighed. "No. You may have noticed that we stopped you from killing the chief last night. Times have changed." He pressed his lips together. There was a finality to it. Dylan felt like it marked the end of the conversation. He thought about the dream again.

"What happened to her? To Arianne?"

"Right now she's living in Madrid with her mate."

It should have been obvious, but hearing that the woman Alec had met three and a half centuries ago was alive and well made Dylan's brain hurt. And Alec had seemed to hate her back then, but the way he spoke about her now was almost affectionate. A far cry from the 'devil woman' of his memory.

"You still talk to her?"

"Of course."

"Why?"

Alec gave him a look that said 'isn't it obvious?' "Because she is my sire. She made me. She is my mother. We're family."

"I don't feel that way about you." There was no use denying it, and he wanted to be clear.

The vampire grinned. "I know. I didn't feel that way about her in the beginning either. But blood runs deep." He shrugged.

Dylan felt like there was something else the vampire wasn't telling him. The monk in his dream had been appalled by the bloodshed and had hated the woman who had turned him into a monster. How did that guy turn into the cold, detached individual in front of him?

"Okay." Alec got up and walked toward the bathroom. "It's still early. Try to go back to sleep." He opened the door and slid inside.

As the door shut behind him and Dylan heard Marie giggling and inviting Alec into the shower with her, he realized they felt comfortable leaving him unsupervised because he couldn't go anywhere.

He groaned in frustration, falling back onto the bed. But he felt too antsy. He jumped up, pacing the room, running both hands through his hair. How was he going to get out of there? Away from Marie and Alec? No matter which way he spun it, he couldn't think of a way out. They outnumbered him.

Slowly, he ground to a halt. How was he going to survive this? He breathed in and out, momentarily forgetting that it wouldn't calm him anymore. Once he remembered, the enormity of everything that had happened came crashing down on him again.

Not only had he survived while the others were dead, but he had also changed beyond recognition. He was no longer human.

What did that even mean? What kind of life could he have now?

He thought about his mom, who was probably crippled with grief. He thought about his bright future at Harvard and beyond that had been ripped away from him now that he could no longer walk in the sun. Tears shot into his eyes.

A part of his brain was surprised that he was still able to produce tears. He looked at his lean perfect hands and felt nauseated. He was disgusted at this cold lifeless body. Why did it have to be him?

Again, he wished he could have died like Molly. It would have been better than this. His vision became blurry, and tears started flowing. He sobbed, wiping at his eyes with the back of his hands. But the tears kept coming.

Deep down, a part of him felt relieved that his body was finally showing a human reaction. He cried harder, trying not to make a sound so Alec and Marie wouldn't hear him.

Fuck them!

He could hear them kissing and giggling in the bathroom. If he'd had actual food in his stomach, he would have thrown up.

He hated these vampires with every fiber of his being. Especially Marie for lying to him like that! He was going to get them back for this. Somehow he needed to regain control over his life. Then he would kill them for what they had done to him. He balled his hands into fists in determination.

The tears let up once he had made the resolve. His gaze landed on his discarded glasses twisted in the sheets. He had forgotten about them. Slowly, he reached out and gingerly grabbed them. They seemed precious to him now.

He turned them over in his hands, taking in the thick smudged glass and the worn temple stems. This was all that remained of his old life.

He scanned the room for a good hiding place and settled on the drawer of the bedside table. It contained nothing but a Bible. He tucked the glasses safely away and sat down on the bed.

So far, he had been acting purely on impulse, but he needed to be smarter. Even if it hurt to leave his mom thinking he was dead, he had to bide his time. She'd be all the more relieved when she found out he was still alive. He had to focus on that.

Yes. He would learn as much as he could and then he would strike.

IV

Berlin, New Hampshire, April 1985

21

So, vampires were able to have sex. Dylan shelved that piece of information in the back of his brain after being forced to listen to Marie and Alec do it for far longer than should have been possible. While they'd been distracted, he had considered using the phone on the bedside table to call his mom, but the line had been cut. Marie and Alec must have thought ahead.

Now, Alec stood half naked in front of the closet, picking out clothes to wear, while Marie was getting dressed in the bathroom. Dylan tried hard not to, but he couldn't help but sneak glances at Alec's flawless back and his taut muscles twitching with every move.

A knock at the door interrupted his thoughts.

Marie stuck her head out of the bathroom, looking questioningly at Alec. The vampire tensed, eyes darting to the door and back to Marie.

"Marie? Are you in?" a voice called from outside.

Everything happened way too fast. When Dylan realized who was at the door, he jumped up from the bed, feelings of terror overwhelming the relief he felt at hearing that delicate, worried voice. He darted to the door, but Alec's arms snaked around him, one of his palms pressed on Dylan's mouth. The vampire yanked Dylan away from the door, every inch of the growing distance making Dylan's heart sink deeper. He struggled against Alec, but the vampire didn't even seem to notice Dylan was fighting him.

Alec dragged Dylan into the bathroom, shutting the door behind them. He whispered into Dylan's ear, "If you make a sound, she dies. Got it?"

Panic flooded his system. He knew what they were capable of. All he could do was nod into Alec's palm still pressed tightly to his mouth. Slowly, the vampire released him. Dylan immediately tried to put some distance between himself and Alec, but as he took a step back, he banged into the toilet. The seat clanged loudly on the porcelain bowl. His eyes darted to Alec's in terror.

Alec's face was dripping with disdain, but he let it slide.

"Susan? What brings you here?" Marie's voice rang clearly through the door. She sounded concerned and innocent. Dylan balled his hands into fists. She was such a skilled liar.

Susan sighed. "I'm worried about Dylan. He didn't come home last night. There was a fire at the old sneakers factory, and they found five bodies there, but—"

Marie hushed her. Dylan heard his mom take a deep breath. "He can't be one of them." Her voice broke. "They say they found his truck by the side of the road, but why would he even go there? It doesn't make any sense!" She started sobbing.

Dylan wished he could comfort her. It was so frustrating. He was right there. All he had to do was call out to her. Tell her that he was alive…

And then Marie would kill her.

He reached out, laying his palm flat on the door. He could feel Alec's warning glare burning a hole in his head.

"I don't know, Susan. I haven't seen him." Marie sounded sympathetic. Dylan wanted to scream at Susan to run. He couldn't stand the thought of his mother being in a room alone with a vampire. One that hadn't eaten yet.

"When he didn't come home after his shift, I thought he might be with you…"

"No, I haven't seen him since his birthday party."

Mention of Dylan's stupid birthday party made Susan cry harder. Marie hushed her again. "Have they confirmed that he's one of the bodies?"

Silence.

"Well, then he might still be alive."

"But where would he be?" Her voice had jumped up an octave. "If he's not with you then…"

Then there weren't any other options. He didn't have any friends. And besides, Susan had come to the right place, only she didn't know it. Dylan wanted to slam his fist into the door.

"Molly's missing, too," Susan said. "Martin is beside himself. I don't know what to do."

"That's awful. I'm so sorry." Dylan almost laughed. Marie did sound convincing though. If he didn't know for sure that she had hated Molly, he'd actually believe her.

"What else did the police tell you?" Marie paused. "It was the police who talked to you, right?"

"Uh, they said the bodies are badly burned and unrecognizable." It took her a moment to continue. "They took them to the medical examiner. They're trying to pull dental records…"

"When did they tell you that?"

"This morning."

"Who do they think the bodies are?"

Now Susan was sobbing hysterically. Marie tried to hush her again, but it wasn't helping. After another beat, Marie said calmly but decisively, "You're going to calm down now."

Susan miraculously stopped crying.

"Now, tell me exactly what the police said to you."

Susan started repeating what she had just said, but this time her voice sounded robotic, mechanical. She added, "The Barnes twins and the Halston boy are also missing. They think the five bodies are them, Molly, and Dylan. The Barneses' truck was found at the scene as well."

Dylan was stunned. He had never heard his mom so devoid of emotion. And she had been crying just a second ago. How...

It dawned on him that Marie had to be using mind control on her. His eyes darted to Alec, who was returning his gaze calmly. "Is she using mind control?" He mouthed the question.

Alec nodded, putting a finger to his lips.

Dylan wanted to hit him. And then he wanted to storm into the bedroom, kill Marie, grab his mom, and run as far away as he could. But fear rooted him in place. Fear of losing and causing Susan's death. Fear of the afternoon sun still beating down mercilessly outside. And – even if he didn't entirely want to admit it – fear of killing her himself once he got too close.

He choked down a sob and fought back tears, refusing to show weakness in front of Alec.

"Okay, good," Marie said after Susan had finished. "Go home and wait for news. Don't come back here. If they tell you anything else or if anything happens, call this number." She dictated what Dylan assumed was the motel's number. "If I'm not in, leave a message with the front desk. You can call anytime. Even late at night."

"Okay."

"Now, try to stay calm. Nothing has been confirmed yet."

Susan sighed, sounding more like herself. "You're right. Maybe it's all a big misunderstanding..."

Dylan's heart ached for her. She said goodbye to Marie and exited the room. When Dylan heard the door close, he rushed out of their hiding spot before Alec could stop him.

"How dare you use your mind tricks on my mom!?"

When he inhaled to say more, he caught a whiff of what he assumed was the scent of Susan's blood. It smelled like cotton candy. The sweetness of it was intoxicating, but Dylan tried hard to ignore it.

Marie stood with her back to the door, her gentle expression morphing into a mask of contempt. She crossed her arms in front of her chest. "Would you rather she have a nervous breakdown?"

Dylan almost exploded. "No, I want you to tell her the truth!"

She rolled her eyes at him, and it took every ounce of self-control he possessed not to hit her. He glared at her instead, but she ignored him, moving her attention to Alec.

"I need to go to the ME's office and make sure they identify him correctly."

Before Dylan could scream at her some more for excluding him from the conversation, Alec said, "Okay. Sunset is in half an hour. I'll take him to the mall while you're there."

"To the mall?" Dylan asked incredulously. Images of colorful store fronts, girls in tracksuit jackets and pink legwarmers slurping iced caffeinated drinks and mothers dragging their kids away from toy stores and arcades flashed in his mind. And he couldn't picture grumpy Alec who seemed to mostly wear black in the mix.

"Yeah, you need some clothes." He looked Dylan up and down. "You can't keep wearing mine. Plus..." He paused, his eyes fluttering to Marie and then back to Dylan. His lips formed a slight smile. "You can practice being around people."

* * *

The nearest mall was an hour away. To Dylan, the whole endeavor felt like a huge waste of time and like a ploy to get him out of the way and far, far away from home. But he reminded himself that he had decided to bide his time and play along until an opportunity presented itself to strike.

Being stuck on an hour-long drive with Alec was something Dylan hadn't accounted for though. Unsurprisingly, the vampire preferred sitting in silence to having the radio playing – now Dylan understood why Marie liked to blare music when she was driving alone. In fact, he was wondering more and more what the two saw in each other. They seemed to be complete opposites in everything: Marie seemed generally happy and up for anything whereas Alec looked like he was being chased by a rain cloud over his head and like he would rip the head off of anyone who looked at him sideways.

Maybe the saying was true, and opposites really did attract. Then again, they both were ruthless killers.

Angry, that he had even thought about them that way, Dylan forced himself to focus on something else. He didn't want to see his captors as people. They were monsters.

He gazed out the window, watching the scenery whoosh by. The night sky looked as bright to him as it did the day before, and he was surprised at how normal that already felt. Like drinking blood. What else would he get used to that had seemed unfathomable just two days ago?

"Do you have any more questions?" Alec asked tentatively.

They still had half an hour to go, but Dylan couldn't think of anything to ask. He needed to learn as much as possible, but he felt momentarily overwhelmed. So he shrugged. "Not really."

"Not even about your body? How it's changed?"

He suddenly felt fourteen again, remembering his mom gifting him a book for his birthday with the apt title *Changing Bodies, Changing Lives*. Back then, he had blushed from ear to ear and prayed for the ground to swallow him whole.

The prospect of talking about sex stuff with Alec of all people didn't make him feel much better. "No, I'm good."

"You're a virgin, aren't you?" Alec asked out of nowhere, ignoring Dylan's unease. Dylan tried not to react. He was only eighteen. Being a virgin at eighteen wasn't anything unusual, he tried to tell himself.

Alec took his silence for confirmation. "Don't worry. You won't be a virgin forever," he said with a weirdly threatening smile. Dylan gulped, but before he could tell Alec to mind his own business, the vampire continued. "Oh, speaking of, you should know that immortals don't procreate like humans do. The only way to make another immortal is by feeding our blood to a mortal with the aura. We only have sex for pleasure. Our reproductive organs are inactive. Female immortals don't menstruate, and male immortals don't ejaculate."

Dylan sank deeper into the car seat. He did not want to have this conversation, but the last part made his ears perk up with curiosity. He pulled himself together, refusing to come across as prude to Alec.

"So, we don't have orgasms?"

"Yes, we do. Just without the mess." He grinned. "And we have more stamina than human men as well. We can even have multiple orgasms." He winked at Dylan.

That explained his and Marie's marathon session that morning. Dylan fought a smile. Maybe not everything about this life was awful...

"So, how do people phrase it these days... Ah, yes, what are you into?"

Dylan blinked. "Excuse me?"

Alec briefly lifted his hands from the steering wheel. "What are you attracted to?"

Dylan thought about it for a moment. That was dangerous territory. The truth was he was attracted to girls. All kinds of girls. He knew that for sure. But sometimes he caught himself checking out another guy's muscles in a way that was more than appreciation. He had always been careful to hide those feelings, not wanting to make his life any harder than it already was. The last thing he needed was more bullying.

He wasn't sure if Alec would understand. Besides, he certainly didn't want to reveal something so personal to the vampire.

He squirmed. "Well, I…"

Alec raised his eyebrows expectantly.

"I like nice girls?" Why did he make it sound like a question?

Alec sighed. "I mean physically."

He instantly thought of Madonna and the naked women in the magazines he snuck into the bathroom sometimes when he was alone at the gas station.

"Blonds. I like blonds."

Alec smirked. "I see." Seemingly satisfied, he said, "Those won't be hard to find." He didn't say anything else.

Dylan didn't want this vampire to find him a girl. He wanted to decide on his terms where and when and especially with whom he was going to lose his virginity.

When they finally reached the mall's parking lot, Dylan was more than eager to get out of the car, but Alec held him back.

"Wait. There will be a lot of humans in there."

"I'm aware of that." Dylan tried to shrug Alec's hand off his shoulder, but the vampire's grip tightened.

"Remember what almost happened with the chief last night?" he asked pointedly.

Dylan shuddered despite himself. He had nearly bitten the chief. Cold dread ran through his veins.

"And that was outdoors," Alec continued. "We're about to step into a large space that has been teeming with humans for hours. The air will be saturated with their scents."

Dylan gulped, suddenly scared to enter the mall.

Alec said, "It's okay. I'll be there to help. But you have to be careful and pull yourself together."

Dylan felt sick. He didn't even want to be there.

Alec turned to get out of the car, but when Dylan didn't make a move, he turned back and added, "This is important, Dylan. You need to learn to be around humans without hurting them; otherwise, you'll never be able to move around freely."

The younger immortal inhaled sharply. As much as it pained him to admit it, Alec had a point. He didn't want to hurt anyone, and to avoid that, he needed to expose himself to the scent of human blood. Get desensitized … if that was even possible.

Determined, he nodded and followed Alec toward the building.

A couple strode past them, both carrying heavy shopping bags. Dylan inhaled their scents as he passed them. Her sugary smell mingled with his tart one to form an interesting amalgamation. Dylan stopped and sniffed as they walked on. He could smell something almost like cherry coming off her – not the artificial candy type flavor but the natural fruity one.

"Dylan," Alec called. He was already a hundred yards ahead.

Dylan realized in shock that he had been analyzing the smell of blood again and rushed to catch up with the vampire.

"When we go inside, I want you to hold your breath, okay?"

Dylan nodded, for once eager to comply with Alec.

22

Dylan had been to this mall before, but even though he knew what to expect, the space still assaulted his senses as he stepped through the doors. Neon hues of pink, green, blue, and orange jumped out at him from the various window displays of clothing stores and toy stores aimed at children. He could hear the whirring and beeping sounds of the second-floor arcade as loudly as gunfire. People of all shapes and sizes were rushing past them, running after-work errands or going on shopping sprees.

He tried to ignore his surroundings and focus on Alec, following the vampire deeper into the building.

Dylan was still diligently holding his breath, not daring to add another sense to the mix. Though he almost caved when they reached the food court and he spotted a mouthwatering display of donuts.

He was wondering if he could still eat those but didn't have enough breath to ask Alec. The vampire was motioning for Dylan to take a seat at a table that stood a few feet away from the rest. The place wasn't crowded anymore – it was after eight o'clock – but people were still scattered around the court, resting from excessive shopping or busy days out. Dylan tried not to focus on the humans.

Alec muttered, "Okay, now take a little whiff."

Dylan stared at Alec with wide eyes. He was just supposed to inhale? Without instructions? Had the vampire lost his mind? Or did he intend for Dylan to fail?

Alec nudged Dylan. "Only a little whiff. Come on."

Giving the vampire the benefit of the doubt for the moment, Dylan carefully did as he was told, drawing in only the tiniest amount of air. But even that was enough to ignite every nerve-ending in his body. He felt like he was going to snap. The room was full of so many delicious smells, all blending, complementing, and enhancing each other. The blood smells working in tandem with the food smells created a spicy mix…

"Jesus… Look at me!" Alec yanked Dylan's head to the side, so he was facing him. "We don't want anyone to notice your eyes turn crimson and your fangs pop out."

Alarmed, Dylan slapped his hand over his mouth. How annoying! He felt like a thirteen-year-old boy hiding a spontaneous erection from his classmates. He ran his tongue over his teeth, making sure his fangs had receded before slowly dropping his hand.

Alec grinned. "Okay, you're good. Try again."

Even more carefully than the first time, Dylan drew in another tiny breath, all the while focusing on Alec's shoulder. He braced himself for the onslaught of smells. But still, this time, they were even more magnificent. He could make out notes of lemon mixed with mint and all of it was tinged with something that smelled like excitement. The food smells were only adding to the mélange of scents, enhancing the properties of the blood scents. His fangs pierced his lower lip, and he pressed his eyes shut.

"Are you all right?" Alec asked.

Dylan nodded, eyes still pressed shut. He tried to think of something disgusting to turn himself off the smell, but thinking was hard right then. He couldn't focus on anything other than the blood. But out of nowhere, Molly's dead body appeared in his mind's eye. His heart sank. If he couldn't control himself, he would end up killing somebody.

He shivered.

He did not want to be a monster.

Amazed, he realized his fangs had disappeared, and he opened his eyes again. Alec was nodding encouragingly. "Good. Whatever you were doing, keep doing it."

He only had to remind himself of the consequences. Easy-peasy… He pictured Molly's face. Not her dead face but her face in life. In his head he saw her frown and her hazel eyes full of pain. She hadn't deserved to die…

He inhaled again. Longer this time. The scents were still there, but they didn't hold as much power over him as before. Everyone in here could be a Molly.

"Well done!" Alec sounded surprised but appreciative. Dylan couldn't help but grin. He had always been a teacher's pet – even if the teacher was a psychopath. "You didn't react physically this time."

"How do you manage not to kill everyone in here?" Dylan couldn't fathom how somebody without a moral code could have any scruples at all about murdering a room full of people. Plus, Alec's memories had shown Dylan that the vampire had done it before.

"You get used to the way humans smell after a while. It's only this hard in the beginning."

Dylan sighed – which was a bad idea because then he was out of air to speak. He focused on Molly's face and inhaled again.

Alec's approving look told him he hadn't vamped out. It got easier, but it still required all his concentration not to give in and eat everyone in there.

He thought of his mom and her lingering scent in the motel room earlier, and his stomach clenched. He needed to pull himself together if he ever wanted to speak to her face to face again. And he needed to do so soon. She was devastated because of him, and he was the only one who could remedy that.

The sooner he got done with all of this baby-vampire stuff, the better!

"Okay, we need to get you some clothes. Let's see if you can keep it up." The vampire slapped Dylan on the shoulder and motioned for him to follow.

Not daring to breathe normally yet, Dylan held his breath again and hurried after Alec, who was heading for the nearest Gap.

Dylan was momentarily stunned by their selection. He usually thrifted his clothes to save money. Alec picked out several items without even looking at the price tag, tossing them at Dylan.

Every now and then, he reminded Dylan to breathe, and after a while the younger immortal realized it got easier every time.

When it seemed like Dylan was hugging one of every item the store had to his chest, Alec ushered him to the changing rooms.

"Hurry up! You still need shoes," Alec shouted through the curtain.

"No!" Dylan shouted back. "I have shoes." He refused to let go of his sneakers. The pair of beat-up navy blue Converse reminded him of his old life. It gave him hope that all was not lost.

"You need new ones."

"No."

Alec let out a huge sigh behind the curtain. "Okay, then. Suit yourself."

As Dylan went through shirt after shirt and pants after pants, he realized he could choose what he liked best, instead of just going with what was available in his size at the thrift store. For a moment, he was thrilled, picking out fashionable light blue denim and T-shirts in various colors and cuts.

But then an inexplicable feeling of dread washed over him. Had he just enjoyed himself while Molly was dead?

He swallowed the bad feelings and the good ones, trying to detach himself from the present moment.

"Are you almost done in there?" Alec called out.

Dylan grabbed the pile of clothes he had chosen and joined Alec outside.

The vampire paid the exorbitant amount that Dylan had racked up in cash. Without blinking.

If they were this rich, why did they stay at a run-down motel in the middle of nowhere? There was still a lot Dylan didn't know about Alec and Marie, he realized with a start.

They picked up a few toiletries, and Alec bought a large suitcase for Dylan to put everything in. At first, Dylan insisted he wouldn't need it, but then he figured he shouldn't look a gift horse in the mouth. If Alec wanted to spend money on him, he'd let him. Plus, it was the least he could do after turning Dylan into a vampire.

Hauling huge shopping bags, they were making their way toward the exit, when Alec abruptly stopped. Dylan craned his neck to see what had halted the vampire and realized Alec was staring at the window display of a bookstore.

"We're not in a hurry, are we?" he muttered mostly to himself as he crossed the store's threshold.

Confused, Dylan followed him. They had moved quickly until then – the only thing that had taken some time was Dylan's acclimating to the scent of humans.

Alec made a beeline to the thriller section, which caused Dylan to shudder and chuckle at the same time.

"You like crime?" he asked once he caught up with Alec.

The vampire looked startled for a second, like he had forgotten Dylan was even there. "I like good fiction," he said. He slid the shopping bags from his right hand to his left and grabbed a copy of Frederick Forsyth's *The Fourth Protocol*.

"Espionage?" Dylan asked.

Alec gave him a look. "What's wrong with that?"

Dylan shrugged. "Nothing. I just thought a guy *your age* would be a little more sophisticated."

The comment was meant as a jab, but Alec didn't seem to get it. His brow creased. "What do you mean?"

"I just figured you'd be reading Shakespeare or Hemingway or some other highbrow literature."

Alec chuckled, turning his gaze to the blurb on the book.

"What?" Dylan asked when the vampire didn't elaborate.

Alec shrugged. "It's just funny to me that you consider Shakespeare highbrow. Back when they were written, his plays were entertainment for the masses. And as for Hemingway, I've read his books. I read them all right after publication. I want to read something new. Something I don't know yet."

That shut Dylan up. He wondered what it was like to be over three hundred years old, to have traveled the world, to have witnessed history unfold in real time.

It hit him that he might find out exactly what that was like. He was immortal now. What would he do with all the time stretching out before him?

Alec checked his watch and hurried to pay for his book.

* * *

When they finally exited shoppers' paradise, Dylan felt confident that he could be around humans without killing anyone – with a little effort. Still, he took a deep breath of fresh air once they were outside, allowing himself to relax a little.

That's when he caught a strong whiff of alcohol and something else he couldn't identify. It smelled like death.

Dylan's gaze shot around till he caught the source of the stench. A homeless man had set up camp near the shopping carts. But this was more than lack of hygiene. Something was in the man's blood.

Once they were out of the man's earshot, Dylan turned to Alec and asked him about it.

"He's sick. That's what cancer smells like," Alec explained while tossing the shopping bags into the trunk. Something clanked loudly underneath. "It's unappealing to you because we only drink the blood of the healthy."

Dylan wasn't sure what to say. "We can smell diseases?"

Alec nodded gravely.

Dylan mulled over this as they got into the Audi and Alec put the car in reverse.

"But then we could help diagnose people. Identify pathogens before they get out of control. We could save lives!" Dylan gestured frantically to the homeless man through the windshield.

Alec looked sharply at Dylan. "No, we can't. Do you know how many humans there are on this planet?"

It sounded like a rhetorical question, but Dylan couldn't help himself. "Four point eight billion," he answered without missing a beat.

"Exactly. And do you know how many immortals there are on this planet?"

Dylan was interested in the answer to that. He waited.

"Maybe two hundred. If that."

"You don't know for sure?"

"No. We don't exactly keep count." Alec had an exasperated look on his face. "My point is we are greatly outnumbered. We might be faster and stronger than them, but they're not stupid. If they knew of our existence, they would hunt us down, lock us up, study us in their laboratories…" His expression had become erratic. He rubbed his temple and closed his eyes for a second. "They can't know we're out there. Understood?"

Alec's emphatic reaction startled Dylan. If what he said was true, it made sense for them to be careful, to remain in hiding. He hadn't been planning on telling anyone about the vampire part anyway because he was sure nobody would believe him, so he didn't mind the secrecy.

"Yes," he said since Alec was waiting for an answer.

"Good. Then let's go back." He pulled onto the freeway, speeding back to Berlin.

23

Dylan was dying to get out of Alec's clothes. He'd been wearing them for nearly twenty-four hours at that point. He had even slept in them! Even though his body couldn't produce sweat anymore, he felt dirty. Maybe it was the prospect of new clothes, tucked away in plastic bags in the trunk, or maybe it was the lingering feeling of guilt. People had died because of him. He tried to shove those feelings down, not wanting to have a mental breakdown in the car next to Alec.

By the time they got back to the motel, Marie was already waiting for them in their room. "Oh, wow, you bought half the mall!" she exclaimed, as they hurled their purchases onto the bed.

Marie curiously peeked into one of the bags, pulling out a V-neck beige T-shirt with white sleeves and a chest pocket. "Bland but okay… We don't want to draw attention anyway."

Dylan rolled his eyes, grabbed a pair of underwear, white tennis socks, tight light blue denim jeans he'd never have worn until yesterday, and a dark blue T-shirt with an oversize fit and a white stripe across the chest.

"I'll take a shower and change." He escaped into the bathroom. Being around Marie was harder than being around Alec. She had lied to him from the beginning. Dylan realized that, so far, Alec hadn't lied to him once. He chuckled at the irony.

Before he stepped under the deafening stream of water, he caught

Marie saying to Alec: "I made sure the dead wolf was identified as Dylan. They're informing the families and the press as we speak."

Dread flooded his system. An image of his mom flashed in his mind, melting into a puddle of tears on the floor as she took in the news of her only child's death. His heart broke and his vision became blurry, eyes brimming with tears.

He tried to calm himself down, reassuring himself that he would set it right. He would find his mom and show her he was still alive. Picturing the elation on his mother's face instead of her grief, he stepped into the shower – glad he could no longer hear Alec and Marie in the other room.

* * *

"Come on, we're going out!" Marie wrapped one arm around Dylan as he exited the bathroom in his new clothes. He squirmed at her touch, but she ignored it.

"Where are we going?"

"To a party." Her smile was so wide it looked grotesque.

"What?"

She finally let go of him. "On my way back, I overheard a group of guys your age talk about a party at Kudowski's place."

"Freddie Kudowski?"

She shrugged. "Maybe."

Freddie Kudowski was another senior. He was on the hockey team with Fletcher – or rather, used to be, when Fletcher had still been alive. He had never given Dylan the time of day, which Dylan hadn't minded. No attention was better than getting the wrong kind of attention. Freddie and Fletcher had been rivals on the team, but

Dylan never would have expected Freddie to throw a party a day after Fletcher's death.

"He's throwing a party when four of our classmates are dead?"

Marie rolled her eyes. "People die all the time. Human lives are short. They're making the best of it." She grabbed a blood bag from the fridge and tossed it to Dylan. "Drink up! Just to be safe."

Dylan caught the bag. "You want to go to a high school party?"

"Sure. Why not?"

He took a closer look at her. She was wearing a tiny denim miniskirt, white leg warmers, white sneakers, and a tight bedazzled black top that showed off her cleavage. She looked like she had jumped out of a music video. There was no way in hell she could pass for a teenager. Dylan threw a glance at Alec, who was lounging comfortably on the couch, engrossed in his new book.

"And how are you going to explain why you're there? Everyone knows everyone at our school. They'll know you don't go there. Plus, you don't look young enough to be in high school."

She scoffed and Alec let out a snort – not so preoccupied after all. "If she shows up there looking like that" – he indicated Marie's ensemble – "nobody will question her presence."

"And you're not coming?" Dylan asked, ignoring Alec's comment about Marie's looks.

"No," he replied without looking up. "I definitely can't pass for a teenager."

Dylan's gaze hung on the stubble on Alec's face that had already grown in again even though he had heard the vampire shave earlier in the day. Dylan couldn't even grow a decent mustache yet, let alone a whole beard. Alec's sharp facial features stood in contrast to Dylan's own. His face had gained some more contours with the transformation, but his cheeks were still on the softer side, giving away his age.

No, Alec could definitely not pass for a teen.

"We'll just tell them that we're someone's cousins or something. Visiting from out of town," Marie said while applying some pink lipstick.

Of course she'd pull a lie out of her ass. Dylan balled his fists. He didn't want to go to some party. He wanted to go see his mom.

But maybe he could lose Marie at the party. Alec wasn't coming, so he would just have to get rid of her… It seemed feasible. Now that he knew how to handle a crowd, he might be able to disappear.

"Okay, then," he said. He never thought the next words would come out of his mouth: "Let's go party."

* * *

As they drove to Kudowski's place – which wasn't too far from Dylan's – speakers blaring Billy Idol, Dylan couldn't help but think back to all the other times he had sat in this car with Marie. The familiarity of the situation felt off considering everything had changed.

"I think we're in the right place," Marie muttered as she drove up to a house visibly bumping with music and brightly lit from the inside.

She squeezed into a tiny parking spot at the end of the street since cars were parked bumper to bumper around the property. It seemed like the entire school was there. Dylan was shocked. Did none of them care that so many people had died?

As they got closer to the house, Dylan could make out hundreds of voices inside, all shouting over each other and the booming music. He realized that he'd be able to hear individual conversations if the crowd was smaller. But as it was, too many voices were overlapping, drowning each other out.

"What are we even doing here?" he asked Marie as they stepped up to the front door. She had never expressed an interest in partying before. He suddenly wondered if she was looking for fresh human blood.

No, then she wouldn't have made him drink another blood bag before leaving.

"We're having fun. I think you need a little fun in your life, Dylan."

He didn't believe her for a second, but he couldn't figure out her true motives either. "What are we going to do if anyone recognizes me?" he asked calmly, trying to provoke her.

She demonstrably looked him up and down arching one eyebrow and curling her lip. His heart sank. Yes, he knew as well as she did that he was unrecognizable – especially to people who hadn't paid much attention to him before anyway. He sighed.

"Okay. Well, after you…"

She didn't bother ringing the doorbell. Instead, she opened the door as if the house belonged to her and they stepped into the crowded hallway.

A wave of mingled scents hit Dylan like a ton of bricks. Fruity fragrances were mixed with smoky smells, savory aromas and flowery undertones working together to form an intoxicating mix that went straight to Dylan's head. Everything was wrapped in the smell of alcohol which somehow made each aroma more intense. Not even the lingering heavy cigarette smell could cover it up.

He was panicking and salivating at the same time.

He immediately stopped breathing. Cutting off his sense of smell helped somewhat, but he could still feel the rich air clinging to his skin, taunting him to let go.

People were bustling around the house. He saw movement everywhere. And everything was clouded by hazy cigarette smoke. A group of girls in skimpy outfits holding solo cups stood by the stairs. They were eyeing Dylan and Marie with interest. Dylan recognized them from school. As he looked around, gazing into the crowded living room, he realized he knew most of the people there. Nervousness was creeping up inside him.

Being there felt like walking down a hallway at school during lunchtime. He couldn't shake the feeling that he was being watched, judged, and ridiculed. He fought the urge to make a run for the door.

"Come on, let's get a drink!" Marie shouted over the music – something off Michael Jackson's latest album. She grabbed his hand and yanked him with her. They were meandering through the crowd, possibly heading for the kitchen when someone smacked into Dylan from the side.

"Oh my god, I'm so sorry," a girl shouted in his ear. "I hope I didn't spill my drink on you." She started wiping at his dry T-shirt sleeve.

Dylan almost cringed when he recognized the blond hair and round face. Juliette Wheeler, a junior, who had started several rumors about him. Once she had told the entire cheerleading squad that he'd been spying on them getting changed and jerking off to it, only because she had seen him walk by their changing rooms on his way to work.

Juliette had stopped dabbing at his dry sleeve and was openly feeling up his triceps. She obviously had no idea who he was.

"It's fine. You didn't spill anything on me." He jerked his arm back and stepped to the side, putting some much-needed distance between them.

"Oh, okay, good." She blinked flirtatiously a few times, her green eyes sparkling. "I don't think I've seen you around here before. What's your name?"

He had to inhale to answer, so he braced himself for the onslaught of smells. But breathing in still felt like snorting a line of cocaine – at least what he imagined that would feel like. He tried to suppress the rush as he inhaled her strawberry scent heavy with alcohol. She was wasted.

He didn't even want to talk to this girl.

A tap on his shoulder made him half turn around. Marie was looking at him expectantly.

"I didn't realize you had a girlfriend," Juliette said too sweetly, her face lighting up like it was the loveliest thing ever. Her eyes darkened though.

Dylan cringed again. He didn't want to be associated with Marie in that way. And he wanted this obnoxious blond with the bad dye-job to leave him alone.

Marie's eyes fluttered from Dylan to Juliette and back again. She leaned in and whispered something in Juliette's ear. The girl's face went blank, and she turned on her heel and stalked off.

"What did you say to her?" Dylan asked, confused.

Marie grinned. "I told her to mind her own business."

This mind control thing was weird.

"You didn't seem to enjoy her company," she said.

Dylan debated whether to tell her the truth. He was about to shrug it off and tell *her* to mind her own business, but then the expression on her heart-shaped face changed slightly and he remembered all the times she had stood up for him in the past. Granted, she had had ulterior motives, but that didn't change the fact that she had saved his ass multiple times.

"She … she was always a bitch to me at school."

Marie nodded knowingly. "I see." Her expression turned grim, and her gaze wandered to the doorway Juliette had disappeared through.

Dylan was suddenly afraid for the girl's safety. "Stop. She's no one." He reached out and touched Marie's arm. Maybe it was because he had been thinking about what it used to be like between them, but in this second, he realized her skin didn't feel cold to him anymore.

Because, now, they were the same temperature. He bit his tongue trying not to react, shoving the feeling of dread down.

Marie glanced from his hand on her forearm to his face, and a tentative smile spread across her face.

Dylan immediately let go. "Didn't you want to get a drink?"

"Yes. Come on."

With a wave of her hand, she indicated for him to follow her through the crowd. There was no way to move around this house without bumping into people, and whenever Dylan felt another warm arm or shoulder touch him, he held his breath, bypassing the oncoming whiff of blood. But even without the olfactory stimulation, the urge to rip into everyone's throat nearly overcame him. It took his full concentration to fight it off.

After what felt like years, they finally reached the kitchen where only three people stood in one corner, immersed in a conversation, and every flat surface was covered in cups and bottles. Marie grabbed a stack of solo cups, loosened two from it, and looked inside to check if they'd been used. Dylan smirked. Even if they had been, it wasn't like they could catch anyone's herpes or germs.

She poured a little of the contents from two bottles on the counter nearby – rum and coke – and handed him a cup.

"Cheers," she chimed, smiling her private joke smile at him – only now he finally got the joke. He felt sick.

She downed half her cup before he had even taken his first sip. "Oh, and take it slow with the booze, okay? When you get drunk, it'll be harder to control your … *urges*." She gave him a warning look.

"Then why drink at all?" It was a genuine question. Why would they make their lives unnecessarily harder?

She raised two eyebrows like it was obvious. "Because it's fun."

He couldn't refrain from rolling his eyes. If he heard her say the word 'fun' one more time, he would explode.

"Come on! Try it!" She gestured to the drink in his hand.

He sighed. Tentatively, he took a sip from the mixture. It tasted weirdly sweet and acrid at the same time. Nothing was appealing about it. When the liquid hit the back of his throat, he involuntarily made a face. How the hell was this fun?

His scrunched-up face made Marie laugh. "Okay, I know the taste is not great," she conceded, "but the effect is pretty good."

He took another sip, forcing more of the disgusting liquid down his throat.

While Marie was focusing on his reaction to the alcohol, he scanned his surroundings. A side door in the kitchen led out to the backyard. People were coming and going through it. Maybe he could step outside for a minute and run off? But Marie would never let him go alone.

A girl whose name he couldn't remember approached them. She was a junior and a cheerleader. Her blond perm was imposing like a lion's mane, and she obviously had gone heavy on the make-up and self-tanner. She wore a miniskirt that was even shorter than Marie's, and her breasts were threatening to spill out of the skin-tight pink crop top. She also sported a fringed leather vest and cowboy boots like a country singer, which reminded him vaguely of Dolly Parton.

"Hi," she said with the confidence of someone who had never been rejected in her life. "I'm Greta. I don't think we've met before. Are you guys new here?" Her mouth was smiling, but her eyes were calculating.

Dylan looked at Marie, who was the expert liar, wondering what story she was going to spin.

"I'm Sally and this is my brother Eric," Marie answered without missing a beat. "We're Gordon Foster's cousins. We're just in town for the week."

Greta's brow creased. "I don't know a Gordon Foster… Does he go to Berlin High School?"

If Dylan's body had still been able to produce sweat, he would have had to wipe the beads off his forehead by then. How could Marie keep all these lies straight?

"Yeah, he's a senior," Marie answered with complete confidence.

"He is?" Greta was visibly confused.

"Yes." That was all Marie said, but her tone didn't leave room for argument.

Greta's face smoothed and she exclaimed, "Oh, right, yes, Gordon! Of course, I know who he is." She waved a hand in front of her face. "How long are you guys here for?"

Dylan was pretty sure Marie hadn't used her mind tricks on Greta. Why the girl was pretending to know 'Gordon Foster' was beyond him though.

"Oh, just for a week or so. We're here for our uncle's birthday."

Greta nodded enthusiastically. Her eyes wandered from Dylan's face down his body appreciatively. It was clear she was picturing him naked. Her gaze made Dylan uncomfortable at first but then he felt weirdly turned on.

"Is Gordon here, too?" Greta asked with a sexy smile.

"Uh…" Dylan had no idea what to say.

"Yeah," Marie answered for him. "He's here somewhere… He went off with a guy from his English class who needed him for something." She gestured in the general direction of the living room.

"I see." Greta took a step closer toward Dylan, her smoldering blue eyes never breaking his gaze.

He dared to take a tiny breath, curious what she would smell like, but when he caught her scent, expecting it to be something flowery and delicious like peaches and cream, he wrinkled his nose in surprise. Greta's blood smelled off-balance somehow. It was too bitter, like very strong coffee.

Dylan took a closer look at the human. There didn't seem to be anything wrong with her. Nothing but a perfectly healthy young woman.

"So, where are you guys from?" she asked, when neither he nor Marie spoke.

"Boston," Marie answered without hesitation. Okay, that was all right. He could fake being from Boston. He had been there before.

"Nice! I go there a lot. Every other weekend actually … to see my dad…"

"Really?" Dylan spurted out. He hadn't meant to say anything, but it took him by surprise that others at his school had parents who were divorced.

Greta nodded, her expression unreadable. Dylan tried to remember if he had ever spoken to her before, but he was pretty sure he hadn't. A girl like her would never have given his human self the time of day.

"You know what? I think I'm going to go look for Gordon." Marie put her drink on the counter and gave Dylan a little wink. Puzzled, he stared back at her.

"Okay…?" But she had already pivoted and was stalking out of the kitchen toward the living room. What had she done that for?

Whatever the reason, Dylan was finally alone. He had a chance to escape.

"So, are you a senior as well?" Greta asked, softly touching his forearm. Dylan groaned internally. How was he going to get rid of her? He didn't know how to use mind control yet. As morally wrong as the concept felt to him, he had to admit it could come in handy.

He needed to get out of there.

"Uh, yeah. Yeah, I am… Hey, do you want to go outside for a bit?" He gestured toward the side door. "It's kind of hot in here."

A smile spread across her bright red lips. "Sure."

To his surprise, Greta hooked her arm around his as they made their way outside. The warmth radiating from her body was like a shock to him. He tried to ignore it as best he could, but he felt his resistance slowly melt away. Once they were out the side door, he looked around, trying to find his bearings. The Kudowski property bordered another section of the woods. He noticed giggling couples hiding behind trees and wondered briefly if Greta could see and hear them too. He was already having trouble remembering what it was like not to see in the dark.

Before he could turn to Greta to excuse himself and make a run for it, she started pulling him toward the dark trees. Startled, he stopped in his tracks, halting her with him. Her small body was so frail beneath his touch that it made his heart skip a beat.

She looked at him with large doe eyes. "Is there something wrong?"

"No. No…"

A smile spread across her lips that awoke something deep within him. As her face moved closer to his, his heart was pounding with nerves. Her bitter scent enveloped him, momentarily breaking her thrall. But when her lips softly touched his, every thought left his brain.

She clung to him, her hands wandering around his torso and down his back. Every cell in his body was electrified as if a current ran through him, accelerating his heartbeat. He kissed her back fiercely, pressing himself against her. She spread her lips slightly, running her tongue along his mouth. She tasted like beer and cigarettes.

The warmth emanating from her became more intense. She opened his mouth with her tongue. He wrapped his arms around her, pulling her even closer. He could feel her heartbeat against his chest. When he focused on it, he could hear it, too. It was pounding in a steady rhythm, pumping her blood through her body.

She broke the kiss, threw a glance over her shoulder to the house and, with a devious smile, took him by the hand and pulled him toward the woods again. This time, Dylan complied, eager to find out what would happen next.

He couldn't keep his eyes off her as she stumbled about three hundred yards deep into the forest, all the while never letting go of his hand. She stopped and pushed him against a tree trunk. Dylan let it happen, unable to resist her.

Her lips found his again. She pushed her tongue into his mouth, playing with his, eliciting a moan from him. But just as suddenly as she had come on to him, she pulled away.

Her hands slid down his torso, and she smiled wickedly, making his heart skip a beat. His lips twitched. Encouraged by her advances, he cupped her face and kissed her again, marveling at the softness of her lips. And the whole world melted away.

After an eternity or just a few moments – Dylan couldn't tell anymore – she pulled away again, giving him another wicked smile as her hands wandered to his groin. Her smile deepened as she stroked him through the denim, almost making him squeal. Hypnotized by her touch, he could do nothing but watch as she slowly undid the button and zipper of his jeans and freed his erection from his underwear.

He could hardly believe it when she dropped to her knees and took him in her mouth, her hands grabbing his butt tightly. The sudden warm slickness enveloping him almost sent him over the edge. He ran his hands through her hair, needing something to hold on to as her tongue flicked up and down his length, sending delicious ripples through his body.

In that moment, he would have done anything she wanted. He was putty in her hands, and he loved it. She worked him harder, making his heart pound faster and his muscles contract. He wanted to thrust into her so badly, and it took every ounce of self-control he possessed not to.

The pressure kept building with every flick of her tongue until he couldn't hold back any longer. He came hard, moaning with pleasure.

She paused what she was doing, looking at his softening penis. He quickly stuffed it back in his pants as she stood frowning at him.

"Did you not finish?" she asked pointedly after a beat.

"Uh…" It took him a second to realize why she was asking. Embarrassed, he grappled for an explanation. "Yes, I did. It's just … I have a condition where I don't ejaculate."

She raised an eyebrow, crossing her arms in front of her chest. "Sure. And I'm Cyndi Lauper."

"No, I swear." He didn't want her to think she had done a bad job. It had been glorious. "Seriously." Mind control would have been really useful right then. He cursed himself silently.

Her skepticism seemed to be waning. "All right. Well…" She fluffed up her perm. "I should get back. They're probably wondering where I am…" Without another glance at him, she turned on her heel and stumbled back toward the house.

Dylan let his head fall back against the tree. He took a deep breath, relishing the cool, clean night air. Did that really just happen? A laugh bubbled up in his stomach and soon he was chuckling hysterically. A wave of joy hit him. He couldn't remember the last time he had laughed like that. For a moment, he didn't have a care in the world.

"There you are." Marie sauntered up to him, a wide grin on her face. She glanced in the direction Greta had gone and then back to him. "Did you enjoy yourself a little?"

Dylan felt himself blush, and his heartbeat accelerated with panic. Had she seen the whole thing? He hadn't paid attention to his surroundings at all…

She let out a laugh. "Don't worry, I wasn't spying on you. I just got here." Her eyes wandered down to his groin and back up. "But you look like you had a good time."

His blush deepened as he glanced down at his pants, finding his zipper still half open. He tried not to let on his embarrassment, quickly zipping up his jeans and meeting her gaze head on.

She smirked and opened her mouth to say something else, but somewhere deeper in the forest, a piercing scream interrupted the silent night.

24

Marie's smile waned, and she threw a worried look at Dylan, whose senses had gone into overdrive. He was straining to hear more from the person who had let out the scream, but he couldn't make out any human sounds among the rustling of the nocturnal forest that had suddenly grown so loud he was wondering how he'd been able to ignore it before.

"Maybe it was just someone goofing around, scaring other people…" Marie ventured.

Dylan shook his head. "That sounded like genuine fear."

Before he had actively made the decision, he took off in the direction the voice had come from. He didn't know what he was going to do once he found the source, but he was tired of being powerless, unable to affect anything.

He vaguely registered that Marie had come after him, but that didn't matter. He kept listening yet heard nothing but the soft crunching of the forest floor beneath his feet.

A sweet smell that didn't belong in the earthly and flowery palette of springtime nature made his nostrils flare with intrigue.

Marie's arms slinked around his torso, stopping him in his tracks. She was squeezing him so hard she would have crushed his bones had they still been breakable.

"What the—?"

"Shush!"

Something was up. His gaze darted around nervously, but all he could see was the tranquil forest. She abruptly let go and stepped in front of him, stretching out her arms protectively as if shielding him from something.

"What's going on?" he whispered. He couldn't think of anything that might be dangerous to him now except maybe other vampires. The face of the one he had seen the previous night through the motel room window flashed in his mind.

But what was that sweet smell? He took another whiff. He recognized the soft notes of human blood, but it was tinged with something intoxicating. Like caramelized sugar. The more he inhaled the scent, the more it taunted him. His mouth was watering and his fangs grew long.

"What is that smell?"

Marie's voice was so low he was sure no human would be able to hear it. "It's a werewolf."

"What?" Dylan's heart almost jumped out of his chest. "I thought you killed them all."

"So did I." She was still shielding him from the invisible enemy. She continued in the same low voice, "When I tell you to run, run back toward the house. I'll be right behind you."

"But what about the scream we heard? Somebody's in trouble. We have to do something." Stacy Yelander's mutilated body appeared in his mind's eye. Nobody should have to die like that.

But Marie shook her head. "There's nothing we can do. I'm sure that person's dead by now."

Dylan's blood ran cold, and he stiffened. He became even more alert, hyperfocused on his surroundings.

Even though the night wasn't dark to him anymore, he still felt intimidated by the maze of trees surrounding him. He whirled around, suddenly not wanting his back to be exposed. Back-to-back with Marie, he stared into the night, listening for the tiniest sound, not daring to think about what would happen if a wolf like the one that had chased them jumped out at him.

"Dylan?" Marie's voice sounded as tense as he felt.

"Yes?" He gulped.

"Run!"

Her instruction ignited him like a fuse. He took off at rocket speed, sprinting back to the house, his feet barely touching the ground.

That's when he heard it: A high-pitched howl rang through the forest followed by the falling of heavy paws. And the sounds were getting closer.

Dylan's heart pounded in his ears. He picked up speed, but so did the wolf. A deep growl made the hairs on the back of his neck stand up. He didn't dare turn his head to see if it had almost caught up with them. He knew those things could run fast.

The house couldn't be far. They hadn't ventured deep into the woods, had they? Between the blow job and the running, he was completely disoriented at this point.

He suddenly remembered the humans sneaking off into the forest behind the house. He and Marie were leading the monster directly to them! He veered off the path, redirecting the wolf elsewhere.

"What are you doing?" Marie shouted behind him.

"It'll kill the people in the forest next to the house!" Dylan shouted back. She groaned.

Instead of running back toward civilization, he steered the wolf deeper into the woods, praying it wouldn't catch up. He listened intently for the beast's paws hitting the forest floor as he darted toward the river. Maybe they would be able to lose it in the water?

But then the wolf's footfalls stopped.

Surprised, Dylan turned around in time to see the wolf lunging straight at him, its claws raised and its mouth wide open, baring its razor-sharp teeth.

He was paralyzed with fear.

Marie jumped up, locked her arms around the werewolf's throat, and put it in a stranglehold. She dropped to the ground with it, the monster writhing to break free. It kept snatching at her, but she wriggled this way and that, avoiding its teeth.

"What are you waiting for?" she shouted to him. "Get out of here!"

But he was locked in place, staring at the struggling wolf. Unlike the other one, this one was black. It was just as huge as the other wolf though, easily three times Marie's size. It looked like an oversized wolf except for one thing: Its paws weren't actually paws at all. They were claws that looked a lot like human hands. Did it have thumbs? Dylan couldn't be sure. But it definitely had long fingerlike appendages covered in hair like a gorilla's hand but pointy and sharp at the end like an eagle's talons.

That's where the scratch marks on the bodies had come from. Dylan shuddered.

"Dylan! Run back to the car!" Marie yelled.

"But…" He couldn't leave her like that. But what was he going to do? Fight it? How?

The wolf clawed Marie's thigh, leaving long deep bloody gashes, but she didn't even flinch. She managed to get up, the wolf still struggling against her stranglehold, and started spinning around. Faster and faster. The wolf growled at her, unrelenting.

She flung it into the trees with full force. The cracks of splintering wood were deafening. The wolf's impact had snapped several trees in half.

The look in Marie's eyes was wild. "Now run, goddamn it!" She grabbed him by the hand and yanked him in the opposite direction of the werewolf. The sudden movement made him snap out of his paralysis, and he started running like his life depended on it – which it did.

"It's not dead, is it?" he asked Marie while they were darting back to the house.

"No. I think I broke a few bones. But it will heal fast. So less talking more running!"

He took that to heart and picked up speed.

They left a large perimeter around the house and hit the street they had parked on a few blocks away. From there, they had to slow down to human speed lest they be seen. They scanned their surroundings meticulously and made it to the car without interference.

Marie floored the gas pedal as soon as the doors were shut.

"What are we going to do?" Dylan was frantic. Another one of those monsters was out there, and people were still dying.

"We're going to leave." Her lips pressed together tightly, and she kept her eyes fixed on the empty road.

"What? What do you mean?" He held onto the car headliner as she turned the corner at a neck-breaking speed.

"I mean we're going to leave town. It's too dangerous here."

It took Dylan a beat to process what she was saying. He couldn't leave. His mom still thought he was dead. "But… No!"

She hit the brakes, which almost catapulted Dylan through the windshield. They were already back at the motel.

"Quick, get out of the car!" she instructed, already out the door herself.

Dylan hurried to catch up with her. They were heading straight for their room. He threw a glance at the other vampire's window, but the curtains were drawn, and the lights were off inside the room. Maybe he was out. Did he know about the werewolf?

"Back so soon?" Alec asked without looking up from his book. He was sitting in the exact same position as when they'd left.

Marie slammed the door behind Dylan. "We didn't get all of them."

His eyes widened with terror, and he looked up, gaze darting from her to Dylan and back again. "What?"

Marie proceeded to the closet, pulled out a suitcase, and threw it on the bed. She started packing both their belongings.

"I'm not going anywhere," Dylan announced, crossing his arms in front of his chest.

Alec locked eyes with him for a moment, his face unreadable. He marked his page, set the book aside, and put all his attention squarely on his wife. "Tell me what happened."

"There's another wolf. Possibly more than one." Marie spoke without breaking focus from her self-imposed task. "It attacked a human in the woods, then it came after us. I knocked it out so we could get away, but I didn't have any silver with me."

"The thing about silver is real?" Dylan asked. He found it hard to believe that jewelry could harm that monster. They ignored him.

"Did you get bitten?"

That's when Dylan remembered Marie's thigh had been scratched. But now there wasn't a trace of the deep gash the wolf had left.

"No. But it was close."

Alec's gaze rested on Dylan. Was that concern in his eyes? They bored into Dylan's with such intensity, the younger immortal had to look away.

"Pack your things, Dylan. We need to get moving. There are only a few hours left till sunrise," Marie instructed.

"Why do you suddenly want to leave so badly? They've been here all along."

She didn't answer. Instead, she tossed Dylan the suitcase Alec had bought him. "Start packing."

Dylan dropped it. It clanked to the floor. "No. I'm not going anywhere." His mind was set.

Alec's worried glance darted back and forth between them. It finally rested on Dylan. "So, it was one wolf?"

"Yes."

"Marie." She pretended not to hear him. He got up, and the next moment, he stood beside her, a hand on her arm. She stilled and slowly tilted her head up to him.

"It's one wolf. There are two of us. We can handle it."

She held his gaze for a beat and slowly shook her head. "I'm not willing to risk his life. And if you knew what it felt like, you wouldn't—"

"I know." Something unsaid passed between them. "We won't let him out of our sight."

"Are you talking about me?" Dylan didn't like where this was going.

Both their heads snapped toward him, and he got a good look at Marie's face. She wore that deeply sad and anguished expression again. Her eyes were watering, on the brink of tears, and her heart-shaped face suddenly looked a decade older. It made him want to reach out and hug her.

Then he remembered Molly, who had always had a similar sadness in her eyes and who was now dead, thanks to the two vampires in front of him.

But even Molly had gotten it wrong. Those two weren't the only monsters in town, and it seemed to Dylan like the wolves were the bigger threat. Another person had been attacked that night. And something told him the killing wasn't going to end unless they put a stop to it.

He tried to remember what they had told him about werewolves.

"Last night you said you had tried to stop them from coming after me."

Marie nodded.

"And that they could smell that I'm a—" He couldn't say it out loud.

"That I was one of you."

She nodded again.

"Were they stalking me before? Was that why they attacked my neighbor Stacy?"

His words seemed to spring her back into action. "Most likely but you don't have to worry about that now, Dylan. They won't get to you."

"But you're no longer watching my house." Now he was the one starting to panic. "What if they go after my mom?"

Neither one of them said anything, but he could sense their uneasiness.

"You think they will." His heart was hammering. "We need to protect her. I can't let anything happen to her." He darted to the door, but Alec was faster.

He blocked the exit. "Dylan, calm down." He held up a hand.

"Let me go! I can't let anything happen to her!" Dylan tackled the vampire, trying to get to the door. Alec grabbed him by the arms, holding him at bay. Dylan struggled to free himself, but his strength was still no match for the older immortal's.

"Dylan, please!" Marie's voice called from behind him. "Please, calm down. I'll go to her house right now, okay? I'll protect her. But please, you need to stay here where you're safe." Her voice sounded strained and desperate, like she was fighting back tears. It made Dylan stop and look at her.

Marie was full-on crying. Stunned, he took a step back.

"I'll go and protect her if you stay here." She didn't try to wipe away the tears streaming down her face. Her hands were balled into fists at her sides.

"I want to come with you." There was nothing he wanted more. He needed to see his mother.

But Marie shook her head vigorously, sending a few tears flying.

"No, it's too dangerous. If there's more than one wolf, I wouldn't be able to protect you and they would overpower you. You don't know how to fight them."

"Then teach me." He looked from her to Alec, who was still stoically blocking the door. The vampire's jaw was working.

Marie answered for him. "No. You need to stay out of harm's way."

"I don't care what happens to me if they get to my mom! And besides" – he ran his hands through his hair in exasperation – "I want to do something. Too many people have died. Please, let me help you get rid of these wolves."

Alec looked at Marie questioningly. Dylan followed his gaze. Marie's lips were pressed into a fine line, her hands still balled into fists, but she had stopped crying.

"We'll teach you how to defend yourself." The next thing Dylan knew she was at the door. "I'll go watch over your mother."

She reached for the doorknob, but Alec took her in his arms. He held her tightly, eyes closed, his body cocooning her tiny frame. She hugged him back, her shoulders shaking with silent sobs. He pressed his lips tenderly to her temple.

She broke the hug, kissed him swiftly on the lips, and was out the door.

Alec tilted his head, listening.

"What—" Dylan started, but Alec held up a finger, silencing him. He stayed like that for a few seconds, then he dropped his hand and looked squarely at Dylan.

"I'm going to teach you more than self-defense. Come on."

25

Curious, Dylan followed Alec out to the Audi. The vampire seemed distracted, looking over his shoulder multiple times.

"Get in," he ordered, nodding toward the car.

"Where are we going?" Dylan asked once Alec had started the engine.

"Somewhere we can train in peace." He took a few turns out of town.

As they sat beside each other in the car this time, the silence did not weigh heavily. In fact, Dylan was glad to have some quiet to process what had happened.

Marie had saved his life. He didn't even know how many times she had saved his ass by now, but this time was by far the most significant. He felt suddenly grateful to her. Not something he wanted to feel, but he had to admit that the wolves weren't her fault. Neither was him having the aura. Those monsters would have come after him with or without her there – and he was lucky she had been there to protect him.

He hated the thought. It would be so much easier if he could just blame her for everything!

He considered his first werewolf encounter. Marie had seemed calm and collected. Was it because they had been inside the safety of the car? This time, she had gotten rattled.

"Why did Marie get so upset?"

Alec stayed silent for so long, Dylan thought the vampire was ignoring him. "It's not my place to tell you. Suffice it to say, she has a complicated relationship with werewolves."

Weird. Up until then Alec had been forthcoming with answering Dylan's questions. This was clearly a sore subject.

"Can you pull out the calendar from the glove box?"

"Uh, sure." Dylan opened the glove compartment and rummaged through the paperwork inside … insurance papers, driver's licenses, registration papers … there it was: a beat-up wall calendar like you'd find at your grandmother's house. Flowery patterns were printed on each monthly page. It was still turned to March 1985. Dylan flipped the page to April.

Alec had stopped the car in front of the paper mill. The building was silent at this time of night.

"What moon phase are we in?" Alec asked.

"Why do you need to know that?"

"Why do you think?" Alec turned to Dylan with an expression that said *isn't it obvious?* When Dylan didn't answer, he continued, "Because of the wolves. Their strength depends on the moon. They're the strongest on a full moon, but they can't shift on a new moon. So what moon phase are we in?"

"Uh…" This was weird. Even weirder than the fact he now lived off blood. Dylan checked the line for April 1. "Waxing gibbous. Full moon's on Friday."

"Fuck." Alec thrummed his fingers on the steering wheel. "Well, I guess we should start training you sooner rather than later." His brown eyes brimmed with emotion, which took Dylan by surprise. The moment didn't last though. Alec got out of the car, and Dylan followed closely behind.

The vampire opened the trunk, and Dylan blinked in astonishment at its contents: heavy silver chains and gleaming silver knives, the handles of which were solid silver as well. Some of the links on the chains were coated in blood.

"Whoa…"

"Yes, we need to polish those." Alec indicated the chains. "But the knives are ready to go, and we can use the chains for training purposes. Grab one."

Dylan took out one of the heavy chains, which rattled dully against the trunk floor, while Alec grabbed four of the silver knives.

Despite his heavy load, Dylan had no problem jumping the paper mill's fence. He should have known by then that physical activities were no longer a challenge, but after a lifetime of being chosen last in PE class and getting winded from climbing stairs, he had a hard time adjusting to this new reality.

Alec broke the lock of one of the side entrances with his bare hands and held the door open for Dylan. Stepping inside, Dylan was bathed in the intense, unpleasant smell of paper and machines. He felt like he was blind, like the smells could mask any other finer scents in the room that might alert him to danger. Relying so heavily on his olfactory sense seemed animalistic, which made him feel even less human.

They found themselves in a darkened factory room. Several enormous machines were accessible by metal staircases that crisscrossed the entire area, creating lots of hiding spots, but Alec seemed confident that they were alone.

"If a werewolf were here, you would definitely smell it," he explained. "Their blood smells very sweet to us. It's supposed to be inviting."

"Why?" It was beyond Dylan why anything would be made to attract vampires.

"Because it's poisonous to us. It'll make you very sick for weeks. And then you'd be an easy mark."

Dylan nodded. "So, they're like colorful mushrooms?"

Alec snorted. "Yes, I guess you could say that."

Alec indicated for Dylan to stop in a wide open area. He took a few more steps and turned around toward the younger immortal. He tossed him one of the knives, which Dylan caught with ease – not without being thrilled that he could do so.

"Okay, so, werewolves were created to hunt us, so they share many of our strengths."

"Hold on," Dylan interrupted. "Marie already said that last night. But what do you mean by 'they were created to hunt us'?"

Alec pursed his lips. "The short version?" He gestured with the hand that wasn't holding the knives. "About twelve-hundred years ago witches created werewolves by invoking the power of the moon to protect themselves and humans from immortals. Think of them as witches' guard dogs.

"But eventually the guard dogs grew tired of their mistresses and decided to go off on their own. Their disdain for us is so ingrained in them, though, that they never stopped hunting us. By the 1600s it got so bad that most immortals were steering clear from forests altogether."

"Do they only live in forests?" Dylan asked.

"Mostly, yes. They need to be near nature; otherwise, they go crazy. Once the Industrial Revolution set in, they avoided highly populated areas completely."

Dylan's head was spinning with all this new information. "But Molly was a witch. How did she not know about this?"

Alec shrugged. "Witches don't keep public records. And I think most of them consider the werewolf project a failure, so they never really talk about it. Plus, there are not many wolves left. A witch could live her entire life without meeting one of them."

Anger boiled inside Dylan. If Marie had been honest with him, he might have been able to convince Molly that she wasn't responsible for the murders and Molly would still be alive. His hand tightened around the knife's hilt.

"But remember that they're almost as strong as you, they're certainly as fast as you, and they heal almost as quickly. So, if you wound them, you better make it a fatal wound." He took one of the knives in his other hand and held it up. "Silver is highly poisonous to them. A wound inflicted by silver takes hours, if not days, to heal. And if you pierce their skin often enough or hit any vital organs, they'll die."

Dylan nodded, thinking of the sliced-up man from the warehouse – the one they had used to fake Dylan's death. That meant that all the gashes on his skin had been caused by these silver knives. He shivered involuntarily. On the one hand, he wanted to fight back and get rid of those monsters, but on the other hand, he had never killed anything bigger than a fly or a spider. Some of his peers had gone on hunting trips with their dads, but his mom wasn't into that stuff, so he had never even held a gun in his hand. He stared at the knife he was holding. Would he be able to use it against a living, breathing thing?

"The chains are sometimes more useful than the knives. If you manage to trap a wolf in a silver chain, it'll quickly die from the exposure to the metal."

Dylan had forgotten about the chain still slung over his shoulder. He took it off and ran his fingertips along the links. Maybe this would be easier…

"Okay, pretend I'm a werewolf and try to kill me."

Dylan's head snapped up. His attention was squarely on Alec now. The vampire held his hands open in invitation. Dylan sized him up. Pretending to want to kill Alec wasn't going to be difficult. After all, he'd wanted to kill that guy since he'd been turned. But he couldn't shake the feeling that this was some kind of trap.

Alec was stronger than him, so he had to try to stay as far away from him as possible lest the vampire get the upper hand.

"Wow, take your time," Alec said with an eyeroll. "If I were a wolf, I would have chewed you up by now. You've got to act faster than that."

The next second, Dylan was on his back on the floor. Alec was straddling him, pinning him down by the wrists. The knife had clanked to the floor, but Dylan hadn't lost his grip on the chain.

He struggled underneath Alec, but he might as well have been trapped under a full-grown fallen tree.

"Now, it would be very easy for me to rip your throat out. You'd be unconscious and your body would take hours to heal. During that time, I could leave you out in the sun to roast," Alec explained calmly, all the while not moving an inch.

Dylan felt utterly humiliated. And he had had his fair share of humiliation in his life. Flashes of Fletcher's smug face ran through his head, a slideshow of every time the bully had kicked his ass. He thought of the time Fletcher had literally made him eat dirt by smacking him facedown into the ground while the whole school was laughing at him.

And now, even as an immortal vampire, he had to take this shit? From Alec, from the wolves…

Rage flared inside him.

"What are you going to do, Dylan?" Alec taunted him. "Hm? What are you going to do?"

With a desperate flick of his wrist, he hurled the chain at Alec. The vampire didn't let go of Dylan, but the flying metal chain caught him by surprise. He jerked back a little, loosening his grip enough for Dylan to wriggle his right arm free.

He didn't waste time. He didn't think.

He turned his head to the side and up, looking for the knife. He stretched, reaching for it with his freed arm. And only a second after the chain had hit its mark, he rammed the blade into Alec's side using all the force he had.

He felt it scrape a rib as it cut through skin and flesh like butter. The feeling was nauseating rather than satisfying.

Alec didn't even flinch. He let go of Dylan, got to his feet, and held up his left arm to get a better look at the knife lodged in his side.

Dylan scrambled to his feet, putting some distance between himself and the vampire.

"Not bad," Alec exclaimed with a nod. "You hit my lungs, and I can feel the blade scraping against my heart. If you had aimed a little higher you would have incapacitated me."

He yanked the knife out. Blood gushed from the wound, but he pressed his hand to it, wiping the knife on his jeans.

"If I were a werewolf, I'd be in a lot of pain right now, and the silver poisoning would spread through my lungs… But then again, you wouldn't even have gotten that far because I would have ripped your throat out way before you started fighting back."

He tossed Dylan the knife. The younger immortal was still staring at the injury he had caused, which would have been fatal and extremely painful to a human but didn't seem to be more than a minor inconvenience for the vampire. When he caught the blade, the wound had already healed.

Alec smirked. "Stop gaping at me like that. You know it takes a lot more to cause us pain."

In theory, Dylan did know that, but it was a different story when he actually got to see it. He shook his head in disbelief. "So, that didn't hurt at all?"

Alec shrugged. "It felt slightly uncomfortable." His face turned serious. "But you can't even let it get that far. Never let a wolf get the upper hand! You have to attack first before they have the chance."

Dylan nodded, understanding. "Is this what Marie doesn't want me to do?"

The corners of Alec's mouth twitched. "She thinks you'd put yourself in harm's way, but I disagree. I think offense is the best defense." Alec's voice sounded like that of a 1950s radio football commentator on that last part. Dylan couldn't help but wonder whether that was where the vampire had picked up the phrase.

"Okay." He bent over, reaching for the chain, never breaking eye contact with Alec. Trying to think fast, he didn't wait to attack until he was upright again. Rather, he thrust out his other arm, hurling the knife at Alec before the vampire knew what was happening.

Dylan could hardly hide his surprise when Alec caught it midair before it pierced his abdomen. "Good. Try throwing the chain next time though. That'll make it harder for the wolf to dodge the throw."

They continued like that for what seemed like hours to Dylan, but no matter how he approached it, he couldn't catch Alec off guard. He couldn't help but wonder how hard it would be to actually go up against the vampire. He definitely needed to gather more information before he could start planning his takedown. There had to be some way to beat him.

By the end of the training session, even though he had nicked Alec a few more times, he didn't feel confident he'd be able to fight a werewolf. The truth was, those sharp gleaming white teeth and fingerlike claws scared him to death. He couldn't say for certain that he wasn't going to freeze up again in the presence of another wolf.

When they got back to the motel, Marie was still out, which made Alec visibly nervous. He paced around the room, only stopping to peek out the window behind the curtain now and then.

"Do you think something happened to her?" Dylan asked, sitting on the bed, shoes off, ankles crossed. He had intended to sound disinterested, but he couldn't hide the concern in his voice. He told himself he was worried about his mom's safety since she might be in grave danger if Marie had been attacked.

Alec stilled. "No, I'm sure she's fine." He sounded convinced, meeting Dylan's gaze head on, his soft brown eyes full of confidence.

"Then why are you so nervous?"

"The sun will come up in ten minutes."

Dylan sucked in a breath, instantly remembering the searing pain from the day before. It reminded him that he was never going to walk in the sun again. He wanted to squeal in desperation but ran his fingers through his hair instead, pulling his knees close to his chest.

He thought back to his birthday when he had taken his truck out for a leisurely drive on a spring day, windows rolled down, soaking up the sun. His heart ached. He'd never be able to do that again.

Alec was gazing out the window again.

"You haven't been in the sun for over three hundred and fifty years. How do you not miss it?" Dylan asked.

Alec frowned at him. "I don't remember what the sun felt like before it was deadly to me." He turned back to the window.

Dylan was stunned. How could someone forget something as basic as the warmth of the sun? Would that happen to him eventually if he lived long enough? He shuddered. He never wanted to live that long. He didn't want to be immortal. He wanted his old life back.

"Finally…" Alec muttered and opened the door. "You cut it close," he admonished Marie as she stepped inside.

She seemed tense. Her whole demeanor was rigid, and her eyes were wide and alert. "Sorry, just wanted to make sure…"

Alec took her in his arms, kissing the top of her head. Her arms wrapped limply around him.

"So?" Dylan prompted impatiently. "Is my mom okay?"

Marie broke the hug and smiled weakly at Dylan. "Yes, she's fine. There were no wolves. Did you guys train?" she asked Alec.

25

Alec nodded, but before he could say anything, Dylan asked, "And what about now? Who is going to watch over her during the day?"

They both looked at him like he was missing something.

"What?" He was getting annoyed.

"Werewolves can only shift at night, Dylan. During the day they're in human form," Alec explained. "They don't have any of their strength or enhanced senses when they're human, so they can't harm anyone."

That explained why they had only attacked at night.

"Since they were created to hunt us, their creators figured they wouldn't need their powers during the day because that's when we can't go outside." Marie's voice sounded bitter, detached. Her face was stone-cold.

"So, they're regular people during the day? Does that mean they could be anyone?"

They both shook their heads. "No. They live in the woods away from humans, kind of like cavemen in prehistoric times." Marie didn't try to hide her disgust.

Alec smirked. "Yes, you could put it like that. But they're more intelligent. They know how to go undetected by humans. Even though I'm quite sure that some of the human myths like Bigfoot or the Yeti are based on daytime werewolf sightings…"

That made sense.

"It's frustrating. We can still smell them in their human form. It would be easy for us to hunt them down and kill them during the day when they're at their weakest but…" She indicated the closed curtains.

"Well, that's what new moons are for," Alec said with a slight smile.

"Right, they can't turn on a new moon…" Dylan muttered. He thought about everything he had learned about real werewolves and about everything he knew from movies. "But can they turn regular humans into werewolves? Is that how you missed that one from last night?"

They looked at each other, concern knitting their brows. It looked like they hadn't thought about that.

"The one that attacked us didn't seem like a newbie," Marie said to Alec.

Alec sucked in a breath and turned to Dylan. "Technically they *can* turn humans into werewolves. All it takes is one bite." He held up a finger. "And they're not limited to certain people like we are. Anyone can turn except people who can be made immortal."

"Ah." Dylan nodded.

"But…" Alec took a seat on the couch. "They never turn anyone. We're not exactly sure if it's lack of self-control or if they just don't want to."

"Then how are new werewolves made?" Dylan asked.

Alec shrugged. "They breed. Just like humans."

"They don't like to mingle with humans. I guess that's why they don't want to bring in new wolves from the outside." Marie crossed her arms in front of her chest.

"So you don't think they bit anyone."

They shook their heads.

"We must have missed one." Marie rubbed her eyes with the heels of her palms. Alec got up and put an arm around her, rubbing her back. "Hey… It's fine. It'll be all right." He cupped her chin so she had to look at him. "It'll be all right."

After a beat, she nodded and let out a breath.

"We'll get that last one, too. I promise."

26

The priest had provided blood for him in a bowl which he had placed right outside his cage so he was able to reach it. Slowly he moved into a crouched position, his enclosure being too small for him to stand up. He reached for the bowl, his blackened and burnt hand sending shots of stinging pain up his arm. His mouth watered at the prospect of the life-giving liquid touching his lips. But the vessel was too wide to fit between the bars. He had no choice but to inch forward until his face was pressed against the barrier, stick his tongue out, hold the bowl at eye-level, and carefully tilt it so the blood could trickle into his mouth. But as soon as he tasted it, he gagged in disgust.

It wasn't animal blood this time but human. Normally, he would have considered this an improvement, but he could taste the disease in it. The person this blood belonged to must have been bled into this bowl to be healed of their ailment. The taste of death and decay made him retch.

He wanted to toss the vessel across the room. The priest's desk was only three feet away, and he would have loved to spill blood all over the man's important correspondence. But the unrelenting pain in his charred body made him stop.

It was either this or nothing.

And he needed it. He pressed his eyes shut and downed the vile liquid as quickly as he could. He flung the empty bowl across the room. It clanged against the opposite wall and clattered onto the wooden floor. Exhausted, he curled into a ball, his head spinning. He closed his eyes in defeat. He should have listened to Arianne. He should have stayed with her.

He could feel the diseased blood coursing through his body. It was trying to repair the damage the sun had caused with the little life left in the liquid. It felt like sand grinding inside his veins. These days he wasn't sure what was more agonizing: the continued exposure to sunlight, making his flesh melt, or his body's efforts to heal itself. Just as he was using up the blood he had consumed, his body demanded more, struggling to repair the damaged tissue with the little it received. Sometimes it was better not to feed to avoid this pain. But if he didn't feed at all, his insides felt like they were digesting themselves and every fiber of his body screamed in agony. And then he was unable to sleep – thus denying himself the only reprieve.

The heavy wooden door opened, and the priest entered. He was wearing his everyday black cassock. His dark hair was thinning dramatically, and his blue eyes were deceptively kind. The priest didn't spare him a glance, but he paused in front of the empty bowl on the floor. Slowly, he bent over, picked it up, and walked to the cage, crouching in front of it.

"Remarkable. Even the diseased blood is affecting you."

The smell of fresh and healthy blood emanating from the priest was maddening. The vampire lurched forward, gripping the so-called man of God by the wooden cross dangling from his neck. But the priest only laughed and easily loosened the vampire's blackened fingers from the ornament. He made a show of wiping it and got up.

"You might get something stronger in a moment." He sat down at his desk. "But only if you behave." The priest chuckled and turned to his correspondence. After a while he started humming a tune.

The vampire held his hands over the remnants of his ears so he wouldn't have to listen – no longer shocked at the feeling of his burnt hairless scalp.

A knock at the door interrupted the priest. "Enter." His servant opened the door and led three young women in. Their scent was irresistible, full of life. The servant was dismissed, and the priest proceeded to orate to the three women.

"I promised you a demon from hell, didn't I?" He kicked the cage, making it rattle. The girls shrieked at the sight of the scorched creature behind the bars. "Now if you are willing to sacrifice a negligible amount of your blood, I can show you his true wickedness."

They had done this more times than he could count. Each of the girls would cut her wrist and bleed into a goblet. The vampire would drink from said goblet and heal enough for his skin to grow back but not enough for his strength to return. They'd be amazed at the display, crossing themselves and mumbling prayers. The priest would open the blinds and let sunlight stream in through the window next to his cage and douse the vampire with it. He'd burn all over again. And this so-called man of God would tell these innocent women lies about how he had been chosen by the Lord to warn people of the devil and his servants and if they wanted a sure way to salvation, all they had to do was lie with him. Occasionally, one or two refused, but they were quickly brought to reason. The priest always got what he wanted in the end. One way or the other.

And sure enough, when the vampire was once again covered in fresh pink skin, the priest opened the blind. By now the sensation was familiar, but it still felt like a shock to his system as the glistening sun hit his naked body like liquid fire from hell itself. He covered his eyes with his hands to keep from going blind, stifling a scream as the freshly regrown skin was melted off his flesh once again.

When the priest put the blind back in place, the torture abruptly stopped. His muscles – or what was left of them – automatically relaxed. The pain dwindled from a sharp burning sensation to a glimmering sting. He hardly remembered what the complete absence of pain felt like.

During the first two years of his captivity, he had still hoped for death to take him, then he started believing he had brought this onto himself and he deserved nothing less for being a monster. But now all he wanted was revenge. He wanted to tear this priest limb from limb, then heal him, then tear off his limbs again.

As he was forced to listen to the priest bedding his naïve flock, he kept thinking about how wrong he had been. There was no God. He felt foolish for ever believing so. Now, all he believed in was himself.

Consciousness tugged at Dylan's senses. He turned over onto his other side, not yet ready to join the waking world.

This time Dylan was aware that he was dreaming. He was looking at Marie, only she appeared different. Her face was gaunt, and her clavicles protruded her skin sharply. She was wearing an old-timey dress and staring at him with curiosity. But there was also a hint of mistrust in her eyes. She had her guard up. The black glow around her was impossible to miss.

The image changed. This time, Marie's body was beaten and bloodied, her eyes staring up at him in fear and terror. He felt desperate to save her...

Another image. Marie, the way she looked now, a fierce immortal, her face lighting up with triumph and joy. His heart warmed at the sight of her. He loved her so much.

Then another face. Another girl. Dark eyes, brown skin, long black hair. Milena. The name rang inside his head. Her dress was in tatters, and she looked like she hadn't bathed in a while, but he could see the black glow surrounding her. She was one of them.

The image changed again. This time, he saw the immortal Marie screaming in pain, doubling over. He didn't know what was happening. He panicked, reaching for her, trying to calm her down. But when Marie looked up at him, he froze in terror. Her face was contorted in a mask of pain and anguish. She grabbed onto her hair, threatening to pull it from her scalp, and dark red tears of blood were running down her cheeks.

Dylan snapped awake. His heart was pounding in his ears. He sat up and ran a hand down his face, trying to banish the images from his dreams that were still haunting him. Alec's pain, Marie's tears of blood... His heart ached for them.

It was just memories. All of that had happened a long time ago. As he tried to calm himself down, a voice inside his head sneered at him: *Why do you care? They're the bad guys. They deserve everything that's happened to them.*

He shook his head, trying to empty his mind of all thought and to focus on the here and now.

Marie lay next to him in bed, dressed like the day before in nothing but a T-shirt. Unlike the day before, though, she seemed to be resting uneasily. Her heart-shaped face was twitching in her sleep, and her arm and leg muscles kept jerking.

Alec wasn't sleeping on the couch this time but was curled around Marie, his half-naked body pressed flush against hers. His arms were tightly wrapped around her.

Dylan felt like a peeping tom intruding on this private moment. And then he promptly felt bad for feeling bad. He looked away, trying to remember when he had fallen asleep. It must have been shortly after sunrise, while Alec had been showering. He was still wearing last night's clothes.

One glance at the curtains told him the sun was still up. That meant he couldn't go anywhere.

For some reason that didn't feel as frustrating as the day before. Maybe he wasn't fully awake yet or maybe he was just glad that his mom was still safe from the wolves while it was daytime.

Nervousness bubbled in his stomach. With images of werewolves tearing his mother up in his head, there was no going back to sleep.

A knock on the door made him jump. He whipped around, thinking in his agitated state of mind that the wolves had found them. Alec awoke and jumped to his feet while Marie was blinking groggily at him.

"Who is it?" Alec asked.

"It's Bernie. I got a message from Susan Harper."

Dylan's heart leaped at the mention of his mom's name, but before he could respond Marie had a hand pressed to his mouth.

Alec opened the door only a foot, staying fully behind it. "Come in," he instructed Bernie, who squeezed in through the tiny space – apparently not considering Alec's behavior strange.

His eyes looked oddly empty, and Dylan realized the man was under their mind control. Once that knowledge sank in, he stopped his futile attempts to get Marie's hand off his mouth and sank deeper into the bed in defeat.

She let go, and he threw a withering stare at her, which she ignored.

"Speak," Alec ordered.

"She says the bodies have been positively identified as Fletcher and Amanda Barnes, Richard Halston Jr., Molly Kirkgaard, and Dylan Harper."

Alec and Marie breathed sighs of relief, while Dylan balled his hands into fists, trying to fight the tears of rage forming in his eyes. His mom thought he was dead. He couldn't imagine the pain she had to be going through.

"Funeral arrangements are being made for all five teenagers. It'll be held two days from now."

Alec and Marie looked first at each other, then at Dylan, who was trying very hard not to let on how much this upset him. He didn't want them to know how hurt he was – how much *they* had hurt him.

"The fire has been declared arson. Police suspect the teens lit it themselves, then got stuck inside the warehouse."

"Is that it?" Alec asked.

"Yes," the old man answered tonelessly.

"Okay, you may go." Alec started opening the door again.

"Wait," Marie said. "Have there been any more dead bodies?"

Bernie looked at her without seeing her and answered, "Yes, two more teenagers have been found dead in the woods after they had been reported missing by their parents. All scratched up like the previous ones."

Dylan's stomach churned, his own misery momentarily forgotten. The wolf had killed two people last night? They had only heard one scream. It must have murdered someone else after they had outrun it.

Alec let Bernie out the same way he had let him in.

Once they were alone, Dylan said, "We have to do something about this. I don't want anyone else to get killed."

Marie's face darkened. "*You* are not going to do anything, got it?"

Dylan jumped up, shaking his head furiously. "Try and stop me!"

"Calm down!" Alec grabbed Dylan by the shoulder, forcing the younger immortal to look at him. "You are not going to do anything because you are two days old and can't hold your own against a werewolf. *We* are going to take care of it, and then we are all going to leave."

"*Leave?*" Dylan's fury and fear turned into panic. "I can't leave! My mom thinks I'm dead!" he blurted out.

"As she should," Marie said calmly. "Dylan…" She marched over to him, taking his hands in hers. He glared at her. "Please, you have to understand…" Her gray eyes were sparkling with an intensity he had never seen before. "Your old life is over. Dylan Harper is dead. There's nothing keeping you here. You're free to go anywhere, be whoever you want to be and do whatever you want! Isn't that what you've always wanted?"

He froze. It was true, he had always wanted to leave this place. He had told her as much himself. But not like this. He wanted to leave on his terms. And he certainly didn't want to leave his mom behind.

"I wanted to go to college, have a career, a family, build a life for myself," he spat. "None of my plans involved becoming a vampire and running off with the two of you."

They flinched at his use of the v-word.

"You were meant to be immortal," Alec said sharply.

"Yes, and it is better than being human," Marie added.

Dylan scoffed.

"No, really. Okay, I'll admit, it hasn't been great so far, but once we get out of this town and you get to see the world, you'll see that it's—"

"Oh my god, you're delusional!" He tried to pull his hands back, but she was gripping them hard. The ensuing desperation brought back that day's dreams. "News flash," he spat, while still trying to wriggle his hands free. She abruptly let go.

"Back when you guys were human, it might have been better, but nowadays people don't end up getting tortured or kidnapped! Being a human is actually pretty great these days."

Marie stared at him with her mouth gaping open, while Alec furrowed his brow.

"What are you talking about?" the oldest vampire asked.

"I just meant in general." Somehow Dylan didn't want to get into what he'd seen. He didn't want to know more. "I'm going to take a shower," he muttered. He needed to get away from them.

Before they could say anything else, he turned on his heel and rushed into the bathroom, slamming the door shut behind himself.

He did need to take a shower, so he turned the water on, but he also needed a moment to think. Being under constant supervision was grinding his nerves harder than anything else.

Once he stood under the stream of hot water, his muscles started to relax. He was running out of time. Marie and Alec weren't going to let him help take out the wolves, so maybe he could use their hunt as a distraction. It was more important than ever that he talk to his mom. Maybe he could persuade her to leave town with him. They could both hide out somewhere until he figured out a way to get rid of Alec and Marie for good.

After the party last night, he was confident that he wouldn't lose control and hurt her. If he could manage being in a room full of people he didn't care for and not kill anyone, he could handle being around his own mother.

Plus, he didn't want to be a monster. He could pull himself together. He'd figure things out and maybe it would all work out in the end.

* * *

While he was getting dressed, Marie went to take a shower, and Alec – now fully dressed in his usual all-black attire – was staring broodily at the closed curtain. Dylan couldn't be sure, but it felt like the vampire was anxiously awaiting sundown.

Dylan got dressed in dark blue denim pants and a turquoise T-shirt that showed off his newly toned arms. The more he looked in the mirror, the more he got used to his new looks, but he still didn't feel comfortable. Everything still felt off. He idly wondered if Greta would have wanted to suck him off if he had looked like his old self. *Of course not*, he answered his own question. *She knew the 'you' from before and she never looked at you twice.*

It made him feel like a fraud. Like he had lured her in under false pretenses.

"You had another memory dream, didn't you?" Alec suddenly asked. The vampire was no longer staring at the window but at Dylan.

Dylan considered lying, but what was the point? Alec would never believe him.

"Yes."

"What did you see?" He tilted his head, barely hiding his curiosity.

Dylan swallowed. He didn't know how to approach this. "You were … held captive by a priest."

Alec's face lost all color, making him look even paler than usual

– which Dylan hadn't thought possible. He avoided the younger immortal's gaze. Dylan could see his jaw working.

"How was this man able to capture you?"

Alec's hands balled into fists, his knuckles turning white. His mouth became a thin line. Dylan crossed his arms, waiting for an answer.

"I was reckless and stupid." Alec's voice was calm, but his rigid demeanor told Dylan that the vampire was about to snap.

Dylan grinned. Provoking the vampire made him feel immensely powerful and deeply satisfied. He wanted the tables to turn.

"What do you mean?" he asked innocently.

Alec sighed deeply and met Dylan's eyes with a withering glance. If looks could kill, Dylan would have dropped dead on the spot. But instead, he put on an innocent expression, meeting Alec's gaze unafraid.

"It was about fifteen years after I was turned. I hated what I was so much that I turned to a priest for help. I asked him to free me from my miserable existence so I could be with God. He saw an opportunity and locked me up." Alec shrugged, trying to seem casual, but Dylan could see his hands were trembling.

"For how long?"

Alec's Adam's apple was working, and his eyes turned glossy. He had fixed his gaze on a point over Dylan's shoulder. "Five years."

Dylan's eyes widened with horror as Alec's words hit him. "How did you get out?" His voice had dropped to a whisper.

"Arianne saved me." Alec looked Dylan in the eyes again. "I would have died if it hadn't been for her." He swallowed hard. "If only I had embraced my nature from the very beginning, I could have saved myself all that pain and suffering." He paused, and his tone became even sharper. "So I'd strongly advise you to get over the loss of your mortal life and accept what you are."

Dylan didn't know what to say. He remembered the sun's fiery pain from the day before. And it had only affected his face and arms. He couldn't even imagine his entire body getting burnt repeatedly over the course of five whole years. The unspeakable agony Alec must have lived through made Dylan's heart ache for the vampire.

Stop it! He kidnapped and turned you against your will. He's the bad guy.

"Is that all you saw?" Alec asked, eyeing Dylan suspiciously.

He shook his head. "The rest was vague. I didn't get much…"

"Okay, then my blood has almost left your system. There won't be any more dreams." When Dylan didn't react immediately, he asked, "And what else did you see?"

Dylan listened to check if Marie was still in the shower. He could hear the water running, hitting the porcelain tub at different angles, which meant she couldn't hear a word of their conversation.

"I saw Marie. First as a human and then as a vampire…"

Alec huffed, shooting Dylan a warning look. "Stop using that word."

Dylan rolled his eyes. "Well, it was strange. She seemed to be in a lot of pain, and she was crying tears of blood?"

Alec's eyes widened for a fraction of a second.

"What happened there?" Dylan asked, unable to hide his curiosity.

If Alec had been able to sweat, Dylan figured the vampire's forehead would be glistening right then. "It was nothing."

"Didn't look like nothing."

"Just forget about it. It happened over a century ago. It's not important."

"Well, if it's not important, then there's no harm in telling me, right?" Dylan was enjoying this. Alec's discomfort was growing by the second.

Alec shook his head and said, "It's not my place to tell you."

He had said the same thing the night before when Dylan had asked him about Marie's intense reaction to the werewolves. Were the two things connected?

Alec bent over and pulled a blood bag from the mini fridge. Their supply was dwindling fast. They only had about ten bags left. Dylan didn't want to think about what they would have to do once they had emptied their stash completely.

Dylan had thought Alec was grabbing the bag for himself, but the vampire tossed it to him. "Here, you need to build up strength, just in case the wolf gets to you…"

But Dylan wasn't done with Alec yet.

"Who's Milena?" he asked innocently.

Alec froze. Then, in the blink of an eye, he was grabbing Dylan by the throat, pressing him into the closet door, crushing his windpipe.

Dylan struggled to break free. His eyes bulged from the pressure Alec was exerting on his throat.

"Do not mention that name again," Alec whispered in Dylan's ear. "Ever." Then he let go, leaving Dylan massaging his broken windpipe. Alec's attack hadn't hurt, but it had felt extremely uncomfortable, and it had rendered him utterly powerless.

"Have I made myself clear?" Alec asked sharply, handing Dylan the blood bag he had dropped.

All Dylan could do was nod. His larynx was still crushed, and he couldn't make a sound. Frantically, he ripped the blood bag open and guzzled its contents. He could feel his throat heal with every swallow. When the bag was empty, he could talk again, but he was still ravenous.

He helped himself to another blood bag, daring Alec to stop him, but the vampire had retreated back to his spot by the window.

As he finished his second helping, Marie emerged from the bathroom. She was wearing the same all-black outfit as the day they had met: tight black T-shirt, tight black jeans, and black combat boots. A heavy silver necklace adorned her neck, and she wore silver rings on each finger. Dylan was speechless for a moment as he stared at her.

She looked ready for battle.

"Okay, let's kick some werewolf ass."

"You're right on time. The sun is about to set," Alec muttered with a smile. His love for his wife was evident in the gentleness of his eyes. The same eyes that had sparkled with threat only moments earlier.

Dylan had to suppress a shudder.

"So, what's the plan?" he asked as he tossed the empty blood bag in the trash.

"We're going to track down the wolf and kill it," Marie answered matter-of-factly.

Dylan scoffed. "Sounds easy enough, but what if you can't find it?"

"We will find it," Alec answered with determination. "The sooner the better. We need to get out of this place…"

Dylan tried to ignore that last part, asking innocently, "And what about me? I'm assuming you won't let me come with you?"

Marie's eyes widened with terror. "Absolutely not!"

Dylan crossed his arms, waiting for her to elaborate.

"You are going to stay here."

"What? You're going to trust me to stay by myself?" he retorted sarcastically.

They shared a look, and Alec said, "Yes, Dylan, we trust you. Plus, we can cover more ground if both of us go, and if there is more than one wolf, there's safety in numbers. So we don't really have a choice. And…" A devious smile spread across his face. "There isn't really anything you can do now. You've been legally declared dead. The murder cases have been closed. All the loose ends are tied up. We know you won't go to see your mother because you might kill her, and you wouldn't want that. So you're fine on your own. And this is where you're safest." He gestured toward the unused TV set. "Watch TV or something while we're gone."

Dylan couldn't believe the audacity, but he forced himself to remain silent. Being left alone was all he needed. He pressed his lips together.

"We won't be long," Marie promised. And with that, they exited the room.

Dylan forced himself to wait a good five minutes after the door had clicked shut, then he slipped out into the night, used sheer muscle to break into the Audi's trunk – and it didn't even take a lot – grabbed one of the silver knives, and ran.

27

He had no time to lose. There was a good chance that Alec and Marie would hunt down the wolf quickly and return to the motel only to find their room empty. And then the first place they would go to look for him would be his house and he would be busted.

He darted through the woods alongside the main road, trying to remain invisible to passing humans while not venturing too far into the forest. The last thing he needed was another run-in with the monster from last night.

The air was clear and a little crisp for the season, and he kept sniffing for that caramel smell that would alert him to the wolf's presence. With every inhale he relaxed a bit more: no sign of the wolf. All he could smell was clear night air.

He had picked up Alec's and Marie's scents when he had crossed the road into the forest, but they had gone off in a different direction. And he planned to steer clear of their scents, too.

What would have been a five-minute drive turned into a two-minute run, and he would have been even faster if he didn't have to stick to the shadows. But his heart leaped with joy when he finally saw his house in all its chipped-paint glory.

His truck – the one his mom had gotten him for his birthday – was parked by the side of the street. The sight of it made his stomach clench. Martin's car was in the driveway behind his mom's old Chevy.

Dylan stopped dead in his tracks. He had been so busy focusing on his escape that he had never thought about how he would reveal himself to his mom – especially if Martin was there, too. He didn't want to get the man's hopes up that his daughter might have survived as well, only to crush him with the news that she hadn't. Plus, he might give Susan a heart attack when he appeared on her doorstep alive and looking so different.

"I don't understand," came a voice from inside the house. It rang out as clearly as if the person were standing right next to him. "Why would they go to that warehouse? And what happened there?"

He noticed light streaming out of the living room window and inched closer. It was dark outside, so they couldn't see him from inside, but he kept a safe distance nonetheless.

Martin had one arm wrapped around Susan. They were sitting on the couch, Susan sobbing into a tissue. A bunch of used tissues were crumpled up around the tissue box on the coffee table. Martin also had tears in his eyes, which he tried to dab at stealthily with his free hand.

Dylan's heart shattered into a million pieces seeing them like that. It wasn't fair. Martin had lost his wife and now his daughter. And Susan had only ever had Dylan.

"I can't believe he's gone." Her voice broke, and she pressed her eyes shut, which made a torrent of tears spill out. She buried her face in her hands, her shoulders trembling with silent sobs.

Dylan couldn't stand it. He wanted to comfort her so badly it hurt. He automatically reached out, but before his palm touched the windowpane, he stopped himself.

Martin squeezed her tighter. "I know," he choked out. "I can't believe it either. I knew Molly was unhappy and that she was missing her mom, but I figured we would have time to work things out. I didn't think—" He pressed his lips together, his jaw tightening.

After what seemed like several minutes, Martin inhaled sharply. "Dylan was a good kid. He should still be here."

Dylan's vision became blurry, and the tears spilled over, running in cold streaks down his cheeks. This wasn't right.

"I just don't understand why he would go off with the Barnes kids and that Halston boy. They weren't friends. And why would they light a building on fire!? Dylan has never broken a rule in his life!" She had gotten up and was pacing the room.

Martin shook his head. "Who knows what those kids were up to. Maybe it was some kind of prank that went horribly wrong."

Susan stopped, her back to Dylan. "Do you think…" She swallowed, but her voice became thicker anyway. "Do you think they were in a lot of pain?"

"No…" Martin's tone was assertive and sure, but his face said he was thinking the opposite. "No, I'm sure they didn't suffer."

That was it. Dylan had heard enough. He had to tell them the truth. He owed it to them. He wiped the tears off his face and zipped over to the front door, but before he could press the bell, a voice he didn't recognize called out to him: "Don't do it."

He whipped around.

The vampire from the motel was standing at the edge of the driveway. He was wearing a beige trench coat and had his hands stuffed in his pockets. When their gazes met, he smiled at Dylan, who suddenly felt threatened. But then he remembered that this guy would be way more dangerous to his mother than to him. And he didn't intend on letting that vampire past him into the house.

He took a few steps toward the other vampire and stood in a wide stance, his back squarely to the front door.

He had no idea what to do when meeting another vampire. Were there any rules of conduct he didn't know yet? The man was coming closer. No, he had to lead him away from his mom's house! He took a few more strides toward the vampire and braced himself for whatever was coming next.

"Don't worry. I mean you no harm." His voice sounded American, but so did Marie's and Alec's. Accent didn't mean anything with these creatures.

"Who are you? And what do you want?"

The man was standing farther away than usual during a conversation. Dylan assumed the vampire kept his distance to make him feel less threatened. Make him let his guard down. Well, that wasn't going to happen.

The vampire ignored Dylan's questions. "You can't let your mother see you like this. Humans can't know. Let her think you're dead. It's easier that way."

How did he know that Susan was his mother? Had the vampire eavesdropped on him, Alec, and Marie? "What do you care?"

The vampire's lips twitched. "I've come here for you." His tone was casual, as if he had told Dylan he read the paper every morning.

Dylan's senses turned to high alert. He listened intently for any other immortals or wolves in the area, his gaze darting nervously up and down the street. "Why?"

The man sighed. "Why don't we take a little walk and talk?" He nodded up the street. And even though Dylan didn't want to leave his mom, he also needed to get this guy away from her.

"Why should I trust you?"

"Because I know who you are, Dylan." He smiled. "You were born in Boston on March 30th, 1967, and you and your mother Susan moved into that house when you were only a couple months old. You've lived here ever since."

Dylan was flabbergasted. "How do you know all this? Who are you?"

The man turned. "Come. I'll tell you." When Dylan didn't move, he added, "Aren't you the least bit curious?" He winked and smiled.

Dylan was indeed curious, and he figured if the vampire wanted to hurt him, he would have done so by then. So he gave in and followed the man. They strolled at a leisurely pace up the street toward the forest.

They walked in silence for a while. Dylan waited for the man to speak, but he didn't.

"So?" Dylan finally prompted. He was losing precious time. He had no idea how long it would take Marie and Alec to figure out he was gone.

The man stopped, suddenly seeming nervous. Dylan halted beside him, waiting for an explanation.

The vampire's gray eyes fixed on Dylan's blue ones. He stroked his beard. "I don't know how to say this, so I'll just be blunt."

"Okay…"

"You're my son." He paused. "I'm your father, Dylan."

He had heard the words, but he didn't comprehend them. "What?" His eyelids fluttered.

"My name is James Mayhew. I met your mother, Susan Harper, in Boston in the spring of sixty-six. She was working at a department store, and I was an accountant. She was eighteen and I was twenty-three."

"How— I— What?" Dylan felt numb. This couldn't be real, but deep down he knew it was. He saw it in James's hands that were shaped like his, in the curve of his upper lip that had been replicated perfectly on Dylan's face…

The man he had hated for as long as he could remember was standing right in front of him.

He had often imagined what it would be like to meet his father. Even thought about what he would say to him. But now he was speechless.

He had no doubt that James was telling the truth, even though he looked too young to be Dylan's father: not a day over twenty-five. But then again, this man was a vampire.

"It was love at first sight." He smiled. "We went out a few times, and after only a month I knew I wanted to marry her. We took the next step and…" He trailed off, shrugging. "When she told me she was pregnant, I was over the moon. We set a date for the wedding. I put a down payment on an apartment…" His smile faded. "But then everything changed. One night, as I was walking home from the bar, this guy came up to me. He introduced himself as Vincent, and next thing I knew, he dragged me into an alley and turned me into an immortal."

"That's why you left?" Dylan could hardly believe it.

"Yes. I'd killed people. I couldn't go back to her. It was too dangerous." He stopped, his jaw working. "I did what I could. I made sure you had a comfortable place to live, and I kept tabs on you over the years."

"Hold on." Dylan held up a hand. This was too much. "What do you mean you made sure we had a comfortable place to live? We moved into my mom's aunt's house. How—" His heart skipped a beat.

James's brow furrowed. "She didn't have any relatives except her brother and Susan. I knew the house would go to your mother when she died."

"You killed her." Dylan shuddered. The house he had grown up in had been obtained by murder. Susan's favorite aunt had died because this man thought her home could be put to better use. He felt sick.

"It was the only way I could provide for the two of you!"

Dylan shook his head in disgust. "And make sure we wouldn't leave, right? You knew Mom wouldn't sell that house."

James's lips widened into the cruelest smile Dylan had ever seen. It made a shiver run down his spine. "Well, I needed to keep tabs on you, son. The first time I saw you was when you and your mother moved into that house. You were two months old, but I could already see the black shimmer around your tiny body." He paused. "As you grew older, you resembled your mother more and more." He gave Dylan a quick once-over. "Even more so now."

Dylan realized with a pang of pride that he did look even more like his mom now that his face wasn't covered in acne and he had lost the extra weight. Maybe this new body wasn't so bad after all.

"But you take after me." The proud expression on James's face made Dylan want to punch him.

"I am nothing like you."

"Sure you are. You inherited the immortality gene from me. You definitely didn't get it from your human mother…"

The disdain in his voice made Dylan ball his hands into fists. The reverie with which James had spoken about her earlier was gone. It took everything Dylan had not to beat the crap out of this man.

"I checked in once a year around your birthday." He shrugged. "Just making sure you were okay. I was going to wait until you left for college and then I was going to turn you."

Dylan nodded slowly, processing the information. "So, it wasn't enough that you left. You were going to take me away from her, too. Do you have any idea what it's been like for her since you abandoned her? You say you loved her, but did you ever make sure that she was happy? Did you not see how much she's suffering right now because of everything that happened!?" *Do you know what it's been like for me?* He wanted to shout at his father. But he didn't want to show him that he cared. He didn't want to admit that his father had hurt him.

James waved him off. "She was fine. She got over it. And she's fine now, too. She's still got that boyfriend." He grinned. "And that hunter talked to her for the better part of an hour last night. She was consoling her, telling her she'd be okay." He scoffed and shook his head. "I don't think I would have bothered with that. Susan is human after all. Their lives are short and tragic, and they get over things pretty quickly." He tilted his head. "I guess they have to. Otherwise, they'd be sad all their lives."

Dylan tried not to react to his father's harsh words, but inside he felt cold. He had already assumed the worst about this man, but somehow, his father still exceeded his expectations. "How long have you been here?"

"I got into town a few weeks before your birthday. Kept a low profile. Hardly left the motel with those wolves running rampant. Kept my distance from those hunters, too."

"You mean Alec and Marie?"

"Yes." His brow furrowed again. "I had heard of them. They're old, but most European immortals are. Heard they've been hunting werewolves for about a century. Eradicated them in Europe and almost hunted them to extinction here in North America. All because one pack killed their child."

"What?" They'd had a child?

"From what I know, they turned a girl somewhere in Europe in the mid-1800s. The continent was infested with wolves. She was trapped by a pack, and the wolves killed her. Those two have been on a vendetta ever since." His face hardened. "I guess you're supposed to be the replacement."

A face flashed in Dylan's mind's eye. The girl in rags from Alec's memory. Milena. That's why Alec hadn't wanted him to mention her to Marie and why Marie had reacted to the wolf encounter the way she had. He felt a pang of guilt despite himself.

He scoffed. "You know nothing about them." He couldn't believe he was speaking up for Alec and Marie, but he felt like his father was doing them wrong somehow, and he didn't know why but it bothered him.

James smiled. "Well, they can't be that great if you ran away from them."

Dylan's heartbeat accelerated. He felt strangely exposed. "I didn't. Just needed to run an errand."

"Sure you did." James's smug smile turned into concern. "But you're too young to be on your own. You're only two days old. There's so much you don't know yet."

"I'll manage."

James shook his head. "No, you won't. You have no idea what you're getting yourself into. But I can help you." The smile on his face was more off-putting than anything else. "I'm glad you left them because now we can be together. You and me. The way it was always meant to be." He put his hands on Dylan's shoulders, and his eyes bore into Dylan's with an intensity that made Dylan want to look away. "I can show you how to get all the blood you want." He grinned. "I can teach you how to dispose of bodies and remain undetected. You don't have to live off blood bags anymore."

Another shiver ran down Dylan's spine. This was worse than anything he had imagined. His father was insane. A psycho killer. He took a step back, shaking off James's hands. "No."

"You see, my blood might not be running through your veins anymore, but I am still your father. I wish I had been the one to turn you, but those old ones beat me to it by only a few months. I've waited for this your entire life." He reached out to Dylan.

Dylan recoiled. "You're my father. You should have been there for me. Instead, you watched from a distance and let my mom raise me on her own. And then you were going to swoop in and turn me into a monster?"

James rolled his eyes. "Your life was pathetic anyway, son. You hated it. I know you did. I was there. I saw it all. How you got bullied and ridiculed by your peers, how you didn't have any friends—"

"And yet you did nothing." He balled his fists tighter. He wanted to hit this man so badly. But James wouldn't feel that pain. And he wanted to hurt his so-called father.

"I was going to give you the ultimate gift: immortality." He spread out his arms.

That's when an eerie howl split the silence of the early night.

"Well, you didn't even give me that," Dylan spat. "So I don't want to join you. In fact, I never want to see you again. Go to hell." He turned on his heel, not sparing his father another glance, and started walking back to his mother.

James grabbed Dylan by the shoulder and spun him around. "Just give me a chance. You don't know what you're doing. They'll find you sooner or later."

Dylan scoffed. "Don't touch me." To his surprise, he easily shrugged James off. He had never been able to do that with Alec and Marie. They were a lot stronger than his father.

"Wait." James grabbed both of Dylan's arms, staring at him with wild eyes.

But Dylan had had enough. He freed his right arm and, with one swift motion, punched his father squarely in the face. James hadn't expected that. Stunned, he stumbled back a few steps, letting go of Dylan's other arm.

Dylan took the opportunity to zip back to his house, not caring who saw him. He stopped in the same spot in front of the door, trying to collect himself before ringing the doorbell.

He needed to figure out what to say to his mom, but his head was spinning. Had he really just met his father? The magnitude of the encounter hadn't sunk in yet. One thing was certain though: James was even more disappointing than he had imagined.

His father had wanted to turn Dylan right when he would have started college. That meant Dylan never would have gotten to go to Harvard. He never would have gotten to live his dreams. He was always going to lose his mother, and his mother was always going to lose him. This fate had been unavoidable. Inescapable.

He ran his hands over his face, trying hard to keep it together. Tears were forming behind his eyelids, but he forced them down. He needed to talk to his mother, then everything would be okay. He would tell her what a piece of shit his father was, and they could put the entire thing behind them.

He raised his hand again to ring the bell and took one last deep breath. He caught a whiff of caramelized sugar. He whirled around, and as his gaze darted to the end of the driveway, he froze, his heart skipping a beat. There, in the spot James had occupied before, the black wolf stood and waited.

28

The wolf growled, baring its teeth, fixing Dylan with eyes that were far too intelligent for an animal. Dylan's first instinct was to run, but then he remembered where he was.

He had led the wolf directly to his mother.

It was bending its hind legs, ready to pounce. Dylan's heart lurched. Every fiber of his being was screaming at him to run, but instead, he charged the wolf.

He pulled the stolen silver knife from the waistband of his jeans and thrust it at the wolf's chest.

The monster stood up on its hind legs like a person and slapped the knife from Dylan's hand.

Dylan dove after the knife as it skidded down the sidewalk. He grabbed it and flipped onto his back as the wolf came hurtling down on him. Another thrust with the knife, blindly, at anything within reach – the weapon found its mark. The wolf howled as the silver pierced its left shoulder. Wisps of smoke emanated from the wound.

Dylan pulled the knife out while the monster was still reeling with pain. His heart was pounding in his ears as he scrambled from underneath the beast and took off into the woods at full speed. Hoping the wolf would follow him instead of taking out its rage on his mother, he was ready to turn back and fight it tooth and nail if it got any ideas about switching targets.

A few seconds later he heard heavy footfalls coming after him and a growl so low and menacing, he could almost hear the wolf shouting *"You'll pay for this."*

At least his mother was safe.

But he couldn't fight this thing by himself. Alec and Marie had to be there somewhere. He noticed a massive scratch on his forearm that was slowly healing. He hadn't even felt the creature claw him. But he knew a bite would hurt like hell.

He ran faster, not daring to look over his shoulder. He could still hear the thing's footfalls and it seemed to be gaining on him.

His gaze darted left and right, frantically looking for a way out, a hiding place, a miracle, something! But he was surrounded by nothing but trees.

The wolf's footfalls stopped abruptly, and as Dylan was amping himself up to turn his head to check what had happened, the creature's claws dug into his back, the monster's weight knocking him to the ground.

As his face bit the forest floor, a twig dug itself deep into his right eyeball. Panic flooded his system at the prospect of losing his eye, but it was like Alec had said: not painful, just uncomfortable.

What was even more uncomfortable was the wolf slicing up his back with its massive claws, slashing again and again. Dylan struggled to turn around so he could fight it off, taking a few more slashes to the arms and chest. He was facing the wolf's open mouth, shrinking at the monster's neat rows of sharp teeth.

The wolf's caramel scent engulfed him, filling his head with thoughts of sugary treats, and the urge to bite it became almost unbearable. Every instinct told him to bite the thing, to drink its blood, to kill it. He held his breath, cutting the scent off, as the monster went for his throat.

He rolled onto his side to dodge the bite and, taking advantage of the wolf's momentary confusion, buried the knife deep in the monster's abdomen. The wolf howled. Dylan scrambled to his feet, leaving the knife where it was.

He didn't linger. The wound was far from fatal, and he needed to get away. Ripping the twig out of his eye socket, he charged through the forest, frantically trying to come up with an escape strategy.

He had lost his only weapon, and the monster was still coming for him. If it jumped him again, he'd be toast – quite literally once the sun came up.

He stumbled through the forest, his blind eye making it harder to navigate all the tree branches. A part of him marveled at his lack of pain. His heart was the only organ that reacted like it was supposed to, beating frantically, telling him to run, to get to safety before he bit the dust.

He could hear the wolf furiously charging after him, though the stab wound was slowing it down some. It was tearing through trees, growling and snarling menacingly, which made Dylan panic. He desperately wished for Marie and Alec to save him.

And then there were no more trees – and no more ground.

Dylan narrowly avoided falling off a cliff three hundred feet down into the river. He whirled around. The wolf was charging toward him with murder in its eyes.

He was trapped. He could already feel the monster's teeth ripping out his throat and tearing out his insides. He imagined the venom would feel like the searing pain of the sun, burning him from the inside – and then he'd be paralyzed and exposed to the approaching dawn.

He realized he didn't want to die. Even if he had to live the rest of his life as a vampire, even if he had to live off blood and would never be able to walk in the sun again, he didn't want it to be over.

He had no choice and no time to think.

As the wolf snatched at him, he jumped off the cliff, hoping against all odds for survival. He pivoted in his fall and saw the wolf standing at the edge, tilting its head back and letting out a frustrated howl.

The water was as hard as concrete when Dylan broke through the surface. The river engulfed him completely, and tiny tingling air bubbles crawled all over his skin as the silence of the water settled over him. He didn't need to breathe so didn't need to come up for air. The dark and cold of the water didn't bother him either. His whole body exhaled with relief in the peace and quiet of the river.

He closed his eyes – the stabbed one having already healed – and floated away with the current. He thought about his father – the man he had hated for so many years – who had somehow turned out to be even worse than he had assumed. He thought about his mom, who still believed he was dead, and how utterly devastated she had looked earlier that night. How could he live with knowing how much pain he had caused her?

But was he really the one who had caused it?

Alec had turned him, but Dylan couldn't blame the vampire anymore. James had been planning to turn him since the day he was born. He had never stood a chance. If anything, Alec and Marie had saved Dylan from an eternal life with his piece of shit father.

But what about his mom? She didn't deserve to be punished for something he had been born with. Something he had no control over. He had to talk to her, to let her know he was okay. He owed her that.

Determined, he cracked his eyes open and swam to the surface.

The cool night air felt like a slap to his face. The sound of rushing water filled his ears, drowning out everything else. He whipped around, trying to get his bearings.

He had been washed out of town by a few miles. He needed to get out of the water before he was carried away much farther. But as he made his way to the riverbank, he hesitated. His eyes scanned the dark trees on each side of the river for the wolf. He checked upstream, but the monster was nowhere to be seen.

He was dripping with water as he waded the last few steps out of the river. When he reached the riverbank, he tried to wring out his T-shirt but realized it hung in tatters down his torso. He ripped off the remnants of his shirt, examining his taut new skin. His body showed no sign of injury, even though his shirt was proof that he had been severely hurt. He shuddered. He wouldn't have survived the attack if he'd still been human.

He touched the eye that had been stabbed, expecting it to be sensitive, but it was as good as new. He let out a huff in amazement.

His stomach suddenly clenched tightly like someone had reached inside his body and was squeezing it. He doubled over, hugging his belly. The sensation spread into his whole body. His heart was pounding in his ears and his fangs had snapped out and were pinching his lower lip.

Dylan panicked. Had he been bitten? Was there a delay in the venom?

The clenching subsided after a few beats, but his body still felt like all his nerve endings were laid bare. It took him a solid minute to realize that he was starving.

Of course he was. He had lost so much blood, his eye had been stabbed… He needed to feed.

Grunting, he clutched a tree, trying to steady himself. He needed to get back to the motel. They still had about eight blood bags left. He could fuel up, and then he'd go to see his mom. Right then, he was in no condition to speak to her. He shivered partly with arousal, partly with terror as he thought about what her blood might taste like.

He started off toward town but stopped after only a few paces. He couldn't trek through the woods and risk running into the wolf again.

His heart skipped a beat. He imagined the wolf tearing through the front door of his house and ripping into his mom because it hadn't gotten to him.

The crippling hunger he had felt was forgotten. Silently cursing himself, he climbed up the steep hill toward the road. Maybe he could flag down a car and hitch a ride to the motel. It was his best shot.

As he reached the shoulder, a truck rounded the bend, its headlights blinding Dylan. He launched himself onto the lane, not caring if he got hit. The truck's brakes screeched as the vehicle ground to a halt only inches away from Dylan.

Since the headlights were no longer in his sightline, he could see the driver, a broad-shouldered middle-aged white guy with a full beard. His eyes were wide open in shock.

Dylan wondered what he might look like to the guy: half naked, soaking wet and with wild eyes jumping out onto the road from the middle of nowhere... He'd be scared shitless if he had encountered someone like that in the middle of the night.

He forced a smile and held up his hands, trying to put the guy at ease.

The man rolled down his window, stuck his head out, and shouted, "Hey, man, are you okay?"

Dylan noticed the man hadn't turned off his engine, presumably ready to take off if the situation went south.

He tried to come up with a reasonable explanation. *This mind control thing would come in really handy right now.*

"I'm sorry, sir," he said. "I ... I got drunk with some friends. We were having a bonfire by the river. And ... I don't know, I must have fallen in..."

The man's eyes narrowed slightly, but he didn't drive off.

"It's all pretty hazy. I don't remember... Would you..." He tried his best to look innocent. "Would you mind giving me a ride into town?"

The man considered it. Dylan's heart was pounding with anticipation.

The man shook his head in a way that Dylan interpreted as 'young people.' "All right then. Hop in, boy!" The man waved a hand in an inviting gesture, and Dylan sighed with relief.

That feeling didn't last long though as the moment he slipped onto the passenger's seat, tucked into the warmth of the driver's cabin, the man's smell hit him like a bucket of cold water. The enclosed space was rich with it, the air heavy with the scent of fresh popcorn and peanut butter and something he couldn't identify but which smelled so intriguing he found himself inhaling deeply.

His fangs snapped out, and he immediately held his breath, panic rising within him. *It's just a short drive, Dylan. You can do this.*

"Where to?" the man asked as he put the truck into drive.

"Can you drop me off at the gas station?" He'd make his way back to the motel from there. There was no need to expose himself to this scent any longer than necessary.

"Sure." The man started driving.

Dylan had cut off his sense of smell, but it seemed like he could feel the guy's blood. It permeated every pore of his exposed skin, tempting Dylan to take a bite. The man's heart was beating steadily, becoming louder and louder in Dylan's ears. Soon he couldn't focus on anything else. It was hypnotizing him, forcing him to think about the delicious liquid it was pumping through the man's body...

His mouth started watering, and he had to swallow. It seemed like even his saliva had acquired the taste of popcorn and peanut butter. He closed his eyes, trying to dispel it, but that only made him focus harder on the beating of the man's heart. It was singing to him, luring him in...

Without consciously deciding to, he took a deep breath, letting himself be filled with the delicious smell. His entire body was aching, yearning to take a bite.

He leaned over the center console, inhaling more deeply.

"Hey, what are you—"

Dylan vaguely noticed the driver hit the brakes, stopping the truck. He didn't care. He needed the blood.

In one swift motion, he pulled the guy toward him and bit into his neck. If the stranger screamed, he didn't hear it. All that mattered was the delicious lifeblood running into his mouth. It had been singing to Dylan before, but tasting it felt as if a choir accompanied by a full orchestra was playing a symphony on his tongue. His body was rejoicing with the sustenance, demanding more.

A part of him noticed that blood bags couldn't hold a candle to this. He had never considered that fresh blood was warm. And the change in temperature released the flavors in an entirely different way. It was like the difference between eating a freshly made hot meal versus cold leftovers the next day times a thousand.

The popcorn and peanut butter blood trickled onto his tongue like caramel. The rush from it was a hundred times stronger than any sugar rush he'd had in his life. Tightening his grip, he sucked harder, craving every drop of the delicious liquid.

A pair of strong hands yanked him off his food. He wanted to protest, but the only thing that came out of his mouth was a guttural growl. An ironlike arm snaked around his chest, dragging him out of the truck. He tried to fight it off but couldn't.

With the blood intake cut off, he noticed the truck's horn was blaring loudly. The man was pressing one hand down on the horn and the other on his bleeding neck. He stared at Dylan in horror.

That's when it hit Dylan what he had done.

He had bitten a human. And if nobody had stopped him, he would have killed that human. Without thinking about it. Just to satiate his hunger. He had let his instincts take over, and his instincts had told him to kill.

Dylan's blood ran cold.

Marie opened the driver's door, removing the man's hand from the horn. She bit her wrist and made the man drink from it. His wound healed within seconds. She helped him sit upright. "You're fine. Forget us. Forget any of this happened." His face went blank, and he nodded once.

Marie closed his door, and Alec shut the passenger's side door with his foot, still holding onto Dylan. Once all the doors were closed, the guy took off.

Dylan had stopped fighting Alec at that point, so Alec loosened his grip. The severity of his actions hit Dylan even harder. He could have killed someone. After telling himself and everyone else that he would never do anything like that, that he would never be capable of killing anyone, he had attacked an innocent man.

His knees buckled under the weight of his guilt, and he broke down. He crouched on the ground, buried his face in his hands, and sobbed. All of this was too much. How had he turned from a normal eighteen-year-old boy into a killer?

"Dylan, baby, it's okay." Marie gently rubbed his shoulders. "He's fine. You didn't kill him."

But he could have. He sobbed harder.

"Dylan. Dylan, hey…" Marie removed his hands from his face. She pulled him up to his feet and hugged him tightly. "It's okay."

The motherly tenderness of her embrace quieted his sobs. But the tears were still streaming down his face. He hugged her back. "I'm sorry…" he whispered. "I didn't mean to."

"I know." She rubbed his back again.

A third hand touched his shoulder. "Let's get you home, okay?" Alec's voice was surprisingly soft, but the word 'home' conjured up memories of his mother and of his plan to get back to her.

Dylan squeezed his eyes shut, pressing out the remaining tears. He had been a fool. What had he been thinking? That he could just waltz up to his mother and explain that he was a vampire now? Then resume his old life working shifts at the gas station? He almost laughed at the absurdity of the thought.

Too much had happened. Too much had changed. It was time to face reality: He was never going back and he was never going to talk to her again.

His pain at that realization was worse than the one inflicted by the rays of the sun. The pieces of his battered heart shattered into even smaller fragments. He was drowning in the endless ocean depths of his sorrow.

Alec stepped around them and looked Dylan in the eyes, a sympathetic look on his face. "It's okay, Dylan. We got you."

Dylan found something reassuring in that. At least he wasn't alone.

He nodded meekly and let go of Marie. She had tears in her eyes as well, looking up at him in relief. "Come on. Let's go."

29

"What happened to you? Why are you wet?" Marie asked as they followed the road back to town.

"I..." He felt embarrassed admitting it. "I snuck out and got attacked by the wolf—"

Before he could say anything else, she stopped and forcefully spun him toward her, inspecting every inch of his exposed skin. Her face looked tense and strained. His heart skipped a beat as he realized why Marie was so concerned. Why she was so paranoid about the wolves... If she had lost someone... He gulped.

"It's fine. It didn't bite me. I'm okay." When her face didn't relax, he added, "Really. I promise."

"How were you able to escape?" Alec asked with wide eyes.

"I had taken one of your knives. I stabbed it and ran away. I jumped off the cliff into the river, and it didn't follow me."

They shared a look.

"I'm fine, I swear! I got scratched up pretty badly, but it healed. The only thing that didn't survive was my shirt." He smirked, trying to lighten the mood.

Marie wrapped her arms around him and hugged him tightly. "You could have been killed," she choked. "If there had been more wolves..."

A shiver ran down Dylan's spine as he pictured Milena being surrounded by ten werewolves, all of them jumping her at once, covering her in bites. He didn't want to imagine how awful her death must have been.

He hugged Marie back. "I know. I won't sneak out again, I promise."

Alec squeezed Dylan's shoulder, but mid-squeeze, his hand was ripped away. Startled, Dylan turned his head and caught sight of the black wolf rolling down the forested hill with Alec, disappearing between the trees.

"Alec!" he shouted.

Marie let go of him, and they darted after Alec and the wolf, Dylan grabbing a knife from Marie's belt, where she had tucked several.

They found Alec a few yards into the wooded area, leaning against a tree and cradling his arm to his chest. His face was contorted in pain. Blood was gushing from his arm.

The wolf's growl alerted them before it jumped from its hiding spot between the trees – straight for Marie. She pulled two knives from her belt. "Get away, Dylan," she instructed calmly, fixing her gaze on the wolf.

"No, I'm not leaving you behind," Dylan shouted.

The wolf found its target. But Marie was quick. She sliced both knives down the length of the monster's body, making it howl in pain and leaving smoking slashes in its fur.

It dropped to the ground but got up again quickly. Its murderous stare was fixed on Marie, its teeth bared and its handlike claws digging into the ground.

"Dylan, run!" Alec screamed from where he was crouching, apparently still unable to move.

"No!" Dylan shouted. He had to do something. He'd had enough of running. Enough of being pushed around and told what to do. Enough of being the good boy and following the rules. He tightened his grip around the knife and charged the wolf.

"What are you doing!?" Alec screamed.

Dylan hurled himself in the air, coming down hard on the wolf, aiming his blade right between the monster's shoulder blades. He hit his mark with a crunch, rolling off the wolf's back and crashing into a tree.

The wolf howled again, reaching for the blade with its front claws, but it was unable to get to it. Dylan scrambled to his feet, and Marie tossed him another knife.

He had never seen her eyes look so cold. Her face was a mask of ruthlessness when she paced forward and, with one swift motion, sliced the monster's throat.

The wolf howled louder than it had before, the howl turning into a high-pitched scream. The creature shrank, its fur receding back into its body, a tuft of long black hair growing from its shrinking head, and soon the wolf was gone entirely. In its place stood a naked woman who couldn't have been older than twenty-three. She sank down to the ground, her throat gushing that deliciously sweet blood, the knife Dylan had attacked her with still lodged in her back.

Dylan's mouth hung open in surprise. He had not expected the werewolf to be female. In her human form, this girl didn't look threatening at all. She was unkempt and dirty with long clawlike fingernails, but apart from that she looked like a normal person.

If he didn't know better, he would have considered it unimaginable that she had been the one who had attacked him.

The young woman was writhing on the ground, her body fighting the silver poisoning. Marie squatted before the werewolf, her expression still stone-cold. "This is what you get for attacking my son," she snarled, the fury in her voice making the hairs on the back of Dylan's neck stand up.

She raised the hand holding the knife high over her head and brought it down hard, burying it in the woman's chest. The werewolf gasped as Marie twisted the knife once, permanently lodging it in the woman's heart. Her writhing body stilled as her pulse stopped and her last breath left her lips.

All Dylan could do was stare, until Alec nudged his shoulder. He looked up at the immortal, who held one arm to his chest and the other out toward Dylan.

Dylan grabbed Alec's hand, letting the immortal pull him to his feet. Alec tried not to show it, but there was pain in his eyes, which swam with tears. He patted Dylan's shoulder. "Well done." A tight smile spread across his lips, and he pulled Dylan into a half-hug.

"Did she bite you?" Marie asked, grabbing Alec's arm and taking a look at it.

A plate-sized bite-mark covered Alec's forearm. It was festering, oozing blood and a clear secretion, like a cold glass of water on a hot summer day. The edges of Alec's skin moved like tiny bugs, trying to close the wound, but it didn't heal.

"Yeah… She jumped me. I wasn't paying attention," he berated himself.

Marie released his arm and tenderly caressed Alec's cheek. "She surprised us all."

He gave her his warmest smile in response.

Marie turned to Dylan, concern on her face. "Are you okay?"

He nodded. Despite the gnawing hunger he still felt and the mental exhaustion he had been through, he felt great. He had fought back. And they had won. The town was safe again. "I'm fine." He couldn't help but smile.

Marie's answering smile was dazzling, and she pressed her lips to his cheek. "Regardless…" She bent over and hoisted the dead werewolf onto her shoulders. "No more werewolf hunting for you."

"What!? But I'm getting so good at it!" Dylan exclaimed in fake outrage.

Alec laughed, putting an arm around Dylan's shoulders, pulling him close. Dylan smiled, putting an arm around Alec's waist, helping the immortal back up the hill. That bite seemed to affect him more than he let on.

They stuck to the shadows of the trees as they made their way back to the motel. Once they had to leave the cover of the forest, they made sure the coast was clear and darted to the car. Marie stashed the werewolf and their weapons in the trunk and pulled out a first-aid kit. When she tried to lock the trunk and failed, she shot a look at Dylan, who shrugged innocently.

They climbed the stairs to their room.

Dylan's eyes darted to James's room, but the lights inside were off and the curtains drawn. Maybe he had already left town. Dylan hoped so.

Alec rested more and more of his weight on Dylan, and the younger immortal was getting worried. When they finally made it back to the safety of their room, he helped Alec take a seat on the couch.

"Are you going to be okay?" Dylan asked.

Alec winced but nodded. "Yeah, it's just the venom spreading…"

"She bit you hard," Marie said matter-of-factly while examining the bite wound. She took out a vile of blood from the first-aid kit and used a dropper to drip a little on the bite. Alec sucked in air as some of the venom droplets that were still sweating from the wound evaporated with a soft sizzle when the blood touched them.

"Whose blood is that?" It didn't smell like human blood.

Without breaking focus from her task, Marie answered, "It's the blood of a very old, very powerful immortal. She was kind enough to provide it to us for cases like this."

Dylan wanted to know more, but the hunger was gnawing at his insides again. Remembering the blood in the mini fridge, he helped himself to a bag, grabbing two more for Alec and Marie.

When he turned back to them, Marie was bandaging Alec's wound.

Dylan paused for a second, remembering Alec pulling a knife from his lungs without flinching and healing on the spot. "How long will it take to heal?" he asked as he handed one of the blood bags to Alec.

"Thank you." Alec accepted the blood with a soft smile that made Dylan a little uneasy. The immortal had never smiled softly at him before. "A couple days. It's annoying… Makes you feel like a human." He laughed at his own joke.

Marie grinned as she finished bandaging him. "Nothing you haven't been through before." They shared a long loving look that made Dylan feel like he was intruding.

He focused on his blood, chugging the whole bag. He immediately felt less anxious and more calm but not nearly satiated. Glancing toward the fridge, he was wondering if he could take another bag from their dwindling supply when Alec was sick.

"Go ahead, take another one," Marie said.

"Are you sure? There isn't much left."

"Then we'll get more tomorrow night. You need it. Go ahead," she urged him.

He nodded, grabbed another bag, and downed it as fast as the one before. This time he noticed how bad the stuff tasted compared to fresh blood and flinched at his thoughts.

He tossed the empty bags in the trash and turned toward Marie and Alec, only to find the two staring at him worriedly.

"What?" he asked with trepidation.

"Take a seat." Alec indicated the bed in front of them. "We need to talk."

30

Dylan sighed, knowing exactly what Alec and Marie wanted to discuss. "Can I change first?" He was still half naked, and his pants and sneakers were drenched.

"Of course," Marie said, waving him off to the bathroom. He quickly put on a white T-shirt and a comfortable pair of green chinos and slipped back into the bedroom.

They hadn't moved. He took a seat on the bed across from them, pulling in his legs and hugging his knees. His bare feet burrowed nervously into the covers of the unmade bed.

"Dylan…" Marie said after a moment of silence. "Why did you sneak out?"

He couldn't meet her gaze. It all seemed so silly now. "I wanted to go and be with my mom." Without looking at them, Dylan knew both of them had stilled and were exchanging alarmed looks.

"But you didn't… Did you?" Marie's voice pitched an octave higher.

"I didn't talk to her." They exhaled. "I watched her through the window though. She's in bad shape…" His voice broke. He couldn't continue. It was too painful and too unfair.

"I know. I was with her last night." That made Dylan look up. He remembered James mentioning something about Marie being with his mom, but with everything else his father had said, he had forgotten until then.

"I tried to console her." She held up a hand. "Don't worry, I wasn't using mind control because I know you don't want that."

Dylan smiled meekly. He couldn't be mad at Marie anymore. She had been on his side since the day they'd met. But the unfairness of it all made him furious. Why did his mom, who was not involved in any of this supernatural stuff, have to suffer the most? Maybe it was okay to ease her pain by supernatural means. They owed her, after all.

"I take that back. Can you make it easier for her, please?"

Their mouths hung open in surprise. "O-of course, but…" Marie paused.

"Why the sudden change of heart?" Alec finished.

Dylan took a useless deep breath. "I ran into another vam—immortal." He corrected himself when he saw their expressions. "He introduced himself as James and told me he was my father."

Their faces fell. This piece of news clearly took them by surprise. "It was bad. He told me he'd been keeping tabs on me since I was a baby. He was going to turn me once I left for college."

They exchanged another worried look. "I'm sorry, Dylan. If you'd rather be with your father, we won't stand in your way—"

"No." He cut Marie off, shaking his head violently. "No. I never want to see him again. He was going to take me away from her after abandoning us. He killed my mom's aunt…" He sucked in more air. Alec frowned. Marie looked confused. "I'd rather stay with you."

He couldn't believe those words had come out of his mouth. Until a few hours ago, he had despised these two immortals, but now he was voluntarily choosing to stay with them. Molly's accusatory face appeared before him, but he pushed it aside.

"You saved me from him. If you hadn't turned me, he would have done it about five months from now."

Marie pressed her lips together, nodding in sympathy.

The truth was that he had resigned himself. All of this had been inescapable from the start. He had never been the architect of his own life. He had to learn how to deal with that now. And Alec and Marie were the far lesser of two evils.

"We hadn't planned on turning you yet. We would have waited at least another four years, but you finding out about us forced our hand. I wish it would have gone differently." Alec sounded contrite, and he was avoiding Dylan's gaze.

"Well, if you had waited, James would have beaten you to it, and I'm grateful he didn't."

They smiled at him.

Dylan uncurled. "I understand why my mom has to believe I'm dead." She couldn't be sucked into this. She'd be safer not knowing the truth. Especially safer from him. And Dylan would never be able to explain why he looked so different without telling her what he had become. "But can you ease her pain? At least a little? And Martin's as well?" His heart was screaming at him as he said those words, but he knew it was the right thing to do.

Marie nodded gravely. "I will. Don't worry."

"Does that mean we'll stop hunting werewolves?" Alec asked, looking probingly at Marie.

She grinned. "For now, yes."

He turned to Dylan. "Where would you like to move?"

Dylan's head bobbed back in surprise. "I get to decide?"

"Yes."

"With a caveat," Marie interjected. "We can't stay in North America. But any other part of the world is open to you."

"Uh…" He was overwhelmed. All his life he'd lived in one place. Sure, he had wanted to leave, but the traveling part had been on the back burner. He'd always been too focused on finding a college and getting a career. The thought made him laugh now. How incredibly naïve he'd been!

"Maybe Europe?" Alec suggested when Dylan didn't say anything.

Europe sounded nice. Only he didn't speak any other language besides English, so he had limited options if he wanted to be able to communicate with people.

"England, maybe?" He looked at them questioningly.

Alec nodded approvingly. "Yes, we can go to London. We haven't been in a while. How long has it been?" He frowned, looking at Marie.

"Eighty-five years, I think," Marie answered, like it wasn't weird.

"We can check into a hotel and then look for something more permanent." Alec was clearly already planning the whole thing out in his head. "Yes, that would be perfect." His brown eyes fixed on Dylan. "You still have so much to learn, and London will be a great environment for teaching."

Dylan's stomach clenched at the thought of what he might still have to learn, but he set his worries aside for the moment. He was immortal after all, and nothing was going to change that. It was time he started moving forward.

He had never given immortality much thought. Too many other things had been occupying his mind. But now he began to understand that he would live forever. He tried to wrap his head around that idea but couldn't. All his life he had lived with the certainty that he would die one day. Having that taken away felt strange and surreal.

"I'm going to make a few calls." Alec jumped up, his determination making him forget about the werewolf bite he'd suffered. "And you two should talk." He left the room.

Marie sighed, her eyes wandering slowly to Dylan. Alec was right. They did need to talk. But he didn't know how to broach the subject he wanted to talk to her about. Something that his father had said was bothering him and he needed to know the truth. He felt nervous.

"Dylan, I…" she said at the same time he said, "I wanted to talk…" They both stopped, embarrassed.

"You go first," she insisted.

He swallowed. "My father said something else."

She frowned.

"He said that you and Alec had lost someone."

Tears welled in her eyes, and she looked away.

"I'm sorry," Dylan whispered.

She shook her head and turned to him again. Her face was all serious, but Dylan could tell it was a mask.

"You have to understand something about us immortals, Dylan."

He tilted his head, listening.

"When we create another one of our kind, we form a bond with them. A very strong bond. The blood runs deep." She stopped, her jaw working. She pulled one knee up to her face, hugging her shin. "It is stronger for the sire than the scion, though. That's why you're probably unaware of it."

He thought about his relationship with Alec. In the beginning he had hated the guy. He had even been a little scared of him, even though he would never admit that to the immortal. But now the hate was gone, and he felt somewhat sympathetic toward Alec.

"I don't know. It does feel like I've known Alec much longer than I actually have."

She nodded. "It's because you've seen his memories. And not just seen them but lived them."

He thought back to the night Alec had been turned, the horrible torture he had been subjected to later, and his memories of Marie…

"Was it the same for you when he turned you?"

"No. We were in love, and I knew what he was before he turned me. And the bond is different for mates. We share blood."

He frowned. "What does that mean?"

"Well, you know how he fed you his blood to turn you?"

"Yes."

"He did the same to me, but then he drank from me too. That way he saw my memories as well. We've been sharing blood ever since when we sleep together. All mated immortals do. It makes us equals."

Dylan found that strange. He couldn't imagine drinking the blood of somebody he loved.

Marie laughed. "You'll see some day." Her expression turned serious again. "But if the immortals aren't mated, it's a different kind of bond…"

Dylan could tell this was hard for her to talk about.

"It's like you're giving a part of who you are to another person, and they in turn become a part of you. Your blood runs in their veins."

Something James had said came back to Dylan: 'My blood might not be running through your veins anymore, but I am still your father.'

"So, technically, my father isn't my father anymore." The thought ignited a spark of hope within him.

Marie answered with a knowing smile. "No, and I'm guessing that's why he was mad. He can't claim you as his own now."

Dylan found that incredibly reassuring. He didn't want to be associated with that man at all.

Marie continued. "Unfortunately…" Her voice broke. She swallowed. "Sometimes, even us immortals get killed. It is rare. Much rarer these days than it used to be." She pulled herself together. "There was a time when werewolves roamed the world. They were everywhere. They need nature to survive, so they steered clear of cities, but they thrived in the forests. And up until a hundred years ago, there were a lot more of those in the world."

"That's why they like it here," Dylan interrupted without meaning to.

She looked at him, her face sad. "Exactly." Her gaze landed on her shoes again. She seemed to be transported to another place, seeing something else. "You held your own very well tonight, but you were only up against a single wolf and you had Alec and me by your side. If you were faced with an entire wolf pack…" Her voice broke again. She wiped a tear from her eye.

Dylan's heart ached for her.

"In 1847 we were living in Austria. We found a twenty-one-year-old Romani woman there who had the aura. She had been orphaned at a young age and was trying to get by on her own."

"Milena," Dylan muttered under his breath.

"I turned her." She swallowed hard. "And only a decade later, in 1858, she…" The tears were streaming down her face. "She was killed by a pack of wolves." Her voice turned bitter and hateful. "There were ten of them. They had trapped her in the woods, attacked her, and left her to bake in the sun."

Dylan didn't know what to say or do. His skin crawled as he imagined what it must have been like for Milena to burn to a crisp. He moved over to the couch next to Marie and tentatively laid a hand on her back, rubbing it lightly.

"I didn't know at the time, but when your scion dies, you feel every part of it as if you were dying. You cry tears of blood as you lose a part of yourself." She hugged her knee tighter.

Dylan was shocked. That's what he had seen in Alec's memory. Her pain had been evident on her face and in her screams. Of course she had a hard time talking about it.

"I'm sorry," he whispered.

She shook her head. "You should know." They were silent for a beat. "I never want to go through that again."

He understood. He put his arm around her shoulder and hugged her tight. "I understand you took revenge on those wolves," he said, trying to redirect her thoughts.

She scoffed. "Yes, and then some. We've been hunting wolves ever since. There are no more werewolves in Europe now and only a few packs are left in North America, but we'll get those too, eventually." She wiped her eyes and turned to him. There was so much sorrow in her expression, but she managed a little smile anyway. "They'll have to wait for a while though." She booped his nose.

He snorted. "I see. Taking maternity leave, huh?"

That made her laugh. "Sort of, yes."

She seemed better now, but he needed to know one other thing. "Am I meant to be a replacement?"

That startled her. She leaned away from him, staring at him with surprise. "No! No, of course not. Nobody could replace her. I wanted to turn you because I like you and not because…" She stopped. "Alec did it because I couldn't."

That made sense. She never wanted to go through the pain of losing another child. "Well, you won't have to worry about me," he reassured her.

She smiled meekly. "I know but I will anyway. And so will Alec."

Strangely, Dylan believed her. Alec wasn't one to show his emotions to anyone other than Marie, but a subtle change in his attitude lately made Dylan feel like the immortal cared more about him than he let on.

Dylan wondered how the blood bond between sire and scion could do that. He had forged a friendship with Marie over several weeks, but had only really gotten to know Alec a couple of days ago… He wondered how else it affected them.

"Just out of curiosity, what happens when your sire dies?"

"*If* your sire dies – which won't happen – you'd definitely feel it."

"How?" he asked.

"Well…" She hesitated. "I obviously haven't experienced it myself and neither has Alec, but from what I've heard, it feels like your heart stops for a moment, sort of, like a human having a heart attack. And afterward you feel like some vital part of you is missing."

That sounded awful. He hoped Alec would never die so he wouldn't have to feel that pain. The thought made him grin since he had wished for the immortal's death only the day before.

They sat in silence for a minute, Dylan's arm still resting on her shoulders.

"I swear I'll make it easier on your mom, Dylan. Trust me, I know what it's like to lose a child." He hadn't expected that. He turned to her in surprise. She met his gaze and hers was smoldering with truth.

It hit him hard. He knew she was being honest. He nodded. "Thank you."

The friendship they had built before he was turned was still there. Only now it had changed into something else. Now they were family.

Epilogue

They disposed of the dead werewolf that same night. Dylan had been wondering how they had made the other bodies disappear and now he got his answer. He and Marie drove to a crematory an hour away and broke in. Four hours later, they scooped out the ashes and spread them on the drive back. It was such a relief to Dylan that nobody else was going to die at the hands of the wolves.

A few other items needed to be taken care of before they could leave Berlin for good. Marie found a dealer who would fix the trunk's lock and have the Audi detailed, cleaning out any bloodstains, and sell the car. Neither of them had a lot of luggage, so everything could fit in suitcases they could take on the plane with them.

Dylan learned that Alec had several storage units in various countries where he stashed books he wanted to keep. Apparently, he had some very valuable first editions that he didn't want to part with. Since they had no use for their silver weapons in Europe, they stashed them with the books in the unit in Boston.

Marie and Alec were on their way there and were also going to make a pitstop at the blood bank to restock their supply. Dylan had asked to stay behind so he could say goodbye to his hometown and everyone he would likely never see again.

They had been okay with that, telling him to be careful, so he was on his way to school. He didn't really know why, but he wanted to see the building where he had endured so much agony one last time. As he circled the empty dark building, he glanced through the windows into the different classrooms. When he reached his history classroom, he remembered Mr. Kline's classes. That automatically made him think of Molly, and his heart sank. There was no way he could bring her back to life. She hadn't deserved to die, and that still hurt.

But he had to accept that it hadn't been his fault either. That was easier said than done though. He knew it would take a while. Maybe a hundred years? Two hundred? He still had a hard time fathoming the concept of forever.

He went to the public library next, immediately feeling better when he spotted the building. It was closed this time of night, but he didn't need to step inside. This place had given him so much solace over the years, and it had always been a place of refuge.

He wanted to save his mom's house for last so he could take his time there. Marie had paid her another visit and had taken some of her pain away. Although she had told Dylan that Susan would be able to handle his death better now, he needed to see it for himself.

He was going to check in with Larry at the gas station first though.

As he entered the store, he blinked at the fluorescent lighting inside. The light bulb's buzzing sounded like a swarm of bees in his ears. But when he spotted the counter he had spent almost every evening behind for the last two years, he cracked a smile, and the familiarity with the place set in again.

"Coming!" Larry shouted from his back office. He had no doubt heard the door.

Dylan quickly grabbed a packet of chips from the nearest shelf and met a huffing Larry at the counter. So, he hadn't found a replacement for Dylan yet…

The old man showed no signs of recognition as he looked at Dylan, which felt strange to say the least. Dylan took a tentative breath of air. Mixed into the dry air and stale food smells was Larry's distinct old-man smell he recognized from his mortal days. But now he could also smell Larry's blood, which wasn't particularly appealing. The old man smelled like an overripe tomato mixed with something sour – something that would have been delicious at another time but was clearly past its prime.

He smiled at Larry as the old man rang him up. "Will that be all?" Larry asked after Dylan handed him the money.

"That's it, thanks." Maybe Dylan was imagining it, but it seemed like Larry paused for a second when he heard Dylan's voice. No, he wasn't imagining things.

Larry was eyeing him suspiciously. "Do I know you?"

Dylan shook his head, panicking. "No." He tried to make his voice sound deeper. "I'm just passing through town."

Larry's eyes rested a beat longer on Dylan, but the old man shrugged. "I could have sworn… Well, I must have been wrong." He smiled at Dylan. "Have a safe onward journey!"

"Thanks. Take care." And with that Dylan pivoted and walked out the door for the last time.

After exiting the store, he took a moment to look at the gas station, committing every detail to memory. As he was standing there, a car pulled into the parking lot. Dylan recognized the driver immediately. It was Patty, Connor's wife. Her dark blond hair was in a messy up-do, and she was wearing her waitress uniform, probably running an errand after the end of her shift.

Dylan realized how weird he looked, standing in front of the store with a packet of chips in hand, staring teary-eyed at the building…

He didn't want to look like a weirdo. But as he turned to leave, a gust of wind hit him from Patty's direction, and with it the most incredible scent he had ever smelled filled his nostrils. He inhaled deeply, trying to make out the different components. It was fruity.

Most prominently strawberries. Then cherry, raspberry, grape… And something heavier… Dark rich chocolate.

It filled his entire body with yearning. Everything melted away except this heavenly smell.

He didn't notice himself follow the scent. He didn't even notice himself leaning in toward its source and inhaling deeper. It was all a haze.

Next thing he knew, he was holding onto Patty, pressing one hand on her mouth and burying his fangs deep into her neck. When her blood hit his tastebuds, he wanted to cry out with pleasure. All the flavors were running smoothly over his tongue, urging him to drink more. He could taste a hint of rose now, which he had missed before.

He bit her again, making the blood flow quicker, listening to her heartbeat pumping more blood through her body directly into his mouth. It was like her heart wanted him to relieve it from its duty.

And he obliged, sucking more and more blood from her until her heart stilled completely. In that moment, he felt a high akin to the one he had experienced when he was turned. Her warmth spread through his body, eliciting a tingling that turned into a rush that almost made him burst into giggles.

He licked his lips to catch the last remnants of blood and couldn't help but smile. But as quickly as the high had come it was dissipating, slowly bringing him back to Earth. Suddenly he noticed the heavy weight in his arms.

He looked down, but it took him a while to process what he was seeing. Patty lay limply in his arms, her skin white as a sheet, her eyes wide open but unseeing, and her red lips slightly parted and smeared with lipstick. Two deep bitemarks on her neck had oozed a trickle of blood down her throat onto her white waitress uniform.

He listened for her heart, but it was silent. Her body was already growing cold. A wave of terror washed over him as he realized what he had done.

She was dead. He had killed her.

His heart started hammering in his chest, like it was beating for both of them. He looked around frantically, realizing with a start that he was in a public place, right in the middle of a parking lot.

Nobody was there. Not as far as he could see anyway. He glanced through the windows into the convenience store, but Larry had retreated to his office.

For lack of a better option, he carried Patty to her car, opened the trunk, and hastily laid her inside.

He grabbed her car keys, got in on the driver's side, and started the engine.

The next thing he knew he was speeding out of town, fighting back tears, feeling only hatred for himself for the horror of what he had done. Patty was a mother; she had a two-year-old child and a husband waiting for her at home...

But she wasn't coming home. She'd never come home again.

Nothing would ever be the same.

TO BE CONTINUED IN BOOK 2 OF
THE IMMORTAL BLOOD GIFT SERIES

Acknowledgments

This book has been a long time in the making and it certainly would never have been written and published if it weren't for a lot of people who have supported me along the way.

First off, I'd like to thank my editor Karen for polishing up my writing and making my manuscript read like a real book. Your work has been invaluable.

I'd also like to thank my cover designer Hampton, who came up with the insanely cool cover art. I mean it speaks for itself…

A huge thank you also to my beta readers Sarah, Nora and Sophie. Your input has helped me tremendously.

The one person I owe the most gratitude to is my sister Verena, who is always the first to read my manuscripts and without whom the story wouldn't be what it is now. Seriously, I love you and I can't thank you enough, big sis!

I certainly never would have finished writing if it wasn't for the support of my friends and family: Verena, Matthias, Julia, Melli, Änne, Nora, Sophie, Johanna, thank you guys for listening to my endless prattling about plot structure and publishing. And thank you for always being there for me when I needed you the most!

Mom, even though you'll never be able to read this book, thank you for always being my biggest cheerleader. I love you.

A big thank you goes out to Julia for setting up my website and to Melli for taking author photos of me in the blazing summer heat. I don't know what I'd do without you guys.

I also really appreciate the support of everyone in Alys's writers club. You guys have been with me every step of the way. You are the best.

And last but not least, I never even would have started writing this book if it hadn't been for Alys Arden whose writing has touched me like nobody else's has. I'll always look up to you. Thank you for everything you've taught me and everything you do.

And of course, thank *you*, who took the time to read this book. I hope you love this story and its characters as much as I do.

About the Author

Marina Rehm has been a fan of vampires and witches for as long as she can remember, devouring every story she could get her hands on. When she was a teenager, she began to make up her own vampire stories.

   When she's not writing or reading, you can find her at the movie theater.

Follow her on Instagram: @_marina_rehm_

Visit her website and sign up to her mailing list: www.marinarehm.com

www.ingramcontent.com/pod-product-compliance
Lightning Source LLC
LaVergne TN
LVHW041035170726
843494LV00004B/133